ACTS OF TREASON

A MAX KENWORTH SUSPENSE THRILLER, BOOK 2

PATRICK PARKER

BOOKS BY PATRICK PARKER

Six Minutes Early: A Max Kenworth Suspense Thriller (Book 1)

Acts of Treason: A Max Kenworth Suspense Thriller (Book 2)

War Merchant: A Dydre Rowyn Suspense Thriller

Treasures of the Fourth Reich

CHAPTER 1

Saturday, February 13, 2016
Chez Vous Restaurant on French Street
Istanbul, Turkey

ALTHOUGH THE TEMPERATURE was in the low forties, the bright afternoon sun made it a pleasant time to be out and the street was filled with people as usual. George stuck his hands inside the pockets of his tan jacket as he pretended to window-shop one of the displays at the many shops on İstiklal Avenue, one of the busiest streets in the world, near the intersection of French Street. After several minutes, he casually strolled to the next display. Having already scouted French Street and the restaurant, he was now scrutinizing the area in all directions while waiting for his contact, who was due to arrive in the next several minutes.

There was an uneasiness in the air that caused his senses to work at a furious pace, seeking to ensure he hadn't been followed or wasn't walking into a trap. His training in the US Army Special Forces and later in the CIA Clandestine Service Trainee program had instilled in him to be ever vigilant while preparing to react effectively and efficiently in a variety of hostile situations. Changes taking place in the country had brought him there. He had done this many times before and knew very well that if he was discovered, he would be executed.

George spotted a beautiful woman in a short skirt approaching. Brunette hair pooled on the fur collar of her brown coat that was buttoned at the waist. Her demeanor was poised, making it easy to see her ample amount of cleavage on display. Once again, he scanned both sides of the street as she stopped beside him.

A possible setup, he thought. *I'll play along.*

For the next several minutes, George monitored his surroundings to determine who might be with the woman and to watch for his contact. It didn't take him but a moment to determine it was a setup for a mugging.

"Those look delicious," she said, pointing a well-polished nail at one of the chocolates displayed as she leaned closer to George. Her silky voice seemed to warm the crisp air.

"They do." He smiled and looked into her brown eyes, then beyond her.

George spotted his contact, Erol, several meters behind the woman. Erol continued his pace past the two without acknowledging George. He needed to continue his pretense with the woman for a few moments to ensure no one followed Erol.

"Would you like one?" she said. "I'd like to get something warm to drink." Her coat gaped open a little more.

"Oh, I don't know." George shifted his stance and dropped his head, playing bashful and nervous as he checked his surroundings one more time. Satisfied no one had trailed his contact, it was time for him to leave. As he turned to step away, his eyes landed on her breasts that looked like they were about to pop out of the lace bra. "Sweetheart, I must be on my way."

"Honey, you are very handsome. Why don't we go to my apartment? It's just around the corner."

George said firmly, "You are enticing, but I simply don't have time."

She leaned into him. "I—"

"No. You and your three boyfriends across the street move on or I'll call the *polis*."

"A girl's got to make a living." She shrugged and walked on.

George watched her go until she disappeared into the crowd. *Within a half hour, some poor sap'll be her victim,* he thought. *Sorry I couldn't prevent some dope from bein' mugged.* He casually stepped around the corner, onto French Street where the brightly painted buildings decorated with awnings and plants resembled a Paris street. He proceeded to Chez Vous to meet with Erol, whom George had met with several times previously. Erol worked on the Turkish Special Forces staff and was his key contact inside the military.

The restaurant, on the European side of Istanbul, had been specifically chosen for this meeting. They wanted a quieter restaurant to meet in and one that was in proximity to such a busy street where you could easily blend into the crowd and practically disappear. The restaurant fit their requirements much better than those on İstiklal. Opening the solid oak entry door, George stepped inside, slid the zipper of his jacket down, and first noticed only three couples at tables scattered around the room. Erol, seated alone by a window, brushed the sleeve of his cream-colored wool sweater, then gave a slight nod—a signal that it was safe. George walked over to the table, seeing that it was set for two with a plate of white cheese in the middle and drinks at each setting. He assumed they were raki—an anise-flavored liqueur similar to ouzo or sambuca. The men exchanged greetings as if they were friends, and George slid onto the chair across from Erol.

"These are very dangerous times," Erol said, his gaze darting around the room before he sipped the liqueur.

George glanced out the window. "What do you have for me? The situation?" He sipped his drink and nibbled on a slice of cheese.

Erol leaned forward, closer to George. "As you know, the situation is bad and deteriorating. The prime minister and President Kağan are at odds with each other. Corruption is bad in the government, and the president is consolidating more power. He is afraid he will be overthrown. Relations between Turkey and our neighbors are strained, and especially with the US. The administration supports the Muslim Brotherhood, and they are firmly within the government. The hardline move of the administration is not sitting well with the military."

"What's the military planning?" George asked, then pinched off another piece of cheese and sipped his drink.

The mention of friction between the military and government was of particular interest. George knew Turkey was no stranger to coups d'etat. The country had already experienced four, the most recent in 1997. Anything can happen during or after such an event, especially if that country is the second-largest military in NATO. The Muslim Brotherhood compounded the problem.

"I don't know." Erol sipped his drink and fidgeted in his chair. "Many are disgruntled."

George studied him for a moment. "You don't know, or won't tell me? Is it across the board or local? Will they revolt against the government?"

Erol lowered his head, then nodded. "I am afraid they will. From what I can tell, it is mostly at the senior levels. The conscripts just do as they are told and don't know anything. How far and wide, I don't know. I don't know *when* either. One must be very careful and not ask a lot of questions."

George scanned the room, then asked, "Is Turkey going to continue to participate in fighting ISIS?"

"I believe so. For now, anyway. There is a lot of friction between the military and government." Erol finished his drink and said, "I must go now. This is for you." He slid his hand across the table, allowing his hand to linger until George's hand approached his.

George accepted the hidden USB drive and slid his hand back to his lap. "Keep me up to date on what the military is going to do and when." He locked his eyes on Erol's.

Erol nodded. "One more thing. If the situation deteriorates more, I want you to get my family and me out of the country. Not to the US. The Muslim Brotherhood is entrenched in your government as well. They will kill me."

George nodded.

Erol stood and turned to leave, and George watched him walk out of the restaurant. Erol was smart and knew how to elude anyone who may be watching. Not being seen and the ability to disappear in the crowd would add points to his and Erol's safety. George scrutinized the couples at the other tables again and could not pick up any indication that they were interested in him or Erol. He casually finished the slice of cheese and his drink, then left the restaurant. He had no way of knowing what the flash drive contained but knew if he was caught with it, he and Erol would undoubtedly suffer severe consequences. If Erol risked his own safety to get the information to him, it was important and he needed to pass it to Field Station Ankara.

Within ten minutes, George was at a location where he could safely contact the desk officer about transferring it. The coded response back directed him to rendezvous in eight minutes at the predesignated location—the Pera Museum near the *Portrait of the Countess of Vergennes in Turkish Attire.*

The desk officer at Field Station Ankara retrieved the information on the flash drive, entered it into the database, and notified the analyst for review. The data was then flagged and a note was sent to the military attaché in the embassy and one to the Middle East desk officer at headquarters in Langley.

Monday, February 15, 2016
Office of the Deputy Director
CIA Headquarters, Langley, Virginia

At the urging of Deputy Director Trent Weldon, Deputy Secretary of State Aaron Fitzgerald and Deputy Secretary of Defense Wes Brock joined him in his office for a meeting. The three men and Weldon's secretary sat around the small meeting table near the window overlooking the courtyard below. The flat-screen TV on the wall played the news with the sound off.

Fifteen minutes into the meeting, Trent turned to his secretary, who was taking notes, and said, "Sally, would you please get us some coffee. We'll take a short break."

Sally placed her pen next to her pad and stood, then said, "Just coffee or does anyone want anything else?"

"Coffee," "Just coffee," and "Coffee is fine," they said with nods and smiles.

Sally walked out of the conference room and closed the door.

As soon as the door latched, Weldon stood and stepped to the window and peered out, then looked back at the others. This part of his meeting was not to be included in the minutes, nor did he want anyone outside of the three of them to know what was discussed. "I don't need to remind you," he said, his brow dipping, "the election is in nine months and we've gotta keep a positive light on the president and the party or we'll be without jobs in January." He returned to his chair and sat, then ticked off an item on his notepad. "You may've seen the intel out of Turkey that came in over the weekend. There was a note about a possible coup d'etat. Downplay it. It may not amount to anything. For God's sake, we can't let this be tied to the Muslim Brotherhood or the Arab Spring. Shut down any communications if it goes in that direction."

"Trent," Wes Brock said, "we've got a lot of civilians in Turkey. If something is about to happen, we've gotta get 'em out of there. It'll take a little time to get the resources in place to evacuate them."

"I haven't seen the intel yet," Aaron said as he looked at Wes, then Trent. "If something is about to happen, I've got people to evacuate as well. We'll need to get a travel advisory out. If we don't get people alerted and evacuate them, it will look bad for all of us to not have been out in front of this."

"Relax, it's just a bunch of grumblings," Weldon said. "We're checking it out. Besides, we could use this to our advantage. You can always blame it on the republicans, or perhaps, Russian meddling."

"If there's about to be a takeover, we have a significant problem at Incirlik Air Base," Brock said. "We've got nuclear weapons there. We just can't throw them on a transport and fly 'em out." He pitched his pen onto the table and leaned back. "We need time to coordinate with NATO and figure out where we can put 'em. Even worse, there's forty of 'em allocated to Turkey."

"I'll keep you posted on what I find out. Just sit tight for a while," Weldon replied.

"How the hell are you going to keep something like this quiet for a while?" Fitzgerald asked, his voice raised and full of astonishment. "The British and Saudis also have troops at Incirlik. The Germans are also considering stationing people there. I'm sure they know what's going on with Turkey."

"Listen, I'll work the intel side and have everyone downplay it. Don't bring it up unless it comes from outside. If either of you is pressed, we're watching the situation. *End of statement!*" Weldon said in a commanding tone as he leaned forward. "I'll talk to the British and have them keep it quiet. Aaron, the Secretary of State, will say anything you want him to say. If he hears about it, tell him we've talked about the issue and believe it's overblown. Just a few disgruntled soldiers. Wes, don't bring it up. If the generals mention it, tell them the same. If they persist, they'll decide to retire. Got it?"

Fitzgerald and Brock both nodded.

At that moment, the door clicked open and the room fell silent. Sally entered carrying a tray with a carafe and four cups. She set the tray on the table, filled each cup, and passed it to each man. Taking the last one, she sipped it and placed it on the table as she sat back down. Looking to Weldon, she smiled and dipped her head slightly, acknowledging that she was ready to continue with the notes.

The meeting continued another twenty minutes. A number of topics were discussed, mainly dealing with terrorism. Turkey was not mentioned.

Leadership within the US government seemed to fall into limbo and only the most demanding situations were addressed, many of them often placated. It appeared the outgoing president was not interested in the international arena. His domestic agenda seemed to favor the Muslims at every turn. The propaganda machine from inside the Beltway was in high gear and, at times, rivaled that of Hitler's favorite propagandist, Leni Riefenstahl.

Presidential campaigning was already in full swing with the administration and much of the country focused on the conventions in July. Obviously, the democrats wanted to remain in power and the republicans wanted to replace them. The news was constantly filled with stories or tidbits about the candidates and potential candidates while border security, the Middle East, and a host of other scandals competed for the spotlight in the news but could never push the campaign out of the limelight.

The presumptive democratic nominee and expected first female president, Jenny Gareth, took every advantage to grab the spotlight—the same as the other candidates, making it difficult to know who to believe. Her well-funded campaign and notoriety kept her ahead of any other candidate, the odds-on favorite to win the election thanks to her spin doctors. It wasn't long until the Beltway propaganda incorporated Jenny's marketing efforts and even the president started campaigning with her—an unusual maneuver.

Many within the government supported Jenny and, despite controversies surrounding her political career, were undeterred. With the backing and endorsements of high-profile figures and staff across the government, her poll numbers remained high. Senior employees jockeyed for positions in Jenny's administration. Money flowed and deals were made behind the scenes. For those who didn't openly support her and for whom other means didn't work, arms were twisted and, in some cases, worse. Murder was suspected but never investigated. Jenny would win, no matter what.

— • ♦ • —

Tuesday, February 23, 2016
Headquarters, US Special Operations Command
MacDill Air Force Base, Florida

Headquarters for the US Special Operations Command, commonly referred to as SOCOM, was a secure site located in the center of MacDill Air Force Base in Tampa, Florida. The Unified Combatant Command stationed there was responsible for overseeing all the special operations forces of the military.

Highly-decorated Major General Hugh "Chugs" Matherson was the Director of Operations, or J3, at SOCOM. The moniker, Chugs, had originated from his college days and held true throughout his early air force years as a young lieutenant. Even to this day, Chugs never passed up the opportunity for good beer. Although known for his fondness of beer, this lanky officer was in excellent physical condition.

Helen, Major General Matherson's secretary, opened the door to the general's office for the two men who'd just entered their office suite and said, "Gentlemen, the general will see you now." She held the door open until the two men entered.

Max Kenworth went first. "Thank you," he said as he passed in front of her.

Max, a former Delta Force officer now retired from the army, worked as a civilian for the J3 and headed up the highly classified program at SOCOM having to do with nuclear weapons planning and counterproliferation of weapons of mass destruction. He was one of the foremost authorities on nuclear weapons and often called upon for advice and expertise. As one might expect, he was in excellent physical condition and every bit of what his name signified—short, jet-black hair, and built like a freightliner.

Lieutenant Colonel Andy Johnston followed Max. "Thank you," he said, nodding as he entered. Though in civilian clothes, Andy worked for the Defense Intelligence Agency (DIA).

After the formalities, Matherson gestured for the two men to sit at the small table in his office and then sat down with them.

Andy looked at Max as the three of them settled into their seats and said, "I read your report on the incident in Panama and the SADMs. That was very close. Good job."

"Thank you. I hope I don't need to do that again," Max said with a nod.

Chugs handed Max a file with a *Top Secret* cover. "We might have a problem in Turkey. Get familiar with this, Max. The bottom line is that one of the CIA's contacts in Turkey has passed information to us that indicates there may be a pending coup." Chugs looked to Andy and nodded. "The military is not happy with the hardline approach of the Turkish president."

Max's gaze landed on the file as Chugs handed it to him. He opened the file and scanned over the summary as Andy started to brief them on the situation.

"We don't know when and believe they're still in the planning stage," Andy said, focusing on Max. "You'll see that it's pretty conclusive. It barely made a blip in the reporting. If it hadn't been for a diligent analyst, we could have missed it. The administration doesn't want this to get out. The president doesn't want to get involved in the internal affairs of Turkey or any of the other Middle Eastern countries. He is deferring or tabling everything outside of his domestic agenda."

Max glanced to Chugs, then back to Andy and said, "The US and Turkey are not exchanging greeting cards now. Turkey supports the Muslim Brotherhood, and they are firmly in their government. It is seventy miles from Incirlik Air Base to Syria, and Turkey has NATO's largest nuclear weapons storage facility." He raised his eyebrows and took a deep breath. "I'd say we are discussing a major problem. I'm having a bit of déjà vu."

"That's about it," Andy continued. "Last week, the air force tried to brief the president, but he wouldn't see them. He sent a note back from the golf course that simply said, 'Keep the damn things locked up.'"

Max started to speak, then simply shook his head as he wrinkled up the corner of his mouth.

"Included in your information is a summary of the analysis on Turkey," Andy continued, his demeanor serious. "In short, the president has created a disaster in the region. The US is battling ISIS and wants the president of Syria removed. Turkey wants the president of Syria removed too, and is more interested in fighting the PKK than ISIS. The US secretly struck a deal to back Turkey and ISIS in an attempt to get rid of the Syrian president. Turkey wants to return to the Ottoman traditions and doesn't trust the West. Strained relations with the US has pushed Turkey into the Russian camp, and Turkey is a long-standing member of NATO, with nuclear weapons. Oh, and of course, Iran is a close ally and supports Syria in the civil war. You get the picture."

"Yeah, the Middle East is on fire and our nuclear weapons are in the middle."

"Take a look at the last page," Andy said, motioning to the paper in front of Max. "The information the contact supplied indicates a substantial amount of money going to the Muslim Brotherhood in the US and to the Gareth foundation. Jenny's reelection campaign is a recipient as well. On that list are the people in our government who we believe support or are members of the Brotherhood. It is safe to assume that whatever we do, Turkey will know about it. This is extremely sensitive. We just don't know what the military or the president of Turkey is going to do."

Max looked at Chugs and asked in a cold voice, "Okay, General, what exactly do you want me to do?"

"For now, get familiar with everything in that file and the nuclear weapons in Turkey. Colonel Johnston will feed you information as he gets it," Chugs said, as he glanced to Colonel Johnston, then Max.

"And?" Max locked eyes with Chugs.

"I'll let you know, but be ready to go there. You'll assess the security of those nukes and make a recommendation on what to do."

"That's really getting into the air force's business, sir." Max's statement came out as more of a question.

"The air force has asked for our help on this."

Max simply nodded.

CHAPTER 2

Friday, February 26, 2016
Headquarters, US Special Operations Command
MacDill Air Force Base, Florida

B EHIND CLOSED DOORS in Chugs's office, Max and Chugs sat discussing Turkey and ISIS. The war in Afghanistan was not going well for the president. The Taliban had pledged support for ISIS and been making steady gains in Helmand Province—the largest in the country and located in southern Afghanistan—where they were on the verge of capturing another district. The opium fields in the province were the most lucrative in the world and a major source of income for the terrorists, corrupt government officials, criminal gangs, and anyone else strong enough—or crazy enough—to compete in this very deadly region. Protecting the opium trade was a high priority for the terrorists. They were not going to lose it at any cost. The province shared a porous border with Pakistan, the leading drug route out of the country.

"We've finally gotten through to the president," Chugs said. "He's ordering more troops to Helmand Province to provide force protection for special forces and provide training and assistance to the 215th Corps Afghan National Army, which is about to collapse."

"Have his rules of engagement changed?" Max asked, knowing the answer before Chugs could say it.

"No, still a disaster. The deployment isn't big enough and will only prolong the inevitable." Chugs locked eyes with Max.

Max sat back in his chair, knowing Chugs well enough to know that the bad news was about to come.

"I just wanted to give you the latest update," Chugs continued. "ISIS is gaining ground and posing a threat to Turkey. Iran is still stringing the president along while plotting to destroy our way of life. And the president isn't helping with either ISIS or the strained relations with Turkey. If there is a coup in Turkey or ISIS decides to go after Incirlik Air Base, we'll have a problem I'm not sure we can handle."

Max leaned forward in his chair and said, "You want me to go over there and assess the situation?"

"Exactly. You'll fly into Incirlik Air Base under the auspices of a no-notice Nuclear Weapons Technical Inspection (NWTI). Do not send your report over the classified network or discuss anything about your trip." Chugs paused for added emphasis. "We know that some of the systems have been compromised by unauthorized servers being used in the State Department, and we even know of a couple the SecDef is using. We're taking steps to isolate our systems, but that's causing a few problems with some of the operations. I don't wanna take any chance that you or your mission will be discovered. If Turkey suspects we are about to do something with the weapons, I don't know what they'll do. As you are very well aware, nuclear weapons are a highly coveted commodity in the Muslim world. Colonel Johnston is doing an assessment on their possible actions but thinks Turkey may retaliate."

"I understand, General. This type of inspection usually has several people doing the evaluation, and I've got an excellent team. How many men am I authorized to take?"

"Not necessary. The team is already assembled and you're just going along for the ride, so to speak. You'll officially be a team member, but you do your assessment. The NWTI team chief is the only one of the team who knows about you and your mission. You'll rendezvous en route. Helen has a packet with additional information for you."

Max stood and smiled. "We haven't had that game of chess."

"Let's see if we can have it when you get back. I'll ice the beer down. Oh, I received your wedding invitation. I'll be there. We'll have you back here in plenty of time for you and Danya to tie the knot in May. Good luck, and be careful, Max."

The two shook hands, and Max walked out of the office.

———— ◆ ◆ ◆ ————

Friday, February 26, 2016
Presidential Palace of the Republic of Turkey
Ankara, Turkey

President Hakan Kağan was hosting a dinner at the palace for several members of his cabinet and representatives from a few other countries in the region. The presidential complex, officially opened in October 2014, was built at a reported cost of over $600 million and reported to be the most extravagant presidential palace in the world. The expenditure had brought Kağan tremendous criticism for wasting the nation's resources on something so opulent.

In a private, ornately decorated Ottoman-style dining room decorated with paintings and statues, President Kağan met alone with Abdal al-Ghazāli, the Muslim Brotherhood representative.

"Your transition to rebuild the Ottoman Empire is progressing well, Hakan," al-Ghazāli said as he adjusted the white fabric of his *thawb*, crossed his legs, then sipped his raki from a gold-inlaid glass. "Remember, a gradual approach."

Kağan picked the napkin up from his lap, blotted his lips, and nodded. "I know. I am afraid there is going to be a coup against me. I do not want to wind up the same as Morsi." Mohamed Morsi had been a Muslim Brotherhood candidate in Egypt who won the first democratic election in 2012 as a result of the Arab Spring and was then overthrown by a military coup d'etat in 2013.

"Morsi was impatient and didn't do as we instructed." Al-Ghazāli lit a cigarette. "You have already curbed the military's political power. They won't be a threat. Whom do you suspect will overthrow you?"

"I am not sure. I am concerned about the Americans. I do not trust them." Kağan brushed a crumb off the sleeve of his tailored dark blue suit.

Al-Ghazāli held up his hand, indicating for Kağan to stop. He took a drag from his cigarette. "This could work to your benefit. We will watch and find out who wants you removed. We will make a list, then when the time is right, you can remove them. Let the planning proceed, so we can identify everyone involved. You list who is loyal to you and the Brotherhood."

"What about the Americans?" Kağan placed his napkin on the coffee table, stood, and stepped to a small desk to refill his glass of liqueur. He motioned to the bottle as he looked to his guest. "Another for you?"

"No. The Americans will do nothing. Neither will the UN. The US president is loyal to the Brotherhood, and he is focused on his domestic agenda along with the elections. The UN will do what he tells them. Jenny Gareth will win the election and will not interfere. The Brotherhood is giving her campaign a lot of money. If she tries to object, we will leak information on her supplying Stinger missiles and money to ISIS."

Kağan studied him as he returned to his seat, then replied, "If she should *not* win?"

"Do not worry, it is fixed. If by chance she should lose, it will all be done and the new American president will not do anything. It will be too late. The Americans will not attack another nation with nuclear weapons."

"What about NATO?" Kağan knew very well that NATO would not interfere in Turkish politics, but the member countries would be worried about terrorists getting the weapons at Incirlik—that was a problem. His brow dipped slightly as he held a wary eye on al-Ghazāli.

"As soon as we find out who is involved with the overthrow and when they plan on the coup, you will take over and blame it on the military. Of course, you can blame the Americans if you choose, but the military will be better. You surround the air base, shut it down, and take the weapons. By the time NATO can react, you will have solidified your position. You will have purged the military of the disloyal ones, taken control of the weapons, and then if you want, sever your agreement with NATO."

Kağan nodded, his face void of expression as he thought on what al-Ghazāli proposed for a moment. Then a slight smile emerged on his face. "What will my costs be?"

"You will be on your way to creating the New Ottoman Empire. A small contribution will be welcomed." Al-Ghazāli locked eyes with Kağan, sat back in his chair, and waved his hand in the air.

Although al-Ghazāli had tried to make the payment for the Muslim Brotherhood's help sound small or insignificant, Kağan knew better. He had to weigh the offer very carefully. If he miscalculated, the military would oust him and his fate would be the same as that of Morsi or, worse, that of Gaddafi in Libya.

"A few of the nuclear bombs at Incirlik and a partnership in the New Ottoman Empire," al-Ghazāli continued, his expression serious. "We will be able to control the West and the world will be ours."

Kağan sipped his drink, then simply said, "We should rejoin the others." He slid his chair back to stand.

Lips pressed together, al-Ghazāli set his glass down on the table and then stood with his host.

Both men walked out of the room.

———— ◆ ◆ ◆ ————

Monday, February 29, 2016
39th Air Base Wing
Incirlik Air Base, Turkey

Max entered Washington Dulles terminal in DC to change flights for the next leg of his trip to Incirlik. He proceeded through the busy terminal to his departure gate. Along the way, he began to focus on five other men in civilian clothes apparently going to the same gate. They all had close-cropped hair and appeared fit, with a military bearing, except for the few pounds around the waist. On the tram, Max turned to the man next to him and said, "Where're y'all headed?"

"Turkey," the man replied, taking a closer look at Max.

"I'm headed there too," Max replied.

The man held his gaze on Max a little longer. "Are you Max?"

"I am."

"I'm Charlie." The man shifted his briefcase to his left hand and held out his right. "I was told to watch for you. I'll introduce you to my team. We don't usually link up with new team members like this. It's kinda interesting. We just go as a team to different installations, do our inspection, then return home."

Grasping the talkative man's hand, Max said, "Good to meet you. We'll talk when we get to the gate."

Charlie nodded, getting the message that Max didn't want to talk on the crowded tram.

At the gate, Charlie introduced Max to the others as the new team member, then he and Max strode off for something to drink. The four men made themselves as comfortable as possible in the waiting area. Several minutes later, Max and Charlie returned to the lounge and waited for their flight.

When Max and the team arrived at Incirlik Air Base, the NWTI team chief initiated the inspection with an Emergency Action Message (EAM). Every aspect, from receiving the EAM through the actual loading of the B61 nuclear bombs on different NATO dual-purpose aircraft, would be evaluated. Primarily interested in the physical security and reaction force protecting the weapons, Max would be evaluating that force during the inspection over the next several days.

The 3,320-acre air base was a beehive of activity with dual-purpose, cargo, and other types of aircraft providing support to NATO and operations in the Middle East. In southern Turkey, the base was roughly six miles east of Adana and twenty miles inland from the Mediterranean Sea. Turkish contract workers provided maintenance and custodial services, and from the start, Max sensed their inquisitive eyes watching his every move. The Turkish Air Force personnel didn't try very hard to mask their distrust of the Americans either. In fact, they distrusted all the Westerners at the base. Max began to make a mental note of the workers he saw routinely and those who displayed more overt curiosity than others.

Any one of these guys could be spying and passing information to a foe or the Turkish officials, he thought. *If there's going to be a coup, you can bet some are watching the military. But who, and which side are they spying for?*

When Max was able to see the security procedures and the reaction force, he evaluated them not only for their technical and tactical competence but also their professionalism. He was an expert in evaluating and maintaining tactical capabilities of small unit forces. The security force had to be able to defend the nuclear storage facility for thirty minutes—supposedly the amount of time needed for the Turkish Army to respond with a force to defend the site. Unfortunately, the thirty-minute time standard was to defend against a hostile threat to Turkey such as a terrorist attack. An inside threat, such as from the Turkish military, was a completely different scenario and the answer was readily apparent. There was no way for Max to know who would be involved in a coup—factions of the military or the entire military—or if ISIS would be involved since they were only seventy miles away.

By Thursday, Max had developed an excellent understanding of the unit's ability to protect the weapons. Seated at a workplace provided in the SCIF, he wrote a summary of his analysis of the physical security of the air force's B61 thermonuclear weapons, capable of producing a yield of 340 kilotons, and the security force assigned to protect them. His analysis would be included in the team leader's final report for the commander. If any unauthorized individual saw the report, it would appear complete and not raise questions. Keeping a copy for himself, he made arrangements and returned home.

— ◆ —

Thursday, March 3, 2016
Senator Archibald Chapman Residence
New York, New York

Approximately one hundred people attended the three-thousand-dollar-per-plate fundraiser dinner for Jenny at the senator's residence. The catering staff continuously filled glasses with champagne, ensuring no glass was empty. The unobtrusive staff circulated through the throng of people with silver trays of hors d'oeuvres ranging from stuffed mushrooms to canapés with red and black caviar to assorted seafood delicacies.

Stew, Jenny's husband who ran the Gareth Foundation, captured more attention than Jenny and guests migrated to him from the onset. It was widely known that Jenny wasn't a cordial person. In fact, it had been said that she was so cold hearted you could etch glass with her tits. Stew was the main reason the people were there, as he made favors happen—for a price, of course. After several minutes of pleasantries, Stew guided the guests to Jenny. His function at the dinner was to support her and, of course, solicit contributions for the foundation.

One of the men Stew guided to Jenny was Nassar, an Arab who spoke excellent English. He was dressed in an expensive European suit and had close-cropped hair and beard. After a round of pleasantries and smiles, Jenny led Nassar to one of the adjoining rooms as she had done with previous guests.

"Please, be seated," she said as she closed the door. "Would you like another drink?" She motioned to a small table with several bottles of various alcoholic beverages and a silver ice bucket with a bottle of champagne.

"Bourbon will be fine."

Jenny poured about two fingers of bourbon into a glass, then turned back to him. "Ice?"

Nassar simply nodded.

Jenny covered the cubes in the glass with bourbon, then stepped to Nassar. She handed him the glass and sat in the leather chair beside him. She got right to the point. The guests knew why they were there—exchange of favors for money. "I want to continue our relationship after I'm elected. I will continue to support and fight for your cause," she said bluntly, a smile appearing on her face. "It takes a lot of resources to get to the convention, which is still about five months away. I need your help. Can I count on you?"

"I want the US border kept open."

Jenny nodded.

"I do not want the Americans to go into Syria. You must keep them out."

Jenny nodded.

"Your president is sending more troops to the Helmand Province. Why? We asked you not to let that happen."

"Don't worry," Jenny said, her tone reassuring. "It is just a small number of soldiers for protection and a few more special forces troops to advise the Afghan National Army. They are not to enter the fighting unless it is necessary. It's just a show to appease some people."

"We are making steady gains and don't want the poppy fields destroyed. Protect them." His tone was stern. "You must keep me informed about the military."

Jenny nodded. "Anything else?"

"For now, no."

Jenny leaned closer to him and said with a straight face as she locked onto his eyes, "Then I can count on your contribution?"

"You will receive one hundred thousand dollars."

"For my campaign, and one million for the foundation."

His eyebrows raised slightly. "Agreed."

Jenny stood and extended her hand. "Thank you for your contribution. Enjoy the rest of the evening." She stepped to the door, opened it, and escorted him back into the crowd.

Stew, seeing her emerge from the room, guided the next guest to her.

She was familiar with the guests and knew about what she could extract from them as long as she supported their cause. As long as she led in the polls, the money would continue to flow in. Jenny and her husband were very experienced at raising money through their connections—a lot of booze, plenty to eat, and lots of promises had always ensured money gushed into the coffers.

As Jenny escorted the last guest back into the crowd, she latched onto Senator Archie Chapman and, after several minutes, extracted him from one of the ladies. The woman was a bit over-the-hill but still attractive and with more money than scruples. She liked to party, and liked the senator. He liked her money and, of course, romps in the sack with her.

"In here, Senator," Jenny said in a low voice. The smile reappeared on her face as she nodded and led Chapman through the crowd and into the adjoining room. As soon as she closed the door, she said, "We've done well tonight." She flopped in the chair next to the senator. "Tomorrow, you start making the rounds. The borders and immigration have been hot topics this evening. The president has assured me that he will not do anything on either. We need the cartels' money for the campaign. Also, criticize the president for sending more troops overseas. Make a big deal out of it. You got that?" She looked down her nose at him.

"Tomorrow is Friday. I won't be able to. Perhaps—"

"Tomorrow morning, Senator!" Her tone was harsh. "I know tomorrow is your day to screw around with that bimbo while your wife plays bridge, but we've got a fucking campaign to run. I don't want to hear any shit from you. We've got a lot to do."

Senator Chapman gave a sigh of submissive agreement.

Jenny stood and led him into the next room.

His smile reappeared as he stepped through the door behind her.

———— ◆ ◆ ◆ ————

Monday, March 7, 2016
Headquarters, US Special Operations Command
MacDill Air Force Base, Florida

Max met with General Matherson the morning he returned to SOCOM. Meeting with the general in his office, the two men sat at the small table and Max summarized his finding on the security of the nuclear weapons at Incirlik.

Max looked up from his notes and leaned in. "One thing we have going for us is the size of the nukes," he said in a reassuring tone. "They are roughly twelve feet long and thirteen inches in diameter. The weight is the biggest deterrent, at almost twelve hundred pounds."

"What about just the warhead?" Chugs asked, his inquisitive mind working through each possible scenario.

"It weighs approximately two hundred ninety pounds. That's a pretty heavy lift for just two men."

Chugs nodded.

"Four weapons are suspended from a steel rack in each protective aircraft shelter. The rack is then lowered into a reinforced concrete foundation in the ground. There are twenty-five of these weapon vaults with only ninety nukes at the base. The hardened vaults in the ground and dispersed aircraft shelters add to the security of the weapons. However, the Turkish Air Force is allocated forty nukes, so, by agreement, they have the right to inspect them. And they did when they found out we were there."

Chugs sipped his coffee as he studied him. "What's your assessment?"

"Depending on the size of the force, I believe a hostile force could capture at least four nukes. They could take the entire bomb or just remove the warhead." Max locked eyes with Chugs. "Another scenario is if the air base is overtaken by a hostile force, they gain access to the weapons, load them onto the F-16 that is right there in the shelter, and fly four nukes out. Turkey flies the F-16 as well, so there'll be plenty of trained pilots in the country."

"What about the airmen providing security?" Chugs asked, still analyzing every word Max said.

"They're good men. Although they met the minimum standards on the evaluation, I think they are the weakest link. They have lost their edge. They have fallen victim to the president's speeches about nuclear disarmament and think their jobs are over. When I checked the records, their training has become lax. There are high personnel turnovers and shortfalls. Little emphasis is on their mission."

Chugs had suspected the weapons were vulnerable before sending Max, but Max just confirmed it. Chugs would reply to the air force and anticipated a request for help in securing the base until additional trained personnel could arrive at Incirlik. Unfortunately, the president's latest commitment to training and advising the 215th Corps Afghan National Army further strained his already-limited resources. He didn't have the personnel available to help the air force.

With his fingertip, Chugs pushed a folder across the table to Max. "Colonel Johnston sent this over for you."

Max slid it closer and opened the front cover.

"It's more info on Turkey," Chugs continued. "He updated his assessment. Corruption and payoffs are worse than they originally thought. He is working with—well, trying to work with—the CIA on this. The senior staff at the CIA is pushing back on this, and we can't figure out why." He paused in anticipation of a question from Max.

"Muslim Brotherhood?" Max asked as he looked up from the folder.

"Possibly. Johnston was able to get some information about the drug trade and a possible connection to Turkey. He's promised more on that."

"Drugs and Turkey? That doesn't fit." Max's eyes narrowed as he tried to make the connection.

"We believe it's more than that. One of the CIA boys in Latin America is following it. Johnston believes the Muslim Brotherhood is more influential in the Turkish government than in the past. He's trying to connect all the dots, but not much on Turkey is coming out of the CIA right now. Imagery analysis hasn't shown any increase in poppy fields in Turkey."

"It's the election, sir," Max said, the frustration in his voice noticeable. "A friend of mine told me that politics within the senior staff is nauseating. The agencies have been staffed with incompetent people for political payoffs. Also, the Office of the Director of National Intelligence is inept. They just pass papers around in a circle. They're worthless."

Chugs gave a slight nod and struggled to suppress a grin. "I'm just concerned about Turkey, Muslim Brotherhood, and drugs all mentioned in the same report. The Secretary of State tried to call Turkey's President Kağan, but he wouldn't talk with him. He's still upset with our president. Johnston said the CIA is not sharing much of the information they received from their contact in the Turkish Army. You'll note that he still lists the possibility of a coup d'etat as probable."

Max nodded. "That brings us full circle. The nukes at Incirlik."

"That's keeping me awake at night."

CHAPTER 3

Wednesday, March 9, 2016
Senator Archibald Chapman Residence
New York, New York

Senator Chapman was hosting one of the regular campaign meetings with Jenny, her husband Stew, and Deputy Director Trent Weldon in preparation for a round of upcoming interviews on the national networks.

In the den of the well-appointed home, the four sat at a round oak card table. A wet bar was built into one wall. A flat-screen TV tuned to CNN hung on the wall. Several paintings adorned the walls of the room. Chapman had hung his favorite, a charcoal drawing of a woman's legs, titled *The Perfect Legs,* next to the bar. Numerous memorabilia from his years in office were on display around the room.

Stew, as usual, kept everyone on track and focused on his meeting topics as they reviewed each item.

Jenny finished off her third Glenlivet XXV and set the glass down on the table with a clack. "Trent, your position as the Director of CIA is solid when I'm elected." She tilted her head slightly forward, and her eyes seemed to roll down her nose toward him. It was her signal that she didn't want any of the intelligence bureaucracy to get in the way. "Anything since we talked that I should be aware of? Do you have the notes I asked you to look at?"

Trent withdrew three stapled-together sheets of paper from his inside coat pocket and handed them to Jenny. "These are the points you wanted me to answer. Everything has been sanitized. Just stick to the points and you won't need to worry about anything that's classified. Stay with the domestic issues and you'll do well."

"That's a good point," Stew said. "Get back to the work you did with the children. That always goes over well." He took a couple of sips from his single malt scotch. "Avoid the international issues. That'll give the opposition a point to attack you on." He placed the Cuban cigar in his mouth and puffed, then blew it out, letting the smoke swirl above his head.

Jenny batted at the smoke with her hand to dissipate it as she glared at Stew. "Stew, if you don't mind, don't blow that fucking smoke into my face." She looked back to Trent. "What's the latest on Turkey?"

"So far"—Trent shot a look toward Stew—"I've kept a lid on all reference to the Muslim Brotherhood and downplayed the rumored coup. Be aware that the DIA is taking a closer look based on the information our source provided three weeks ago. I don't think it's anything to worry about, as that is something DIA would normally look at. In any event, should it come up, acknowledge it, downplay it, and return to one of the safe domestic topics."

"Can you hush it up?" Jenny asked. "I don't want anything negative making the news that could come back on us."

"I'll call the president," Stew said, holding a crooked finger in front of him. "I'll tell him to promise President Kağan the latest upgrades of the nuclear bombs in Turkey if he keeps the situation under control and calm. That'll pacify Kağan for a while."

"Better have the Secretary of State pass the word, as Kağan is still not speaking with the president," Trent said. "The FBI is asking questions about leaked classified information and unauthorized servers in the government."

Jenny turned to Stew. "Talk to the attorney general and tell her I'll announce that she'll stay on in my administration. Make sure she understands there'll be no investigation."

Stew nodded. "I'll back channel and see what Kağan wants. We can turn this into a positive event if we work this just right."

Jenny looked back at Trent. "Keep an eye on the DIA. I don't want to be caught off guard if something does happen in Turkey. I want to be able to influence any situation there."

Trent nodded.

Jenny sat upright in her chair. "Archie, nose around and find out what the DIA and military are planning. Specifically, if there is anything to the rumor about a possible coup, what'll they do? We're getting a lot of money from the Muslim Brotherhood and Turkey…the foundation is."

"Jenny, I—"

"Do as I said, Senator. No whining. As you make your rounds, keep spreading the word about police brutality and the military killing innocent civilians. Keep the news focused on those issues and reinforce that Islam is a peaceful religion. Make damn sure no one talks about the Muslim Brotherhood."

Senator Chapman's face turned red, and he downed his scotch.

"One last thing," Trent said as his gaze darted between the others. "The FBI is going to pull one of your staffers in and talk with him."

"Which one?" Jenny leaned toward Weldon. "What're they going to talk to him about?"

"David Johnson," Trent replied. "I was told it was about the private servers, mishandling of classified information, and possible money laundering."

"I don't want him talking to the FBI," Jenny replied in a vile tone before turning her attention to Stew. "Tell the attorney general to let the director of the FBI know, I don't want him questioned." Jenny gave Weldon a hard stare. "Get rid of Johnson. Dead men tell no tales. Be sure and sanitize his apartment thoroughly."

"Jenny, I don't like that," Chapman protested. "There's got to be another way. Perhaps—"

"Shut the fuck up, Archie! Well, Trent?"

Weldon nodded.

———— ✦ ✦ ✦ ————

Friday, March 11, 2016
Temple of Augustus and Roma
Ankara, Turkey

In the open-air museum amid the ruins of the Temple of Augustus and Rome, George rendezvoused with Erol. The two appeared like any other visitors, conservatively dressed, strolling along in the sun-filled morning, viewing the ruins, and reading the historical markers. People from all over the world visited this site dating back to 25 BC. The diverse crowd made it easy for the two men to blend in.

"ISIS and the Muslim Brotherhood are working together," Erol said in a low voice while seeming to read one of the markers.

"That's not new. I need the latest information," George replied firmly, maintaining his gaze on the marker.

"ISIS wants the nuclear weapons at Incirlik and is pushing the Brotherhood. That, along with President Kağan's hard line, is causing friction with most of the military. The Brotherhood is spreading a lot of money around to get what they want."

"Is there going to be a coup?" George asked.

"Yes. The military, or most of it, objects to Kağan's hard line. They know the Brotherhood is causing problems throughout the region. Be very aware of them." Erol moved to another marker.

"Go on," George said.

"I think the fight against ISIS is more of a show. As you know, Syria is causing a lot of problems. Iran is pro-Assad and Turkey is anti-Assad. Our two countries have had good relations. The Brotherhood is pushing Kağan, but I don't know which way he is going."

George gave a slight nod.

Erol inched closer to George and held his cupped hand between the two of them. "This is the latest on the coup and those whom I have determined, so far, are going against the hardline approach of the government."

George raised his palm under Erol's cupped hand and received the flash drive. "When is the coup going to happen?"

Erol shook his head. "Don't know. It is very dangerous now. You will need to get my family and me out of the country soon."

"Understood," George said as he deposited the flash drive into his pocket.

"I must be on my way," Erol said, then he turned and walked away.

———◆◆◆———

Monday, March 14, 2016
Headquarters, US Special Operations Command
MacDill Air Force Base, Florida

Helen opened the door to the J3's office, stepped just inside, and said, "General, Lieutenant Colonel Johnston, DIA, is here."

"Thank you. Show him in," Matherson said. He and Max stood as Johnston entered the office.

The three men sat at the small table after the traditional greetings.

Johnston retrieved three folders from his briefcase, then handed one to the general, one to Max, and laid the third one in front of himself. "I've completed an analysis on Turkey. In short, I believe there'll be a coup, but I'm uncertain when. They're probably still in the planning stage. It's our belief that President Kağan is going to play both sides on this. He's collecting information on who's plotting against him and who's loyal. It's possible he's staging the coup to purge the military and those who oppose him in his efforts to move back to Ottoman traditions. He could also be allowing his opponents to plot against him so he can identify who they are, then remove them. In any event, he's playing a dangerous game. The Muslim Brotherhood is pressuring him, and they want those weapons. NATO is concerned with the course of events in Turkey and for the safety of the ninety B61 nuclear bombs."

"The president is reluctant to authorize the movement of the weapons out of Turkey," Chugs said as he glanced at the two men. "He believes the situation there is overblown and has authorized them the latest upgrade to the weapons. The president's denial is the problem."

"NATO is not happy with the president's decision," Max said. "I was on the phone earlier with the OND (Office of Nuclear Deterrence) at the Pentagon. They're uneasy with the situation in Turkey and want my recommendation. A senator has asked that Congress be briefed on the situation. I'm going to OND on Wednesday to give them a copy of my report and analysis. I'll encourage them to move the weapons to another country."

"President Kağan wants to keep the weapons in Turkey," Chugs said. "Our president believes that if there is an incident in moving the weapons, or word gets out that we're moving the weapons out of Turkey, it'll look bad for the election and Jenny."

"We're basically screwed." Max pitched his pencil onto the table and leaned back. "There's about to be a coup in Turkey, and they host the storage of ninety of our nuclear bombs. A coup happens in Turkey,

Turkey takes control of the weapons, and the hardline Muslims have our nukes. Some of them could end up almost anywhere and possibly used against us. It boils down to Gareth's election. Well, that's just great." Max's frustration was unmistakable.

"The SecDef won't even talk about nuclear weapons," Johnston said. "He thinks they should be eliminated. Iran is going full speed ahead with their nuclear development program, and North Korea is working on perfecting their strategic missile capability."

"It appears that the Muslim Brotherhood and ISIS are working together on plans to acquire some of the nukes," Johnston said. "One more thing. We think the Brotherhood knows about your real mission to Turkey and suspects the US is going to move them. They may make a move before we can get them out."

"We have a leak somewhere?" Chugs asked, his expression serious.

"I don't know if it was a leak or not," the lieutenant colonel replied. "It's just a good suspicion. We're looking into it. Just be careful, and I'll let you know what I find out."

A possible leak was devastating news. SOCOM depended on secrecy, and their mission demanded it. If Turkey or the Muslim Brotherhood knew of Max's trip to the air base under the guise of the NWTI inspection, that meant they were ahead of SOCOM and could prevent the American military from taking any proactive measures to safeguard the weapons. They could also strike the base first.

"We've got people scattered all over the world," Chugs said, his tone stern. "If we have a leak, it must be stopped immediately or a lot of people could get killed."

"I wanted you to be aware of it and know we're working on it," Johnston replied as he shifted in his chair.

— ◆ ◆ ◆ —

Tuesday, March 15, 2016
J. Gilbert's Steak House
McLean, Virginia

At a linen-draped table in one of the private dining rooms of J. Gilbert's, Senator Archibald Chapman cut into his center-cut filet Oscar. The ample portion of crabmeat and hollandaise sauce oozed down the side of the steak and dripped onto the pants of his off-the-rack suit.

Chapman's title assured privacy without question. The room, with subdued lighting and rich library paneling, was cordial and suited to a senator's status. The staff was unobtrusive and attentive to the desires of the guests.

Chapman slid the fork into his mouth and promptly placed the hunk of meat into his cheek, then said, "This is very good. How's the crab bisque?" He pointed with his fork.

Nassar nodded, wiped his mouth, then placed his spoon on the saucer. "It is quite nice." He glanced around the room to ensure no one was nearby. "Is the military going to increase the troop strength in Afghanistan?"

"No, no plans that I am aware of. The president won't authorize any more troops."

"Good," Nassar said. "What about Syria? Is he going to go beyond the air force striking in Syria? Any plans for ground troops? We are concerned with the recent events. Your information has saved a number of our fighters in Syria and Afghanistan." He retrieved an envelope from inside his coat pocket and slid it across the table to the senator.

Chapman scooped up the stuffed envelope faster than he'd attacked the dinner and placed it in his coat pocket. "Nothing. He's not interested. He just wants to protect his legacy and help the party win the election. Although he and Jenny aren't the best of friends, he's doing all he can to get her elected. She believes focusing domestically is what the people care about and that's what matters to win. She'll then turn her attention globally, and that'll help our president and Kağan with their future goals."

Nassar leaned closer into the table. "What are his plans for Turkey?"

Chapman shoved another piece of steak into his mouth. "He's loyal to the Brotherhood. Not to worry."

"If there should be a coup d'etat, what will he do?" Nassar asked, his voice low and gaze fixed on the senator.

Chapman never slowed down in devouring his meal, answering without looking at the man across from him. "Is there going to be one?"

"Possibly. If so, what will he do?"

"Hell, man, I don't know."

Nassar's eyes narrowed. "That's not the right response. You are on the Senate Select Committee on Intelligence and are paid for information. Quite well, I may add. One more time. What will he do?"

Chapman cleared his throat, then took a swallow of his cabernet. "Probably nothing." He wiped his mouth.

"I want to know *specifically*. I don't want any interference from the US."

"All right. I'll see to it."

Nassar sipped his cabernet, then wiped his mouth. "There are ninety nuclear bombs at Incirlik Air Base."

Chapman nodded, then the color drained from his face as he realized what Nassar was suggesting. "No, you can't take them. Those are not negotiable."

Nassar leaned forward again. "You will do as I tell you and provide me whatever I want."

Chapman wiped his mouth then his brow with the napkin. "You're asking too much. I'm severing our relationship." He slid his chair back and started to get up from the table.

Unflapped, Nassar replied, "Senator, you have made a number of trips to a private Caribbean Island with Jenny and Stew Gareth. I believe it is referred to as *Pedophile Island*." He slid his hand inside his coat and when it reappeared, he was holding two photos. He flipped them onto the table face up. "It looks like you are enjoying yourself. The first one, that little girl, is about thirteen. The next one, the little boy is twelve. If those made it into the media, I don't think you would be in Jenny's cabinet. They could even cost Jenny the election and your reelection. I doubt that your wife or Friday piece would like it either."

Chapman looked as if he was going to be sick. He scooped up the photographs and shoved them into his pocket with a trembling hand. "What do you want me to do?"

"I will let you know. Keep me informed on anything to do with Turkey. If the military is going to move the bombs, I want to know immediately."

———•••———

Thursday, March 17, 2016
Sheraton Hotel
Washington, DC

In his hotel room, Max was preparing to leave for the scheduled meeting at the OND when his cell phone rang. "Hello," he said into the phone, somewhat surprised to be receiving the call.

"Max, Andy," came the familiar voice. "I know you're about to head out to your OND meeting. Have you got a few minutes?"

"Sure, what's up?"

"Have you seen the news this morning?"

"Earlier, yes. The same old bullshit about the election. I couldn't take much of it. It was too nauseating this early in the morning."

"No, a body was found early this morning in DC."

"What's so unusual about that? It's a common occurrence here."

"This one got my attention. The body was David Johnson, one of Jenny Gareth's staffers. At first, the name didn't mean anything to me, until I realized that the FBI was pulling him in to question him about mishandled and leaked classified information. I had seen his name and the reference to the leak during my research for the analysis on Turkey."

"What happened?" Max asked, his curiosity piqued.

"Early this morning, he was out jogging and, according to the report, he fell or stumbled and smashed his head against a rock. When they found him, he was unconscious. He died at the hospital without regaining consciousness. The police say it's simply an accident."

"An accident? He's connected to leaked classified information, the Gareth campaign, and was about to be questioned by the FBI. That sounds kinda fishy to me."

"I thought so too. I'm going over to talk to the DC police and see if they can provide any more information. I'll also go by the FBI Field Office to see what they have, or if they can provide any more on Johnson now that he is dead."

"Okay. I'm heading to my meeting. I'll call you when I finish."

CHAPTER 4

Thursday, March 17, 2016
National Mall
Washington, DC

MAX AND LIEUTENANT Colonel Johnston strolled along the National Mall in Washington, DC, near the Lincoln Memorial, steering clear of others. In the low sixties with a partly cloudy sky and light breeze—a reprieve from the dreary DC winter—it was too pretty a day to be inside.

"How did the meeting go at OND?" Johnston asked as he slid the zipper down on his Levi's jacket, his voice low and his stride steady.

"About what you'd expect with a room full of bureaucrats—bad coffee and stale pastries," Max said with a grin. "OND is very concerned with the situation in Turkey. They're going to schedule a briefing to Congress as soon as possible. I don't think it'll be before sometime next month. They're going to recommend the weapons be relocated out of Turkey based on the current situation there. A NATO representative was at the meeting, and he told me they want the weapons to remain in theater."

"They've asked us to help them with an assessment of possible storage locations," Andy said as his pace slowed. "Turkey has pledged to double their efforts to protect them. President Kağan is pressuring the US not to move them and says it's a slap in the face to Turkey to even consider it." Andy stopped walking and faced Max. "Don't trust 'em. I don't like it."

Max nodded. "You mentioned before I went to my meeting about the body of David Johnson being found this morning. What did you find out about Gareth's staffer?"

"The DC police are calling it an accident and *case closed.* The FBI is frustrated—at least that's what it seemed like. Apparently, Johnson had access to classified information although he didn't have clearance. There've been a lot of rumors about Gareth's handling of classified information. Johnson was mentioned a couple of times in reference to Turkey in intel reports and has connections to a Muslim Brotherhood lobbyist."

"What was the reference to him in the reports?" Max's eyes narrowed, his expression growing more serious. "Does the CIA have anything?"

"Our liaison at the CIA told me he can't get access to anything related to Johnson. All reference to the possible coup d'etat in Turkey is being passed off as grumblings. Reference to the Muslim Brotherhood and Turkey has been minimized as well. All of a sudden, that information is practically impossible to access. The FBI did tell me Johnson is known to have met with the lobbyist several times."

"Who's the FBI agent in charge of this?"

"Her name slips me right now. I'll get it to you. Why?"

"Curious mostly." Max was more than curious, but he wanted Andy to find out all he could from his sources before committing. His mind was already working through the bits and pieces—classified information leaks, nukes, Muslim Brotherhood, Turkey, a dead staffer, and a presidential campaign. He was uneasy about the scenario forming in his mind. "I just don't have a good feeling about all this," he said in a cold tone as he slid his hands into his jacket pockets. "Keep digging around and see what you can find. It seems odd that a lobbyist is meeting with a low-level staffer. See if you can find out about those meetings. He could be a messenger boy. If he is, what was he delivering? Something's up, and I don't mean the temperature."

Andy nodded. "Talk to you soon."

———✦✦✦———

Saturday, March 26, 2016
Senator Archibald Chapman Residence
New York, New York

"Here ya go, Archie," Stew Gareth said as he entered the senator's house, handing Archie a wrapped bottle. Cigar smoke flowed over the shoulders of his Brioni suit as he stepped through the door. "I got that from one of our contributors. It's a single-barrel bourbon from Garrison Brothers in Texas. Damn good bourbon!"

With bottle in hand, Archie ushered Stew into the living room where Trent Weldon, Aaron Fitzgerald, Wes Brock, and Nassar, the Muslim Brotherhood representative, sat engaged in idle conversation while awaiting Stew's arrival. He greeted and shook hands with each of them.

With a broad grin, Stew looked back at his host. "Archie, pour us a round of that bourbon. Y'all watch out for that stuff—it's not for the faint of heart. I think you'll enjoy it." He eased into a vacant wingback chair across from the couch.

Nassar stood, grasped the leather handle of the briefcase that sat on the floor next to him, and stepped to Stew, placing it beside his chair. He didn't speak. Everyone knew it was stuffed with cash as the briefcase had appeared several times before and then contributions would occur later.

The meeting was one of the regular gatherings for the Gareth campaign. All was going well, and the money was flowing in—a necessity to be successful. Stew, well connected throughout the world, never hesitated to use those connections to benefit his causes. Jenny's campaign was one of them. He called the shots and ensured his key players left nothing to chance. Winning the election was their main focus, and Stew kept everyone on target. He made sure potential negative information about Jenny was suppressed. As one would expect, previous campaign stops and video from the media outlets were reviewed with recommendations for future events.

"Trent," Stew said, pointing with his glass of bourbon. "I read in the paper about Johnson having an accident when he was jogging the other morning. Too bad."

The deputy CIA director nodded, interpreting Stew's statement as a compliment for a job well done. "The FBI doesn't have anything that can get back to us. DC police are in line as well."

Stew puffed his cigar, holding his gaze on Weldon. His subtle way of asking, *What else ya got?*

"The DIA has been poking around and looking for intel about Turkey and the nuclear weapons stored there," Weldon replied.

Wes Brock coughed after he took a sip from his glass.

"Ya all right there, Wes? Little sips. Don't get in a hurry. This stuff is real sippin' bourbon."

Wes wiped his mouth with his hand, then said, "What's DIA doing?"

"There is a lot of hand wringing because of the report about a possible coup d'etat in Turkey," Weldon said, his eyes darting back and forth between the others. "NATO is nervous about the nukes stored there. Not to worry, the information is being suppressed."

Stew puffed his cigar and said through the swirling smoke, "You know, we might be able to use this in the campaign. Let me think about it for a while. Keep any reference to the Muslim Brotherhood and Arab Spring low-key. I don't want either of them becoming an issue. We've gotta get past the election." He looked toward Nassar, then back to the others. "Oh, and if anyone should ask, *we are very saddened by the untimely death of David Johnson.* Then drop it and go to the next topic."

"I want to know immediately what NATO or the military plans to do about those nukes," Nassar said, his voice calm but demanding. "You have assured me that the US will not interfere with President Kağan."

"Archie," Stew said, pointing with the smoldering cigar between two fingers, "that's your department. If you hear anything, let me know immediately. Downplay the talk and make a fuss, if you do."

"OND held a meeting last Thursday on the nukes," Archie said as he poured more bourbon into his glass. "They've requested to brief Congress and have referenced an analysis of the situation, which came out of SOCOM."

"Block the meeting," Stew said with a harsh tone as the smoke swirled above his head. "Why's SOCOM doing an analysis? That's air force territory."

"The air force asked SOCOM for help because of the problems they're having with the nuclear surety program," Wes said. "They've had a couple of rounds of their nuclear people flunking inspections, and a number of them have been fired. You may have read that the air force fired the general in charge of the nuclear forces for misconduct. Well, in reality he didn't want to play ball and has been advocating that the weapons in Turkey be moved. Aside from being shorthanded, the air staff isn't comfortable with their nuclear program right now and it's in chaos."

"What does the analysis recommend?" Nassar asked.

"Move the nukes," Wes replied.

"I don't need to remind you that the Brotherhood has spent a lot of money and effort in setting all this up, from the Arab Spring to Jenny's election. In just a few months, the New Ottoman Empire will be born and there will be a new world order."

"Aaron, you and Wes keep a close eye on this. If you hear anything about moving the nukes, get in touch with me immediately," Stew said. "Trent, keep an eye on DIA and SOCOM. If they keep nosing around or digging deeper, get with me right away."

Trent and Wes nodded.

———— ✦ ✦ ✦ ————

Monday, April 14, 2016
Headquarters, US Special Operations Command
MacDill Air Force Base, Florida

Max's meeting with Chugs in his office had become a regular occurrence, and the topic was always Turkey and nuclear weapons. A large wall TV tuned to Fox News with the sound muted focused on the conventions and upcoming election, although neither man seemed to pay any attention to the broadcast. Jenny's organization was exceptionally successful in getting the media outlets focused on her. The international news continued to take a backseat to anything other than the most notorious events and, of course, Jenny. The current headline the pundits were feeding on was several leaked documents and the promise of more by WikiLeaks. It was, in fact, detrimental news for Jenny's campaign, but it also shed light on the government, corruption of the politicians, and exposed the vulnerability of government computer networks, drawing America's attention away from international events.

"Max," Chugs said as he glanced at the TV, "the NATO commander is livid and wants the nukes out of Turkey. The leaks of classified documents are making it difficult for all of us to operate. Remember back in March when I gave you Colonel Johnston's update on Turkey?"

"Yes, sir," Max replied, his eyes raised to meet the general's.

"The Agency's guy from the Latin America Division who was following up on the drug trade and a possible connection to Turkey connected the dots. Supposedly, he obtained a list of President Kağan's loyalists and their plan to take the nukes from Incirlik," Chugs said in a serious tone.

Max breathed a sigh of relief. "That's good news."

"That's only part of it. He's disappeared. The NATO commander thinks the CIA may have him located, but they can't get to him. Unfortunately, the Agency is keeping a lid on this, which is making it hard for all of us. The NATO commander has asked for our help. He needs that information, but, based on the leaks in the government and now the WikiLeaks, he wants to get it before the CIA. If they get it first, he thinks they will bury it and we won't get access to it until it is too late. Something is going on at the upper echelon in Langley, which is complicating our efforts."

Max leaned forward with an owlish look. "The Agency hasn't asked for our help in getting him back?"

"Nope!" Chugs replied. "They know we have teams all over the area, and it almost seems like they are writing their guy off and don't want the intel. Johnston is trying to get the operative's location. Work with him and get that info. Just keep me updated on where it takes you, but above all, be careful. Once you've got it, figure out our best course of action. We've gotta get ahead of Turkey on this, otherwise, they may split from NATO and take our nukes with them. If they do, the Muslim Brotherhood and ISIS will have them."

It was becoming very obvious that the CIA wouldn't be helping Max get the information from their man who had disappeared. In fact, Chugs believed the CIA was closing the file on the suspected coup in Turkey and possibly planning to eliminate the operative. Although his head kept discounting that possibility, his gut instinct was screaming something different. This made it difficult for Max, and a lot more dangerous.

Johnston had been around a long time and interacted with the CIA on numerous occasions. He had contacts and had already started developing vital information before the CIA ended its assessment on Turkey. Whatever knowledge the missing operative possessed, it was believed to be vital information necessary for the protection of the nukes and a potential confrontation with a NATO member, or worse, ISIS gaining the weapons.

In Max's assessment of the nuclear security at Incirlik, he outlined two other options for the weapons. Both were unacceptable. The first was to keep the bombs securely locked and in the subsurface locations. However, this option was not feasible, as Max ascertained that a hostile force could overpower the guards protecting them and gain access to the weapons. The second option was to use the command disable mechanism incorporated in each of the B61s. However, this option would require going to each of the ninety nukes and actuating the mechanism. This would render the nuke useless by literally frying the internal circuitry of the bomb. Unfortunately, the nuclear material would still be in the warhead. The terrorists or rogue nation would want that component, therefore, leaving the plutonium was not an acceptable option, which left the only viable option to evacuate all B61 bombs to a safe NATO location.

"It sickens me, but I have a feeling the CIA is going to liquidate their operative," Chugs said with a sigh.

"Another Benghazi," Max said as he nodded.

Chugs dropped his gaze. He knew the CIA and possibly the entire government security community would not be in favor of Max's mission. Chugs did consider Max's suggested possibility—another Benghazi. If it was, what was the government doing, and what was it all about? He would also be throwing Max into the middle of it. He didn't like that, or the odds for Max's success. "Find the operative, get the information, and then let's figure out how we can get the nukes out of Turkey without causing an international incident, or worse. I don't need to tell ya, but be extremely careful."

Max nodded, then stood to leave.

——— ◆ ◆ ◆ ———

Monday, April 25, 2016
Chez Vous Restaurant on French Street
Istanbul, Turkey

George agreed to the unusual meeting with the two men but preferred to meet in this restaurant, as he could trust the owner and the money he paid him was an added inducement. George knew well the escape route out of the restaurant but had never had to use it.

The three men sat at a table near one of the windows overlooking the entrance. Two other tables across the room were the only others that were occupied, and those patrons were oblivious to George and the men with him. The waiter placed a platter of white cheese and three glasses of raki on the table.

Andy looked up at the man and said, "Thank you." He turned his attention back to George.

The waiter nodded and stepped away.

Max's gaze followed the man until he was at a safe distance from them.

George shot a glance out the window, then sipped his drink. "Turkey is a mess," he said, his voice low. "Be very careful here. The president has his spies everywhere."

"Is there going to be a coup?" Andy asked.

"Yes, but I don't know when," George said, his gaze darting between the two men.

"What about Incirlik?" Max asked, his face void of expression.

"It is just one of the pieces. I have made a detailed report—twice actually. Somewhere along the line, it's changed. Now Langley, as far as I know, has limited the info on Turkey and the situation. The state of affairs here is worse than you think." George slid a piece of cheese into his mouth, then reached for his drink as the waiter passed their table on his way to another table. "The Russians, Iranians, Americans, Syrians—all are stirring the pot."

Andy gave a slight nod. "You're aware that one of your people from the LA Division is missing?"

"I haven't paid attention to the Latin American Division. What's the story?" George replied.

"He was following up on a possible connection between Turkey and the drug trade. He's somewhere in the region."

"That sounds familiar. I did hear something, but the story was a bit different. I'll see what I can find out."

"Are y'all going to get him out?" Max asked. "What the hell is going on here?"

"I'll get back to you on our guy. Be very careful in Turkey. It isn't just about ideology, though that is a part of it. It's about money."

"Are you saying Incirlik is not a problem?" Max shot back.

"They are just one piece of it. Despite what the governments say in public, it is about money. Turkey is on the transit routes between the oil- and gas-rich countries and Europe. A gas pipeline was planned from Arabia and Qatar to Israel and across Turkey to Italy for sale through Europe."

"These countries are aligned with the West." Andy sipped the anise-flavored drink.

"Correct," George said. "Russia also wants to sell its oil and gas to the European market. The planned pipeline would push them out of that market and relieve Europe from its dependence on Russian gas. In 2006, an agreement was reached to build an extension of the Trans-Arabian Pipeline through Syria to the Turkish border and connect to the Turkey-Austria gas pipeline. In 2009, Syria backed out of the deal and blocked transit."

"They blocked it because Syria is an ally of Russia," Max said, his head dipping slightly.

"The US then got the bright idea to overthrow the Syrian government and replace it with one more in line with our way of thinking." George bit off a piece of cheese. "Who do you suppose came up with that idea? I can't remember who first said it, but remember the quote, 'Whoever controls the government controls the state's resources, and by extension, the wealth derived from them.' "

"Jenny Gareth," Max said as the corner of his mouth wrinkled up and his head bobbed. "Where does Incirlik come in?"

"Again…money." George took another sip of his liqueur. "President Kağan wants money. Russia wants the pipeline access, and so does the US. Who's going to pay him the most? The nukes are a prized possession. Will we pay him not to steal them? Will we pay him not to withdraw from NATO? What else does he want? He doesn't respect our president, and he suspects we're going to participate in a coup against him. The price will be high. You can bet that Iran, ISIS, the Muslim Brotherhood, and even Russia would love to get their hands on those nukes."

"We can't trust the Turkish military to safeguard the weapons," Andy said.

"Correct," George replied. "Russia would love to see Turkey back out of NATO. Then Russia could move in unobstructed. As I said before, this place is a mess…a powder keg ready to explode."

George had confirmed Max's and Andy's suspicions that it wasn't going to be easy to get the nukes out of Turkey. Max had experienced the scrutinizing eyes of the Turkish military and civilian workers at Incirlik. It was about to get worse. The Turks would soon discover who he was and why he had been there. It appeared that Turkey was a NATO member in name only and could act at any time. Max had to locate the missing operative and get the information he possessed without any delay. Hopefully, George could provide more information after he had the opportunity to research the missing man. They had little to go on and even less help.

CHAPTER 5

Friday, April 29, 2016
Esans Hotel
Sultanahmet District, Istanbul, Turkey

SEATED AT A corner linen-draped table of the Esans Hotel restaurant, Max and Andy sipped coffee. The large windows offered a magnificent view onto the bay of the Sea of Marmara. The hotel, built in the nineteenth century, was of Ottoman style and located in the old city on the European, or western, side of Istanbul. George had recommended the two men stay there as it was an easy walk to the main square and the train station and was tucked away, around the corner from the noisy part of town. The two men watched a ship as it made its way into the Bosporus Strait that connected from the Black Sea. The view and the pleasant morning made the real world of problems in Turkey seem far away.

Max's cell phone rang, interrupting the tranquility of the moment. He looked at the display, then to Andy. "Time to go to work."

Andy nodded.

"Yes," Max said into the phone.

Then Max looked to Andy and nodded, indicating it was the expected call from George.

"We'll be there," Max said into the phone, then the connection went dead. He laid the cell phone on the table and took a sip of his coffee. Returning his demitasse cup to the saucer, he looked to Andy and said, "We meet with George at nine this morning. Topkapi Palace Museum."

Andy acknowledged the meeting with a nod and then sipped his own coffee. He checked his watch, then withdrew his cell phone and tapped the keys. "It looks like about a ten-minute walk from here."

Max nodded.

They finished their coffee, then stood and made their way out of the hotel. Acting like tourists taking in the panoramic view, they were actually checking to see if they were being followed. Crowds of tourists had gathered at the front entrance of the palace by the time Max and Andy arrived.

The Topkapi Palace was the main residence and administrative headquarters of the sultans between the fifteenth and nineteenth centuries. The most beautiful and well-known site in Istanbul, the palace was converted into a museum in April 1924, two years after the Ottoman monarchy was abolished.

Once inside the entrance, visitors milled about, picked up maps, and began their visit to the palace, taking a myriad of paths. George seemed to appear out of the throng of people and greeted Max, then Andy as though he was their tour guide.

George steered them into the Fourth Courtyard. Only a few other tourists had made it that far into the palace, making it easy for the three men to meet in private. They nonchalantly strolled along in the tulip garden, avoiding others. Flowerbeds decorated with brightly colored roses, tulips, hyacinths, carnations, and jasmine flowers made for a pleasant walk. But unfortunately, it was work and not pleasure.

George told them he had an update that he had discovered since their meeting on Monday. "President Kağan is a bit irritated with his neighbors, to say the least," he said, his voice low as he maintained a casual behavior. "The rest of the world doesn't see things the way he does, and internally, the situation between him and the prime minister continues to deteriorate. The prime minister and Kağan are at odds on just about everything. I think the coup we keep hearing about *is* going to happen."

"That's what I'm afraid of." Max stooped to pick up a pebble. "That brings us back to Incirlik."

George withdrew a folded paper from his inside coat pocket and handed it to Max.

Taking the paper, Max slowed his pace and unfolded it to reveal a photo of a bearded man in a courtyard of a bombed-out building.

"That's a satellite image taken two days ago. It's suspected to be the man you asked me about the other day, the one who has the information on Kağan's loyalists and their plan to take the nukes from Incirlik."

"Is the Agency canceling the guy or are they going to get him?" Andy asked as the three men faced each other.

"That's just it. I can't find out anything," George said. "That image was taken in Aleppo, Syria. I was lucky to get it."

"Aleppo? That place is in chaos." Andy's tone was one of astonishment. "Why would he be there? If he was captured, was he taken there or was that where they got him?"

As the three men continued to stroll along the path, George said, "I know. All good questions. I can only guess. It's a very dangerous place now. Langley may have decided it's too risky to go in after him. I just don't like the entire setup on this guy."

"Langley hasn't asked for SOCOM's help," Max said, then pitched the pebble several meters in front of them. "Are you sure it's our guy?"

"As best I can tell," George replied. "I suggest we go to Aleppo and have a look for ourselves. It'll take a day's travel time to get there. It's about 750 miles by car from here. We can leave early in the morning and be in position by nightfall."

Max and Andy nodded.

"I'll make the arrangements," George said. "See you in the morning." He left the two and walked out of the courtyard.

Fighting in Aleppo had raged on since July 2012 and seemed like everyone was fighting everyone else—complete bedlam. As one could imagine, the city had taken a heavy toll in destruction and casualties. Food shortages, increased infectious diseases, lack of basic services, and a tremendous number of people had become refugees as a result of the carnage. The hostilities in this no-man's-land were between the Syrian opposition, which included the Free Syrian Army and other Sunni groups, such as the Levant Front and the Al-Qaeda-affiliated Al-Nusra Front. They fought against the Ba'athist government, which was supported by Hezbollah, Shia militias, Russia, and the Kurdish People's Protection Units.

George's suggestion that they go into this mayhem was an extremely dangerous proposition. Making it into the city and locating the man was only a small part of it. They weren't even sure the man in the image was their target. And getting the information or the man out was a different problem all together. Of course, their top priority was not to be shot or captured by any of the various factions—a challenge in itself.

Later that evening, Max planned to call General Matherson to give him a status report and tell him of his planned trip the next day. He also needed the general's approval since he would be entering a very hostile area, as well as clear agreement on an exfiltration plan if, and probably when, something went badly wrong. The paucity of information and intelligence on the situation concerned Max. He did consider the possibility that if the CIA was going to eliminate the man, anyone near him would be taken out as well and that it could very well be him.

Max checked his watch. *I'll catch Chugs just before lunch,* he thought. He punched in the number on his secured cell phone. Irritated at the news on the TV, Max switched the channels to a local show. Although he didn't understand Turkish, it was for background noise to help mask his end of the phone conversation.

"How's the beer over there?" came Chugs's usual question when Max was away from the office.

"Not bad, actually, much like the German beers," Max said with a smile. "Efes produces a nice dark beer you'd like."

Chugs uttered a throaty, "Uh-huh," then said, "Whatcha got?"

"My contact here gave me a satellite image of a man he believes is the guy I'm looking for."

"Do they have 'im? Are you goin' to talk with him?" Matherson asked, his tone serious.

"They don't have him but know where he is."

"Where is he, Max?" His voice was full of concern.

"That's the problem. Aleppo."

"That damn place is a disaster. What's the Agency doing? Are they going after him?"

"My contact doesn't think so," Max said. "He says Langley has labeled it too dangerous."

"That's one of the smarter things they've done lately."

"We're wanting to go there tomorrow to get a closer look at the guy and see what the real situation is."

"I don't like it, Max."

"It's just for a look, then out," Max pushed.

The general's tone was stern. "Max, I have to agree with Langley this time."

"Sir, we don't have much choice," Max insisted.

"Max, I can't give you any support and you'll be on your own. If either side in Syria picks you up, they'll have a heyday with you. You'll be paraded around on every news channel all over the world. It'll be a disaster for us and the president. I don't think I can get you out."

"I know. I don't know how else to get the information. If Langley is writing him off, which they could be, we've lost the intel. If they do get him, they'll bury him and the data."

"Damn it, Max!" The general was more frustrated at the situation than Max. He knew there was a high probability Max would be apprehended, or worse. He didn't like being in that situation. "Be careful, Max. Keep me posted and call me when you get out."

"Will do, sir."

Max sighed and ended the call, the reality of being on his own settling in to stay.

—— ✦ ✦ ✦ ——

Friday, April 29, 2016
Gareth Residence
New York, New York

At any given time, poll numbers continuously released by various polling companies maintained that Jenny was dominating. Even after the recent sixth straight win in the primaries by her party challenger and socialist, the numbers remained in her favor.

The war in Afghanistan was still not going well for the president, however. Another district in the Helmand Province fell to the Taliban—the fifth. Military casualties were still returning home from the Middle East on stretchers or in coffins without any end to the fighting in sight and the situation seemed to be at a stalemate. The president's foreign policy was a disaster, and he was still more interested in the November election than events around the world. His ongoing domestic agenda gave fodder to both sides, for and against.

Strong feelings spread across the country. The disinformation, or propaganda as the case might be, continued unabated. Many Americans became sickened by this situation and avoided the news altogether. Media outlets skewed their reports to support their preferred candidate. It was truly *high stakes politics*—win at all costs.

Both parties hammered away, taking opposing positions on most topics. Border security, healthcare, and government spending took the top three spots, and Jenny's propaganda made it appear that the majority of the country agreed with her take on things.

Deputy CIA Director Trent Weldon, Deputy Secretary of Defense Wes Brock, Deputy Secretary of State Aaron Fitzgerald, and Stew Gareth had been on a conference call with Senator Archibald Chapman for over half an hour.

Senator Chapman sat in his den, his shirt sleeves rolled up to his forearms as he watched the news and drank coffee. He held the phone to his ear but was more interested in the broadcast.

Stew said, "Archie, did you get the OND briefing to Congress canceled?"

"I'm working on it," the senator replied.

"Archie, get it canceled," Stew said, his tone stern.

With a meek tone, Chapman replied, "I will."

"What the hell have you all been doing?" Stew stood as his face reddened, sensing Archie was not focused on the phone call. "That socialist has won too many primaries. The last six. Now this WikiLeaks shit. Jenny is the next president. Got that?"

"Yes. Got it. Yes. Yeah," came their mumbling replies.

Stew, his tone unmistakably punitive, continued, "Trent, how the hell did that WikiLeaks guy get all that information? Clean this mess up."

"I'm already on it." Weldon chose his next words carefully. "We have crafted a report and are blaming the Russians. The people will buy it. We've tried to get the WikiLeaks guy, but he has asylum in the Ecuadorian embassy in London. We've gotta be very careful with this. Supposedly, he has a ton more information ready to be released that will destroy Jenny's election and put us in jail. He has a *dead man's switch* on it. If we take him out, the information will automatically be released."

"I like the story blaming the Russians," Stew said with a chuckle. "Keep that going. Stay on the WikiLeaks."

"The NATO commander is pushing our president to remove the weapons from Turkey," Brock said. "Turkey could be an issue, the Muslim Brotherhood."

"Okay." Stew rolled the ash from his cigar into the ashtray. "Wes, tell the commander the nukes remain. I'll tell our president they are to stay in Turkey, we don't want them moved."

"Will do," Brock replied.

Stew continued, "Aaron, tell President Kağan the bombs'll stay in Turkey."

"Okay," Fitzgerald replied.

"Stew," Weldon said. "DIA is digging into the Turkish situation. I think we have just about all the information blocked, but there could be another problem."

Stew laid his cigar in the ashtray. "What is it?"

"Our operative is missing," Weldon replied, referring to a CIA operative stationed in Panama who worked directly for him. "He has a list of those loyal to President Kağan and information on the planned coup in Turkey. He could tie it all back to us."

"You said *missing*, as in captured?"

"Don't know. He could just be unable to communicate. I have a Special Ops team looking for him, and they think they've located him. They just can't get *to* him. If he's compromised or gone on his own, the information he has will look bad for us…if it gets out."

Stew picked up his coffee cup and sipped. "Find out his situation and get it under control. If he's gone rogue, do what needs to be done. No more scandals."

Brock shot a glance out his window, then said, "Understood."

"Aaron, what's the status with President Kağan?" Stew asked sternly.

"He was receptive to the upgrades on the bombs, but I think he wants more money," Fitzgerald replied.

"I'll get Nassar on it," Stew replied. "Jenny's got a big fundraiser tomorrow in New York and we need to pull in a lot of money. I don't want the donors getting jittery over Turkey. Archie, you work the folks on Capitol Hill and shut down any talk about Turkey. Aaron, put out something from state that says there is nothing to the coup rumors. Have your people spin it."

———•♦•———

Saturday, April 30, 2016
No-Man's-Land
Aleppo, Syria

Max, Andy, and George passed through two checkpoints after displaying the press credentials supplied by George and the guards' inspection of their car. They were cautioned at both stops about the dangers of entering the area as the sound of sporadic automatic weapons fire could be heard around the city. Displaying a cavalier and obnoxious attitude common to press people, they were grudgingly allowed to proceed. Haze filled the air, and the buildings displayed the signs of fighting. The closer they got to their destination, damage to the buildings was more severe and many destroyed vehicles set vacant on the side of the trashed streets. Only a few vehicles were seen sporadically moving along the roadways. The abandoned area was dark, quiet, and stunk from uncollected, rotting garbage. Smoke from nearby smoldering fires lingered in the night air.

After parking their car in a partially destroyed structure near their target's location and camouflaging it, they maneuvered to a bombed-out building across the deserted street from the house with a courtyard their suspected target reportedly occupied. They set up in what used to be a bedroom on the second story. Bombing had blown out the windows, and holes marred the ceiling and floor. Pockmarks from bullets and shrapnel decorated the two walls that had managed to remain standing.

Max inspected the rest of the building for signs of both recent use and to plan an escape route, while Andy and George prepared their observation position with cameras, scopes, and improvised rear cover. Although larger caliber and automatic weapons would have been preferrable, all they had were .45 caliber pistols supplied by George. Larger weapons were too difficult to conceal in the car, and press personnel didn't carry rifles. Their black-market handguns could easily be disposed of and were not traceable. Getting comfortable, if that was even possible, was not an option. It appeared no one had used the building for quite a while, but as a precaution, Max rigged several obstructions as noisemakers and motion sensors for warning, in the event someone decided to enter the building. Satisfied with his preparations, he rejoined the other two.

For almost two hours, the three men peered into the darkness, hoping to identify their target. There was nothing—no one could be seen anywhere. The night seemed full of tension and the threesome sensed the prying eyes of combatants, like rats in a garbage pile at night. They knew they were there but just couldn't see or hear them.

Max turned his head to the other two and said in a low voice, "Let's try to get some sleep. We'll take turns on watch. I'll take the first shift."

"I'll take the second," George murmured.

Andy and George found places to sleep near the window and used the equipment bags for pillows, covering themselves with poncho liners and laying their pistols where they could easily grasp them if needed.

Max kept his attention on the target and courtyard across the street, alternating between the night scope and just his eyes. It was black and nothing moved. No light and no sounds. The overcast sky blocked illumination from the moon, and a mist began to fall. Almost thirty minutes had passed when Max tensed, his senses warning him something was present. Then he detected a faint smell of cigarette smoke as it drifted on the humid air. He scanned the building, courtyard, and adjacent structures and methodically scrutinized the windows, doorways, the street, and any place a person could hide. No cigarette glow anywhere. Someone was nearby, but Max couldn't locate him.

Is it one or several? he wondered. He strained his vision to search the blackness again.

After several minutes crawled by, he spotted the telltale glow as it punctuated the blackness of the courtyard. The figure was black but the red dot unmistakable. *There is someone there, but who? Friend or foe?*

Max wanted to identify the smoker and who was with him, if anyone, but venturing out into hostile territory in the black of night would not be a wise move. There was no way to tell who he would meet. Most likely, they would shoot first and ask questions later. Whoever was out there would be more heavily armed and, probably, outnumber Max. For now, all he could do was keep watch on the courtyard and wait for daylight.

Max checked his watch. *George's turn,* he thought. As he reached out to tap him, a crashing sound emanated from the floor below. "George," he whispered, grasping his shoulder and giving a gentle shake. "We've got company."

Without uttering a sound, George reached over and tugged on Andy's arm. "Company," he said softly.

Both men seized their pistols and crouched behind the makeshift rear cover they'd erected earlier.

Max stepped through a hole in the wall to the adjoining room. Anticipating the visitor would inspect their observation room first, he hoped to gain the advantage over him if he proved to be hostile. He had a clear field of fire and observation of the door from behind his barricade. The gentle footsteps continued crunching on the debris-strewn floor as they slowly made their way up the stairs. Max signaled with his hand to Andy and George that he was ready.

Both nodded.

CHAPTER 6

Sunday, May 1, 2016
Bombed-Out Building
Aleppo, Syria

T HE MIST TURNED to light rain by 0200 local time, which made it difficult to hear the footsteps approaching. Three men, ready to fire, strained their senses. Whoever was advancing on their position was a skilled fighter—there were no noises other than unavoidable soft steps on the debris-strewn floor. Each step was slow and deliberate in the dark hall. Max detected a second set of faint footsteps, but then the rain increased in intensity and practically drowned out all sound.

This could be dicey, Max thought. *Lady Luck, watch over us. Our pistols will be no match against automatic rifles.* He motioned with his hand to get the other men's attention, then held up two fingers as a signal to George and Andy that he'd detected two bodies advancing on them.

Both gave a slight nod, then returned their attention to the doorway.

"Press…hold your fire. Friendlies," came a man's low voice in good English from beyond the door.

George shot a look to Max and caught his nod as a signal to admit them. George knew that Max would remain silent until they were sure the men in the hall were friendly. If they were not, hopefully, Max could take them out before serious damage would be done. They anticipated the second person would remain protected in the hall until he was satisfied that it was a safe situation.

"Enter," George replied in a subdued voice.

"Coming in," the man said, then stepped into the room.

"Put your weapon against the wall and step forward," George commanded, observing the silhouette as best he could.

The dark figure turned and placed his weapon against the wall, then faced back in George's direction and stepped forward.

"Tell your buddy to come in and place his rifle against the wall," George ordered.

The man turned his head over his shoulder and said, "Come in. It's clear."

The second figure entered the room and placed his weapon against the wall.

"Sit and cross your legs," George commanded. "Who are you?"

The man complied, and the other figure followed suit. "I'm Dave, and this is Sandy." He motioned with his thumb. His accent was midwestern US. "We're both Americans and with the YPG."

The precarious cessation of hostilities in Syria had been in effect since February 27th as a result of the meeting in Munich between Russia, the US, and the International Syria Support Group. The Islamist fighters—who controlled a major portion of the country—were not covered in the agreement. This left the Kurdish People's Protection Units, or YPG, fighting ISIS in the north. The YPG was aligned with the Kurdistan Workers' Party, or PKK, a US- and Turkey-designated terrorist group. Turkey considered this relationship a challenge to their national security, and the US had supported the YPG with arms and ammunition, which strained the US-Turkey relationship. US Aircraft from Incirlik Air Force Base supported the YPG in Syria while the Turkish Air Force bombed PKK targets in Iraq and southeastern Turkey. As a result of this disastrous situation, Turkey was suspicious of the US.

andy picked up his tactical flashlight and passed the small beam of red light over Sandy's face, her uniform, and highlighted her YPG patch. He did the same to Dave, illuminating his YPG patch, then his Ranger tab.

Max stepped through and said in a low voice, "They're friendly." He entered the room and sat next to George. "You took a big chance coming in here."

"Probably did, but I didn't think the press would shoot us." Dave pointed to the blue flak jacket on the bag beside George, then withdrew his canteen and unscrewed the cap. "We've been watching that building for three days." He pointed in the direction of the building with the courtyard. His eyes glanced toward the equipment George and Andy had set up by the window, then drank from the canteen. "We spotted you as you came in. I'm guessing you're watching the same one."

"Could be," Max said, wanting to know more about the man and woman before revealing anything. "How long have you been with the YPG?"

"I've been here a couple of years, and she's been here about eighteen months."

"You were in the US Army previously?" Max asked as he studied the man.

"Ranger Regiment for eight years, two tours in Afghanistan and one in Iraq," he replied, then pointed to the woman. "Sandy spent four years as an MP, two tours in Iraq. She doesn't like to talk about it, but she received the Bronze Star for valor during her second tour. She's as good as any Ranger I know."

"What's your interest in that building?" Max asked.

"I'll ask you the same thing." Dave held a steady gaze on Max. "It's suspected to be ISIS. Our commander sent us here to watch it. We're to try to find out who they are and what's going on. Word has it, the cease-fire is going to be called off tomorrow, and the Syrian Army is surrounding the city. All hell is getting ready to break loose. You guys have wandered into a lion's den."

After the man's silence signaled he was awaiting reciprocation, Max shrugged his shoulders and said, "Just looking for a story. It was getting late when we got here, and we decided to take shelter in here. We spotted the guys in that building and wanted to see what was going on there. Any way we can get closer to them, possibly do an interview?"

"Not likely," Dave said. "Those blue flak jackets kept you from getting shot. Everyone wants the press on their side to support their cause, so you probably won't be shot at unless you start nosing around. Don't push your luck."

"Have you identified any of the men in there?" Andy asked, his gaze darting between Sandy and Dave.

"There're about four or five Middle Eastern men and what looks like a Caucasian man. That's not the big problem. There's a two-man team on the second floor of that building diagonally across the street. I can't tell who they are, but they've got some heavy firepower and are watching the same building we are. They came in a couple of days ago. I've seen a few others in some of the buildings at times, but I don't know about them either. I see 'em mainly at night, and they don't stay long. It's damn hard to figure out who is who. I've lost count with over a hundred and sixty factions fighting. Hell, everybody is fighting everybody else. I suggest you guys clear out of here first thing in the morning. I'm guessing our commander is going to pull us out of here tomorrow."

Though the information Dave provided aided in their situational awareness and strengthened the possibility that the person they were looking for was in that building, he also painted a far more hazardous situation than anyone had originally thought. And it appeared to be deteriorating rapidly. Max did consider that the two-man team in the building diagonally across from them could be a team to eliminate the CIA's man who, supposedly, had disappeared. If Max tried to get to the Caucasian man to identify him, he could be shot by the ISIS fighters, the shooters in the building across from them, or anyone else in the area, for that matter. He had no alternative but to wait and hope an opportunity arose that would allow him to get to the man. Strolling over there and knocking on the courtyard gate was not an option.

Dave and Sandy had opted to spend the rest of the night in the company of the Americans rather than risk another journey back into no-man's-land. They fixed themselves places on the floor next to each other.

Max and Andy returned to their places on the floor of the former bedroom by the window. George finished out his time on an uneventful watch, then was relieved by Andy.

———— ◆ ◆ ————

Saturday, April 30, 2016
Office of the Deputy Director
CIA Headquarters, Langley, Virginia

The deputy director received an urgent message from Aleppo at 10:30 p.m. local time. Excited and thinking this would get him on Stew's good side, he punched in the numbers and listened to the phone ring.

"Stew," Trent said into the phone. "We've got our missing operative located in Syria. It's currently raining in Aleppo, bad enough the Predator can't see the target. The Special Ops team we sent out is in an adjacent building."

"I told you to take care of him," Stew's voice blared out of the phone, his frustration unmistakable. "What's the goddamn hold up?"

"Our team spotted three men from the press enter a building near them. They don't want to fire if the press is around for obvious reasons. If the Predator did fire and something went wrong, or if the press saw any of the Hellfire missile fragments, we could have a problem."

The silence before Stew replied was unnerving. "Okay, here's what ya do. As soon as the weather breaks and the Predator can see the target, take it out. Get the press guys too. No witnesses. Be sure and pull your men back to a safe location before the strike. Then have them go in after and ensure both targets are destroyed. Be ready to leak a story accusing the Syrian Air Force of using barrel bombs. Oh, and have them collect any obvious evidence, if there is any. Got it?"

"Yeah. The weather over Aleppo may not clear up until about mid-morning tomorrow, Aleppo time."

"Okay, call me as soon as it's done," came Stew's reply. "Jenny has a couple of campaign stops and a fundraiser this week. When you release the story of the barrel bombs, she'll condemn their use and make a big deal out of indiscriminate killing of children and civilians. She'll appear to be up on world events, and of course, the children angle will be good. Round up a couple of photos of injured children to go along with the story. She can use them too."

"Okay. Anything else?" Trent asked. Anxious to end the call, he was uneasy with his latest orders.

"Yeah, tell Wes that Kağan is upset with our military." Stew's tone turned harsh. "Those special forces soldiers that are assisting the YPG are wearing their patch. Tell them to take 'em off. Turkey is fighting the PKK and complaining that it is unacceptable for our soldiers to wear them. They're accusing us of having a double standard and being hypocritical. Kağan is paranoid anyway."

"I know. I'll pass the word to 'em."

— ◆◆◆ —

Sunday, May 1, 2016
Bombed-Out Building
Aleppo, Syria

A couple hours into his turn at watch, Andy picked up his field glasses and systematically looked over the area beyond the window opening once again. The light rain had stopped by 0530 local time, and twilight had begun to penetrate an overcast sky. The shower had cleansed the air of stench within the neighborhood at least temporarily. Anywhere else, it would be the promise of a beautiful day. Unfortunately, the light revealed the state of destruction that had befallen Aleppo, Syria's second-largest city. In every direction, the streets were filled with rubble and debris from bombed-out buildings, hulks of burned cars, and charred remnants of Russian main battle tanks.

The emerging light of the new day revealed a different perspective of the courtyard they had focused on since the evening before. It, too, suffered the effects of the destroyed city. Rubble from the damaged, nearby buildings, two barrels, trash, and the burned remains of a car littered the ground. Several clumps of weeds scattered about clung to life like the inhabitants of Aleppo.

A Middle Eastern man emerged holding a cup in one hand and a cigarette in the other. His beard was full and heavy. Another bearded man emerged, walked to one of the far clumps of weeds, stopped and unzipped his pants, then relieved himself. The first one finished his drink, set the cup down, and made his way to the same clump of weeds. He flipped his cigarette to the side, then relieved himself.

Andy checked the time on his watch. *Looks like they're waking up over there,* he thought. He placed the binoculars to his eyes again to get a better look at the two men. Studying each man briefly, he then lowered the glasses and picked up the satellite image George had provided. *Neither one is our contact. They're nobodies. I'll give Max and George a few more minutes of sleep.* He watched the two men light cigarettes and meander around the courtyard while talking to each other for several minutes.

Eventually, a third bearded man with a Kalashnikov slung over his shoulder emerged, talking on a handheld radio. He looked around and seemed to be searching the buildings. The other two men joined Radio Man and began scrutinizing the area as well.

Something's about to happen, Andy thought. He reached over and gently shook Max's shoulder. "Something's up. Three men in the court-yard," he muttered, then turned and shook George. "Activity—three men in the courtyard."

Max stepped through the hole and tugged on Dave's arm, who in turn shook Sandy. "Activity in the courtyard," Max said softly.

The four joined Andy around the window.

"The guy with the radio," Dave said. "He seems to be the leader. Three days ago, they did the same thing at about the same time. A car and pickup pulled into the courtyard and another guy got out. I haven't seen him leave. I got the feeling when he arrived that he must be a senior guy based on the way the others were acting. He could be getting ready to leave."

"Or they're going to have a meeting," George said.

"I'd sure like to know who they are and what's going on," Max said, then he turned his head toward Dave. "Can you get me closer?"

"I don't recommend it," he replied.

"We could be just wasting our time, waiting around, hoping to get a story," Max said, more of a nudge to Dave. "If he's a leader, he's a story."

"All right, but we'll both likely be shot." Dave then turned to Sandy, who was already looking at him.

Her eyes told him everything. "I'll get a position where I can provide you some cover. Be careful," she said, then she gently patted his shoulder and slid her hand down his arm.

As the two men stepped out into the hall, their light footsteps crunched on the small bits of rubble covering the floor. Sandy went to the window in the adjoining room and found her position. George and Andy returned their attention to the situation outside.

Radio Man went into the building and, within two minutes, returned with another man—a Caucasian with a heavy beard.

"That's our man," George said without taking his eyes off him.

Andy glanced at the satellite image, then to the bearded man. "It looks like him."

At that instant, a muffled shot pierced the tranquility of the morning. The Caucasian man flinched and dropped to the ground.

Andy and George frantically sought the source of the shot, their eyes sweeping the windows, doorways, roof, and any other place a shooter could be hiding.

The Caucasian man crawled back through the door.

Then terror erupted. Gunfire exploded from several windows, rooftops, and doorways of the courtyard building and two other nearby buildings. The hail of bullets focused on the window diagonally across the street where Dave had pointed out the two men on the second floor. The firestorm was relentless. Bits of rock, stucco, smoke, and dust filled the air. Pockmarks appeared all around the window, the bullets chipping away at the remnants of the window frame. Then an RPG streaked across the street and into the window. The ensuing explosion certainly left no one alive, if they'd still been alive after all the bullets that had entered the window. After the fireball, smoke billowed out of the window and the barrage ended as suddenly as it had begun.

Andy immediately began searching the area for Max and Dave. Anything could happen in this type of situation. The two could have been spotted and shot. It was obvious there was a small force providing security to the inhabitants of the courtyard building. After this exchange, everyone would be on edge, and that made it even more dangerous outside.

"What the hell happened?" Max asked as he entered the room followed by Dave, who continued into the next room and knelt next to Sandy. "We didn't even get out the door before all hell broke loose."

"The guys on the second floor across the way took a shot at our target. We confirmed he's the same guy in the image," Andy said as he held up the paper imprinted with the satellite image.

"Are you sure it's him?" Max asked as he took a position at the window next to Andy. "Did they get him?"

"He crawled back inside," Andy said as he glanced at Max, then back to the courtyard. "He could've been wounded though. I couldn't tell."

The three men maintained a vigilance from the window while Dave and Sandy observed from the window in the next room.

The silence that ensued was deafening. No movement and no signs of life, but the tension was thick in the morning air.

Within several minutes, two combatants carrying Kalashnikov rifles emerged from the building with the courtyard and made their way across the street to the opposing building, obviously to verify there were no survivors. A moment later, one of the men appeared at the window and waved. He retreated inside, then reappeared with the other man, the two heaving a body from the window, then a second one. Both bodies landed on the rubbish below with a thud, sending up a poof of dust.

Less than five minutes after the two men returned to the courtyard building, a BMW followed by a Toyota pickup with four armed, bearded men in the back stopped in front of the gate to the courtyard. The gate opened, and both vehicles entered, circled, and stopped facing the gate. The occupants vacated the automobiles and entered the building.

"Well now," Max said. "Are they getting ready to leave or is this a meeting? Damn, I'd sure like to know what's going on in there."

"Same routine as the other day," Dave said as he leaned through the hole in the wall. "Probably picking up the guy they dropped off." He returned to his position at the window next to Sandy.

Ten minutes later, two men emerged from the building, looked over the surrounding area, then walked to the gate. Four more men stepped through the door, including the Caucasian man.

"There he is," Andy said in a low voice.

Max looked through the field glasses at the four men. He didn't utter a sound as he studied the Caucasian man. Finally, he lowered the glasses, rubbed his eyes, then raised the binoculars to his eyes again. "I know that guy." His tone was cold. "It can't be him."

"You *know* him?" George asked as he lowered his binoculars.

"I…I don't know. I think so, but it can't be who I think it is. Naw, it *can't* be him. It sure looks like him, though. Andy, get photos of him."

"Come in here," Max said in a low voice as he leaned over and looked through the hole to Dave.

"That's the guy I'm looking for, the Caucasian with the three guys," Max said as Dave knelt next to Max. "Can you get word through YPG to follow him or take him, if possible, but not kill him?"

"I don't know. I can try," Dave replied, his expression serious. "If the cease-fire ends today, that'll make it difficult." His gaze darted between George and Andy, then back to Max. "Level with me. I know you're not press. It'll help if I can tell my commander the US'll help us…more soldiers, arms, ammo, money, anything."

CHAPTER 7

Sunday, May 1, 2016
Bombed-Out Building
Aleppo, Syria

T HE SKY DARKENED and moderate rain began to fall again at 0620 local time. Turning his attention back outside, Max watched helplessly as the Caucasian man got into the BMW, the gates opened, and both vehicles sped out of the trashed compound.

Sandy leaned through the hole in the wall and said, "We've got to go. I just received word for us to withdraw."

Dave motioned his acknowledgment to her, then looked back to Max and said, "Gotta go. Can I tell my commander the US will help us?"

"I'll see what I can do," Max replied, then he scribbled a number on a piece of paper and handed it to Dave. "Call me if you get that guy. How do I get in touch with you?"

Dave took Max's pen and jotted his number on a scrap of paper, then handed it to Max. "You guys need to clear out of here too," he said. "Keep your heads down." He grinned as he stood.

The two American YPG mercenaries made their way out of the building and disappeared into the rain-drenched city.

"We'd better get outta here as well, while it's raining," Max said as he looked between George and Andy.

Max's instinct was to call the general and update him, but he checked his watch and thought, *Damn, it's around midnight in Tampa. It'll have to wait till later.* If the Caucasian was who Max thought he was, the situation had taken a serious turn for the worse. That individual was ruthless, cunning, and a formidable foe. Almost three years ago, Max had faced this mercenary and almost lost. However, that guy was supposed to be dead. Had his ghost returned to haunt Max? At the time, Matherson had informed Max the man had been taken care of by the CIA. *Did Chugs lie to me about his death? Or did the government lie to Chugs? Not good either way.*

Their equipment packed, the three men donned their blue flak jackets and were ready to escape the war-torn city. Max looked at the other two but didn't speak. After both men nodded they were ready, he led them out of the building that had been their refuge and into the open street. The rain obscured their movement from any distance, but shooters close-in were a different story. Although the trio's car was close, the journey to it was still dangerous. Open areas had to be negotiated. Sprinting along-side the buildings to limit their exposure as much as possible, they finally reached a place across the street from the camouflaged car. Pausing there, they scanned the surrounding buildings before Max darted toward the car. When he was about halfway, Andy followed. George prepared to do the same when suddenly a shot rang out, then another. A burst from an automatic rifle followed.

———— ✦ ✦ ✦ ————

Sunday, May 1, 2016
Presidential Palace of the Republic of Turkey
Ankara, Turkey

Abdal al-Ghazāli and President Hakan Kağan sat alone at a table draped with linen for breakfast. As the Muslim Brotherhood representative, al-Ghazāli needed to ensure Kağan was doing as instructed as well as providing any necessary assistance to the president to prevent him from being overthrown. He didn't necessarily trust Kağan, but the Brotherhood was necessary for him to achieve his goal to rebuild the Ottoman Empire. In turn, Kağan was necessary to the Brotherhood to achieve their goal of obtaining the nuclear weapons. It was all about money and power.

Al-Ghazāli, a frequent guest at the palace, took special delight in the first meal of the day, especially at the palace. Breakfast, leisurely but business-focused, consisted of bread, butter, jam, honey, olives, toma-toes, cucumbers, cheese, yogurt, cold meats, fruit juice, eggs, and Rize tea. He looked up as he smeared a huge dollop of jam and honey on a piece of warm flatbread and said, "Things are going according to plan. You have done well. I have been informed that the prime minister is going to announce his resignation." He bit off a piece of bread.

President Kağan sipped his tea, then set the gold-rimmed cup back on the saucer. "Yes, he will resign in a few days," he replied.

"You will be provided a name for the new PM."

President Kağan nodded. "The plan is set. I have identified everyone who is loyal to us. I have been assured the Americans will do nothing and the bombs will remain at Incirlik," he said, then lifted the teacup to his lips again.

"Excellent," al-Ghazāli said. "Our man, the American, is making the final arrangements. He is in Aleppo and will return in a day or two."

Kağan nodded. "Good. I want you to go back to all the loyal commanders and make sure they understand what to do and are ready to execute when the signal is given. There will be a lot of chaos at the air base. The power must be cut precisely when the signal is given and the air space closed. The 6th Corps Commander in Adana is key to all this. He will send a force to surround the entire air base and ensure it is sealed."

Al-Ghazāli sipped his tea. "Understand. The American will meet with the commander when he returns from Aleppo to make final coordination and check of the plan."

"Make sure he gets whatever he needs," Kağan said. "The main focus for the media is Ankara and Istanbul. Incirlik will come up, no doubt, but everyone is to minimize comments about the air base. Avoid comment if possible."

"The Brotherhood is ready and in position to facilitate the operation," al-Ghazāli said, then he shoved the remainder of the piece of bread into his mouth.

———◆◆◆———

Sunday, May 1, 2016
No-Man's-Land
Aleppo, Syria

Bullets ricocheted off the pavement and walls of the buildings as the escaping trio zigzagged the final distance. Caught in the open, they had very few options but to crouch and dodge and duck while advancing as fast as they could. Bullets buzzed all around them like mad bees. It almost seemed like the shooters were just harassing the three men—or were they just incredibly bad shots? Stopping to find out was not a consideration. If they were hit, it didn't really matter.

Max looked behind him to check on the progress of the other two and saw Andy fall. Fearing the worst, he turned back and darted to him. George reached Andy just before Max.

"In the thigh," George said, wiping the rain from his face.

Max grasped one of Andy's shoulders, and George grabbed the other. They raised Andy and scurried—Andy hobbling between the two as best he could—the remaining distance to the entrance of the destination building. Once behind what little wall still stood, they placed Andy on the floor so Max could check his wound.

George took a guarded position at the edge of the wall to watch for anyone chasing them.

Max wiped his face clear of dripping water with his hand, then went to work on Andy. "It's not too serious. I don't think the bullet hit any major arteries, but he's losing a lot of blood," he said as he looked into Andy's eyes, then to George. He slid the small medical kit closer to Andy's leg and retrieved the supplies he needed to clean and bandage Andy's thigh.

"You were hit too, Max," George said.

Max made a quick check of his body. "Where? I don't feel it or see any blood."

"Your vest," George said as he pointed to Max's back.

"So much for not shooting the press," Max said as he ripped Andy's pant leg. "I'll have him patched up in a couple of minutes. Get the car ready."

George looked over the wall once again to ensure the other side was clear. Not seeing anyone, he rushed to the car and went to work clearing the debris they had placed around and on the car to camouflage it. When finished, he began loading their gear.

Max stood and said, "He's ready to go."

He handed Andy's things to George, who, in turn, stowed them. Max and George stepped to Andy and again raised him by the shoulders.

Andy groaned as he stood. The two men helped him get into the rear seat of the car.

Max closed the car door and looked around their immediate area to ensure they had left nothing behind. "Let's go," he said, getting into the car.

Their first priority was to get out of Syria safely, and the next was to get Andy to a doctor. Wandering around Aleppo, or any other place in Syria, looking for a doctor was out of the question. The closest medical facility in safe territory was at Incirlik Air Base in Turkey.

Their route back to Istanbul took them to Adana and then on to the air base on the east side of the city. Unfortunately for Andy, it would take about three and a half hours to reach the hospital there. George drove with speed, dodging the debris in the street and avoiding as many potholes as possible. Andy moaned each time the car jolted over one of the hazards.

"Sorry, Andy," George said as he worked the wheel. "I'll slow down when we get out of this area."

Andy grimaced and forced out the words, "I'm okay. Just get us the hell outta here!"

George soon slowed the car when it appeared they were far enough away from their last position. The street was in better condition with fewer obstacles than the past several blocks, which provided Andy relief from the jostling. Max and George remained vigilant as they made their way out of the city.

George glanced at Max and said, "You stated you know the Caucasian guy back there. Who is he?"

"It can't be the guy I think it is. He's supposed to be dead, but it sure looks like him."

"Who do you think it is?"

"A mercenary named Bart Madison. An ex–special forces officer who worked for me a short time in Afghanistan. A smart officer, but he got a little carried away and I reprimanded him. He was later court-martialed and forced to resign his commission. He dropped out of sight for a while and then turned up with the FARC as an adviser."

"Sounds like a pleasant fellow," George grinned.

"There's more. Madison led an attack with the FARC on one of our classified storage facilities in Panama and made off with four man-packed nukes. They practically wiped out the entire site."

"I kinda remember reading something about that." George shot a look to Max, his expression serious.

"Yeah, the FARC sold two of the nukes to ISIS and they planned to attack the heartland of the US."

"I remember now. That was you?" George said with a hint of surprise in his voice. "Hmm. He almost got away with it, didn't he?"

"Yeah," Max replied as he thought back to Hoover Dam, the place where Madison had almost killed him and a lot of other people. "He knows nuclear weapons. My boss at SOCOM told me the Agency took care of him."

"Maybe he survived somehow. Unlikely, as the Agency makes sure you're dead when they eliminate you. Are you sure it's him?"

"No. My eyes tell me one thing, and my brain says something else. I can't believe my boss would lie to me."

"Perhaps the Agency didn't tell your boss the truth. They're known to lie and be very convincing, ya know?"

"I know," Max muttered. "If it is Madison, that raises the stakes. He's ruthless and capable of anything. Is there any way you can find out if the Agency actually eliminated him or not?"

George held his gaze on the road in front of them. "Hmm, I don't know. It could be a bit tricky trying to find out. Any information on him will be compartmented, and only a select few have access. I can't just start poking around as that will set off alarms and then I'll have a problem. Let me think whom I might be able to contact. There're a few people who owe me."

"If it is Madison," Max continued, "that makes it all the more imperative we locate him again, and fast."

———✦✦✦———

Sunday, May 1, 2016
Gareth Residence
New York, New York

"I haven't heard from you on that issue in Syria, Trent," Stew said into the phone in an icy tone. "Are you having phone problems? I was expecting your call hours ago."

Trent took a deep breath. He'd known this call wouldn't go well. "No. We can't get in touch with our people in Aleppo," he replied. "We're trying to find out what's going on."

Stew's harsh voice shot back, "Well, is the issue taken care of or not? I haven't seen anything on the news about a barrel bomb in Syria." He puffed on his cigar, then slurped his drink.

Trent replied, "Both buildings were destroyed. Two missiles each. The damage assessment was verified by the Predator feed. I don't have any confirmation on casualties. I've already sent a Special Ops team in to find out what happened."

"Damn it, what's wrong with your guys? You had a team right there, across the street, watching. What the hell is so hard about walking over there and checking the bodies?"

Trent took a deep breath, then proceeded with caution, choosing his words carefully. "Stew, as soon as the rain stopped and the Predator could see the target, it destroyed the buildings. The cessation of hostilities ended in Aleppo this morning, and the place is in chaos."

"So, you don't know if the target was neutralized and any fragments picked up? Hell, for all you know, those three press guys are interviewing our man and filming the fragments. You do want to be the next director, don't you?" Stew's words were so sharp they could have sliced a steak with ease. "I told you—*no more scandals.*"

"Yes, Stew. The team I sent in to check is en route to the location now and moving as fast as they can."

"Hell, Trent, that's all we need is some kid picking up a piece of missile shrapnel and turning it over to the press. Or worse…. Your rogue operative could be running around peddling the information on the coup. If that information gets out, it will embarrass Kağan. That would also force our president's hand and give the NATO commander enough ammunition to remove the nukes from Incirlik. Do you understand what I'm saying?"

"Yes, Stew. I do. I'm working on it and will take care of it."

"I expect a call as soon as you have. Don't forget your story about the barrel bombs."

The phone went dead.

———◆◆◆———

Sunday, May 1, 2016
39th Medical Group
Incirlik, Turkey

By midafternoon, Andy was admitted to the base hospital after surgery to inspect and clean his wound. The surgeon who'd operated on him preceded Max into the room. After the cordialities, the surgeon said, "I need to check you over to make sure everything is okay." He then looked at Max as a signal for him to wait outside.

Propped up in bed, Andy said, "Let him stay, Doc. You can talk in front of him."

The surgeon nodded, then turned to Max and said, "You were a good medic." He looked back to Andy and began examining him, the bandage, and the IV entry. "The projectile traversed deep into the rectus femoris muscle of the quadriceps and exited, leaving no fragmented foreign bodies." He pointed to the bandage and indicated the path of the bullet. "The femur was not involved. However, I want to keep you in the hospital for a few days to allow better pain management and IV antibiotics to prevent infection in view of the delay in treatment. Any questions for me?"

"How long will I be laid up?"

"That depends on your body. Let's see how you do in the next couple of days. Stay off the leg and let those muscles heal. I'll check on you tomorrow." The surgeon nodded, then walked out of the room.

"I figured they were going to keep you," Max said. "You need anything?"

"I don't think so. I'm good to go."

"Since we'll be hanging around for a couple of days, I'm going to try to accomplish a few things here. I've got a meeting with the security officer and his commander. I want to take another look at their security and readiness." Max's cell phone rang. He retrieved the phone from his pocket and saw Matherson's number displayed, then looked to Andy and said, "It's the boss calling me back." He placed the phone to his ear. "Good morning, General." Stepping to the side chair, Max withdrew his notepad and pen from his pocket, then sat in the chair.

"I was in an early morning meeting, Max," the general said. "Helen said you called. Things are heating up again in your neck of the woods. Glad you made it okay. What'd you find out?"

"Andy took a bullet in the thigh, and they've admitted him to the hospital here at Incirlik. It's only for a couple of days. While I'm here, I'm going to work with the security people. We did confirm that's the guy we're looking for," Max said.

"Did you learn anything from him?"

"We couldn't get close to him. He pulled out this morning surrounded by guards, but Andy took pictures of him."

"Good. It wasn't a total loss then."

"That's not the important news, General. I got a good look at him. It's Bart Madison." Max listened intently for what Chugs was about to say but also how he said it.

There was a long pause before Chugs spoke. "You said Bart Madison?"

"Yes, sir."

The telltale pause was longer this time. "Max, you must be mistaken. The Agency took care of him."

"No, sir. It's him. I'll be sending you some of the photographs Andy took and a summary this afternoon."

"Who did he leave with, and any idea where he went?"

"Our best guess is ISIS. He wasn't a prisoner. No idea where he went. Our contact here is trying to find out anything he can on Madison. If he turns up something, that may tell us where he is heading."

"Max, I want you to know, I personally spoke with the Agency and they told me Madison had been taken care of. I'll get with the commander and try to get this sorted out. I'll get back with you when I find out something."

Max dropped his eyes to the notepad, then to Andy. "Yes, sir. It just occurred to me that in Agency speak, *taken care of* is not always dead!"

———•◆•———

About an hour after Max spoke with Chugs, Bart Madison made a reconnaissance of Incirlik Air Base. He made contact, as directed by the 6th Corps commander, with a local maintenance worker who was actually an agent of the state intelligence agency of Turkey—the National Intelligence Organization, or MİT in Turkish—assigned to collect intelligence at the NATO Air Base. The MİT Agent guided Madison around the perimeter of the airfield, pointing out protective shelters where the B61 nuclear bombs were stored.

Madison compared the research of the air base he had conducted on the internet to his actual view of the base. Analyzing the terrain, he determined the best route to the shelters and egress upon completion of his mission and noted the double security fence and other obstacles that could pose a threat. Most of all, he determined where the security forces would try to establish their defensive positions.

Madison and his guide drove to various locations around the airfield, periodically stopping to give the appearance of their inspection of something specific, such as the grounds, fence, or road, all the while studying the airfield from different vantage points. On the last stop, Madison scanned the area with field glasses. His field of view stopped on one of the protective shelters, where a man in civilian attire and an airman stood talking. The civilian pointed to several locations, which piqued Madison's attention.

On closer examination, he murmured, "Son of a bitch—Max Kenworth. The US Military suspects an attack on the base. But why is Kenworth here? This is air force territory." He lowered the glasses and said to the agent, "I've seen enough. Let's go."

CHAPTER 8

Monday, May 2, 2016
Headquarters, 6th Corps
Adana, Turkey

Lieutenant General Devrim Çakmak, 6th Corps commander, sat across the large, wooden conference table from Abdal al-Ghazāli and Bart Madison. Thick dark hair grew from Çakmak's ears like clumps of weeds that seemed to challenge his wide mustache. Just as the cordialities ended, a soldier entered the room carrying a tray with three small, tulip-shaped glasses of black tea. General Çakmak raised his hand slightly as a signal for the men to be silent. Without speaking, the soldier carefully set a glass in front of each of the three men, then left the room, closing the door behind him.

Çakmak raised his glass, displaying the unit's crest—his fingers dwarfing the glass—and took a sip. Al-Ghazāli and Madison followed. The general returned the gold-rimmed glass to the matching saucer, looked to Madison, and said, "You have walked the terrain on the objective, and you know the plan of the operation. Do you have any recommendations?"

Madison glanced to al-Ghazāli, then to Çakmak. He had been briefed in detail on the powerful general and had dealt with his type several times in the past. The intel and his experience would prove invaluable in dealing with him. He needed the general's trust and confidence to do the job he'd been hired for. "A few things, General," Madison said. He knew the commander would challenge him—his type always did. He would want logical and coherent recommendations from someone confident in what he was saying. "I believe information on the mission has leaked out. When I agreed to this job, one of the conditions was complete secrecy."

Çakmak's eyes seemed to burn into Madison, his distrust of the American apparent. "What makes you say this?"

"Max Kenworth," Madison said, his tone cold. "Kenworth, a retired Delta Force colonel, works for SOCOM. I saw him at the air base yesterday. He's their nuclear weapons expert and wouldn't normally get involved at Incirlik. My guess is that someone leaked the plan and he was tasked to beef up security at the base."

"Kenworth is that big of a concern to you?" Çakmak studied Madison. "One man?"

"Yes, sir. That one man. I must assume he's analyzing security and preparing a force to defend the nukes. He will, no doubt, bring in additional soldiers. If your operation is to succeed, I'll need to make a few changes. Our attack must be fast and hard, because the Americans will be ready."

Çakmak studied Madison, sipping his tea. "Any changes will delay our plan. What do you have in mind?" It was obvious the general was cautious and a politician, but he was no fool.

Madison withdrew two folders from his briefcase, then slid one across the table to the general and handed the other one to al-Ghazāli. He watched Çakmak open his and scan the first page, then the second. "That's a quick sketch of the changes and a list of additional resources needed," he said. "If you approve, I'll work with your planners to make the detailed updates. The next thing will be rehearsals. There must be deliberate actions and no hesitation. Each task must be executed on schedule and exactly as I have noted. We will hit Incirlik before they can react."

Çakmak, with a stone-faced expression, said, "We will discuss your recommendations, then let you know. Will there be anything else?"

"Yes, sir," Madison said, his reply matter-of-fact. "Take out Kenworth immediately. Cut the head off the snake and that'll hamper the Americans. He's a threat and must be eliminated."

Çakmak wrapped his large fingers around the glass of tea, lifted it, and took a sip. "Perhaps he could provide us information or be useful in some other way."

"That won't happen, sir. He's too well trained."

"Perhaps," Çakmak said. "He has a weakness. Every man has. We just need to find it." His gaze shifted to al-Ghazāli. "Spend some time with Madison and learn all you can about Kenworth, then see if you can find out anything from your people in the US. I want a detailed file on him—likes, dislikes, family, girlfriend…anything and everything."

Al-Ghazāli nodded.

"I will direct MİT to start watching him," Çakmak said. "If he attempts to leave the country, they will apprehend him."

"He could just leave the base, fly out of Incirlik on a US Military aircraft," Madison said.

"Possibly, but we have our ways," Çakmak replied, his arrogance apparent.

"General," Madison said, "there must be absolute secrecy about this entire operation and about me. Reevaluate your OPSEC and stop the leaks. This entire plan is *need to know* and at the highest security level. President Kağan and al-Ghazāli assured me this would be the case."

Çakmak's face flushed slightly and his eyes narrowed at Madison's words. It was obvious he didn't appreciate his bluntness or criticism. However, he knew that ignoring Madison's instructions would not enhance his career either. His gaze shot to al-Ghazāli, then back to Madison. "I will see to it."

Al-Ghazāli, somewhat unnerved by Madison's directness, said, "Everyone involved, outside of the military, is already being cautioned that this is *need to know* and of the highest security, General."

——◆◆◆——

Wednesday, May 4, 2016
Office of the Deputy Director
CIA Headquarters, Langley, Virginia

"That's correct, Stew," Weldon said into the phone. "Both of the men we sent in to take care of the problem in Aleppo were killed. The missile fragments have been recovered."

"Hell, that took long enough. What about the press guys?"

"No trace of them." Weldon shifted in his chair and tensed.

Stew rolled his eyes and took a deep breath. "See if you can find out who they were. They're loose ends. What's the status of the missing operative?"

"He's disappeared. I have people dedicated to looking for him. We'll get him."

"Yeah, right. Before or after he tells the world what he knows? Damn it! Trent, you'd better find that guy and those press people. You had a simple task, and you blew it. Turn over every rock and *find 'em*. Get rid of 'em!"

"Yes, Stew. I'm on it."

Stew was quiet for a moment, then said, "Trent, I want you to put out another intel paper on Syria. Highlight the people fleeing their homes and going hungry. Put in there about the barrel bombs and how the poor children are casualties of this savage tactic. The last one did get some buzz with the media. Throw in several pictures of maimed children. I want this to tug at the heartstrings of the mothers and grandmothers in the US. Do ya get where I'm going? Send it over to me when you have it finished. Jenny will refer to it and hammer her opponents with it. That'll help her in the polls and the primary next week."

"Got it. I'll get someone working on it."

"I gotta go, Trent. I'm giving a campaign speech for Jenny. Call me this evening. I want a status update."

The phone went dead before Trent could say another word.

Jenny had come in second to her competitor in the past two primaries, which had everyone on edge and tempers short. Her competitor was simply a prop, put up by her party, to make Jenny look good, and the Gareth machine had been very successful in showing Jenny winning with the highest poll numbers. Unfortunately, the primaries' results showed Stew couldn't control the voters the way he'd anticipated. Jenny was supposed to win, so Stew was now challenged to call in more favors, twist more arms, make a few more payoffs.

———— + + + ————

Tuesday, May 4, 2016
Atatürk Airport
Istanbul, Turkey

Andy had developed a slight infection, so the doctors decided, over Andy's objection, to keep him in the hospital on a day-by-day basis.

Max met with the security officer and planned a number of tasks for him to accomplish, to enhance defense of the nukes. George returned to his station to seek leads on information concerning Madison's whereabouts and his ISIS connection as well as the pending coup. High on his agenda was to arrange another meeting with Erol as soon as possible, in hopes he could provide some of the needed intel. Unfortunately, the trail leading to Madison had gone cold with his disappearance in Aleppo. It would take time for George to work his contacts and develop new intelligence. This left Max with little to do in Turkey, so he decided to return to Tampa.

Waiting to board his flight, Max sat in the gate area of the Atatürk International Airport, checked his watch, and then sighed. With two hours remaining before his scheduled flight, like the other travelers, he was restless and struggled to find something to occupy his time while he waited. The terminal was bustling with passengers from all over the world going in all directions, and the PA system regularly blared out announcements in multiple languages. It was a noisy place, but Max soon managed to tune out the noise and settle into reading a book.

When a man sat down across from him, Max glanced up to observe him, then returned to his book. The man, casually dressed, didn't seem interested in him. A few moments later, another man sat down next to Max. A quick glance did not reveal anything alarming. It was a natural occurrence for travelers to wander in and sit nearby. They were there for the same reason, waiting on their time to depart. Then a third man took the seat on the other side of Max.

Although a glance revealed nothing unusual, Max began to feel uneasy. His eye caught a policeman standing ten feet away and facing in his direction. His instinct was to get out of there, but there wasn't really a good place to go except into the moving throng of people. He began searching for the best escape route. The airport was crowded, but the three men were too close for him to make a fast break. He hadn't committed any crime in Turkey, so there was no need to make an abrupt escape.

Casually stand and walk to the restroom as though nothing is wrong, he thought. No need to call attention to myself. He slipped his book into his briefcase and started to stand.

The man seated across from him opened his coat with his left hand, exposing a pistol, and said, "Kenworth, you are to come with us. We have a few questions."

The three men stood, and the two on either side of Max grasped his arms.

"What's this all about? Questions about what? Who are you? I've got a plane to catch. I haven't done anything wrong!"

"You will come with us peaceably or the policeman standing behind me will arrest you," Pistol Man said with good English syntax. "That will not go well for you."

Max saw he didn't really have a choice and didn't like the circumstances. However, Pistol Man's English told Max the man was not a conscript, he was a professional. The best option was to go with them and not commit any offense that would keep him in Turkey any longer than necessary. He had seen this type of setup before. A paranoid dictator suspects everyone and has those people picked up whom they deem to be a threat. Those poor souls were then roughed up to extract information and used for propaganda. The unlucky person was usually released in twenty-four hours, unless they divulged information the regime deemed as vital intelligence.

What the hell is this about? he thought. *Maybe I can pick up some intel as well. Looks like I'll miss today's flight.* "You're MİT, aren't you?" Max said. He knew the answer but wanted to see how easily they would talk. "I want to make a phone call first."

"Let's go," Pistol Man said as the two men tugged on Max's arms, moving him toward the exit.

"Where are we going?" Max's tone was stern. "I have done nothing wrong. I want to call the American embassy."

With no further discussion, the men ushered Max out of the terminal to a waiting Peugeot van with darkened windows. Pistol Man slid opened the side door, and the man on Max's right entered the vehicle and sat in the rear seat. Pistol Man motioned for Max to enter next, and the other man followed. As soon as he sat, Pistol Man closed the door and sat in the front passenger seat. The van sped away just as he pulled the door closed.

———— ♦ ♦ ♦ ————

Thursday, May 5, 2016
Contractor's Hill
Panama City, Panama

Danya Mayer leaned on the railing guarding the drop-off overlooking the Gaillard Cut of the Panama Canal. The bright sun was high in the cloudless sky, and a light breeze caressed the hilltop. She brushed her short, wavy brown hair from her face as she looked around. She then checked her watch, thinking, *Come on, where are you? I need to teach you how to tell time. It's getting hot out here.* She was there to meet a man, and like most of the men she dealt with, he was not very punctual nor of the upper crust of Panamanian society.

Danya was an Israeli intelligence officer for Mossad in Panama, there to meet with one of her contacts for updated information on Hezbollah and MS-13—the international criminal gang operating in the United States, Canada, Mexico, and Central America. Hezbollah was using MS-13 to smuggle ISIS fighters across the US-Mexico border and conduct narco-terrorist operations along the southern states of America.

Iran was exploiting what they saw as a weak and inept current US president who would be out of office within eight months. Stew Gareth and his political party continuously pushed the president to keep the borders open. The cartels and Muslim Brotherhood contributed huge sums of money to Jenny's campaign in exchange for those open borders. Iran had recognized the opportunity and accelerated their plan to install sleeper cells in the US, ready to rise up in jihad against the Americans before a new president was sworn into office. Iran, by way of Hezbollah, was also a contributor to the campaign. Hezbollah and the Muslim Brotherhood had teamed up in their efforts to invade the US. Once the US had been severely weakened—militarily and psychically— and chaos instilled, Israel would be destroyed. Since America and Israel were the bulwarks shoring up the West against ISIS and Islamization, Danya played a pivotal role in intelligence collection and disrupting the threats to Israel. Of course, Israel did share appropriate intelligence with the US to ease the tense situation between the two longtime allies.

Three years ago, Danya had seen firsthand the cunning, ruthless extremes these Islamists were willing to go to in their cause. The West had almost lost when the terrorists stole four nuclear weapons from the US Military. Danya was a member of the team that foiled them. At that time, the intelligence community had known they might not be so lucky in the future and that the fanatics would not give up their cause.

The man she was waiting for she knew as Carlos, a Hispanic in his midthirties. She had developed him over the past eighteen months. He had provided accurate information in the past, when he wasn't doped up, but she trusted him about as far as she could throw him. It was a simple meeting to exchange cash for information—low threat and quick. She pressed her hand against the pocket of her pants and felt the Glock 19. She knew that anything could happen with the type of creatures she met with, and was prepared.

It wasn't long until a beige Lexus appeared and eased to a stop near Danya, its wheels crunching on the pebbles. She watched Carlos get out of the driver's seat, then two more men emerged from the rear doors. Both men had thick black beards and appeared to be Middle Eastern. The one approaching her on the right was stocky, his face pockmarked, and a scar ran down his forehead into his left eyebrow. The other was taller and slim. Sunglasses shielded their eyes. The men casually walked toward her and stopped with Carlos in front of her, almost making a semi-circle around her. The three men towered over her.

Although no threatening movements or weapons were displayed, Danya's defenses went up. In a slow movement, she slipped her right hand into her pocket and grasped the handle of the Glock. *Three on one is not good odds,* she thought. "We were to meet alone," she said as she held her gaze on Carlos and took a step back.

"These are my friends," he said, shifting his stance.

The three men stepped closer to her.

"Back off!" she said as she motioned with her left hand. She could almost feel the other two men's scrutinizing eyes from behind their sunglasses. Her eyes darted between the three.

Carlos looked to the others, then back to her and shifted his stance again.

Son of a bitch is doped up, she thought.

"They just came along for the ride. You don't need to worry," Carlos said. "We will proceed with our business."

"Not today, Carlos," Danya said, her tone firm. "I said *alone*, and you brought a crowd. Call me when you can meet without a chaperone." She started to back away.

"I need my money," Carlos said through clenched teeth and stepped closer to her.

She stepped back again. "I need to piss too, but not now. Meeting over." Danya's eyes narrowed and shot between the men.

It was going to go down, and she couldn't stop it.

At that instant, a car raced over the crest of the hill and slid to a stop near them.

The man to her right, Scar Face, lurched just as Danya started to withdraw her hand with the pistol. She dodged, freed her hand from her pocket, and fired. Carlos went down. Scar Face grabbed her waist and pulled her to the ground. Her sunglasses flew from her face. Then Slim Man stepped on her arm with the pistol, forcing her to relax her grip.

Danya struggled, twisted, and kicked her legs, but Scar Face was too big and had a hard grip on her. "You bastard! Get off me." She struggled and tried to bite, scratch, and knee the man, but she was pinned beneath him, unable to inflict any damage.

"Shut up, bitch!" Slim Man said as he grasped her Glock. "We can do this easy or hard. The choice is yours."

Danya paused to catch her breath, then angrily said, "What do you want?" while trying to knee Scar Face in the groin.

"You," Slim Man said as he looked down on her.

Danya continued to struggle but could not reach any vital points on the man. The pebbles dug into her wrist as Slim Man pressed harder.

Scar Face popped her in the face.

"You want it hard? Okay," Slim Man said and increased the pressure of his foot on her wrist.

Dazed from the blow, she forced out the words, "You slimy pigs! You're disgusting. You're going to rape me out here in the open in the hot sun. Both of you are pathetic."

Scar Face punched her again.

Slim Man knelt and said, "Don't flatter yourself, bitch." He withdrew a syringe from a small case he carried in his pocket.

Danya saw the needle and fought with every ounce of her body, twisting and kicking to no avail. Scar Face was too strong. She felt the prick of the needle and knew she didn't have much of a chance but continued to struggle. It didn't take long until her strength started to drain and her movements became sluggish. She couldn't focus her eyes, and it became harder and harder to resist the man. Her vision was distorted and blurry. Then nothing.

———•◆•———

Friday, May 6, 2016
Headquarters, US Special Operations Command
MacDill Air Force Base, Florida

After Max failed to return from Turkey the day before as planned, Chugs began the process of trying to find out what had happened to him. Matherson reached George through Andy.

"Missing?" came George's voice through the secure phone. "The last thing Max said to me was that he was heading home and was glad he didn't have to change his vacation plans. He told me he was going to spend a week at the beach with his girlfriend."

"He was supposed to leave tomorrow," the general said. "This is unlike Max. We've worked together for years. He is more than just a subordinate and friend, he's a *key man*. He knows the nuclear plans, status, and location of all the classified nuclear storage sites that belong to SOCOM. We need the information he garnered for the protection of the nuclear bombs in Incirlik. The only thing I know is that he's missing, presumably in Turkey. He'd have contacted me if he wasn't in trouble. I need your help."

"What do you need me to do, General?"

"Help me find Max. I don't want this to go through official channels. I have a suspicion there's a problem in Langley that could compromise our efforts and even cost Max his life."

"Off the record," came George's mumbled words, more to himself than to Matherson. "If this turns to shit, Langley will hang me out to dry, and possibly you too."

"I'm very concerned that Max is in trouble," Matherson said, his voice lowered. "The rumored coup could happen at any time. If it does, the ensuing chaos'll make getting Max returned difficult and a lengthy process, if at all."

"That's what I was thinking. If something does happen, I'll probably be locked up next to Max." The meaning in George's comment was very clear.

"I understand," Matherson said. "I won't forget."

There was a lingering silence on the line, then George's words came, "Out of official channels, a deal. I'll find Max."

CHAPTER 9

Saturday, May 7, 2016
Abandoned House
Kayseri, Turkey

After making contact with Erol and arranging to meet with him again, George rendezvoused with him at an abandoned house situated atop a hill on the outskirts of the south side of Kayseri. The rock and stucco building appeared to be an old farmhouse that had seen better days. The remnants of a once prosperous vineyard on one side of the old structure seemed to be the only place any attempt had been made to clear the large rocks from the property.

"It is very dangerous now," Erol said as he looked down the hillside, then back to George. "I grew up on a farm much like this one." He looked back at the terrain, a bit of melancholy in his voice. He knew what he had to do and what helping George meant for his future. "Since the prime minister announced his resignation on Thursday, security has gotten very tight. Most think the coup d'etat will happen as soon as the new prime minister is sworn in. Rumors are running rampant. It does, however, seem more and more like Kağan is orchestrating the coup and will name a new prime minister." Erol fixed his gaze on George. "My family—I want you to get them out of the country as you agreed."

"Okay, I'll see to it," George said as he tugged the zipper up on his jacket. "It's a bit cool."

"It is," Erol said with a nod. "The man you are looking for, Kenworth, I think I have located him."

"Go on."

"An American matching your description is at a refugee camp near the Turkish-Syrian border. It is called Kilis *Öncüpınar* Accommodation

Facility, three kilometers from the border. It is operated by the Turkish government and not by the UN."

"You sure it's him?"

"I am trying to get a photograph of the man, but I am almost certain." Erol looked around, first to his right and then left. "It was very difficult to get even the little information I got. Kenworth is not listed in the camp records. I happened to see a message that said he was taken to the camp under guard. A woman was brought to the camp yesterday under the same circumstances. Are you looking for a woman as well?"

"I don't know about the woman." George made a mental note, mention of her and that she was taken to the camp under the same circumstance having piqued his interest. "Where in the camp is the man being held?"

"I do not know. The facility is not a tent city like other camps. They have converted over two thousand steel shipping containers into shelters. Take your pick."

"I need to know exactly where he's located. Can we get him out?"

"I do not know." Erol ran his hand over his short dark hair. "It will not be easy. Many police and soldiers are there. I will come up with something. I will need to do more research on the camp."

"Okay, do it." There was no need to caution him to be careful. He knew his fate if he were caught.

George was troubled to learn that the Turkish government operated the camp and had no listing of Max in their records. They could shuffle Max around and even kill him without anyone knowing of it, and he feared that might be their plan. They could even make a quick dash across the Syrian border and dump him, if need be. The pending coup and paranoia of President Kağan made for an unpredictable situation and might even prevent Max's safe return altogether. Without any evidence of Max's detention, the Turkish government would disavow any knowledge of him.

It's a smart move to stash Max at the refugee camp, George thought.

This particular camp was overcrowded, like most camps, with between 15,000 to 17,000 Syrians. A lot of activity occurred around a facility like this—resupplying the camp, a major presence of military for guards and security, police, MİT, plus additional workers for maintenance, medical, and logistic support. Even though new refugees arrived on a regular basis, the camp had been in operation long enough for all their procedures to be fixed. Any disruption in the camp routine would signal an alarm.

Since the Turkish government operated the camp, the US could not officially enter it. An assault to try to get Max out would be devastating politically for the US and NATO. Such an act would cause chaos, which itself would hamper any rescue. It appeared that Max would disappear at the hands of the Turks when he had outlived his usefulness.

———————— ◆ ◆ ◆ ————————

Saturday, May 7, 2016
Kilis Öncüpınar Accommodation Facility
Öncüpınar, Turkey

Battered and bruised, Max was lying on a bunk inside the makeshift living quarters of a steel container. Sweat streaked down his face, and the fan provided little relief. He scrutinized, once again, the inside of the refurbished container. The interior walls and ceiling were covered with plywood and painted, and there were lights, a bathroom, and a window. Metal doors with locks had been installed for security. Max had seen some of the other containers when he was brought to the camp, and again, when he was taken out for interrogation. They were standard twenty-four by ten-foot shipping containers. Unfortunately, the container he had the luxury of occupying was divided in half and the window wouldn't open. He noticed the steel bar across the outside of the door that secured him inside. A personnel door, although locked, led to the other half of the container.

Obviously, a detention cell, he thought.

He had inspected every inch of his metal box, searching for some way to escape and something to use as a weapon, but his captors had been proficient in denying him both. Since his arrival three days earlier, the Turks had kept Max locked up inside the container, except for numerous periods of questioning by MİT. He had developed a good sense of the camp's routine. He knew he was in a refugee camp—this one was definitely upscale compared to the usual tent city camps with horrid conditions and crime—but he didn't know exactly where in Turkey the facility was located. He could see only a small portion of the compound from his window. Bright lights illuminated the entire facility during the night, and two soldiers stood guard outside his box.

Only a single chevron on their sleeves, he thought. *Most likely conscript soldiers. If so, that could be to my advantage.* Conscripts do exactly what they're told—nothing more, nothing less. They're always afraid of having their service extended because of some infraction.

Although Max didn't have any way to tell the time, he suspected that the major events, such as posting guards, meals, etcetera, occurred on the hour.

Find a way to establish the time, he thought.

During the day about all he could see was a white wall about ten meters in front of his window. Occasionally, he glimpsed people coming into his view, roaming about, and a few children playing games or sports. The facility's interned residents had all but settled down for the evening.

As Max studied his box again, he heard the door open in the other half of the container. *Company?* he thought.

Muffled voices permeated the wall separating the two spaces.

He eased up from his bunk, crept close to the door, and placed his ear to the wall, but all he could hear was a man's voice speaking what he thought was broken English, then silence. A metal sound rang in his ears. *Someone is unlocking the door.* It was the sound of the bolt that secured the door sliding back. He jerked around and quickly returned to his bunk, pretending to be asleep.

The door opened.

Max tensed and waited. *More questioning?* He anticipated the rousting as he sensed the man's presence close by. *Take him now or see what the situation is? Not now, not ready.*

The man stepped back through the door. The next sound was the adjacent compartment's outside door closing, then the unmistakable sound of the bar sliding into position.

What the hell? Who's in there?

Max stood, his bruises reminding him of the past few days, and cautiously eased through the door. Not knowing what to expect, his senses worked overtime. All he could see in the dim light was a small form on the bunk. "I'm a friend," he said as he inched closer, his voice gentle and reassuring. "Don't be alarmed. Are you all right?"

There was no reply.

He continued his slow advance. "Are you hurt?" He realized it was a woman, and her hair covered her face as she lay on her side. "I'm not going to hurt you. I'm a friend." Max knelt beside the bunk and gently brushed the hair from her face. "What did—" He couldn't believe his eyes, and his body went numb. Struggling through the shock, he said, "Danya, what…what happened. Why're you here? Why *you*?"

Danya's blurred eyes gradually opened, then she rolled to her back. "Maaax…" Her voice was labored. "I knew you would come."

"Danya, wake up." Max sat on the edge of the bunk and gently pulled her into his arms, brushing her hair back. "Are you okay? Wake up."

She forced the words, "I'm so *tired*."

Max looked her over but didn't see any wounds or bruises. He eased her back down, stepped to the washbasin in the bathroom, and grasped the towel that hung on the rack next to it. After soaking and wringing the towel, he returned to Danya's side. With care, he dabbed the moist towel over her face and said, "Danya, wake up."

"Not now, Max. I'm so tired. Let me sleep."

"Wake up. You've been drugged."

"You're so far away, Max. Come closer to me."

Max sat her upright on the edge of the bunk and swabbed her face again. It would take time for the sedative to wear off. All he could do was wait, and that was the hard part. *Is she here by chance?* he thought. He needed her awake and coherent before MİT questioned him again. *There's no such thing as coincidences. It's Madison, but how did he know I was here? Did he see me somehow in Aleppo?* He went over every detail that had occurred over the last couple of months and what he had previously read about Turkey. He began to suspect that President Kağan was orchestrating the rumored coup and planned to use his adversaries as the scapegoats. Stealing the nukes from Incirlik would give him status and money, should he sell them. Of course, he would need to convince NATO and the rest of the world that he was the innocent victim. Arresting those *responsible* for the coup would aid in his scheme.

Danya slowly raised her head and looked at Max, then forced the words, "Max, it is you? I thought I was dreaming. I feel like crap." She rubbed her face and eyes with both hands.

"Yeah, it's me." He gave her a small grin. "Do you have any idea why you're here?"

"No. Hell, I don't even know where we are. We were supposed to meet up in the Caribbean this weekend and get married, and I don't think this is the right place. Do you know what this is about?"

"You're right. We're in a refugee camp in Turkey, near the border, but I don't know which one."

"Turkey?" Danya exclaimed in whispered astonishment. She ran her hand through her brown hair. "My head is still mushy. I had just one thing to do before I started my vacation. Make a payment to one of my sources in Panama in exchange for information. Quick and easy, I thought, until two goons with him jumped me. We were fighting, then one of them pinned me down while the other one drugged me. I woke up on a plane and just after it landed, they juiced me again. That's the last thing I remember. What's today?"

"Saturday."

"I guess we're not going to be meeting in the Caribbean today," she sighed. "My meeting was Thursday. No wonder I feel so bad. Any idea why I was brought here?"

Max wiped her face again. "It's beginning to make sense now. You're here to get me to talk."

"About what? I don't even know what you're working on."

Max pointed to his ear, then across the wall to signal that he suspected the room was bugged.

Danya nodded to acknowledge his meaning.

He slid his hand over hers, then leaned close to her ear and whispered, "Remember three years ago when Madison stole the nukes from the facility in Panama?"

Danya nodded her head, and her brow furrowed as she concentrated on what he was saying.

"Madison is planning to steal the weapons from Incirlik."

She turned her head and whispered in his ear, "What? Madison, as in Bart Madison? That can't be. He's dead."

"Apparently, the CIA lied to Chugs." Max decided not to mention the other possibility, that Matherson had lied to him. "I saw him, and it's Madison, all right."

Since his return from Aleppo, Max had begun developing a theory—and their current circumstance supported his hypothesis—that Turkey had teamed up with ISIS. Publicly, Turkey had been reluctant to fight ISIS except in a show to oust the Syrian regime. At least that's how it appeared. ISIS had almost succeeded in their plan three years ago to use nukes against the US. Neither Turkey nor ISIS had any respect for the US and viewed the country as nothing but weak and ineffective. Madison had led terrorists in an operation to steal nuclear weapons once before. Seeing him in Aleppo, Max believed the traitor was making another attempt at such an operation. He was confident that Madison could also be facilitating the use of the weapons against the US. Max believed it made sense, and with President Kağan's desire to rebuild the Ottoman Empire, it was even more plausible. If Turkey joined forces with ISIS, Kağan could blame them, along with his internal adversaries, after his plan was executed. Then fighting ISIS, Kağan would get accolades from the West and possibly eliminate one of his future problems.

Continuing the routine of whispering in Danya's ear to circumvent eavesdropping, Max told her what he surmised.

Danya leaned close and whispered, "You think Turkey will aid ISIS in using nukes against the US and then attack Israel?"

"It's looking that way. I think Turkey will then go after ISIS. Kağan believes he is the caliph and the Ottoman Empire is the caliphate. If something should happen to me, you must get word to Chugs. Tell him what I suspect."

"I will, Max. But nothing is going to happen to you. I won't let it." Danya squeezed his hand. "Why didn't we get married three years ago like we talked about?"

Max bent forward and kissed her gently. "We let our jobs get in the way. It's time we get out of this business."

She smiled, then kissed him. "Just as soon as we finish this." She stood—her stability not fully restored—and made her way to the basin. Splashing cool water on her face was refreshing. She toweled her face and said, "How the hell do we get outta here?"

"I don't know yet," Max replied as he scrutinized her side of the container. Nothing appeared any different from his side—no way to get out other than the door and nothing to use as a weapon. "I'm still working on it."

———— ✦ ✦ ✦ ————

Sunday, May 8, 2016
Headquarters, US Special Operations Command
MacDill Air Force Base, Florida

"General," the secretary said as he walked by her toward his office. "I'm worried about Max. Has anything turned up?" She wrapped her arms around her chest.

"No, Helen, nothing yet," Matherson said, stopping to place a comforting hand on her shoulder. "I'm worried too. The State Department doesn't have any word on him and has verified his passport hasn't been used to reenter the country. The American Commander of the 39th Air Base Wing in Incirlik and I have talked twice in the past twenty-four hours. The last time he saw Max was when Max left the air base en route to the airport. No one else has seen him after that time."

"Thank you, General," her head drooped. "Excuse me," she said as the phone rang. She answered, then quickly replaced the receiver and said, "You have a phone call on your secure line. He said his name is George."

"Thank you." Matherson walked into his office, closing the door behind him. "George, have you turned up anything?" he said into the phone.

"One of my sources said an American matching Max's description was taken to the Kilis Öncüpınar Accommodation Facility three kilometers from the Turkish-Syrian border," George's troubled voice rang down the line. "He's not listed in the camp records. My source is working on getting a photograph of him."

A hint of eagerness came through in Matherson's voice as he asked, "Can we get him out?"

"Not sure. I am working on something. One more thing, a woman was taken to the camp under the same conditions as Max. Are you missing a woman too?"

"Not that I know about. What are you hearing about the coup?"

"Rumors are flying around." George's words carried concern. "There seems to be some confusion about who is behind it, and no one is willing to talk. I think it could happen any time."

The general's tone grew somber. "That's what the staff here thinks as well. In light of the Turkish prime minister's resignation, we're afraid it could be a radical takeover much like what happened in Tehran in November of 1979. This time, a NATO member and nuclear weapons are involved. I *don't* want Max trapped in Turkey if that occurs."

"I understand, General," came George's reply. "I hope it doesn't come to that."

"Thanks. As soon as you have that photo, get it to me. Keep me posted on what you come up with, George." Chugs hung up the phone, then perched his elbows on the desk and dropped his head into both hands.

———✦✦✦———

Sunday, May 8, 2016
Gareth Residence
New York, New York

"Yeah, whatta ya got, Wes?" Stew said into the phone.

"Remember when I told you about SOCOM's recommendation that the air force remove the nuclear weapons from Incirlik?"

Stew slurped his coffee, then wiped his chin. "Yeah, go on. We took care of that."

"SOCOM's guy who did the analysis has disappeared."

"So what's the concern?"

"He was in Incirlik evaluating security. SOCOM wants me to ask the CIA for help. They've made an official request. What do I tell 'em?"

"I don't like it," Stew said, more to himself than into the phone. "Nassar won't be very happy if he hears about this. The campaign needs his money." Stew looked down and tapped the eraser end of a pencil on his desk. "Okay, just tell 'em you've passed the request on to the CIA, but don't do anything. If they ask again, tell 'em the CIA has the action. Just stall 'em."

"All right, Stew. I just don't like playing around with someone's life."

"Sometimes you have to make tough calls, Wes." Stew lifted his cup to his lips and slurped his coffee again. "Put it out of your mind. I'll give Trent a heads-up on this in case he hears something."

CHAPTER 10

Sunday May 8, 2016
Kilis Öncüpınar Accommodation Facility
Öncüpınar, Turkey

MAX AND DANYA were taken, with their hands bound behind them, to a stark room in the building across from their detention container. The lights were harsh and the air stale. A video camera suspended from the ceiling hung above a darkened window and there was another by the door. Beneath the window, a small table held a wooden box about the size of a shoebox with a dial and several knobs. Max and Danya were seated on chairs facing each other with their ankles shackled and attached to the floor by short chains.

The door opened and a medium-build man entered.

Max focused on him, recognizing him as the same one who had picked him up at the airport. *Pistol Man,* he thought.

Following him was a burly man with close-cropped hair, a pock-marked face, and a short scar across his cheek.

He looked evil, and Max didn't like the setup. *He does the dirty work,* he thought. *He's gonna hammer her.* Not that he was going for another round of questioning but that it was Danya sitting across from him was his concern. He knew it was going to be psychological torture to get him to talk, delivered by beating on Danya. His gaze shot back and locked onto hers. *She knows.*

Expressionless, her head moved slightly from side to side, signaling him not to answer.

He felt his heart race and a coldness washed over him. Max had faced danger many times before but never had such a helpless sensation. *Danya,* he thought, *I can't protect you.* The two had planned to marry and live happily ever after, but it suddenly looked like there might not be any marriage or happily ever after. *There'll be no rescue today. Hell, no one knows where I am. Tell them and save her—or watch her die?* Max's gaze darted between the two men.

Without speaking, Hammer walked up to Danya and, with a heavy swing of his arm, backhanded her. His big hand connected, covering a large portion of her face and knocking her off her chair.

She moaned, and Max lurched at the man, but the shackles stopped him, digging into his ankles. He almost lost his balance and fell.

Hammer reached over, grasped Danya's shirt collar, and pulled her upright.

She lifted her head and gave it a shake to clear the hair from her face. Max saw the tears well up in her eyes and the red mark across her cheek. Her eyes locked onto Max's, and she slowly shook her head again. She didn't speak, but Max understood her meaning.

Hammer drew his fist back and released it with great force, connecting with Danya's cheek and eye. She cried out and her body shot to the side, the shackles holding her. As she lay slumped sideways, Hammer grasped her collar again and hauled her upright.

Pistol Man smirked at Max and said, "Kenworth, just so you know, if I don't like your answer, my colleague will demonstrate my displeasure. This was just a warm-up to show you that I want straight answers. I am a compassionate man. Should you prolong my discontent, we will go to other means. I don't want my colleague to get tired or hurt his hand." Pistol Man wrinkled his face and shook his head. "One such means that will demonstrate my unhappiness very well is a little electrical stimulation."

Pistol Man looked to Danya, then back to Max. "Unfortunately, it will require my assistant to remove her shirt and expose her breasts." He pointed to the wooden box on the table and shot a glance to Danya, then to Max. "My colleague will use that control box to indicate my dissatisfaction. He will attach a metal clamp to each of her nipples. The clamps are connected to the control unit. He can adjust the voltage for effectiveness. As you can imagine, the pain is, well…excruciating." He looked to Danya again, then back to Max.

"Okay, asshole. You've made your point. Let her go."

Pistol Man maintained eye contact with Max while making a slight motion with his hand.

Hammer slugged Danya again. She groaned as his fist connected.

Max's gaze shot to her, his fists clenched as he struggled in vain. Her nose was deformed, her eye and both cheeks were red and swollen, and blood streamed from her fractured nose and trickled out the corner of her mouth. Rage masked the pain of the bindings as they dug deeper into Max's flesh. Helpless to defend her, a livid storm consumed his body as he fought against the restraints to no avail. The extreme emotional pain was like the tornado within a storm.

"Kenworth, that response irritated me. Try not to displease me anymore. We will try again. I will ask you questions, and you will answer me correctly."

"Look, I've answered questions from the others. I don't know anything. As I told them, I was just doing an inspection."

Pistol Man glared at Max. "Why specifically you?"

Max glanced to Danya, then back to Pistol Man. "The air force was shorthanded and asked for my help. That's it." He looked into Danya's eyes, trying to signal strength to her.

Pistol Man followed Max's gaze. "Were you planning to remove the B61 bombs from Incirlik?"

"No. I was sent here to ensure the deficiencies from the NWTI in February were corrected. That's standard procedure. You know that."

Pistol Man motioned with his hand again.

Hammer punched Danya, and her head shot back.

Pistol Man's eyes narrowed. "How many soldiers are deploying to Incirlik? What units?"

"I don't know of any units deploying to Incirlik," Max said.

Pistol Man motioned with his hand, and Hammer popped Danya again. She slumped in the chair—out cold. Pistol Man then said, "She has, or *had* a very pretty face. I certainly hope there are no lasting scars or disfigurement. But these things do happen."

"Okay. Okay, I'll tell you what I know," Max said, his voice filled with anger. He knew they were in a no-win situation and believed Pistol Man already knew the answers to some of his questions. Those were to verify that Max was being truthful. Unfortunately, Max didn't know which ones. He would answer their questions as close to the truth without divulging the most sensitive classified information if at all possible.

Pistol Man studied Max briefly, then asked, "How many soldiers are deploying to Incirlik and when?"

"I don't know. There was discussion on the security of the bombs but not on deploying soldiers before I left. I was told the weapons would remain at Incirlik."

Pistol Man nodded, then asked, "Why were you sent here?"

"Like I said before, the air force was concerned by rumors of a coup d'etat. They're shorthanded and asked me to verify that the deficiencies from the NWTI in February were corrected. Part of my inspection was on physical security. I was to report specifically on the security of the bombs and make a recommendation of what was needed in terms of soldiers and equipment."

"Is NATO going to take the weapons out of Turkey?" Pistol Man asked.

"No. The president will not authorize the removal of them and has told the air force to keep them locked in the vaults."

Pistol Man held his eyes locked onto Max's and nodded. "How many B61 bombs are stored at Incirlik? There are three weapon vaults that are vacant. Which ones are they?"

"Ninety B61 nuclear bombs are at the base, and all are serviceable. Give me a sketch or photo, and I'll point out the vacant vaults." Max knew they would have photos and diagrams of the airfield and suspected they already knew which vaults were vacant.

Pistol Man nodded again, then said, "What are the access codes to the vaults?"

"I don't have those codes."

Pistol Man motioned with his hand.

Hammer stepped in front of Danya and drew his arm back.

"Wait!" Max shouted. "I really don't know the codes. The security officer and NCO obtain the codes when directed to open the vaults. The codes are locked in a top-secret, two-man-controlled safe. I was never authorized access. They always change."

Pistol Man nodded to the other man to move back.

The questioning continued for about another two hours. Many of the same questions were asked several times and in different ways to ensure Max was truthful. Some of the questions seemed benign while others were specific. The MİT man was good and had collected a lot of intelligence, but was it what he wanted? Max was well aware of how sadistic Pistol Man could be and didn't want Danya subjected to any more pain, especially the electrical stimulation. He shot another glance to her. His heart ached and nausea filled his stomach when his eyes landed on her swollen face. She looked as if she had gone ten rounds in a title fight. Max knew their usefulness was about to end and they needed to, somehow, get out of the camp.

Pistol Man nodded toward the door, and his shadow walked out. He returned in a few moments, followed by four soldiers. Pistol Man motioned to Max, then looking at the soldiers, said, "Take them back."

Without speaking, one of the soldiers removed the short chain from the floor, freeing Max, then Danya, and escorted them back to their container. Two soldiers had to drag Danya by the shoulders. Max could only hobble, blood oozing into his shoes as a result of the bindings digging into his ankles.

———◆◆◆———

Monday, May 9, 2016
Gareth Campaign Office
Washington, DC

Jenny was still battling it out with her opponent only a month before the last primary. Tempers were short and frustration was high. The Gareth campaign had been spending money at a scandalous rate, and more was needed. In addition to the normal costs of advertising, travel, rallies, etcetera, millions of dollars were spent in buying votes.

In a closed-off room at the back of campaign headquarters, Stew, Jenny, and Archie worked through making the last-minute preparations before her speech. The front office buzzed with excitement as the rest of her staff worked the phones, coordinating the final preparations with the media to portray Jenny in the best possible setting. Making her look good on camera and orchestrating her arrival and departure amid the cheering crowd was their objective. She had to look presidential.

"Pour me another scotch, Archie!" Jenny said in a harsh tone.

Archie's jaw tightened and his brow furrowed as he stood and turned away from her, then stepped to the counter to refill his coffee mug.

"Go easy on that stuff, Jenny," Stew said, shooting a condemning eye at her. "You've gotta talk to the press."

"Back off, Stew! I need a drink."

Archie set Jenny's glass of scotch on the table, then sat as he said, "Stew, that incident last week in Aleppo was a close call. It was a nice touch blaming Syria for maiming the children with the barrel bombs. What's the status on those reporters who were there?"

"Trent's people are looking for 'em," Stew said, then leaned back and eyed an attractive staffer as she walked to the copy machine. "I'm not too happy with Trent over that screw-up. You hearing any rumbles on the Hill about Aleppo?"

"Naw, nothing that we need to worry about." Archie slurped his coffee. "Wes told me about the missing SOCOM guy in Turkey. That entire situation could become a big problem. What the hell is Kağan doing?"

"Nassar and I are meeting for lunch," Stew said as he withdrew the leather cigar pouch from his inside coat pocket. "Want to come along?"

"I've got a few pressing things to do."

Jenny downed the remainder of her scotch, then looked over her glasses and said, "Archie, you're full of shit. We all know you're meeting your bimbo. Get me another scotch."

Archie's face flushed, and his crimson lips seemed to disappear. It was all he could do to keep his mouth shut. He stood, then stepped to the counter to refill the glass.

Stew grinned. "I warned Nassar about taking the guy. He told me Kağan is going to use him as evidence that the US was involved in the coup attempt. In the first speech after Jenny takes the oath of office, she will announce that she and Kağan will meet in a show of solidarity. She will promise to prosecute those US citizens involved in the coup—peace in the Middle East, unity, and a new world order. All that bullshit."

"Hmm. Stew, that sounds risky to me," Archie said from the counter.

"It'll work." Stew lit the cigar. "Besides, the American people will've forgotten all about it by then."

"But what if something goes wrong or someone talks?" Archie said as he picked up the glass of scotch. He stepped back to the table and set it in front of Jenny, then picked up a cinnamon roll from the plate as he sat down.

"I've told Nassar to make sure that guy dies, and the sooner the better. That'll take care of that loose end. I've got a better idea for Kağan anyway. As soon as Jenny is sworn in, she'll tell the SOCOM Commander that if one word leaks out about this entire incident, he'll be fired and then prosecuted. She'll refer to her predecessor firing his CIA director amid a sex scandal. Remember that? The president got dirt on the director, then used it when he wouldn't go along with the program. If Kağan screws up his coup or it doesn't go the way he wants, well…too bad for him. Then who'll care? Besides, we control the media anyway."

"What about Trent's private operative who's missing?" Archie shoved the rest of the roll into his mouth, his cheeks bulging as he chewed.

"He'll be dead soon." Stew rolled the ash from his cigar in the ashtray.

"Damn it, Stew," Jenny said, her face scrunched up. "Get rid of the fucking cigar. It stinks. Archie, another scotch. Fill the damn glass up this time."

Archie licked the frosting off his lips, then pressed them together, resisting the urge to tell her to get the damn scotch herself. He stood and stepped to the counter.

———— ✦ ✦ ✦ ————

Wednesday, May 11, 2016
Headquarters, US Special Operations Command
MacDill Air Force Base, Florida

George contacted the J3 to discuss what he had discovered about Max's situation since their talk on Sunday. The pending coup was causing him problems in gathering information, and the coup could happen at any moment. For over ten minutes, the two talked on secure phones about Max's situation. So far, George wasn't optimistic that an extraction was possible.

"It'll take support from Langley, and I haven't received anything from them, " George said.

"You haven't received any word to assist us in getting Max out?" Matherson replied.

"That's correct, General." The frustration in George's voice was noticeable. "We haven't received any information or direction to assist SOCOM in locating Max. Nothing."

"Damn," Matherson said, more to himself than into the phone. "That figures. When our commander briefed the SecDef that Max was missing, he sought the SecDef's support in asking the CIA for help in locating him, but he was ambivalent and didn't seem all that interested in SOCOM's problem. However, he did say he would look into the matter. We suspected that meant no support from Langley. You just confirmed it. The entire administration is dysfunctional, and everyone is jockeying for a position in the new administration."

"Sorry, General. I'm sending you two photos. One is of Max, and the other is the woman."

"Good, I'll get back to you as soon as we confirm it's Max. I need good intel on the refugee camp. Their routine, where specifically Max is located in the camp, and your thoughts on how to get him out. I need details."

"I'm already working on it," George replied. "My contact has a few ideas. I'm meeting with him later."

"Listen, George, this is very sensitive. NATO says Turkey doesn't know anything about Max and we're getting sluffed off by the administration. Keep as much of this out of official channels as you can. I'm sending you a satellite image of the camp. Can your contact get a message to Max? He needs to know we're working on getting him out. Also, he needs to know that I've notified all US Special Forces operating in northern Syria of his disappearance. If he can get free, they're the closest friendly forces. And they know to watch for him. Have him sign it *Chugs*. That way Max will know it is from me."

"I'll ask him. I'll get back with you soon, General."

— • ♦ • —

Thursday, May 12, 2016
Presidential Palace of the Republic of Turkey
Ankara, Turkey

Al-Ghazāli sipped his Rize tea, then set the gold-rimmed cup and saucer on the edge of President Kağan's desk and said, "Nassar called me. Gareth said to get rid of the American at the accommodation facility."

"I told you before, I want to use him as evidence. No one will believe the coup was orchestrated by the Americans if we don't have proof," Kağan said, then sipped his tea.

"Gareth thinks it is too risky to keep him and is afraid something might go wrong. If he should escape, it will not go well for us or Gareth."

"What could go wrong? We have him locked up and under guard," Kağan said. "We agreed that we would have him shot, then dump his body where it would be found near the palace."

"Gareth said no," al-Ghazāli said, his tone stern. "Get rid of him. General Çakmak told me about the woman with the American. She is an Israeli. This could be bad for us. Gareth can take care of the Americans but not the Israelis. They will come after her."

"What in the hell am I supposed to do for evidence?" Kağan said, his tone harsh.

"If either of those two people is discovered alive, you won't need evidence. You will probably need a coffin. Gareth suggests an alternative. Dump both their bodies across the border in Syria. Blame the Commander of US Central Command when it is over. Gareth assured me the US will not retaliate and will block the UN from acting if we do as he said."

"Can we trust Gareth on something like this?" Kağan asked, gingerly sipping his tea.

"Probably. This is a much better idea. We don't have to worry about Kenworth or the woman. Central Command is responsible for fighting ISIS, and it will be easy to make the case that the general wanted to take over Turkey. Use the fact that the US Special Forces fighting alongside the YPG were wearing their patches. YPG is aligned with the PKK, and we have designated the PKK as a terrorist organization. We have publicly protested this situation as a challenge to our national security. There is your proof."

"Perhaps. Let me think a moment," Kağan said, sipped his tea again, and sat back in his chair. "I will give the word for MİT to dispose of them in Syria."

CHAPTER 11

Saturday, May 14, 2016
Headquarters, 6th Corps
Adana, Turkey

Madison slid a folder across the table to General Çakmak and said, "The results of the training over the past two weeks."

Çakmak held his gaze momentarily on Madison, then picked up the folder and opened it.

"The units are about as ready as they're gonna get," Madison continued. "We've had a few problems with equipment, but I believe everything is ready now. All the unit commanders know exactly what to do. We must go right away. I don't want 'em to lose their edge."

Çakmak's eyes landed on al-Ghazāli. "What is the status of the crews and pilot?"

Al-Ghazāli shot a glance to Madison, then back to the general. With an air of confidence, he said, "I have them, and they are ready. The Brotherhood wants to know the status and the downrange location for the transfer of the bombs. What do I tell them?"

"You can tell them that all the preparations are complete," Çakmak said over the folder. "They will be given the specific details soon."

"General," al-Ghazāli said, his tone full of insistence, "I need to give them the location. Arrangements must be made. We have to coordinate with our brothers of the Islamic state for the transfer."

Çakmak held up his hand as his eyes bored into al-Ghazāli. "In time, those details will be provided. Secrecy is of utmost concern now."

General Çakmak hadn't risen to the rank of lieutenant general by being stupid. He was well aware he was committing an act of treason against his country and NATO. Although he'd agreed to President

Kağan's plan, he didn't want to be a scapegoat if anything should go wrong. He knew that Kağan was going to purge the military of those who had opposed him in his quest for the New Ottoman Empire. Kağan had promised Çakmak a higher position and money in exchange for his agreement to take the weapons. He understood NATO and the Americans very well. If there was any hint that he was complicit in an attack on Incirlik, his career and life as he knew it would be over. Since his forces were the ones that were going to take the weapons from Incirlik, he would be heavily scrutinized afterward. Also, if Kağan were implicated in orchestrating the coup, he was callous enough to sacrifice the general. Çakmak wanted insurance. As long as he kept the plans secret, there was some assurance he would survive for the time being, but he needed more leverage. He had developed his own plan for his post-army existence—one of the B61 nuclear warheads and a secluded compound in South America.

Madison studied the general for a moment, then said, "The pilot'll need to be briefed on the details and where to take the bombs. He'll need to plan out his routes."

"I am aware of that," Çakmak said without looking up from the folder. "I will notify you when the pilot is to be briefed. We must be very careful on this and follow the time-phase sequence precisely on all events. Timing is critical. All air force preparations are complete. The airspace will be closed, power to the airfield will be cut, and roads will be closed in accordance with the timeline. I have directed that all units involved will stay under overhead cover and minimize outside activities until we execute. I suspect the Americans are watching us via satellites."

"Most likely, General," Madison said. "Advise your commanders not to permit any of the A-10s to take off."

Çakmak nodded and, with a flick of his hand, said, "Thank you for coming. I must talk with President Kağan now."

— ♦ ♦ ♦ —

Saturday, May 14, 2016
Kilis Öncüpınar Accommodation Facility
Öncüpınar, Turkey

Max stood silently peering out the window, looking right then left. No one was visible and all he could see was the familiar white wall ten meters in front of his container. After a moment, he caught a glimpse of one of the guards entertaining himself by poking at a beetle with a stick.

The guards are bored, he thought. *Good.* With boredom, soldiers become lax. *This could also mean that MİT is no longer interested in us.*

Stepping into the other half of the container, Max knelt next to Danya's bunk where she was lying down, leaned near her ear, and said, "I have a feeling they're done with us. It's been several days since they've questioned us."

"I was just thinking the same thing," Danya said into his ear. "I haven't figured a way out of here yet. Have you?"

"No." He glanced to the door. "I found a note someone hid in my bunk. Chugs knows we're here and is working to get us out."

Danya sat up and swung her legs off the side of the bunk. A glimmer of hope flashed in her swollen eyes, and a slight smile emerged on her bruised face. "That's good news. What did he say?"

"He's working on a plan to get us outta here. Our forces in northern Syria are the closest friendlies and know to look for us if we can escape."

Danya squeezed his hand, then stood and stepped to the window. Her eyes telegraphed the anxiety in her voice as she said, "Max, we're about to have company." She remained motionless, her nerves twisting inside her as she anticipated what was coming.

The door opened and the bright sunlight spilled into the container. Hammer filled the doorway and said, "Your wrists. We are to go now."

Max stuck both of his arms out in front of him, and the Turk placed the double zip-tie handcuffs around his wrists just like every other time they'd been taken for a round of questioning. He turned toward Danya and placed the handcuffs on her wrists. Satisfied they were secure, he stepped to the side and pushed Danya and Max out the door.

Without speaking, Max and Danya stepped from the container. Instead of leading them to the usual stark room in the building across from their detention container, Hammer and the two guards marched them to a waiting Peugeot van next to the front of the building.

What's up? Max thought, shooting a guarded look to Danya. Just as they reached the van, Max saw Pistol Man emerge from the entrance of that building.

An army private slid open the side door, and Hammer nodded with his head. "Get in."

Hammer followed Max and Danya into the rear seat and closed the door as the private got into the driver's seat. Pistol Man sat in the front passenger seat.

"Where are we going?" Max asked. He didn't like being taken out of the camp, unless they were going to be released, and his instincts told him a release was not going to happen. *Have they discovered SOCOM is working on getting us out?* he thought. *This is going to make it more difficult for them to find us.*

"You are leaving and will know soon enough," Pistol Man said over his shoulder. "Sit there and shut the hell up."

Danya slid her hand to Max's and squeezed it.

He looked into her eyes and knew she was thinking the same thing he was—the end of the line. He saw her eyes dart around the inside of the vehicle. *She's looking for anything to use as a weapon,* he thought, then he glanced to the three Turks and didn't like the odds. *The private won't be a problem, but the other two are.*

The van eased out of the facility and turned, following the signs toward Syria. A few moments later, the Peugeot slowed behind a number of large trucks making the trip across the border and came to a halt. Pistol man flicked his hand, signaling the driver not to wait. The van swerved into the next lane and sped up, passing a seemingly never-ending line of vehicles. As the Peugeot passed each one, the drivers gestured with their hands, indicating their displeasure at the impatient travelers. No interpretation was needed.

Max shot a glance to Danya and caught her nod. *She knows,* he thought. *Looks like our destination is one way to Syria. Probably taking us a few miles inside the country to some secluded location, out of sight of any witnesses, and will shoot us.* He felt Danya squeeze his hand. *There's gotta be some opportunity to get the advantage. Just watch for it.* Max kept working his wrist against the plastic ties.

Stopping at the border, Pistol Man handed a paper to the guard controlling the crossing. As one would expect since the southeastern border province of Kilis had the highest number of refugees in Turkey, the Öncüpınar border crossing was a very busy place. Refugees, on foot and in or on anything they could ride, continued crossing the border. After a quick look at the paper, the policeman motioned with his hand and the Peugeot lurched forward. The terrain beyond the border was mostly farmland with small villages dotting the landscape. Two distinct columns of black smoke rose on the distant horizon—a reminder that they were entering dangerous territory. Potholes littered the road, which had been neglected since the hostilities started. The driver swerved repeatedly to avoid them, and attaining any considerable speed was a treacherous adventure.

Max studied the area, looking for any sign of forces, friendly or otherwise. Even the farm labor was scarce. Not seeing anyone didn't mean no one was there—he just couldn't see them. From his review of the region before going to Turkey, Max knew that ISIS, Syrian rebels, Syrian government forces, Russians, and YPG, to name a few, had been fighting in this area. Somewhere in all this mess were the US Special Forces.

Max saw Pistol Man point to the remains of a severely damaged building ahead, signaling for the private to go there. Time was growing short, and he still didn't have a good plan. His eyes roamed the area again and landed on Hammer. The thug looked drowsy with his hand resting in his lap, clutching his SIG Sauer P229 pistol. Max shifted his gaze to Danya. *She's scrutinizing the area as well,* he thought. *Has she come up with something? Our chances seem to be zero and dwindling fast. Gotta watch her close and be ready in case she makes a move.* The plastic dug into his flesh as he continued to twist his wrist, and he searched the floor for anything he could use to help free his hands.

Danya slowly raised her arms to her chest and gingerly slipped free the two top buttons of her blouse. Next, she sneezed into her clasped hands—a signal to Max so he would know what she was doing—then lowered them to her lap and bowed her head.

The soldier parked near the building and started to get out but stopped when Pistol Man spoke to him in Turkish. The private nodded, then slid out from behind the steering wheel and remained standing by the vehicle.

Hammer opened the door and wrestled his burly frame out of the van, then scanned the area as he turned to face the side door. Stretching briefly, he exercised his arms and neck to become alert as he stepped slightly to the right.

Pistol Man swung out of his seat, closed the door, and withdrew a SIG Sauer P229 pistol from his shoulder holster. He also looked over the area, then stood to the left of his thug. Satisfied no one was visible nearby that could see them, he said in a commanding tone, "Get out!"

Danya, with a sure footing, wiggled her small frame to the exit, glanced to the right and then left, and cautiously stepped down. She had calculated her moves to stop short of the man who had worked her over. "What's the plan now?"

Neither of the MİT men spoke.

Danya took another step closer to Hammer and stood erect, her shoulders back.

As expected, Hammer couldn't resist the enticing view of her thirty-four double-Ds nestled in the lace bra.

"We can make a deal," she said, her voice low and sultry. She inched a little closer to him.

Max stooped forward and followed Danya's path of egress. He couldn't see what she was doing nor hear her. *This it?* he thought as he looked at the back of her. *I'm not gonna make this easy for 'em. What's Pistol Man gonna do? Make a mistake, asshole!*

Just as Max was in the doorway ready to leap, two shots registered nearby. Then a cacophony of rapid gunfire erupted from several locations not too far from their distant front. As suddenly as it had started, silence returned like the flick of a switch.

Max held his focus on Pistol Man and saw him glance over his right shoulder in the direction of the gunfire. *A bit of a leap, but I can make it,* he thought. At that instant, he jumped, pushing off the van with all his strength.

Danya had caught Max's move and kicked Hammer in the groin. Catching him off guard, she took the advantage and unleashed her fury.

As Max lunged, he brought his arms up, knocking the man's right arm, with the pistol, up and wide, freeing the P229. He was inside both of the man's arms and crashed into him.

Danya thrust up her bound and clenched hands with all of her might when the thug bent forward, catching him under the chin. His head shot up, and he staggered backward.

Max brought up his knee just before he connected, striking Pistol Man in the solar plexus. He gasped for air as the two went down. As soon as they both hit the ground, Max jammed his forearm against the man's throat, pressing hard. Pistol Man struggled, twisted, and his arms flailed against his opponent.

Danya lunged into Hammer as he was still dazed, jabbing at his eyes, then plowed into his cheeks with her fingernails. Hammer shook his head, trying to avoid her fingers as he fought against her attack, first at her body and then at her hands that were digging into his flesh. Danya was relentless in her attack, fighting with discipline.

Soon, asphyxia overtook Pistol Man and his body went limp as he blacked out.

Max scrambled the short distance to the handgun and held it between his hands as he stood. He gave a quick look to Danya, then back to the young soldier who was coming around the van. "Halt!" Max commanded as his left hand shot up, palm facing the driver. "On the ground! Hands behind your head." He pointed to the ground.

The startled driver dropped to the ground and placed his hands behind his head.

Max darted to Danya, glancing back to the private.

"Hold it! Stop," Max said, his tone stern. He reached to Danya's shoulder, grasped her blouse, and said, "Danya, stop!" Looking at Hammer, he said, "On the ground! Hands behind your head."

The man complied.

Looking at Danya, Max said, "You all right?"

"Aside from a few bruises, some loose teeth, my eye hurts, and a fucking headache, I'm fine." Her tone was harsh.

"See if you can find a knife or something to cut these cuffs off. We need to get the hell out of here."

Danya nodded and bent over the man at her feet. It was all she could do not to kick him several more times. She slid her hands over his pocket, then stopped and inserted her fingers. Withdrawing them, she displayed a folded knife with a bone handle. Stepping closer to Max, she opened the blade and cut the plastic from his wrists. Max took the knife from her and cut her bands. She then picked up Hammer's pistol that he'd dropped when she kicked him, checked it, and blew the dirt from it.

Max kicked Hammer's foot and said, "Get up." He looked to Pistol Man, who was gasping for air and holding his throat as he struggled to stand.

The thug brushed the dirt from his trousers and stepped to Pistol Man with Max behind him.

Danya stepped to the rear of the vehicle, opened the door, and leaned inside. In less than a minute, she backed away and closed the door. Her hand was filled with several double zip-tie handcuffs. Moving to Pistol Man, she said, "Hands behind you."

"What're you doing?" Max asked, his curiosity piqued.

Without stopping or looking up at Max, Danya snugged the band on the man's wrist and said, "Dead men feel no pain. I want these fuckers to feel pain." After all three were cuffed, she zipped them to the van doors.

Now Max got it—tied to the van, in the middle of a hostile fire zone on a failed mission. Danya was very good at her job.

"Let's get out of the open. In here." Max Pointed to the inside of the damaged building. "We gotta figure out who was shooting and where to go."

———◆◆◆———

Saturday, May 14, 2016
Headquarters, US Special Operations Command
MacDill Air Force Base, Florida

General Matherson and Lieutenant Colonel Johnston sat at the conference table with a secure phone between them. Matherson had contacted Thaddeus Nussbaum—Chief of Mossad Station, Panama, and Danya's boss—when he received the photos of Max and Danya from George. Thaddeus arranged the conference call after he confirmed the photo was of Danya.

"Our source in Turkey," Matherson said into the phone, "has confirmed that Max and Danya are both being held in the Kilis Öncüpınar Accommodation Facility near the Turkey-Syria border."

"Hold on, let me locate it on the map," came Thaddeus's reply. "I see it. Go on."

"We believe the rumors of the possible coup d'etat in Turkey to be true and it could occur anytime," Andy said into the phone. "Max was sent to Incirlik to evaluate the situation and security of the B61 bombs there. We believe Danya was kidnapped to get Max to divulge what he knows about the status of the nukes and the plans to protect them."

"The situation there is not good," came Thaddeus's words through the speaker. "I don't like what you are leading up to. Go on."

For the next ten minutes, Andy and the general briefed Thaddeus on the pertinent background details they had discovered. Andy emphasized their assumption that President Kağan was orchestrating the coup d'etat and that the Muslim Brotherhood was entrenched in the Turkish government, playing a big role in facilitating the coup. Thaddeus expressed his discontent and concern upon hearing the latest intel on the Brotherhood actively working with Kağan.

"Just before Max was taken, he identified a mercenary working for the Turks by the name of Bart Madison," Matherson said.

"Bart Madison!" Thaddeus's tone was incredulous. "He's dead."

"We were quite surprised as well," Matherson said. "I was told the CIA took care of him. Obviously, that didn't mean killing him. We believe Kağan plans to steal several of the nuclear weapons at Incirlik during the coup, blame it on his opposition, and give a couple of them to the Muslim Brotherhood."

"What is the US government doing about this?" Thaddeus asked. "Are they going to remove the weapons from Incirlik?"

"No, the president will not authorize it and simply said to keep them locked up. Our president does not believe the rumors of the coup."

"Incredible! We did this once before, about three years ago, and the terrorists damn near succeeded. What the hell is with your government?"

"The election," the general said. "Very little is getting done. It appears that everyone is focused on getting Jenny Gareth elected and jockeying for a position in her administration." The general looked to

Johnston, then to the speaker. "I suspect there's a problem in Langley. I don't know to what extent, but Colonel Johnston and our source working in Turkey can't get anything out of the Agency. We've asked for their help but received nothing. We're being stonewalled at every turn when it comes to Turkey. Colonel Johnston believes the Brotherhood may be influencing our government and providing support to Gareth."

"I want to get Danya back," Thaddeus said. "How can I help you? What do you need?"

"We can't go into Turkey," Matherson said, concern in his voice. "If they can cross into Syria, our forces are watching for 'em. As you know, northern Syria is a no-man's-land. We're short on intel and assets inside Turkey."

Thaddeus replied, "Do you know where exactly in the camp they're being held?"

"We're working on it. Colonel Johnston believes Max and Danya will be executed when the Turks finish with 'em."

"Understand," Thaddeus said. "You are asking a lot. I'll see what I can do."

CHAPTER 12

Monday, May 16, 2016
Gareth Residence
New York, New York

S TEW STARTED TO lift his coffee cup, then set it back on the desk. "What the hell did you say?" His face flushed crimson and his hands began to tremble as his rage built, his anger unmistakable.

"The man and woman have disappeared," came Nassar's words.

"This is fucking incredible," Stew said into the phone. "I was assured that he was locked up and a twenty-four-hour guard was on him. How the fuck does someone disappear while locked in a steel box with a guard? I told you bastards to get rid of him."

"They were being taken into Syria as you instructed and somehow escaped. We found the mutilated bodies of our men, but no trace of the man or woman."

"If they're rescued, there'll be hell to pay," Stew said, then he picked up the smoldering cigar from the ashtray. "Your incompetence is going to cost Jenny the damn election. Get your best team after 'em and get rid of both of 'em. Do you understand? No mistakes this time. You got that?"

"We have a killer team already dispatched and in Syria now," Nassar said. "I assure you, the man and woman will never be seen again."

"You tell Kağan I want to know immediately when they are eliminated. If he screws this up, Jenny will not support him after she's elected, the US will not block the UN against Turkey, and the nukes will be removed from Incirlik. You got that, Nassar? I want this taken care of… now!"

"I understand. I will call you as soon—"

Stew slammed the phone down, then immediately dialed Trent's number at CIA headquarters in Langley. As soon as he heard Trent's voice he said, "We have another problem."

"What's happened?"

"I just received a call from Nassar. The fucking Turks let Kenworth escape. He and the woman were being taken into Syria and somehow got away."

"Damn. How?"

"I don't know. They're incompetent. Here's what I want you to do." Stew took a sip of coffee. "Put one of your teams on 'em. I don't want their bodies found. You understand what I mean? Don't bungle this. Tell your team to be careful. Nassar said a Turkish team is already after those two."

"I understand."

"What's the status of your missing operative?" Stew mouthed his cigar as he anticipated the response.

"We still don't have a positive location on him. However, based on a couple of reports, we think he's inside Turkey and working for them. We should know very soon if it's him. Do you want us to hit him in Turkey?"

"No, I want you to give him a fucking microphone so he can spill his guts to the world," Stew said, his sarcasm thick. "Hell yes, I want you to get him. Tell your men not to get caught in Turkey. I don't want to deal with Kağan. Remember Aleppo? Make sure that doesn't happen again. I mean it, no screw-ups this time. And this is a busy week for the campaign. Don't make me chase you down for a status report."

"Yes, sir," Trent said, then the phone went dead.

Stew dialed Senator Chapman's office. As soon as Archie came on the line, Stew said, "The Turks let Kenworth and the woman escape. I've talked to Weldon, and he's sending out a team. I want you to nose around the Hill and see if you pick up anything on Kenworth and the woman. If you do, get with me right away. Oh, and Trent thinks the missing operative could be in Turkey but doesn't have confirmation yet. If he screws up either one of these situations, *he'll* fucking disappear."

"Got it," Archie said. "I have an Intelligence Committee meeting this morning. I'll start there."

"Be damn careful what you say," Stew said. "I don't want anyone to think you're getting information from the outside."

"I know."

"I've got a lot going on this week, but if you hear *anything*, call me."

—— ✦ ✦ ✦ ——

Tuesday, May 17, 2016
39th Air Base Wing
Incirlik Air Base, Turkey

The signal was given at 0100 hours to execute the plan. Simultaneously, the airspace was closed, roads leading to the base were blocked, and all communications and electricity were cut, isolating the air base from the rest of the world. MİT had sabotaged the emergency generators on the base, and it would be some time before repairs would be permitted. The normal hustle and bustle came to an abrupt standstill without electricity. Air traffic control could not talk to returning aircraft, and they had to be diverted to other air bases. The usual roaring jet engines were silent, and the only sounds came from the turbocharged diesel engines of the approaching tanks and fighting vehicles.

Under cover of darkness and a dense smokescreen, M60T Sabra main battle tanks and ACV-15 Infantry fighting vehicles raced to surround the air base with precision. On the north side of the airfield, the tracked vehicles penetrated the outer fence and took up positions next to the double-fence surrounding the NATO Area—otherwise known as the *exclusion area*—their target. In front of them were the protective aircraft shelters containing the ninety B61 nuclear bombs.

The Tactical Response Force was able to take up positions to augment the on-duty security force by the time the armored vehicles closed on their positions around the perimeter. Off-duty security personnel had been alerted, but the ACV-15s prevented them from deploying. The armored vehicles had approached the air base from different directions and cut off any attempts at strengthening the security force. The large area of the base and number of aircraft parked spread the duty force very thin as they tried to provide protection for the planes. Bart Madison was pleased with the execution of his plan thus far—Incirlik was caught off guard.

There had been no official intelligence warning of an impending attack on the base and the armored vehicles were NATO allies.

Madison directed the driver of the ACV-15 he was in to occupy a place in the middle where he could observe the entrances of three of the shelters. The exclusion area was on the farthest side, away from the headquarters of the air base. Armored vehicles on the south side kept the airmen on that part of the base inside those buildings. Turkish and other forces stationed at the NATO base were also kept inside their respective buildings.

Madison was unsure how the Turkish military—mostly airmen—inside the base would react. General Çakmak and al-Ghazāli had assured him the Turks would not fight against their own army, at least initially. They would first seek instructions. Without communications to their higher headquarters, that would be impossible. Madison didn't trust that theory completely. He wanted to be out of the area as soon as possible and before the Turkish airmen inside the base decided which side to support during the assault.

Events were unfolding fast and with accuracy. Although the men assigned for protection of the air base were well trained, there was a period—like in any emergency—of chaos at the onset as they analyzed their situation. They were surrounded by an overwhelming force and were outgunned. Diesel fumes and smoke hung thick in the crisp night air and competed with the oxygen, making it difficult to breathe.

The security force inside the exclusion area held their weapons ready and glanced to their officer in charge—First Lieutenant Timothy Brown—with anticipation.

The intimidating 120mm tubes of the main gun on the tanks and the 25mm cannons of the infantry fighting vehicles pointed in toward the base were ready to wreak havoc, though no shots had been fired up to this point. The tension was palpable.

Lieutenant Brown had never faced such a situation, but his instincts told him to hold fire. During that period of initial confusion, he had to decide whether it was some kind of no-notice inspection or test. After a few moments, he realized he had not been advised of a test.

Three floodlights popped on, illuminating the young lieutenant and the three shelters behind him. From somewhere in the darkness in front of him, a loudspeaker blared out in English, "The air base is surrounded. Put your weapons down and no one will be injured. Stay inside the buildings." The voice repeated the instructions again and again as the same instructions were repeated on the other side of the base.

MIT had provided Madison with a list of the members of the security force and the locations of their fighting positions. In a gunfight, one never knows when a bullet has your name on it. Bart knew this all too well and drew on every bit of his experience to avoid that one bullet. Understanding the importance of psychological operations, Bart was skilled in using it. He'd anticipated the young officer would be susceptible, at least for a short time.

"Lieutenant Brown," Madison said over a loudspeaker, "the base is surrounded by an overwhelming force. Do as I say and no one will get hurt. Remove the magazines and place your weapons on the ground." He studied the young man, then scrutinized the others.

In the distance, other voices over more loudspeakers echoed the same commands Bart had just given. Each of the Turkish officers had been assigned a section around the perimeter and were executing in accordance with Madison's instructions.

"Do you understand, Tim?"

Madison personalized the situation when he used the lieutenant's first name. The stage was set. From behind the bright lights, he studied Brown's every move. The man's jaw tightened and sweat emerged on his face as he looked right, then left, searching for the man speaking to him.

"Stay inside the buildings," the voice blared out when the door of one of the buildings across from the lieutenant's position opened.

Several airmen in combat gear darted out of the open door, beelining toward a location to reinforce the lieutenant.

All of a sudden, two quick bursts from the 7.62mm machine gun on one of the tanks pierced the tension like the shattering of a crystal glass. Bullets arched through the darkness toward their targets. Four figures fell to the ground, but a fifth made it to cover behind a vehicle. Another burst erupted, spraying the vehicle. Then a machine gun in the distance opened up with two deadly bursts, signaling an attempt by Americans trying to provide help to the security force or a pilot trying to reach his aircraft.

"I'm sorry, sir!" the officer said. "We cannot do that."

"Tim, look around," Madison said, his tone cold. "You are facing an overwhelming force and will die. My men can easily destroy this entire air base and everyone on it. I will not repeat myself again."

The whine of an A-10 Thunderbolt's turbines competed with Madison as it attempted a quick takeoff. One of the nearby tracked vehicles unleashed the fury of the 25mm cannon, and the A-10 exploded and then rolled off the runway still ablaze.

"You see, Tim," Madison continued. "I mean business. One more demonstration for you."

A nearby tank fired its 120mm main gun, rocking with the violent explosion. The protective aircraft shelter—with an F-16 parked inside—to the left of the one Lieutenant Brown was in front of, erupted in a fireball.

The lieutenant flinched with the explosion, then struggled to regain his composure.

Again, a 7.62mm machine gun fired, spewing death in two torrents. Three more Americans in combat gear fell as they stepped from one of the buildings. Another 25mm cannon fired on an F-16 attempting a takeoff from the field. It burst into flames and skidded off the runway.

"What'll it be, Tim?" Madison said.

Lieutenant Brown swallowed hard, then said, "No, sir!"

A single shot from a HK33 5.56 assault rifle rang out, and the senior airman beside the lieutenant collapsed to the ground. The bullet had struck him above the right eye, and blood had splattered on Brown's face.

Lieutenant Brown removed the magazine from his M-4 carbine, then laid it on the ground. Turning his head, he said, "Do as he says! Remove your magazines and place your weapons on the ground." He turned his head to the other side. "Place your weapons on the ground."

Two other 7.62mm machine guns from across the airfield sounded in the distance, accentuating the tension with bursts. Light from the burning shelter glimmered across Lieutenant Brown's face as he stood with his hands in the air.

Two Turkish soldiers jogged out of the darkness, carrying power saws. Reaching the fence, the soldiers started their tools and began cutting the fence between two posts. Two more soldiers emerged from the darkness, lugging a portable generator, and entered the exclusion area as soon as one side of the fence was opened. Without hesitation, they went to work connecting the generator to the shelter behind the lieutenant. Once connected, one of the soldiers started the machine. The other stood and held his thumb up, signaling their task was completed. Two more soldiers hustled through the open fence with another generator and headed to the shelter to the right of Lieutenant Brown. They performed the same task of connecting the generator.

"Tim," Madison said, "raise the bomb rack out of the vault in the shelter behind you and the one in the next shelter."

"I can't do that, sir," Brown replied. "I don't have the access code."

The HK33 assault rifle registered again.

A staff sergeant next to Brown fell when the bullet entered his thigh, and he lay on the pavement in pain, clutching his leg.

"Raise the rack, Tim," Madison said coldly. "That bullet could have just as easily killed Sergeant Ramirez. Don't make me say it again. If I do, it'll cost you another man. Perhaps Technical Sergeant Ledbetter or Senior Airman Kennedy. I'll shoot you all, if need be. Raise the rack. It's not worth dying for." Madison observed Brown's face, illuminated by the flickering light.

Brown had no choice. "I will need to call operations and get the codes."

"Contact them," Madison said. "Tell them to send one airman with the codes, alone, in a single vehicle."

"Yes, sir," Brown said, then he spoke into his walkie-talkie. Hearing the response, he said, "Sir, they cannot comply with your request."

A single shot from the HK33 rang out again. "Tim, tell operations they just killed Senior Airman Kennedy," Madison said. "Send the codes. They have fifteen seconds to respond positively or that KC-135 over there on the tarmac will go up in flames." He pointed to the tanker to his right front.

"Yes, sir," Brown said, then he spoke into his walkie-talkie. Receiving their reply, he said, "The answer is no."

An M60T recoiled as it released another deafening eruption from its main gun. The KC-135 Stratotanker exploded.

"Tim, I'm getting annoyed. Tell them one airman will be shot and one aircraft destroyed every thirty seconds until they comply."

"Yes, sir," Brown said, then he spoke into his radio and waited for their reply. "They'll comply. It'll take them just a couple of minutes."

"They have five minutes to have someone on the way with the codes."

Brown relayed the message into the radio, then dropped his gaze to his men lying on the asphalt. Looking right and left, he took in each of the airmen's terrified faces staring back at him. Brown then glared toward the direction of Madison's voice, but all he could see was numerous gun tubes peeking out from behind the lights. He gritted his teeth and squeezed his hands into a tight fist. Sweat streak his face. Minutes seemed like hours as Brown waited operations response.

Finally, after a few grueling moments, he received confirmation. His throat was so dry he had to force his words. "The codes are on the way."

Madison looked across the airfield and saw the headlights of a vehicle, its yellow lights flashing as it approached his position. "Very good, Tim."

When the pickup truck arrived, Madison directed the driver over the loudspeaker to get out of the vehicle and take the codes to Lieutenant Brown. The driver, a female in a US Air Force uniform, complied. As soon as Madison saw her hand the codes to Brown, he said, "If those are the right codes, you will be allowed to return to operations."

The airman didn't speak but simply stood waiting for permission to leave.

Lieutenant Brown took the envelope and stepped back inside the aircraft shelter, stopping in front of a panel on the wall. He opened the envelope, looked at the code, then entered a series of characters. The rack began to rise. He returned to the front of the shelter and knelt to check on Staff Sergeant Ramirez.

Madison said, "Airman, you can leave now."

She returned to the pickup and drove back across the airfield.

Brown stood, then walked to the next shelter and entered characters in the panel. That rack began to rise. He then returned to his former position.

Several men—two ex-Turkish pilots and their two ground crews—darted through the fence. One pilot and crew went to the first shelter and the others jogged to the adjacent one. The first pilot immediately started making preflight checks on the F-16 parked inside the shelter while the ground crew began placing the bombs on the loader. The second crew immediately went to work doing the same thing when they reached the raised rack while the pilot performed his checks on that jet.

Madison had only planned for the use of one pilot and ground crew. The addition of the second crew and pilot had come from General Çakmak just before the operation started. He hadn't elaborated on the second pilot and crew, simply telling Madison he was adding a second crew and that they knew what to do. Madison didn't like last-minute changes as they always had the potential to cause problems. He had not worked with these men, nor had he supervised the training of their duties, and now he had to oversee the operations in two shelters. He didn't have any choice about including the men, even though he'd protested to the general. If anything went wrong with the second crew, Madison would sacrifice them.

Machine-gun fire captured Madison's attention, drawing his gaze across the airfield. Muzzle flashes identified the position of two tanks firing. Then a nearby M60T opened fire with its 7.62 machine gun. *The Americans are making another attempt,* he thought as he identified several figures emerging from a building. He glanced to the Turkish lieutenant directing the armored vehicle. *He's got it under control.* Madison checked his watch. *Just a couple of minutes behind.*

Finally, the crew in the first shelter signaled to the pilot, already in the cockpit, that the bombs were loaded and the aircraft was ready to depart. The F-16's turbine engines whined and then roared with life. Madison looked to the second shelter, and the crew indicated that jet was also ready to depart. Hearing its engines come to life, he looked to the first pilot and gestured for him to take off, then to the second pilot. The fighters rolled out of the shelters and taxied into position for takeoff. The F-16s roared down the runway, both loaded with three B61 bombs each.

Madison watched the two aircraft disappear into the night sky. He checked his watch, looked around the area, then stepped to the Turkish officer in charge. "My portion here is complete. You're in charge now."

The officer saluted Madison.

He breathed a sigh of relief that the first phase of his operation was complete. He climbed into one of the Infantry fighting vehicles as the engine started. It backed out of position and departed from Incirlik Air Base, speeding to a secluded location several miles from the base, where Madison rendezvoused with a waiting car. Climbing out of the track, he was greeted by al-Ghazāli, and they immediately got into the car and sped away.

"Did you have any problems?" al-Ghazāli asked with a serious look as he handed Madison a bottle of water.

"Nothing I couldn't handle," Bart replied, then took a swig from the bottle.

"All is going according to plan," al-Ghazāli said with a grin. "Istanbul and Ankara are all that is being talked about in the news. Nothing so far has been mentioned about Incirlik. President Kağan has made a statement on CNN, and Anadolu news agency has kept sending out reports. One of the parliament buildings has been bombed, and tanks have been deployed to those buildings. The Americans are already being blamed, and we are starting to make arrests. As planned, Kağan was safe in Marmaris, southwest Turkey. The special forces headquarters has been bombed. Kağan held a press conference at Istanbul Atatürk Airport when he arrived from Marmaris."

"That's good," Madison said with a nod. "Now the next phase. What's the status at the landing zone? That must be completed and the site cleared quickly."

"The bombs have been off-loaded, and they should have started on the warheads by now."

Bart nodded and took another drink of water. "The US pilots have probably questioned the reason for being diverted. It won't take CENTCOM or the Pentagon long to start asking questions. They'll want to know why Incirlik is closed."

CHAPTER 13

Tuesday, May 17, 2016
Gareth Residence
New York, New York

"I TOLD YOU I wanted Kağan to hold off on the coup until the little problem with Kenworth was taken care of," Stew said into the phone, then puffed his cigar. With Nassar's news, Gareth knew he had lost some leverage with Kağan, a position he didn't like. He was forced to fulfill his part of the agreement and block any UN resolution against Turkey.

"I know, but the timing was critical," Nassar said, implying there was no choice. "President Kağan was advised that his plan might be discovered if he waited any longer. Actions are being taken as you directed."

"What about Kenworth and the woman?" Stew asked, his frustration building. "Has the team got 'em yet?"

"They think they have located the two. It will be finished very soon now."

Stew replied, "It'd better be." He placed the cigar in the ashtray, brushed an ash from the desk, then said, "Be sure and suppress any news about Incirlik until it is absolutely necessary, then make sure it's downplayed. The news reports are only to say the base is surrounded by anti-government forces and there are no casualties. Jenny will release a statement today condemning the coup d'etat. She'll say in the statement that the US supports the democratic process and will not interfere in the politics of Turkey. Of course, it will have all the right words in the full statement, and she'll plead for everyone to be calm and respect human rights. Just after she releases it, I want CNN and Anadolu news agency to broadcast her statement."

"I understand," Nassar replied.

"Oh, Nassar, Weldon is looking for one of his men and believes he may be in Turkey. His name is Bart Madison. Have you heard of an American by that name?"

Nassar was caught off guard by the question, which caused a noticeable delay in his response. He knew the name and that Madison had planned and led the operation against Incirlik. He replied, "I am not familiar with anyone by that name. Why are you looking for him?"

Stew hesitated as he thought about Nassar's words, then said, "Weldon hasn't heard from him and was a little concerned that he may be hurt. I just thought I'd help him out." He didn't know whether to believe Nassar or not. He had to consider that Nassar could be looking for money in exchange for information and if he appeared too anxious for the information, it could get expensive. "If you do hear of him, let me know."

"I will. Al-Ghazāli may have heard the name. I will ask him."

"I've got another call. Keep me posted." Stew hung up the phone without waiting for a reply.

Jenny, looking rough around the edges and with bags under her eyes, walked into the room, set her glass of scotch on the corner of his desk, then flopped into the chair across from Stew. "What's on for today?" she asked.

He shot a glance to the glass, then a disapproving eye to Jenny. "Go easy on that shit. You've got to issue a press statement on Turkey in about an hour."

She sipped the drink, then asked, "Turkey, what's going on there and who gives a shit about them?"

"Jenny," Stew said, his voice full of frustration. "We do. They give our campaign lots of money. We also have quite a few air force personnel stationed at the NATO airbase in Incirlik—the coup d'etat. You need to sound concerned for the Americans and the NATO base. We've talked about this a number of times."

"Oh, right." Jenny's reply was not all that convincing. "Do you have it all written out for me?"

"It's on the desk. Make sure you are very concerned with the situation and sound like you are on top of world events. We want to keep

Kağan happy and in our court so we can keep the Russians from selling their oil through the pipeline to Europe. That means a lot of money to us and the foundation."

"I do remember something about that. Should I blame the Russians for the coup?"

"I'll think about it. We may want to use the Russians for something else. Besides, if we are too heavy on them, they may get annoyed and cut off their money to the campaign. Just go practice your speech and stay on script."

"All right," Jenny said as she stood. "I need another scotch anyway."

------ ◆ ◆ ◆ ------

Wednesday, May 18, 2016
Somewhere
Northwest Syria

Max and Danya continued moving in a southeasterly direction, mostly at night and avoiding the main roads as they attempted to find the US Special Forces. They had to scrounge for something to eat, which usually consisted of scraps, raw vegetables, and anything else they could find. The first two days they had fresh milk—goat on day one and cow on day two. The milk was warm, directly from the animal. The food was not all that clean and always cold, because having a fire to cook anything or to keep warm was out of the question. Food became harder to find the farther they pushed into Syria.

Just before dawn on the fifth day, the two sought shelter in an old stone building that had been converted from a house into—for the lack of a better term—a barn. Like most buildings in the area, the war had taken its toll on the structure. Max kept alert and watched the area for threats or anyone who may have started following them. Being caught off guard was not in his plans. Danya began searching the interior of the barn for anything they could use or eat. Max climbed to the second level, stepped to the door, and resumed his vigilance. Within several minutes, he looked around to see Danya at the top of the ladder.

"I found us something better than muddy water to drink," she said, holding a bottle of wine in front of her as she approached him. A small bag was in her other hand and both of her front pockets bulged. "Our farmer has a nice stash down there."

"Is it any good?" Max asked without taking his eyes off the area beyond the building.

"It looks good and smells good. Let's taste it and find out," she said. "It's not Pinot Noir, though."

"Probably something the owner of this place makes himself. We better get settled in for the day." Max removed the cork and took a sip. "It's okay." He handed the bottle back to Danya, then focused his attention on her other hand. "You look like you've been to the market. What've you got in the bag?"

"Dried figs and dates. I've got pistachios in one pocket and two apples in the other."

His eyes darted to her bulging pants pockets. "Good going. I think I'll keep you around." He returned his attention back outside. "I'll keep watch for a few hours while you get some sleep," he said, a slight concern coloring his voice about what might be lurking beyond their shelter.

"What is it?" Danya asked. "Did you see something?"

"I don't know. It's more of a feeling. I saw two birds land in that tree right over there." He nodded to a large oak tree about thirty yards from them, on their front right.

"Max, you're tired. It's birds. Get some rest. I'll take the first watch," she said as she stroked the stubble on his cheek.

"Perhaps. I'll eat first, then I'll rest." Max took two figs from the bag, returned his attention outside, and placed a fig in his mouth. "Yesterday I got a glimpse of two birds just like those two and didn't think anything about it. I haven't seen any other birds. Have you?"

"Now that you mention it, no," Danya said as she stepped next to Max and peered outside. "What are you thinking?" she asked as his attention left her.

"Drones," Max replied in a low voice without looking at her.

"Do you think we've found the special forces, or they've found us?"

"No, the army doesn't have drones like that. It could be CIA or some other government's intelligence service. I doubt that ISIS or any of the terrorist organizations have anything that sophisticated."

"So what do we do?"

"We need to find out if they're friendly or not. If they're hostile, they could be observing us and we'd walk right into an ambush. If armed, three or four grams of shaped explosives would ruin your day. If I'm right, the operators are nearby. A drone like that has a short range. Whoever it is figures we'll hold up in here for the day. I'm guessing they're observing this barn to see if we leave. After we have settled down, they'll make their move."

"You wanna try to capture one of the drones?" Danya asked. "Or try to locate the operator?"

"The latter is our best bet. If we nab one of the drones, that'll tip 'em off that we're on to them. We need to get out of this barn. A deception will give us a little head start." Max began scooping up armloads of hay and piled it near the door. "Grab that old piece of canvas," he said as he pointed to an oil-stained scrap of fabric crumpled-up in the corner across from them.

When Danya handed it to him, Max stepped in front of the loft door and casually wrapped the material around his shoulders. He stood, momentarily giving the observers ample time to see him wrapped in the heavy, dingy cloth while giving the appearance that he wasn't concerned about being watched and all the while hoping not to get shot. Max casually withdrew out of sight and placed the shroud on the pile of hay, forming it to look like a person's shoulder. Next, he scooted the shape closer to the edge of the opening and then refined his handy work. He had positioned it to give the appearance of someone seated, leaning against the edge of the door with only a shoulder visible.

As soon as the drones start flying again, they'll see it's a deception, he thought. *Just hope we get enough of a head start.* Turning to Danya, he gave her a slight nudge. "Out the back, quick!"

Danya grasped the bag of dried fruit and stepped to the ladder with Max behind her, the bottle of wine in his hand. At the back of the barn, near the corner diagonally across from the tree with the drones, Max saw cracks in the mud and straw mortar that held several of the limestone blocks in place, indicating a weak place in the wall.

"Hold this," he said as he handed the bottle of wine to Danya. "Watch out. The entire corner may collapse when I kick it."

She backed up several feet to where she thought she would be clear if the wall crumbled.

Max raised his foot to the third course and four blocks out from the corner, then kicked.

Nothing happened.

He struck the wall again and felt it give. Striking it once more as hard as he could, he pushed two stones out, both holding by a small portion of the corner. He stepped closer to the wall, then pushed on the blocks and they fell free. Moving back, he assaulted the wall again and again until the opening was big enough for them to crawl out.

Once out of the barn, he darted to a tree-lined stream with Danya following. It provided some cover to conceal their escape. Crouching and wading through the cool, ankle-deep water, the two moved as fast and quiet as possible. After traveling about a quarter of a mile, Max stopped and dropped in a clump of weeds beneath a tree that hung over the bank. Danya landed beside him. The two lay motionless, observing the area around them and the barn. They waited and listened. After five minutes had passed, there was no sign of anyone or, most importantly, the drones.

Danya placed the bag of dried fruit in front of them and said, "Just as well enjoy breakfast while we wait." She placed a fig in Max's mouth, then one in her own. She rolled to her side and withdrew the apples from her pocket, giving one to Max. She bit into the other one, and juice streaked down her chin.

Max wiped her chin with his thumb and said, "Use your napkin." He smiled.

Danya smiled. "Right."

At that instant, the old barn exploded in a thunderous fireball. Debris and smoke rose into the air.

Max pushed Danya's head down as he dropped his. A few seconds later, he eased his head up and watched pieces of what used to be the barn rain down. What remained of the structure was on fire. "Predator strike," he said in a low voice. "Scoot more under that tree." Nudging Danya, he slid into a position with her that gave them more overhead cover from the optical sensors of the bird. "They'll be checking what's left. We'll come in behind them. Still got your pistol?" Max said as he withdrew the P229 he had confiscated from his captors.

"Yep!" she replied. "They certainly aren't friendly."

"Nope! Get ready and stay alert," Max said. Soon he nodded to his left front. "There they are, carrying long guns."

Two men in camouflage clothing crouched and cautiously made their way toward the smoldering remnants of the barn. Reaching their destination, one of the men remained on guard while the other one scoured the barn's remains.

"I don't like the odds," Max said in a low voice. "I've got another idea. Those two are light, probably left their gear behind somewhere. Possibly a third person guarding their rear. Come on." He slithered off the bank and backed into the stream in a crouch.

The two moved with caution, their pistols ready, as they followed the stream. Searching the stream's bank, left then right, revealed nothing but deserted farmland. *It won't be long before whatever farm workers still in the area come to check out the fire,* Max thought. *More chances of being seen.*

They had traveled about one hundred meters when Danya tapped Max's arm and said in a low voice, "Look, there he is." She pointed to their right front and approximately twenty-five meters away from the stream.

The two eased onto the bank near a small bush.

The lone man sat with his back to them, earphones in his ears and watching a screen on a tablet type device with two antennae. A long gun to his right leaned on a boulder.

Max looked to Danya and said, "Go on down about twenty-five meters, and we'll go in at the same time. When we get close, throw a rock to his left front so he'll look in that direction. I'll come in from his right rear. I want him alive."

Danya nodded and slid to the rear, raising to a crouch, then began moving into position.

Max watched her, then returned his focus to the target. She was very quiet as she moved. The seated man was unaware of either Max or Danya as they neared. Max had picked the shortest distance to the target but still had to travel unnoticed for twenty-five meters in open terrain. He glanced back to Danya, who had found her mark and was waiting on his signal to move forward. Max motioned with his hand, and the two started their move toward the device operator. When Max stepped into the clearing, he checked the area in front of him again, then started running as fast as he could, his arms pumping. He motioned for Danya to throw the stone. When it landed, the man looked to his left, then returned his attention to the tablet. Max was two meters from the target when he looked up from the screen at him, too late to react. Max crashed into him, knocking him over. Max had the advantage as he held the P229 close to the man's face.

"On your stomach," Max said, his voice low but commanding. "Not a sound. Put your hands behind your head."

The tablet operator had no choice but to comply or die.

Danya stepped next to Max and said as she removed the earphones from their captive and grasped the walkie-talkie, "You all right?"

"Yeah, I just scraped my forehead when I hit him," Max said and passed his hand across his head. "Check him out, and I'll look at his tablet. See if there's anything you can use to tie him up." He knelt next to the device and picked it up. A live video was displayed on the screen showing the two camouflaged men searching the burning debris. "I was right, those are drones and this is the controller," he said as he glanced to Danya and tilted it toward her, displaying the video.

Hearing a faint sound emanating from the earphones, Danya placed one of the earpieces next to her ear. "Max, I think those guys you're watching are calling him." She motioned to the guy on the ground, then handed the walkie-talkie with earphones to Max.

He placed the earphones in his ears and listened as the voice repeated the call again. If he answered, the caller on the other end would know there was a problem. Max took a breath, depressed the talk button to break squelch, and released it. *That might slow them down if they think he's having radio trouble,* he thought. *It's a crap shoot. Those two'll be here quick.* "Hurry up, we're about to have some company," Max said as he looked to Danya, then looked at their captive on the ground. "Okay, dude, lie there and be quiet. If you try to warn them, you'll be the first to die. Got that?"

He nodded.

"Grab his rifle and get behind those boulders," Max said as he pointed to a spot just a few meters from him. He returned his attention back to the controller.

"Do you know how to operate a drone?" Danya asked as she grasped the rifle.

"No. Do you?"

"Here, you take the rifle and I'll fly the drone," Danya said, handing the long gun to him.

He looked at her, his brow furrowed. No time to ask questions, he darted to the position he pointed out to Danya and took aim in the direction of the two men.

Danya sat behind one of the boulders, crossed her legs, then placed the controller in her lap and said, "Okay, here goes." She feverishly worked her magic on the electronic box. "Not too bad. This one's sensitive. I'll get the hang of it."

"We don't have a lot of time. Do you have a video feed on the two guys?" Max's voice was full of anxiety.

"Got it," Danya said. "They're just beyond that bend in the trail up ahead. I'll show you. Look up and you can see the drone."

"Danya, get down," he said. "Stop playing around. Just keep them in sight and tell me where they are."

"Coming into the bend now," she said as she gingerly adjusted the controls. She pressed the red *Armed* buttoned. "You should be able to see them any time now." She made an adjustment as she focused on the display. A pop emanated from the area to their front.

"What was that?" Max asked as he shot a glance to her.

"The trailing guy dying," she replied. "I'm bringing up the other drone." She pressed one button, then another. Her finger traced the screen with a deliberate touch, then pressed a button. "I'll have the guy on video in a few seconds."

"He's screaming in the radio. Where is he?"

"Just a second," she said, her voice cold. "There he is. On the left, thirty-five meters. Do you see him? He's staying close to those trees."

"I see him," Max said, then spoke into the radio. "Put your weapon down and your hands up."

"Kenworth," came the man's voice over the radio. "I can't do that. I've gotta kill you first."

"Not today," Max said into the radio. *Most likely CIA,* he thought.

A rifle shot cracked, and the bullet ricocheted off the limestone near Max's head. The man was close and had Max's position located.

Another shot registered. The bullet ripped through the leaves on the tree just above Max. Several pieces sprinkled on him.

A pop broke the tension and silence slammed back.

"He's dead," Danya said as she set the controller down. "Are you all right?"

"I'm okay," Max said as he stood. "I'll go check those guys. You stay here and watch him." He pointed to the man on the ground. "I was hoping to get some information from these guys. Try not to kill him while I'm gone."

Danya nodded. "As long as he doesn't piss me off," she replied more under her breath than to Max.

About ten minutes later, Max walked up dragging the corpses and had two rifles slung over his shoulder. "I've got their rifles, pistols, ammunition, and knives. That's about it. They're CIA."

"I've smashed the controller," she said, "Looks like we're stocked up on weapons and ammunition. I emptied out two of their rucksacks and filled them with the water, rations, and extra ammunition they had here." She pointed to two bulging bundles to her left.

"I'll check the weapons and look around to make sure we haven't missed anything. While I'm doing that, take one of the corpses' bootlaces and secure this guy a little better. Put one of the laces tight around his mouth." Max motioned to the man on the ground. "We'll take him with us and work on him later. We need to clear outta here."

Danya stepped to the corpses and began removing a lace from one of the boots.

By the time she finished and had the man sitting on the ground cross-legged, waiting to go, Max had ended his search. "Nothing," he said.

"He's ready. Let's get moving," she said as she stepped next to Max.

The two donned the rucks, then grasped the rifles. "Ready to go?" Max asked as he looked at Danya.

"Ready," she said, then she tugged on the man's arm. "Let's go."

CHAPTER 14

Wednesday, May 18, 2016
Damaged Farmhouse
Jarabulus, Syria

A L-GHAZĀLI HAD ARRANGED for a meeting with representatives of ISIS senior leadership to sell two of the nukes. The meeting took place in a bomb-damaged farmhouse on the outskirts of the town. A mostly intact limestone wall surrounded the courtyard, provided some security. Jarabulus was a small village just inside the Turkey-Syria border on the west bank of the Euphrates River in northern Syria. The compound, in ISIS controlled territory, was heavily guarded by ISIS fighters at the house and for several neighboring blocks.

The squalid meeting room was dimly lit by candles. Debris littered the floor, thick dust covered everything, and a tattered and dingy cloth shielded the windows from outside observation. The house suffered from the effects of the war and years of neglect. Six men sat cross-legged on a worn rug. A young Arabic boy served tea to the men, first to the Muslim Brotherhood guests, Dawud Al'alim and Abdal al-Ghazāli. Moving to the next man—a Caucasian—the child paused, unsure what to do. His inquisitive eyes darted to the ISIS man, whose face was illuminated by the flickering candlelight that dramatically emphasized his features, including the three-inch scar across his cheek. Nabi Ulmalhamah al-Aqrab always intimidated him. Al-Aqrab nodded to the rugged man, indicating he was to be served. Bart Madison accepted the cup with a slight nod. The boy moved to the ISIS side, serving al-Aqrab first, then Ra'id Umar Tarik and Khalid Safar.

Tarik, a slender man with a heavy black beard and stained teeth, was the first to speak—in English—looking first to al-Aqrab and then to

Madison. "Al-Aqrab, you have recommended this American to us, but I do not trust him. He could be CIA. We should kill him now." His dark, piercing eyes remained on Madison.

Al-Aqrab looked to Safar. "What do you say?"

"You have told me many things about him," Safar said, his gaze never leaving Madison. "I want to hear him talk."

Madison knew his life could end that very night. He had faced similar situations in the past and knew the slightest thing could spook these men, resulting in his head being on a stake. Showing any sign of fear would be the start of his downfall. "Al-Aqrab knows me. I worked for him about three years ago. I delivered a nuclear weapon to a key target in the US to inflict great pain on the Americans."

"I understand there were problems," Safar said, then lit a cigarette.

"I was hired to plan, take the nuke into the US, and place it at the target," Madison said, then sipped his tea. "That was what I was hired to do, and I did it. I was later captured in Panama by the CIA. They made a deal with me, in exchange for my life. I am not CIA but was forced to work for them. I worked directly for the deputy director, Trent Weldon, mainly to oversee the drug trade and a few other odd jobs." He took another sip of tea.

"Continue," Safar said, motioning with his hand, which was missing the last two fingers.

"I operated throughout Central and South America. I kept the routes open and maintained a steady flow of the drugs into the US. It takes a lot of money to buy an election." Madison glanced at al-Aqrab and then to al-Ghazāli.

Al-Aqrab nodded. "This is true. I talked with the FARC in Panama and verified what he has said. They had many good things to say about him."

Tarik stroked his beard. "You were forced to work for CIA in Panama. How did you get here?"

"I was coordinating for increased opium shipments into the US when I was tipped off that the CIA had sent a killer team after me. I was no longer of use to them, and I had information about the coup in Turkey that they didn't want made public. I was alone in Helmand Province and made my escape."

Al-Ghazāli nodded and sipped his tea. "I checked out Madison and knew about his background. You can trust he is not CIA."

Madison continued. "Al-Ghazāli hired me to take the nukes from Incirlik. I did that. If I were CIA, I would not have delivered the nukes to the US target, nor would I have taken the bombs from Incirlik." He opened a folder beside him on the floor, withdrew several photographs, and flopped them on the floor in front of Safar. "Those are photographs of the warheads we came to talk about. They're in a safe place. If you don't want to do business, I'll take the warheads elsewhere."

Safar held his gaze on Madison.

It was a power play meant to intimidate him. Madison locked eyes with the terrorist and didn't move. He could see in Safar's eyes that he was desperate to pick up the photographs and look at the coveted items. It was something the terrorists longed for. Not only was it a status symbol for them but it would make them victorious over the Americans. ISIS could inflict great damage on the Americans or simply taunt them into submission. The Muslims believed that the US feared nuclear retaliation, and therefore, if the US knew the terrorists had a nuclear weapon, the Americans would capitulate.

Safar could no longer resist and dropped his eyes to the photographs. He grasped the photos with the damaged hand and held them close as he studied each one.

I win, you bastard, Madison thought. *You don't have a clue what you're looking at.*

Taking the photographs from Safar, al-Aqrab said, "We must talk now."

The three senior ISIS representatives stood and walked into the next room.

Al-Ghazāli touched Madison's forearm and said, "Now we wait. Do not worry, they will buy them. This is another show."

By the time al-Ghazāli lit his second cigarette, the others had re-entered the room and taken their places on the rug. Safar held up his disfigured hand and motioned to the Arabic boy to serve them again.

Tarik lit a cigarette and asked, "The price?"

Al-Ghazāli, with his eyes locked on Tarik, replied without hesitation, "Fifteen million US dollars each."

A flurry of Arabic ensued between Tarik, Al-Aqrab, and Safar. Within a few minutes, Al'alim joined in the passionate exchange. Al-Ghazāli periodically interjected something, but for the most part remained secondary, providing backup to Al'alim.

The meek boy silently served the tea, appearing to magically avoid the animated men. After serving the last man, he left the room without making a sound.

Tarik smoothed his beard and said in English, "Ten million US dollars each for all six warheads."

Al'alim shook his head. "No, fifteen million US dollars each, for two. The Brotherhood has two and that is all of them."

Tarik's eyes remained locked onto Al'alim's as he said, "I am told six were taken from the Americans."

Al'alim replied, "Two are for the Brotherhood, two are for sale to you, and the other two were for expenses." He was not about to tell Tarik that General Çakmak had the other two. Al'alim wanted those available for the future.

The agitated Arabic discussion returned. After a few more moments of the energetic debate, al-Aqrab held up his hand and said in English, "We will take both warheads."

Madison said, "We will deliver them day after tomorrow. I will provide you with the time, location, and bank information for the electronic transfer of the money."

"Agreed," al-Aqrab replied.

———— • ♦ • ————

Wednesday, May 18, 2016
Somewhere
Northwest Syria

Max and Danya continued their southeasterly trek just after sundown. However, with the addition of their captive, they were not able to travel as fast as on previous nights. The trio approached a neglected olive grove. Aided by the bright moon, Max was able to see beyond the grove to the rubble of two farmhouses. The stones were scattered around both dwellings. One stone wall remained on the house to his left and two walls stood in the ruins to the right.

The night was pleasant—if there was such a thing in a war zone—with a slight intermittent breeze. There were no sounds except for the soft crunch of their shoes on the sunbaked earth. No other soul was visible anywhere or, for that matter, there were no living creatures of any kind. The casual observer might have just assumed it was normal for that time of night.

Max tensed. *It's too quiet,* he thought. As Danya stopped beside him, he whispered, "I don't like it. Too quiet. Stay alert."

Danya nodded, turned to their captive, and leaned closer to him. With a stern expression, she placed a vertical finger in front of her lips to signal him to be quiet.

He nodded.

Max strained his senses as he scanned the area again. He couldn't detect any movement or sound. With a deliberate step, he moved forward at a cautious pace. His years of training had taught him to pay attention to his environment—smells, sounds, movements, the wind, temperature, the feel of the earth beneath his feet, and his eyes. He had been right too many times in the past when relying on his senses to deny what they were telling him now. Like earlier that morning, something wasn't right. Focusing on what his body was telling him, he was ready to react to any situation.

The trio had moved another ten meters in the olive grove when Max stopped again. He scrutinized the area as far as he could see, then knelt and held his rifle at the ready. Danya and the captive took a knee as well. She also held her rifle ready to defend their position. No one made a sound or moved.

A female voice just above a whisper, in front of them, penetrated the silence. "Kenworth! Max Kenworth. Friendly. I want to link up."

Max scrutinized the blackness in front of him. Then he replied in a low voice, "Identify yourself."

"YPG friend," came the reply.

"Where did we meet?" Max asked.

"Aleppo, almost three weeks ago," the voice replied.

"Show me your hands and walk slowly," Max commanded. He looked to Danya and saw her nod. He didn't need to say anything, but he knew she was ready. Turning his attention back to the front, he saw a figure begin to emerge from the blackness. He scanned the area to his flanks, then back to the approaching form. He kept his eyes on the shape as it approached and then knelt in front of him.

"Good to see you again," Max said as he extended his hand. "Is your battle buddy with you?"

"You too," she replied and pointed off to the right. "He's on your right flank, just over there."

Max introduced Sandy to Danya. "She's a friend and used to be in the US Army as an MP," he said as he looked to Danya.

Sandy glanced to the man on the ground beside Danya and said, "Who's he?"

"He's not friendly. CIA. He and his two buddies tried to kill us this morning."

Sandy nodded. "We need to move out of this spot. Follow me." She looked to her left and said in a low voice, "Heading your way." She stood and stepped out.

Sandy led them about thirty meters from where they'd met to several boulders at the edge of the grove. The trio followed her around the boulders where they were greeted by her battle buddy. He extended his hand and greeted Max. Sandy introduced Danya to him.

"Sit down," Dave said as he sat. "A lot of people are looking for you—good and bad folks. I see you found the CIA. You were about to walk into an ambush just up ahead. I think there're Turks and possibly a couple of ISIS fighters in that old farmhouse with the two walls. We've been looking for you. I'm to guide you to the US Special Forces."

"Good. When can we get started?" Max replied.

"Whenever you're ready. I've got one thing to do first. I've got that old farmhouse targeted. As soon as I tell my commander I have you, an artillery battery is going to hit that place." Dave didn't wait for a reply. He rose and stepped to a spot about three feet away and picked up his radio. He spoke into it, then put it back on the ground. "Get your heads down," he said as he returned to the others.

Within a minute, three 155mm high-explosive rounds slammed into the old building. The fireballs blinked illumination as smoke, limestone blocks, dirt, and whatever else was in the old structure shot into the air.

Thunderous explosions shook the ground. Nothing could have survived the onslaught.

"As soon as the dust clears, I need to go check it out," Dave said as he raised and looked at the falling debris.

"I'll go with you," Max said, then he looked to Danya. "Stay here."

Danya nodded.

— ◆ —

Wednesday, May 19, 2016
Headquarters, US Special Operations Command
MacDill Air Force Base, Florida

The somber atmosphere at headquarters that morning quickly turned cheerful as the news of Max's arrival at the special forces forward operational base in northern Syria. A message was sent to MacDill as soon as he entered, and coordination was made for Max to call the J3. The next several hours were consumed with preliminary reports, medical checks, a meal, and baths.

"Max, you had us a little worried," Chugs said through a smile, into the speakerphone. "Colonel Johnston is here with me."

"Glad you're okay and back with us," Johnston said as he sat down across from General Matherson.

"Thank you. I was worried a bit myself. The CIA had a team after us. I killed two of 'em and captured the third one. The S2 here has him now."

"I'll coordinate with S2 and see what we can get from him," Johnston said. "We can probably charge him with attempted murder. That may get him talking. I recommend we hold him in Syria. If we return him to the US, he'll be out of jail and will disappear."

"I agree," the general said. "This can get very dicey until we know exactly who ordered him to hunt you and we have a statement. This could involve senior people in the government."

"We don't want to take any chances and will need hard evidence," Johnston said. "Something is wrong with the entire Turkish situation."

"Max, Madison led an attack on Incirlik and made off with six nukes," Matherson said, his tone serious. "Turkey has imposed martial law and been rounding up those who oppose the president by the thousands. I want you to find those nukes—and Madison. Whatever you need, you've got it. If the trail leads you back to Turkey, get in touch with me before you cross into the country. It's a mess, and we don't know who the friendlies are now. Colonel Johnston'll be sending you the intel he's gathered on the attack."

"Danya requests you let Thaddeus know she's okay and is with me," Max said. "She has a broken nose, a bit of an infection in a cut on her eyelid, and they're watching her for a mild concussion as a result of the blows she took from the Turkish thug who worked her over in that camp. Aside from that and a few bruises, she's fine."

"Max, when you find Madison…I don't want him to turn up again later." The general's tone was cold.

"I understand," Max replied with no hint of emotion. "Andy, be sure and send me everything on Madison and especially his contacts in Turkey. He had a girlfriend. I don't remember her name right now, but check her out."

"Will do," Johnston replied. "I'm already on the girlfriend. George is helping all he can. His contact in the Turkish military has disappeared. We don't know if he's been arrested or killed. The Turkish Special Forces Headquarters was bombed during the coup attempt. George is trying to find out what happened to him."

Their conversation lasted another fifteen minutes as Max relayed the details of their capture and escape. *Where to start?* was Max's big question. Numerous entities would have loved to get their hands on the bombs—every terrorist group in the Middle East—but since ISIS and the Muslim Brotherhood were working together, they were most likely the culprits. Although SOCOM believed Turkey had orchestrated the theft of the weapons, it was unlikely they held on to them. President Kağan was portraying himself as the victim in the news and blaming rebel forces for the attempted coup. Kağan was smart enough to know that NATO and the US would be using every asset available in trying to find the nukes. Keeping them in Turkey was too risky. None of the friendly intelligence agencies knew who had the bombs or what Turkey did with them after the attack on Incirlik.

"I've left a message for George to call me," Johnston said. "I'll have him work on ISIS and the Muslim Brotherhood. Langley isn't going to be any help in this. The other day when I talked to him, he said he couldn't get anything out of headquarters. Something is wrong at the senior level."

"I figured as much," Max replied. "Madison is the key, and I want him. Dig deep. Turn over every slimy rock. The smallest detail concerning him could be important. I'll read the intel you send me and get back with you. I'm going back to the S2. He's been working on the CIA guy for a couple hours."

"Will do," Andy replied into the phone.

CHAPTER 15

Friday, May 20, 2016
Old Farmhouse
Karkamiş, Turkey

THE MEETING FOR the acceptance and delivery of the two B61 nuclear warheads took place in an old farmhouse just outside the small village of Karkamiş, a border checkpoint inside Turkey, on the west bank of the Euphrates River and about two miles north of Jarabulus, Syria.

Al-Ghazāli had arranged for the meeting and a meal at the old house. Madison was responsible for transportation and security. He had also coordinated with Nabi Ulmalhamah al-Aqrab on the security for the ISIS representatives. It was a show of good faith to coordinate with ISIS, and Madison did not intend to be double-crossed by the terrorists. He understood that they would be skittish but desired the warheads. If they became spooked, they could decide to shoot their hosts and take the warheads, saving themselves thirty million dollars. Madison did all he could to keep them at ease throughout the exchange, including adherence to their protocols.

No business was discussed during their meal of fried fish, pickles, green salad, and white rice. After the main meal, the men adjourned to another room while the dirty dishes were removed and their places cleaned. Platters of fresh fruit—bananas, grapes, oranges, and apples— and dishes of dried figs with clotted cream were set for them. The men returned and took their respective places, sitting cross-legged on the carpet. Some of them picked at the fruit and two of them picked up their dishes of figs with clotted cream.

Al-Aqrab was the first to speak, indicating it was time for business. "We are ready and wish to inspect the warheads." He looked to the small, bespectacled man with piercing black eyes behind his wire-rimmed glasses, to his right.

The man nodded. He was an addition to the three ISIS men who had been at the meeting in Jarabulus. He had not spoken to anyone other than al-Aqrab, and then it was in private.

Khalid Safar motioned with his hand that was missing the last two fingers, to the young Arabic boy who stood silently by the door, indicating for him to serve tea.

Madison's gaze followed the hand and recognized the boy as the same one who had served them in Jarabulus.

Dawud Al'alim looked at al-Ghazāli and gave a slight nod.

Al-Ghazāli waved his hand in the air and motioned, indicating he wanted the warheads brought in.

A man standing guard at the door nodded and left the room. Within a few minutes, the guard returned leading four men who struggled to carry a wooden crate. Four more men followed them with a second crate. Both boxes were placed on the floor in front of al-Ghazāli, then opened.

The eyes of the ISIS representatives revealed their eager anticipation. They were like children in front of the candy counter. "The warheads," al-Ghazāli said as he motioned with his hand. He stood, and the others followed.

Ra'id Umar Tarik extended his hand to help the bespectacled man stand, and they joined the other men in standing around the crates. A flurry of Arabic arose between the ISIS members. Heads bobbed and turned to each other. Their prize was before them, and their excitement was obvious.

Tarik looked to al-Ghazāli, then to Al'alim. "Our scientist, Dhul Fiqar, will now make an inspection."

Madison looked at the short, weaselly man. He knew the name. He was their top bomb scientist. *Unusual for him to be here,* Madison thought. *He must have a laboratory in the area.*

From a bag on the floor behind him, Fiqar retrieved a digital Geiger counter, a small flashlight, and what looked like a dental mirror. He stepped to the first crate and methodically moved about the warhead, examining each detail of the exterior. Within a few minutes, he opened the small door to reveal the internal components. The little man shined his light and strained to see inside with the help of the mirror. He then grasped the wand probe of the Geiger Counter and inserted it next to the nuclear material. After reading the instrument, he stood, looked to Tarik and then to al-Aqrab, and nodded.

"Praise be to Allah! We accept," al-Aqrab said with a toothy grin as he looked to the others.

The expressions on the men's faces revealed their pleasure as conversations in Arabic ensued.

Al-Aqrab looked to Madison and held up his hand. When the room fell silent, he said, "Once again, you have not failed us. Come with me, outside. I want to discuss something with you."

Madison nodded.

Al-Aqrab turned to Tarik and spoke to him in Arabic, then looked to al-Ghazāli and nodded.

Madison watched the exchange and saw Tarik withdraw a cell phone, punch in a series of numbers, and speak into it. *They're transferring the money,* he thought. *Al-Ghazāli will have the money in a few minutes. Then we're outta here.*

— ✦✦✦ —

Saturday, May 21, 2016
Gareth Residence
New York, New York

Stew Gareth summoned Senator Archibald Chapman, Deputy Director Trent Weldon, Secretary of Defense Wes Brock, and Secretary of State Aaron Fitzgerald to his home for a meeting.

Archie—the first to arrive, by design—headed straight for the pastries and coffee as soon as he entered Stew's office. Stew wanted to discuss the campaign and upcoming events before the others arrived. Although money was pouring in, his wife's campaign was struggling.

"Archie, I want you to get with Jenny's PAC and see what they need," Stew said as he looked over his coffee cup. "Then circulate around the Hill and get the other senators to grab mikes wherever they can and talk up Jenny. Your lady friend is an executive at one of the networks, get her to plug in Jenny. I want to see her on TV or hear people talking about how wonderful she is at any given hour. I'll have her campaign manager get in touch with you. Also, tell your friend, no negative news about Jenny. Got it?"

Archie licked the icing off his fingers, then said, "She knows, and I'll remind her. There're a lot of questions being asked on the Hill about Incirlik and the nukes."

Jenny sauntered into the room and flopped in the chair beside Archie. "What's this about nukes?"

Archie stood and returned to counter where the pastries were displayed, an arm's reach from the scotch, then turned back toward Jenny and said, "Several senators want to know the details on the coup attempt in Turkey and the security of the nuclear bombs."

"Pour me a scotch, Archie," Jenny said as she watched him slide another cinnamon roll onto his plate.

He shot an unflattering glance toward her, but she didn't see it. He retrieved a tumbler from the cabinet, dropped several cubes in it, and sloshed in the scotch.

"Wes Brock has been doing a good job of keeping a lid on the news," Stew said as he slurped his coffee. "I've talked to the president several times about that issue. He's getting nervous. I told him to keep stalling. I don't want the news about Incirlik to get out until we are ready."

Archie handed Jenny the scotch, then nestled his large frame into a chair. The pastry automatically went to his mouth.

Taking the glass, Jenny said, "Oh hell! That little pipsqueak is afraid of his own shadow." She sipped the drink. "Stew, have one of our people work with Wes to prepare a news release. Spin it, of course. I want it to convey that the White House has been closely monitoring the situation and will take the appropriate action when necessary. Have them add something about the exact details being classified and not available to be released yet. Issue the statement late enough Friday evening so no one will pay attention to it. I'll follow up and give a news release about the situation. It'll look like I'm on top of things. Then run new polls showing me with a 5 percent bump. Oh, and have one of the generals give the press release. Wes doesn't do well in press releases. He'll let something slip." She took another drink of scotch.

"Not a bad plan," Archie said, his cheeks bulging. "We should be able to drive the narrative on this and not many people will bother to look up the details, especially after Jenny's release."

"All right," Stew said as he scribbled on the paper that was on the desk in front of him. "We can use the publicity. I like the idea of you following up after the press release with your own release and new polls. That'll cost us, but we need new numbers."

Jenny emptied the glass, looked to Archie, and said, "Another scotch. Not so much ice this time." She didn't see the *drop-dead* look on his face, nor did she care what he thought.

The dutiful Archie stood and took her glass, then stepped to the bar.

"Nassar told me Kenworth and the woman with him are still alive," Stew said, then finished off his coffee and set the cup back on the desk.

"Trent sent a team after him," Jenny said. "What the fuck happened?"

Archie returned and handed Jenny her the glass of scotch before he sat down again.

"The Turks sent a team after them as well," Stew said, leaning into to the desk. "It's time we start looking for a replacement for Trent. He's becoming a liability."

"I'll start making the rounds and get a couple of names," Archie said as he slurped his coffee.

"We want someone who'll do as he's told," Stew said, then leaned back in his chair. "Make sure he's someone who can get confirmed, has no skeletons we need to clean up."

"Understood," Archie said.

"You two find the replacement. I'm too busy." Jenny stretched out her bulky legs and crossed them at the ankles. "Just tell me who you pick."

The doorbell rang, and Stew looked up. "That'll be the others," he said. "Get the door, Archie."

The obedient Archie set his cup on the table, stood and ambled to the door. Within a moment he appeared in the doorway, ushering the three men into the office, Archie pointed out the pastries and drinks, then picked up his cup as he neared the table.

Wes, Aaron, then Archie filled cups with coffee while Trent went for scotch. One after another, they sat in the chairs directly in front of Stew's desk. Jenny and Archie sat on the ends. Stew stood, picked up his cup and stepped to the counter, and refilled his cup with coffee. He was in no hurry as he returned to his desk and sat down. It didn't take long for them to figure out it was a *come-to-Jesus* meeting, and Stew's harsh tone confirmed it.

After an uncomfortable moment, he said, "We've got an election to win. We're in the homestretch and now isn't the time to fuck up. Wes, you've done a pretty good job on keeping the situation in Incirlik quiet."

Wes nodded, with a slight sigh of relief.

"Questions are being asked about Turkey, as you are probably well aware, and the safety of the bombs in Incirlik. We can't keep it quiet much longer. Wes, the Pentagon is going to issue a press release Friday evening on Incirlik. Jenny will follow up with a statement, so she'll look like she's on top of the situation. We'll prepare the announcement and get it over to your office. Have one of the generals issue it."

Aaron, lifting his arm to sip the coffee, lowered it and said, "I'll need to clear it with the president. He wants the people to think he's still in charge."

In a cackling laugh, Jenny said, "In charge? He never has been. He just wants to go play golf."

Stew leaned forward into the desk. "I'll take care of the president."

Aaron nodded, then sipped his coffee.

Stew held his gaze on Aaron as he said, "Increase your efforts in spreading the word that the US wants the refugees. Promise them money and benefits when they get here. Focus on the Latin American and the Middle East countries. Make sure they know Jenny will take care of them. I want those bastards flooding the border. Coach them on what to do and make sure they understand the borders are open. Promise them anything. Better idea, get some people to go to the countries and organize convoys. Bring them close to the borders, but don't cross it with them. It's gotta look good."

"Yes, sir," Aaron replied.

Stew's eyes bored into Trent, his face reddening as he said, "Nassar told me Kenworth and the woman are still alive. I'm also told that your man Madison is still alive."

Trent stiffened. "We have—"

"Get this straight, you *sons a bitches*... I told you all, no scandals," Stew said, his tone scorching. "This is a disaster. What's so hard about getting rid of three people? President Kağan doesn't like the loose ends either. Trent, get your ass on a plane to Turkey. Find out what's going on with your people and get a team after them. Kağan wants to see you when you get there. He'll send another team to Syria after he talks to you. Nassar is concerned that Kenworth is a threat to the Brotherhood's plans for the bombs. I'm meeting with Nassar on Monday and will tell him you are handling the situation. Their bodies are not to be found."

Trent nodded. "Yes, sir."

"Wes, direct the military not to release any information on Incirlik until further notice. If questions are asked, direct them to the State Department." Stew looked to Aaron. "We'll draft a statement for you."

"Yes, sir," Aaron said with a nod.

Stew looked back to Trent. "The campaign needs more money. Increase the shipments of cocaine. Have you got a replacement for Madison?"

"Not yet," Trent replied.

Stew slammed his fist on the desk and, in a harsh tone, said, "Damn it, Trent. What's the problem? Get another guy! We need the money."

Stew continued issuing pointed orders to the men for another ten minutes without allowing discussions or rebuttals. It was all about Jenny's election. The political party, the media, and key influential people were solidly behind Jenny. Her selection as president seemed to be a done deal, so if laws were broken along the way to election, not a big deal and, of course, the money Stew spread around kept people looking the other way. Her indiscretions would be swept under the rug and forgotten about as soon as her opponent conceded the election. The masses loved her, and no one would accuse her, let alone prosecute her for breaking a few little laws.

Archie remained behind for several minutes after the others departed. He and Stew discussed several details of the campaign and cabinet positions, and he was Stew's sounding board after the meeting.

Archie helped himself to one of the cigars in the humidor on the desk. He lit it and slouched in the chair. "You're right about Trent," he said.

Stew nodded, then stood and walked to the bar. He retrieved a bottle of Garrison Brothers single-barrel bourbon from the cabinet and poured two fingers into a glass. "Want one?" he asked as he looked back to Archie and held the bottle in front of him.

"Sure," the senator replied and puffed the cigar.

Stew poured a second glass and handed it to Archie before he returned to his desk. He took a sip, then picked up the receiver and punched in a series of numbers. "He's leaving tomorrow for Turkey. You know what to do, just as we discussed." He returned the receiver to the cradle and took another sip of bourbon.

—◆◆◆—

Saturday, May 21, 2016
Rio Guaire Canyon
El Hatillo Municipality, Venezuela

A team made up of three Mossad agents and three Shayetet commandos watched the estate from a vantage point across Rio Guaire canyon. El Hatillo, one of five municipalities of Caracas, was located southeast of the capital with Rio Guaire as the eastern boundary of the borough. Perched on a hill overlooking a plush green canyon, the beige manor had good visibility of the only road leading up the hill, and a matching rock wall encircled the property. A large swimming pool, complete with outdoor kitchen at one end, was the centerpiece of the rear grounds. The entire estate, upon close examination, was a fortress, and it belonged to Bart Madison. Private security guarded not only the estate but a striking redhead, Maurine Rowen, as well.

For more than three years, Maurine had been Bart's love interest. She was no longer a high-priced escort but had settled into his life for the long term, taking care of his every need and he, hers. Maurine didn't particularly like Bart's occupation but did like the money. She accepted the security guards as a necessity, though she preferred to be alone. Maurine had dropped out of sight not long after Bart's mission to deliver a nuclear weapon into the US. Some thought she was in jail and others thought she had moved to Panama. A few even thought she was dead. No one knew exactly what had happened to her.

Soon after General Matherson notified Thaddeus that Madison was alive and connected to the coup d'etat in Turkey, he had set in motion the process of locating Maurine Rowen. The Mossad agents soon found her in El Hatillo, and for the past seventy-two hours, the Israeli team had observed her, her movements, and the house. They had identified four guards on the property and determined they were not much more than rent-a-thugs, although they were probably the best guards in Caracas. The house also had complete coverage by security cameras and alarms. They had tapped her phone, started inspecting her mail, and intercepted her internet. The team had collected enough information on her to get a good idea of her routine. The agent monitoring her internet learned that she was scheduled to receive a package via UPS that afternoon by three o'clock. Not the ideal time to snatch someone, but they had accomplished similar missions in the past.

Although there was not much time to prepare, the lead Mossad agent made the decision to take advantage of the opportunity and grab her that afternoon. Each man had specific duties to accomplish and immediately went to work.

The last check before the team launched was on the four guards. Two were in the back at the pool. One of them appeared to be cooking at the outdoor kitchen and the other one lounged in one of the chairs. The agent watching the property assumed the other two were inside and planned accordingly.

At precisely 2:59:30 p.m., the UPS truck turned the last curve leading to the beige manor on the top of the hill. One of the Mossad agents cut the power to the property and set up a jamming signal to block cellphone coverage. The truck pulled into the drive as usual and stopped in front of the door. The driver—dressed in traditional brown shorts and shirt—walked to the door with a package in hand, concealing his Glock 21SF underneath the box. He rang the bell and waited. A medium built Latin American man opened the door, looked to the person in front of him, shot a glance to the brown truck, then back at the man in front of him. Perceiving no threat, his posture relaxed.

The driver, in Spanish, said, "I need a signature, please." He casually looked beyond the guard but could not see anyone else. As soon as the thug started to pick up the electronic tablet on top of the box, the Mossad agent raised his hand with the Glock, pointing it at the man's midsection. In a calm and cold voice, he said, "Not a sound. No sudden moves. Back up." He made a slight motion with his head, a signal to the others to enter. The guard had two options—comply or die. He chose the former.

One Mossad agent and three Shayetet commandos sprang from the truck and were almost silent as they entered the house. The disciplined Israelis made their way farther into the house, searching for both the other guard and Maurine. The second thug they were searching for stepped into the room and was startled for an instant when he came face-to-face with one of the commandos. He realized, without a doubt, the soldier in front of him controlled the situation. The Israeli, as he held his M4 carbine pointed at the thug, said in Spanish, "Not a word. On the floor. Hands behind your head." The commando took the guard's pistol from his shoulder holster, and the man went to the floor. Two other commandos went to the back door and observed the two guards at the pool, both oblivious to what was happening in the house.

The driver brought his man in and motioned with his pistol for him to get on the floor next to the other thug.

Maurine, curious about the doorbell, stepped into the room and said, "Who was at—"

Terror filled her body as she stared at the commando. She had been in this situation before, and vivid memories returned. The Israelis terrified her then, and she had no desire to repeat such an ordeal. She bolted to the back door, attempting to escape, but ran right into one of the other commandos.

"Be quiet and you won't get hurt," he said, then took her back into the room where the two men lay prone on the floor.

The agent in the brown uniform produced a syringe, and the commando holding the defiant Maurine slid up the sleeve of her blouse despite her efforts to resist and inserted the needle into her arm. He turned and looked at the two men on the floor and said, "Your turn. Something to allow you to sleep for a while. Any shit from either of you and you will be asleep forever. Got it?"

Both men nodded.

By the time the agent withdrew the needle from the second man, Maurine was limp in the Israeli's arms. A final check was made of the rooms before the commandos withdrew into the truck, one carrying Maurine over his shoulder. The brown truck drove away as though it was off to make another delivery.

CHAPTER 16

Saturday, May 22, 2016
Abandoned House
Kayseri, Turkey

E ROL HAD MADE contact with George and arranged to meet him at the abandoned farmhouse where they'd met before. Someone had picked the perfect place atop the hill for the old structure and most likely admired the view of the city below on many nights. Erol leaned against the opening that once held the long-gone window, keeping a vigilant eye on the road leading up the hill from the city. There were no sounds or lights, and a faint breeze found its way into the confines of the stucco walls. He was not there to admire the scenery, but to meet with an ally who he anticipated would get him to safety. The bright moon provided enough light to see any car, motorcycle, or otherwise in enough time to make an escape if needed.

A black silhouette of a man emerged in the darkness, making his way up the hill toward the house.

Erol studied the figure, the area around him, and didn't see anyone else. When the man entered, he said just above a whisper, "George."

The man stopped and replied, his low voice carrying a cautious tone, "Erol."

Erol made another check of the area and road outside, then stepped closer to George. "It is very good to see you."

George took his hand and said, "Very good indeed. I've been looking for you. I had almost given up, thinking you had been rounded up or killed." Even in the dim light of the moon that found its way into the room, he could tell the man was disheveled and unshaven. The bags under his eyes were unmistakable.

Erol shrugged and said, "I have managed to avoid being picked up by Kağan's thugs. They are arresting everyone."

"By the thousands," George said.

"ISIS bought two of the nukes from the Muslim Brotherhood," Erol said. "The Brotherhood kept two, the last I heard. ISIS wants to target the US and the UK. The other two are going to be used for targets in Israel."

"Six were taken," George said. "Do you know what happened to the other two?"

Erol shook his head. "No. Kağan's plan is in full force. He claims the Gülen movement and the US Central command are the instigators of the coup against him. He is blaming his opponents for stealing the bombs from Incirlik. It is all a distraction while he is transitioning to the Ottoman traditions. Martial law is a cover to purge his opponents."

George focused on Erol. "Do you know where they took the nukes?" he asked.

"Not sure, I heard that ISIS has set up a bomb lab in Aleppo. Possibly there."

George nodded. "That's possible. Come on, I'll get you outta here."

Erol touched George's forearm. "My family, they are safe?"

"Yes, we got them out of the country to a safe place. We need to get going."

A slight smile emerged on Erol's haggard face as he nodded. "Thank you."

George led him out of the building, and the two disappeared into the blackness.

——— ◆ ◆ ◆ ———

Monday, May 23, 2016
Presidential Palace of the Republic of Turkey
Ankara, Turkey

President Kağan met Trent Weldon at the entrance of the palace and escorted him to one of the private rooms for breakfast. Al-Ghazāli stood when the president entered with the US Deputy Director of the CIA.

"This is Abdal al-Ghazāli," Kağan said, introducing Weldon to him. He didn't wait for cordialities between the two men, gesturing toward the linen-draped table as he said, "Please, be seated."

Weldon didn't pick up on Kağan's impatience to commence the breakfast meeting and sat between the two men.

Interested in the first meal more than anything else, al-Ghazāli took a piece of flatbread, then passed the plate to Weldon.

Kağan began the meeting with light conversation as the three ate. He finished his eggs and motioned to one of his staff to bring in more hot tea.

Knowing the meal was about to end, al-Ghazāli took the opportunity to add several more slices of cold meat and a dollop of yogurt to his plate. Then he added more honey to his bread.

The staff member returned with fresh brewed Rize tea and filled their gold-rimmed cups. As soon as he finished with the last one, Kağan flicked his hand and the man left the room, closing the door behind him.

Kağan's eyes locked onto Weldon's, and he said with a stern voice, "There's a term you Americans say…this is fucked up." He slammed his hand on the table. "What are you going to do about the American and the Israeli woman with him? They know too much. They are a liability. Gareth assured me that things like this wouldn't happen. How did your people allow them to get away?"

Weldon shifted in his chair and replied, "I am sending another team after them. I'll have the answer to that question before I leave. There is one problem, though. Those two managed to get to the American Special Forces in Syria. I have a meeting this afternoon and will make sure they're taken care of. They won't leave Syria alive."

"They had better not," Kağan replied. "How do you plan to do it?"

"Perhaps you could contact the Russians and have them make an air strike on the special forces location in Syria. Then we'll call it a case of *friendly fire*. It's not all that certain and will require a team to go in after the strike to ensure we killed them."

"It is risky, but it might work. I will discuss it."

Weldon nodded as he shifted in his chair again, then lifted the cup of tea to his lips.

"What are NATO and the UN going to do?" Kağan asked over his cup as he, also, sipped his tea.

"Nothing. Our president has told the NATO Supreme Allied Commander not to interfere in the domestic problems of your country. He has forbidden him to take any action against your military. The US ambassador to the UN has condemned the terrorists' actions, and the US is blocking any efforts by the Security Council. Just as we agreed," Weldon said with a reassuring nod.

"The statement Jenny Gareth made on behalf of Turkey and against the coup leaders was very good," Kağan said. "Is she still going to win the election? I understand she lost the recent primary."

"Yes, but that happens. In fact, it kinda looks good in the press. Gives a bit of legitimacy to the process, don't you think? However, it is taking a lot of money for the election."

Kağan nodded, then shot a look to al-Ghazāli and back to Weldon. "The US borders are still open?" he asked as more of an order than question.

"Yes, still open."

Displaying a sincere look, al-Ghazāli said, "Nassar told me you are looking for one of your men that went missing. Did you find him?"

"Not yet. He could be injured and can't contact us. I'm sure we'll locate him."

"That is too bad. We will keep watch for him."

"Thank you."

Their meeting lasted another fifteen minutes before Kağan ushered Weldon out, though the conversation was much lighter in the last few minutes. Kağan had gained more information than he gave away. One item was the commitment to get Kenworth and Mayer. Weldon's suggestion to use the Russians was exceptionally appealing. Gareth had invoked the Russian connection numerous times in the past when a news story was getting close to their operation. That always energized the Western media and deflected any light from the Gareths. Jenny's machine had even accused the Russians of meddling in the presidential election. While the world was focused on the two superpowers, Kağan could continue the purge of his opposition and change the Turkish constitution to consolidate his power.

Al-Ghazāli had kept Kağan informed on the Gareth campaign more than anyone would suspect. Kağan knew the Gareths needed money and would do anything for money—anything! It was what motivated them. Money meant power, and Gareth would use it to get what he wanted. Kağan thought of the Gareths the same as one thought of a prostitute—didn't respect them, didn't particularly like them, but got what he wanted. Once Gareth was sworn in, Kağan believed nothing would interfere with his plan to rebuild the Ottoman Empire.

⸻ ✦ ⸻

Monday, May 23, 2016
Esat Caddesi
Ankara, Turkey

Trent Weldon had agreed to meet at a nondescript building on Esat Caddesi—the office of the contractors he planned to use to eliminate Kenworth and Mayer. The meeting was away from the embassy so no record of it or his meeting with the foreign company would be made. After the botched attempt by the American resources, using a foreign contractor would make it more difficult to connect the CIA to the assassination.

In a few months, Jenny would be the new president and any misdeeds by her, Stew, or her staff would be swept under the table to be forgotten. However, murder was serious, and it was Weldon's neck on the line. Just in case something went wrong with the election, he wanted to minimize his risk. It was a departure from security for the deputy director of the CIA to meet outside of the embassy or a secured area in a foreign country. However, the contractors were to provide security for him with snipers at the top floor windows and guards at the entrances for his arrival and departure. Weldon's security detail would accompany him and escort him the short distance from the street to the entrance during his arrival and departure.

The afternoon sky was clear and the traffic on Esat Caddesi was light. The snipers and guards had good visibility along the street and immediate area. No crowds had gathered to protest the government. It was a normal day in Ankara. Weldon had arrived a little more than an hour and a half earlier without the slightest evidence of interest by anyone.

Just as Weldon emerged from the entrance, a BMW swung around the corner and onto Esat Caddesi from the intersection close to the mid-block building of the meeting. The car was already close to the director's entourage by the time the guards or snipers could react. The engine of the vehicle roared, and the car accelerated. Automatic weapons fired, emptying magazines of ammunition into the oncoming car, which didn't waver from its trajectory. Weldon's security turned him around and tried to get him back into the building, but it was too late. The explosive-laden BMW crashed into Weldon's sedan with a tremendous blast. The fireball engulfed both vehicles and the building entrance, shattering windows and demolishing the entire building entrance. When the smoke cleared, the mutilated bodies of Weldon, his security detail, and guards lay strewn about. The detonation also killed the snipers on the top floor.

⸺ ✦✦✦ ⸺

Tuesday, May 24, 2016
Special Forces Forward Operational Base
Northern Syria

The lanky special forces S2 captain placed the intelligence report in front of Max as he talked on the phone. Max held up his index finger, indicating for the captain to wait until he was finished with his conference call with the liaison officer of the British 22nd Special Air Service (SAS). Max ended the call and picked up the paper, scanning it.

"That's from last night's fight," the captain said. "A senior ISIS guy was killed, Ra'id Umar Tarik."

"A senior guy, that's good," Max replied as he looked up at the captain. "Another one bites the dust. Any other big ones get it?"

"No, sir," the S2 replied. "Tarik had a small boy with him, probably about ten or so. Hard to tell. Even the kid doesn't know how old he is. At first, the team didn't think anything about the boy, and he was terrified—in shock, actually. Several times he's mentioned a big bomb and mother of all bombs that will destroy the Americans. I thought you'd be interested in him."

"Where is he now?" Max started to get up.

"Doc is checking him out. He's been abused, has a few cuts and bruises. The kid is filthy, and he pissed his pants when they found him.

Doc wants you to wait a little while. He's trying to get the boy to calm down and clean him up."

Max eased back onto the chair and said, "Okay, tell doc to let me know when I can interview him. What intel did you get from Tarik?"

"He was to meet with a merchant for transportation. That's all I know right now. He had quite a bit of cash, a map, couple of passports, an AK, pistol, and a cell phone. My guys are working on his cell. The merchant was one of our informants, and he tipped us off. I'm to meet with him in about an hour. I may have more after that. You wanna see what we recovered?"

"I've got a meeting in about ten minutes," Max said as he looked at his watch. "Give me a call when you get back."

——— ✦ ✦ ✦ ———

Thaddeus Nussbaum had kept Danya updated on the intelligence Mossad gleaned from Maurine Rowen since they abducted her three days ago in El Hatillo. Defiant at first, as her captivity continued with Mossad, her resistance began to subside. Knowing she had always been meticulous with her appearance, the Israelis had not allowed her to bathe or change clothes since they snatched her. Her toilet was a bucket. They had affixed a mirror so she could see herself, which had been the biggest impact on her. Her red hair was stringy and needed combing, she was void of any makeup, and her own body odor was repulsive to her. The Israeli agents knew her well and used her vanity to their advantage. Liberal politicians—breathing down their neck, accusing them of inhumane torture tactics, trying to make political points—did not hamstring Mossad. The Israelis knew how to get information and always did.

As a result of the intelligence Mossad had extracted from her, Thaddeus believed Israel was a possible target for at least one of the nukes. So far, he didn't know where or when, but as always, Israel took the threats seriously. He had Rav-Seren Jacob Beiser, Shayetet 13 team commander, the rank equivalent of lieutenant commander in the US Navy, to meet with Max and Danya to coordinate their activities and ascertain the resources needed.

Max, Danya, and Rav-Seren Beiser sat around a makeshift conference table in the inflatable tent inside the confines of the special forces forward operational base. Beiser, a rugged-looking man with piercing blue eyes, leaned forward and said as he handed a folder to Danya, "The CIA has been no help in providing information. The intelligence we have gathered is from our sources and what we have gotten out of Maurine Rowen. It is sketchy and doesn't provide much."

"We're struggling for information as well," Max said as he handed Beiser a single sheet of paper. "The warheads have been removed from the six B61 bombs. That'll make them much easier to move around, but they still weigh about two hundred ninety pounds each. I have a CIA agent out of Turkey I can trust, but he's being stonewalled as well. One of our teams killed Ra'id Umar Tarik last night. He was a senior ISIS guy who had a small boy with him who might provide some pertinent information. The boy mentioned a big bomb several times. Unfortunately, he was in shock and not making a lot of sense."

Beiser's eyebrows raised at hearing the name. "Senior ISIS guy."

"Danya is going to see what she can get out of the boy when the doctor says it's okay to talk to him," Max said, then he grasped one of the bottles of water from the center of the table and took a swig. "We thought he might open up to a woman, a gentle voice and soft touch."

"Sounds reasonable," Beiser replied.

"We think Tarik was looking for transportation for the nukes," Max said. "Hopefully, after the boy calms down, we might get more out of him."

"Thaddeus briefed me on that theft of your nukes three years ago," Rav-Seren Beiser said as his eyes shot to Danya, then to Max. "You were lucky. Their bomb scientist had to learn how to bypass your PAL and make the necessary wiring connections to get the trigger mechanism to function correctly. That took them about two weeks. They won't need that much time for discovery this go-round. They already know how to do it." Beiser was referring to the permissive action link (PAL) on the nuclear bomb, an electronic interface requiring a special code to activate the weapon.

"We agree," Max replied as his eyes darted to Danya, then back to Beiser. "They've had eight days to work on it. We must assume they have the trigger figured out and it is now ready to function."

"How they move the nuke to the target will give us an idea how much time we have," Danya said.

Beiser shifted in his chair, then leaned forward. "Thaddeus said that an American, Bart Madison, is advising the Muslim Brotherhood and ISIS."

"Correct," Max replied. "We were led to believe the CIA killed him, but as it turns out, they were using him. He knows our tactics and how to get a bomb into the US."

"He probably has already figured out how to get it into Israel," Danya said as she picked up a bottle of water. "Make no mistake, he is dangerous and cunning."

"Exactly what was Mossad able to get out of Maurine?" Max asked.

"She is providing us some information, and the important items are in the summary I gave you," Beiser replied as he pointed to the folder on the table in front of Danya. "From her computer, we learned she is interested in going to Italy, but no tickets have been booked that we can find. She has received a number of calls from a cell phone. No number, and we can't trace it. All the calls have been rerouted. Most likely a burner."

"Well, that's a start," Danya said. "If you'll remember, Max, Madison set up a rendezvous in Las Vegas with Maurine."

Looking at Danya, Max said, "Coordinate with Thaddeus. Ask him to keep her computer and cell monitored. I doubt we can fool Madison again on a meeting, but we might be able to find out where and when they are going to meet. We may even get lucky and find him. I'm still convinced Maurine warned Madison, somehow, that we had a trap set for him in Las Vegas."

"I agree," Danya replied. "I don't know either. I'll have Thaddeus look for any other phones, numbers, or even email accounts."

"See if Maurine has any other passport other than Venezuelan," Beiser said.

"Will do," she replied. "You're thinking she and Madison may travel as Mr. and Mrs. *Smith* on another passport?"

"Possibly," Beiser replied.

The three continued the conversation for another hour. Max provided Rav-Seren Beiser a summary of the intelligence Andy had gathered. Most of the information was background or circumstantial. Nothing was enough to lead them to a specific location of the nukes, Madison's location, or his targets. George stated in his information that two of the nukes were sold to ISIS and the Muslim Brotherhood had two. He could not account for the remaining two. Those two warheads were particularly worrisome. The US administration was not making it easy to recover the weapons and, at times, Max suspected they were working against him.

Beiser told them he had a Shayetet team on standby and ready to go after the nukes when they were located. Max confirmed he had a Delta team on alert and had coordinated with the British 22 SAS. The three of them tried to determine the routes into Israel, the UK, and the US. However, their intelligence didn't reveal sufficient information to predict an accurate destination or route. They held high hopes that the young boy could give them enough to determine a location.

CHAPTER 17

Tuesday, May 24, 2016
Special Forces Forward Operational Base
Northern Syria

MAX MET WITH the S2 captain in his shelter and sat at a small wooden table. The captain had called Max after he returned from talking with his informant. Prior to meeting with Max, he had assembled all the intelligence pertinent to Max's mission that had been collected to that point, including the treasure trove of information from Tarik's cell phone.

The captain turned his laptop so Max could see the screen, then said, "Thanks to your CIA contact in Turkey, we've located the bomb lab in Aleppo." He clicked one of the tabs to display a map of Aleppo, then pointed to the display. "It's set up here, in this compound. The S3 is working a plan now to raid it."

"No artillery or air strikes," Max said as he looked at the captain.

"That makes it tough," he said as he leaned back.

"I know," Max replied. "But if the warheads are still there and an artillery round or bomb hits one, it could cause it to explode. Not a high-order explosion, but one that would do enough damage to scatter the nuclear material, contaminating the area. We wouldn't know it until our guys got in there and searched what's left of the building. That'd cause us big problems we aren't ready to deal with. Also, I want prisoners."

"The S3 won't like it," the captain replied. "That building is deep in the city and protected." He clicked on another tab to display an intel synopsis. "My informant told us Tarik wanted transportation out of Aleppo. He didn't know where Tarik wanted to go as that was to be discussed when they met. He thought Tarik wanted five SUVs for a day or two. Unfortunately, that meeting never happened."

Max wrinkled up the corner of his mouth and nodded as he said, "That is. Maybe Danya can get a destination out of the Arab boy. What are you getting from Tarik's cell?"

"We did get several numbers. So far, we have identified numbers for two top ISIS members, Nabi Ulmalhamah al-Aqrab and Khalid Safar. Also, two Muslim Brotherhood members, Dawud Al'alim and Abdal al-Ghazāli. As soon as we got the cell numbers, the electronics guys searched their database of captured cell-phone transmissions. They're analyzing them now. So far, most are short coordinating calls. A couple of the calls were in reference to their meeting to sell and exchange the warheads. One call, yesterday, between Tarik and al-Aqrab. Tarik was supposed to contact al-Aqrab as soon as he had the vehicles. Another noteworthy transmission was on the afternoon of 20 May. Al-Aqrab called Abu Bakr al-Baghdadi. We believe that call was after two of the nukes were sold to ISIS. Al-Aqrab confirms to Baghdadi that the American has accepted the contract. They're working on a couple of other numbers. I'll let you know when they have more."

Max leaned back in the chair. "You said the call was made after two nukes were sold. They didn't sell them all?"

"So far it appears that just two have been sold to ISIS. We believe the Muslim Brotherhood still has the others."

His expression serious, Max said, "Madison. I'm guessing they just reached an agreement with Madison to plan the emplacement of the nukes."

"That's what we believe," the captain replied.

"That was four days ago," Max said. "I doubt the warheads'll still be at the lab. Most likely, they're prepositioned somewhere or perhaps in transit. Madison hasn't had enough time to reconnoiter his objectives or finish his plan. He won't execute until he has a thorough understanding of the targets. Lieutenant Colonel Andy Johnston, DIA, will be arriving tomorrow to help out."

"We can use the help," the captain said.

The shelter door opened, interrupting their conversation with a burst of bright light and desert heat as Danya entered. She stepped to the table, slid a chair closer, and sat between Max and the captain. Danya had just finished interviewing the Arab boy. After her brief synopsis of the meeting, she said, "I'm not sure he knows where they were supposed to go. He said *Hims*, but I can't find it on the map."

A blank expression crossed Max's face, then he said, "The city is Homs. It was formally called Emesa, and after the Muslims conquered Syria, the inhabitants shortened the name to Homs or Hims. Some held on to the name Hims. On maps, it is Homs. It's about one hundred miles north of Damascus on the Orontes River and about fifty miles from the coast."

The captain clicked the tab to display the map.

Max's face lit up. "That's it," he said. "They're going to take the warheads to Homs. That makes sense. The Hezbollah militia is supporting the Syrian Army, which controls Homs. ISIS is going to use Hezbollah to transport one of the nukes into the US by way of the drug routes and probably take the other one into the UK the same way. Lebanon is a stone's throw south of Homs, and they could go into Israel either via Lebanon or by going down the coast. Either way, it's an easy shot for Hezbollah. Homs is their distribution point."

"Shit. That's a hornet's nest," the captain replied. " 'The enemy of my enemy is my friend.' It looks like the Muslim Brotherhood and ISIS have agreed to an alliance with Hezbollah and the Syrian Army. Most likely Russia is in there somewhere or at least is aware of what is going on since they support Syria."

Danya glanced to the captain, then to Max. "That's a damn big area to cover. But at least now we have a little better idea where to concentrate our efforts."

"The nukes are probably still in the area, but not for long," Max said as he focused on the captain. "They'll set up another meeting for transportation very soon. Make sure your informant notifies you as soon as they contact him."

———✦✦✦———

Tuesday, May 24, 2016
J. Gilbert's Steak House
McLean, Virginia

In the private dining room Nassar had reserved, he and Senator Chapman finished the main course of jumbo lump crab cakes. Nassar knew how to get what he wanted from the senator, and it wasn't that difficult. A lot of wine, food, and money usually did the trick. In those more difficult situations when the senator developed a conscience, Nassar would entice him with a weekend retreat, and of course, a young plaything. That never failed. Chapman finished his wine as the attentive waiter cleared the table.

"Another bottle of Sauvignon blanc, Senator?" the waiter said as he paused before stepping away from the table.

"Please," Chapman said with a nod. "And we're ready for our dessert now."

"Yes, Senator." The young man spun on his heels and left the private room.

Nassar leaned back in his chair, knowing it was time for business, and said, "Weldon has been taken care of."

Archie shifted his large frame in the chair, then nodded as he fingered the stem of his wine glass. He then wiped his brow with the napkin and placed it back in his lap. "The Gareth campaign would like another contribution from you."

Nassar leaned forward and said, "So soon?"

"It takes a lot of money to buy…to run a campaign."

"You were supposed to block putting troops in Syria, keep the air force from conducting airstrikes in Syria, and the man from SOCOM, Kenworth, is still alive and in Syria."

"Trent delivered a plan to Kağan to get rid of him and the woman with him."

"I know of it, but that's not much of a plan," Nassar replied. "Weak at best. It is very risky and uncertain." His jaw tightened visibly. "The Russians are still unhappy with Turkey for shooting down their jet in November. They may not be willing to do that sort of favor for Kağan."

"Look, you got the nukes, didn't you?" Chapman said forcefully. "We've blocked the Security Council, and the president has forbidden the NATO commander from taking any action. Besides, the Turks missed Kenworth too."

The waiter entered the room, and the two fell silent. He carried a silver tray with two desserts—vanilla bean crème brûlée topped with raspberries—placing one in front of the senator and then Nassar. A second man entered with a new chilled bottle of wine, filling their glasses. Both men withdrew from the room, closing the door behind them.

As soon as the door closed, Nassar said, "I want to know every move SOCOM makes. I also want to know what the British and Israelis know and plan to do in regard to the nukes."

"Not to worry. I understand." Chapman wiped his brow again. "However, getting information on SOCOM is difficult and risky. The British and Israelis are an entirely different situation. I don't have any contact with them. As I mentioned, the Gareth campaign is looking for contributions."

"Information, Senator." Nassar's tone was stern as he locked eyes with him. "You are on the Senate Select Committee on Intelligence. Find out. I also want to know who will replace Weldon. And I doubt the Russians will go along with your plan to get rid of Kenworth and the woman. Get a better one."

Chapman tried to ignore the comment about Kenworth. "A replacement for Weldon hasn't been made yet," he replied, his attention focused on the dessert.

"Come up with a better plan, Senator," Nassar said. "Keep me informed who is being considered as Weldon's replacement. Then I will discuss your request for a contribution."

━━━✦✦✦━━━

Tuesday, May 24, 2016
Senator Archibald Chapman's Office
Washington, DC

Senator Chapman poured another glass of Glenlivet XXV and leaned back in his leather chair. He leaned forward, rolled his chair a little more to the side, and leaned back again. He had positioned himself to get a better look at the young twenty-something brunette staffer. Her skirt was at midthigh, and the top button of her blouse had slipped free, exposing an enticing glimpse of her supple breasts nestled snuggly in a lace bra. Chapman daydreamed of her as she moved about her work area, crossing and uncrossing her shapely legs. His excitement rose when she stood and stepped toward his office. It was all he could do to pry his eyes away from her ample breasts bulging at the top of the lace.

"Senator," she said as she stopped in the doorway. "A constituent, Mr. Paul Hamilton, would like an appointment with you."

Chapman leaned forward in his chair and said, "What does he want?"

"He and his family are in DC for a few days. He wants a nomination to West Point for his son and would like to introduce you to him."

"Tell him I'm in a committee meeting and you are not sure when I'll be out. I am booked the rest of the week. Is he a donor?"

"Yes, sir. One of your bigger ones."

"Tell him to stop by tomorrow and get the information," Chapman said. "Give him my apologies and tell him I am free Monday, if he's still in town."

"He said they are going back home on Saturday morning."

"I thought so." Chapman took the last sip of his single malt scotch, leaned back, and watched the brunette's hips sway as she returned to her desk.

Chapman reached for the scotch and refilled his glass. His cell phone rang as he placed the bottle back into the credenza. He took a sip of his drink and thought, *Who the hell is that? Hope it's not Jenny again, drunk. Not in a mood to deal with her shit right now.* He set the glass on the desk and saw the number displayed. He took another sip of Glenlivet before answering the call.

His hand trembled as he placed the cell to his ear and said, "Senator Chapman."

"We haven't talked in a while," the voice said.

"I can't really talk right now. I'm heading to a meeting."

"Don't give me that bullshit, Senator."

"What do you want?" Chapman dreaded to hear his answer.

"Meet me in Mexico City Friday. I have a suite reserved for you at the InterContinental until Monday."

"I…I'm too involved with the election to get away right now." Fearing he was not convincing, Chapman took another drink of scotch.

"We'll do lunch as soon as you get here, then you'll have the rest of the weekend to relax."

"No, really, now is not good," Chapman said.

The stern voice replied, "Senator, the early flight. Be on it." The call ended.

Chapman sat back in his chair and emptied the glass. After a moment, he swung his chair around, retrieved the bottle from the credenza, and sloshed the glass full as he turned his chair back to the front. He set the bottle on the desk with a clack. Try as he might, he couldn't get his mind off the call. Not even the shapely brunette could distract him from it.

————— ✦✦✦ —————

Thursday, May 26, 2016
Special Forces Forward Operational Base
Northern Syria

Max, Danya, and Andy sat in the operations section, their attention focused on the monitors displaying the video feed of the compound and teams from a Predator drone's night-vision cameras. They watched the special forces commandos' progress as they infiltrated the compound suspected to contain the ISIS bomb lab and recover the warheads. Soldiers seated around the shelter, their faces illuminated by the computers they operated, provided input to the S3. Everyone focused on their area of responsibility for the mission, and no one talked, except to provide progress to the officer in charge or answer calls specific to them. The tension was intense as the S3 major coordinated the teams, ready to provide additional support if needed. Two CH-47 Chinook helicopters with rangers orbited a safe distance away, and air support was on call for the operation. Radios cracked, giving progress reports along the route. The S2's latest intelligence indicated that fifteen to twenty individuals were in the compound. However, his data was referenced to a specific time and was hours old.

The radio grabbed everyone's attention again. "Tango six three, this is tango niner six. Entering the courtyard. Over."

The major replied, "Tango six three, roger. Out." He was like a conductor directing an orchestra in Wagner's *Twilight of the Gods*. His demeanor and calm voice instilled confidence in everyone. Like Wagner, he never missed a beat.

Everyone anticipated that it would be a fight and things could easily go wrong. All battles are filled with chaos and intense terror. But these were elite soldiers, superbly trained to manage that chaos to a successful conclusion. With that transmission, the tension escalated. The teams had reached the compound without incident and presumably undetected. So far, not a single shot had been fired.

Everyone's eyes remained on the monitors as the radio blared out again, "Tango six three, this is tango niner six. Entering the building."

The S3 replied, "Tango six three, roger. Out."

The rest of the soldiers searched the sparse courtyard and took defensive positions as the one team searched the interior of the building.

Soon, the radio boomed again, "Tango six three, this is tango niner six. The building is empty. I say again, the building is empty."

The major looked to Max and slowly shook his head as he wrinkled up the corner of his mouth. It indicated to Max that he was just as disappointed as he was. "Sorry, sir," he said. "We're all disappointed."

"I know. It's not your fault," Max replied. "There's no way of knowing if ISIS was tipped off or simply moved on their own. Either way, they still have the warheads."

The major turned back to the radio and ordered the men extracted from the courtyard.

Max, Danya, and Andy stepped out of the shelter. There was nothing else they could do.

Max stopped and turned to face the others. "I'm not all that surprised the warheads were not there. I'm convinced now they've bypassed the PAL. They wouldn't move 'em if they hadn't figured it out."

Andy waved his arm in front of him. "We have six warheads capable of functioning out there somewhere, and we can only account for four. God help us."

"That's about it," Max said. "Let's focus our efforts on Homs. That's the best we have for now."

"I'll coordinate with Rav-Seren Beiser and let him know we struck out at the lab," Danya said.

"I'll let the 22 SAS know," Max replied.

"The S2 may turn up something when he debriefs the teams," Andy added. "I'll tag along with him. I want to see what the teams recovered from the building, if anything."

"I just have a feeling," Max said. "This has the markings of Madison. Our teams infiltrated into ISIS controlled territory; made it to the compound, which we believe was their lab; searched the building; and not a shot was fired. That bothers me."

"I see what you mean," Andy said.

"They let us in," Max said, then waved his hand in front of him. "They could've moved a hundred meters into any of these buildings and just watched us. Madison probably advised them to move out as soon as they figured out the PAL. If they're still in the area, they might not have wanted to risk a fight and give away their positions. Especially if they still have the warheads here."

CHAPTER 18

Friday, May 27, 2016
Palm Restaurant, InterContinental Hotel
Mexico City, Mexico

THE RUGGED-LOOKING MAN sat in a booth with no other patrons nearby. His cold blue eyes scanned the room as he anticipated the senator entering the restaurant at any moment. He raised the glass of Sauvignon blanc and took a small sip.

Senator Chapman stepped into the doorway and paused to look around the room. It wasn't his usual parade, and he looked as if he was headed to the gallows. Recognizing Bart Madison in a booth across the room, he made his way to him and squeezed his large frame into the seat.

"Bart," Chapman said, more of a nervous reflex than a genuine greeting. "It's good to see you again."

"I bet it is, Senator." Madison sipped his wine, then raised his hand and motioned to the waiter. "I've ordered for us. We'll start off with wine and an appetizer."

The senator scanned the wall, then looked back to him. "This place is just like the Palm Restaurant in DC, complete with caricatures and cartoons on the wall."

"It is," Madison said. "They say this is the place to see and be seen."

"Bart, we shouldn't be meeting together." Chapman glanced around the room to see if anyone was interested in him.

"Relax," Madison said, his tone calm. "No one is looking for me in Mexico."

"They could've followed you."

"No one did," he replied. "I trust your suite is acceptable?"

"Yes, it's very nice," Chapman said, his impatience growing. "What did you need to see me about?"

"Let's eat first," Madison replied, controlling the situation and adding to the senator's anxiety.

A young man approached the table with a large platter of calamari fritti and set it in the middle, then placed small plates in front of Chapman and Madison. Madison picked up a wedge of lemon and began squeezing it over the dish. The waiter returned with an ice bucket and chilled bottle of Sauvignon blanc. After he placed the bucket in the stand beside the table, he immediately filled Chapman's glass. He motioned with the bottle to Madison, who lifted his hand, indicating he didn't want his glass topped off. After returning the bottle to the ice, the waiter left the table.

"How's the election going? Is Jenny going to win?" Madison was just warming up with his questions.

"She'll win, it's all arranged," Chapman replied. "The calamari is delicious."

"I thought you'd like it." Madison watched the large man shove the appetizer into his face nonstop, then pause only to empty his wine glass. In a seamless motion, Chapman grasped the bottle, refilled his glass, and returned the wine to the bucket.

"Who's behind the push to kill me?" Madison asked. "And is the CIA still looking for me now that Weldon is dead?"

"Stew Gareth wants you dead, and he's pushing the CIA. However, it has become a little more difficult with Weldon out of the picture. We're looking for a replacement for him now. Be careful."

Bart nodded. "Where's Kenworth now?"

"At a special forces forward operational base in Syria. He's looking for the nukes."

When Archie refilled his glass again, Bart withdrew a bulging envelope from inside his shirt, placed it on the white tablecloth, then slid it closer to Chapman.

The senator scooped up the stuffed envelope and slid it into his jacket pocket faster than he had attacked the calamari.

"I need information," Bart said as he held the senator's gaze.

"What do you need?" Chapman asked, then upended his glass.

Bart motioned to the waiter, then said as he looked to Chapman, "I want you to keep me informed on the CIA's interest in me, what Kenworth knows and plans to do, and I want the US borders kept open."

Chapman's gaze again fell to Bart's and he said, "The CIA's not a problem. Keeping the borders open is not a problem either. Everyone wants 'em open for the votes. That's even part of the Gareths' plan. Kenworth is a different story. It's too risky trying to get information from SOCOM."

Bart took a sip of wine and with a calm voice said, "We've had this conversation before. What I ask for, you provide. I don't need to remind you that you're on the Senate Select Committee on Intelligence, Senate Committee on Appropriations, and Senate Armed Services Committee, to name a few. You won't have any trouble getting me what I want."

"But, Bart, it's—"

"No buts, Senator. I want information, and I want you to keep me updated. Also, if you hear anything from the Israelis I should know about, don't waste any time getting the info to me. I want to know such things as what the Israelis say about the nukes and any attack plans. Do you understand?"

The waiter arrived before Chapman could utter another word and the table fell silent. He picked up the appetizer dishes, then placed bowls of lobster bisque in front of the men. After checking to ensure the table was in order and the men desired nothing else, the young man left the Americans to their privacy.

"What're you planning to do with the nukes?" Archie's face became pale.

Bart leaned forward. "Don't worry about what I'm planning. You just do as you're told."

"Bart, I…I don't know. This sounds very risky to me."

Bart picked up a folder from beside him on the bench seat. He looked inside, then laid it on the table and slid it closer to the senator. "For you. These are copies. I have some terrific video and audio to go along with them."

Chapman's trembling hand pulled the folder closer to him. Opening it, his face became pallid. Without hesitation, Archie closed the cover and slid the item off the table.

Bart leaned back and said, "I don't think you'd want those pictures of you and your little plaything to go public, especially just before the election. I do think your *Friday piece* in DC is much better than this little toy. How old—twelve, thirteen?"

Archie leaned forward, motioning with his hands, and said, "Bart… Bart, please, keep it down. I'll do what you want."

"I thought you would," Madison said as he leaned forward. "I want you to keep me updated on the US southern border, Kenworth's and SOCOM's plans, and the CIA's and Israel's interest in me. I want an intel update every week. If you learn any critical information that is time sensitive, get with me right away."

Chapman slurped the remainder of the bisque and said, "I understand. I will. I just don't like the sound of any of this. If someone should find out, it would have severe consequences for us."

"I'll do the worrying, Senator. You get your talking points ready—border security, immigration, and the poor souls fleeing their repressive countries. Those are good points for you to campaign on." Bart motioned to the waiter again.

Switching the conversation to lighter topics, Bart worked to settle Chapman down.

Within a moment, the waiter arrived at the table and cleared the bowls, then placed the main course plates of red snapper Milanese in front of the two men. "Another bottle of wine?" the attentive man asked as he looked at Bart.

"Please," Bart replied.

He knew how to get what he wanted from the senator—food, booze, money, and a weekend of sex. Not necessarily in that order, however, or all in one weekend. This was a special occasion, and he didn't want to waste time with the senator's conscience. Chapman was in for a real treat. As soon as a fresh bottle of Sauvignon blanc was in the bucket, Madison was gleaning information from the senator once again. His questions probed many topics and provided him much more than he'd anticipated. Chapman finally got to the cheesecake with raspberry sauce. The fork slid without effort into his mouth, not a crumb wasted.

Bart sipped his wine, then set it back on the table and held on to the stem with two fingers. "A friend of mine, Maurine Rowen, has gone missing. I want to know what happened to her."

Pointing to Bart with his fork, Archie said, "I don't know how I can help with a missing person. You should go to the police."

"I believe she was taken by the CIA, possibly the Brits or another government. I want you to find out who took her and where they're holding her."

Archie slid another piece of dessert between his lips, held it in his cheek, and said, "I don't know if I can get that. Why do you think it was the CIA?"

"They drove up in a UPS truck, surprised my guards, drugged them, then took Maurine. That's an intelligence agency operation. Find out who has her and where. Be quick about it too."

Chapman nodded and wiped his mouth.

Madison placed his napkin on the table. "There are two bottles of Glenlivet XXV and a cute little plaything waiting for you in your room. Don't forget what I have asked you to do, especially the intelligence reports and finding out about Maurine."

"Not to worry. I'll see what I can find out on Maurine and get you what you need. I'll be in touch," Chapman said.

"Sooner rather than later," Madison replied as he stood. "Enjoy your weekend. Remember…I'm waiting to hear from you." He walked out of the restaurant.

— ♦ ♦ ♦ —

Saturday, May 28, 2016
Classified Location
Panama City, Panama

Looking and smelling like a homeless person, Maurine was escorted into the room by a Mossad woman and told to sit at the table. The stark white room was without windows, and the lights were bright. She sat and cupped her hands together, attempting to hide her chipped and broken fingernails. Hearing the sound of the door opening behind her, she unconsciously reached up and attempted to smooth down her dirty, matted hair.

He sat across from her and looked into her bloodshot eyes. The routine was always the same but at irregular intervals around the clock. All concept of time—whether it was day or night—escaped her.

For over an hour, Chief Thaddeus Nussbaum of Mossad Station, Panama questioned Maurine. So far, she had been consistent in sticking to her story that she didn't know what Madison was doing or where he was working. However, she was weakening.

Thaddeus leaned back and said in a harsh tone, "You stink and are filthy. Do you like what you see when you look into the mirror?" He slid a mirror across the table to her, then withdrew a toothbrush and tube of toothpaste from his pocket and laid them on the table between them. Without uttering a sound, he pulled out a bar of soap and placed it on the table too. Then he produced a small bottle of cologne, opened it, and sniffed the light, fresh floral scent, letting the fragrance flood her nostrils. Then he replaced the cap and placed it beside the other items.

Her eyes revealed exactly what he'd anticipated. She could smell the clean, fresh soap. Without even a conscious thought, her hand rose from below the table and inched toward the toiletries. Already dreaming of the cool water carrying the rich lather cascading over her bare skin, she was stunned when she felt his hand come down on top of hers. She heard his words, snapping her out of the reverie.

"You will have to earn them. Answers first. You cooperate, then you can have them. Do you understand?" he said, his tone serious.

Maurine locked eyes with him. She couldn't remember ever being this dirty. Madison had schooled her well, but she was no professional intelligence or military person. She was never, under any circumstances, to tell anyone what he did or where he was if he wasn't with her. She had been around and knew how to play the game with the authorities. However, the Israelis were not like the local police she was accustomed to being rousted by. *These people control every minute of my life,* she thought, looking down at the toiletries again. *I don't know what they know or have tricked me into revealing. They could make me disappear and no one would ever know.* Aside from her fear of her captives, her vanity was getting the better of her. She thought, *I could tell them just a few things but not everything. The insignificant ones. Then a shower and clean up.*

Her gaze went back to Thaddeus. "I have told you over and over, I don't know where he is."

"We're not going to play that game." He started to scoop up the enticing things in front of them.

"Okay. He's in Syria," she blurted out before she realized what she had said. "He is doing a job for the Arabs." Once she broke Madison's rule, she couldn't stop.

Thaddeus's questions appeared benign at first to get her talking, but they became harder and more specific as time progressed. "Madison led an attack on the American airbase in Turkey. Who did he report to?"

"I don't know anything about him attacking an airbase. I have already told you all I know. He never tells me the specifics on what he is doing. All I know is that he works as a military consultant. I really don't know." Her voice was sincere.

Thaddeus held his gaze on her. "Did he ever mention anyone?"

She looked down at her clasped hands. "He did mention a Turkish general a time or two."

"He stole some military equipment from the airbase. Where did he take it?"

She shook her head. "He never mentioned anything about that."

"From your computer, we know you were going to meet Madison in Italy," Thaddeus said.

"I was," she said with a smirk. "I would much rather be on the beach in Italy than here. Obviously, that is not going to happen."

"Why didn't you meet him in Italy?"

"I wish I had," she replied. "He contacted me the day before your people took me. He said he had another contract and needed to postpone the trip. That's all he said."

"Who was his contract with?" Thaddeus studied her expressions.

Maurine shook her head and replied, "He never said."

Thaddeus grasped the bottle of water on the table, opened it, and took a swig. He leaned back as he replaced the cap. Watching tears stream down her cheeks, he calmly said, "Maurine, I need your help. A lot of innocent people—men, women, children, and babies—are going to die unless you help me. When he attacked the American base in Turkey, he stole several nuclear bombs. Nuclear bombs, Maurine! They are capable of destroying cities."

"No, Bart would never do anything like that," she said with force.

He took another sip of water. "You can stop it, Maurine. If you don't help me, you are just as culpable as Bart. You can stop it, right now. Otherwise, you will go to your grave with the death of hundreds of thousands of people on your conscience."

"No! No, you are wrong." Maurine began to sob. Burying her red, tear-streaked face in her hands, she bowed her head to the table as she wept. "What can I do? I don't know anything. You are asking me to betray Bart."

"I am asking you to save hundreds of thousands of lives," he replied. "Think about it, Maurine, people vaporizing and others lingering on, dying of radiation sickness. Babies and young children struggling for their last breath, dying a horrible death. You can prevent it." Thaddeus withdrew several photographs from a folder on the table beside him, flopped them on the table, and spread them out, exposing the images. Then he pushed them closer to Maurine. The photographs were of children and babies all dying from ionizing radiation sickness. Some of them had cancerous growths already appearing, hair loss, redness, and blistering skin. One baby was crying in obvious agony. All of them were lying supine on a bed. Of the ones with their eyes closed, it was difficult to tell from the pictures if they were asleep, unconscious, or dead. "All of those children were dead within thirty days," he said. "They died horrible deaths."

She looked up at him, her face flushed and tears streaking her cheeks. "But I told you, I don't know anything."

"I want your cooperation," he said. "You may know more than you think you know. It is like putting a puzzle together. You may know a piece that completes the picture. It could be a big thing or a small piece. I want you to think about the things Bart talked about, people he talked to, and what he said to them."

"If I do not help you?"

In a serious tone, Thaddeus replied, "People will die. For you, life as you know it will be over. You will live in a cell. You will have no cosmetics and lose your beauty. You will age and develop wrinkles. Your hair will thin out."

"So I don't have a choice?" she replied as she wiped her running nose, then the tears from her cheeks.

"You have a choice, but you will live with the one you make."

"If I help you, can I go home?"

In a sympathetic tone, he said, "After we have the nuclear devices back and have Bart in custody."

"What will I have to do?"

"Tell us everything you know," he replied. "Anything and everything. We may want you to talk to Bart for us or send him email. But if you should warn him, you will be locked up for the rest of your life and never see your home again."

"Bart has always been good to me. He takes care of me. How can I betray him?" She burst into tears again.

"One day, Bart will turn on you," he replied with sincerity. "That is the kind of man Bart is. He will sacrifice anyone when it suits his need. Even you."

"No, no, not Bart!"

Worn down by Mossad, Maurine found herself in a world she was not prepared to deal with. She was torn between her love for Bart and helping Thaddeus save the lives he'd said would be lost. The images of dying children burned in her brain were too much for her. No matter how hard she tried, she could not get them out of her mind. She would never see Bart again, no matter what she did. She hung her head. The Israelis had broken her.

"Think about what I said, Maurine. You have a choice to make." He picked up the toiletries on the table except the toothpaste and toothbrush. "Brush your teeth. We will talk again in a little while. I will expect your answer then." Thaddeus nodded to the Mossad woman seated by the door, then stood and walked out of the room.

Maurine did not respond or raise her head.

CHAPTER 19

Monday, May 30, 2016
Special Forces Forward Operational Base
Northern Syria

Talking with Max and Danya in the S2 shelter, the S2 captain said, "We received a report that ISIS has taken about two hundred people hostage. US citizens are in the group. They're in our area of operation, and the S3 is working on a rescue plan. Resources available to you are going to be very limited until the hostage situation is resolved."

Andy stepped into the shelter and joined the three where they stood. "Max, I got a report that a young man is sick and no one knows what's wrong with him. I'm not sure, but this could be a lead. He's in the city of Saraqib, about fifty kilometers southwest of Aleppo on the Damascus-Aleppo International Way."

Max stepped to the large map attached to the side of the shelter, placed his finger on Aleppo, and traced the highway south, stopping at the city. "That's in rebel-controlled territory and heading in the right direction," he said as he looked at Andy. "What did the report say his symptoms were?"

"It was sketchy and about all it said was that he is in pain, his arms are red, and his hair is falling out."

"See if you can backtrack and find out who made the initial report," Max said. "Also, any other important details, especially his exact symptoms. I want to go see him, but we need to make sure this is a valid lead before we go down there."

"I'm already on it. The CIA is funding and supplying arms to the Free Syrian Army. I'll need to go through them to get us into the area."

The report Andy received was good and bad news for Max and his team. Saraqib, the second-largest city in the province, was considered a strategic location. It was at the junction of two main highways, one going from Damascus to Aleppo and the other going west toward Latakia on the coast. Whoever controlled this major interchange could deny the use of the highway to their opponent. The city had changed hands several times during the Syrian civil war and been used to attack military convoys attempting to use the routes. It was currently under the control of the Free Syrian Army, which was a good thing for Max's team. With the CIA's help, getting in and out wouldn't be that difficult.

Unfortunately, the Free Syrian Army was composed of several militant groups to include the Al-Nusra Front, also known as al-Qaeda in Syria. Also, ISIS was known to operate independently in the area. The jihadist groups were not necessarily friendly to the US, but their goal was to bring down the Syrian government—the same goal of the US. Reports were often published of the Free Syrian Army selling CIA supplied arms to ISIS.

Max held up his hand. "Hold on. This is one of Madison's traps."

Danya's brow furrowed as a serious expression covered her face. "What? I don't understand. Why do you think it's a trap?"

"Think about it," Max replied, his tone serious as he shifted his stance. "Madison knew we were onto him when we went to the bomb lab and probably suspected it long before that. He planned the taking of the hostages to try to draw our attention in another direction, and if we stayed on the trail after him, we would head right into a quagmire. Remember, the CIA tried to kill us and they're supporting the Free Syrian Army. No doubt, they have contacts with ISIS in the area. Also, the intel report was sketchy at best. There were no details in the report except the man's vague symptoms. We were supposed to focus on his hair and launch out. This is bait, and we ain't biting." He wrinkled up the corner of his mouth as he shook his head.

"I see what you mean," she replied. "ISIS has two nukes and, with deceptions, will protect them."

"Right," Max said. "Remember, Madison is smart and cunning. If we charge in, they'll *clean our clock*." Looking at Danya, he said, "We're not taking the bait. Get with Rav-Seren Beiser and brief him.

Tell him to set up his Shayetet team off the coast west of Homs. I'll get with the 22 SAS." He turned to Andy. "Contact the CIA and proceed as though we want to see the sick guy right away and make arrangements for us to enter the area. Find out what you can about him. We'll turn this into our own ruse. I want everyone to think we took the bait, but we'll get Madison and the nukes on the other side. Also, get the latest imagery of the highway and area around Homs. I'll set up some activity to look like we're going there."

Andy smiled. "Will do."

⸻ ✦ ✦ ⸻

Tuesday, May 31, 2016
Gareth Residence
New York, New York

Filling one of the easy chairs across from Stew, Archie balanced a plate containing a large apple crumb Danish on his knees as he took a sip of coffee. After returning the cup to the side table, he took a firm grasp on the plate and sliced off an ample piece of the pastry with his fork.

Stew sipped his coffee, then said, "You look a little tired, Archie. Did you have a good weekend?"

Archie took his focus off the Danish and, with a bulging cheek, said, "It was all right. I worked most of the weekend out of town." He shifted his eyes to the coffee and took a sip.

Stew grinned. "You're a terrible liar, Archie. Nassar'll be here in a little bit. I wanted to talk to you first. Wes Brock and Aaron Fitzgerald will be here as well."

"Why did you want to meet here this morning instead of DC?" Archie shoved another piece of pastry into his mouth.

"I want to be out of the eyes of the media for this meeting. They'll ask a bunch of questions about Nassar, and I want our discussion kept private." Stew grasped the remote and turned on the surround sound as an added precaution against eavesdropping. "There're nine primaries in June. Jenny and her closest competitor are predicted to be neck and neck in California. She's polling high in the Virgin Islands and Puerto Rico. If she takes these three, she'll have the delegates needed for the nomination. That'll give us about seven weeks to focus on the national convention. I want a big showing at that convention."

Archie lifted the coffee cup to his lips, then nodded and dropped his gaze to the Danish.

"Although we're spending a lot of money keeping the delegates happy"—Stew sipped his coffee—"I'm concerned about the general election. I have an idea that I think'll ensure Jenny wins it."

Archie stood, a shower of crumbs falling to the floor from his pro-tuberant belly, and stepped toward the small table. "Not to worry. The election is taken care of."

"I'm concerned," Stew said as he followed the senator with his eyes. "We can't let up. Things can go wrong."

Archie scooped up another Danish. "They do. What're you thinking?"

Stew picked up his coffee cup. "If there was a major incident or catastrophe in the US, Jenny could capitalize on it. She'd then blast her opponent and come out strong on her experience."

Jenny sauntered into the room in what looked like the latest fashion from Target's bed and bath department and flopped into the chair. The shower curtain look-alike billowed slightly as she hit the seat. "What am I going to come out strong with?" Her eyes darted to Archie as he was about to sit. "Fix me a drink."

Archie stood erect and said, "Good morning. Coffee?"

"No, not fucking coffee. Scotch." Her tone was so caustic it should have melted his coffee cup.

I oughta smash this pastry in your face, bitch, Archie thought. *But that'd be a waste of a good Danish.* He set the plate next to his coffee and stepped to the cabinet to retrieve a glass and the bottle of scotch.

Stew's disapproving eyes shot to Jenny as he lit a cigar. "I was saying, if there was an incident or catastrophe in the US, you could capitalize on it. You could blast your opponent and emphasize your strengths. Sound strong on terrorists and all that shit."

"Yeah, if something should happen…that's not bad. But what about the little pipsqueak in the White House? He's gonna want to be out there making a speech."

The senator returned and handed a glass to Jenny, then planted his frame into his chair. Without hesitation, an ample size of the sweet pastry went straight to his mouth.

"Don't worry about him," Stew replied. "I'll handle him. He can make the initial speech, and you can take it from there. I'll even tell him to give you a plug on your ability to handle the situation. And, of course, I'll get some of the other world leaders to endorse you."

"Not a bad idea." She sipped her drink. "You got something in mind?"

"Hear me out. Suppose the terrorists smuggled one of the nukes they stole from Incirlik into the country and detonated—"

Jenny sat forward, sputtered, and spit out her mouthful of booze. "What?"

Archie coughed, almost choking on the pastry. "Oh, no! That's way too risky. Are you serious?"

Stew puffed his cigar, then placed it in the ashtray on the desk. "Yes, now listen. This's what I'm thinking." His gaze went to Archie, then Jenny. "You'll come out swinging, blast the terrorists and lack of border security. You'll hit your opponent's inexperience. We'll come up with great points for you. What do you think?"

Jenny picked up her glass and held it in her hand. "I like it. Our insurance."

"That's right," Stew said as a smirk appeared on his face. "Jenny's going to be the next president. We'll ensure the attorney general, the FBI, Homeland Security, and the police blame the terrorists. None of us'll be implicated. After all, Jenny'll be the president…the first female president."

"No, that's just too dangerous," Archie said. "You'll never be able to keep something like that quiet."

Stew puffed his cigar, and through the blue smoke, said, "Yes, we can. We control all the key people. They work for us, remember? Besides, we've got dirt on all of 'em. We can take care of those who don't want to go along."

The senator finished off the Danish, licked his fingers, then stood and said under his breath as he started to the cabinet, "I need a drink."

Jenny's face began to light up as she thought about Stew's idea. She held her glass out to Archie without looking at him and said, "Fix me another one."

Archie took the glass and lumbered back to the cabinet.

"Go on," she continued. "How are you going to pull something like this off?"

"That's why Nassar'll be here. We use him to arrange delivery of a nuke. We tell him when and where." Stew's head dipped as he glanced at his notepad, then he looked up. "It just occurred to me that the CIA never did kill the guy working for Trent."

"Madison," Archie said as he shuffled back to his chair. He handed the glass to Jenny before he sat.

Holding the cigar between his first two fingers, Stew pointed at Archie. "Right. Nassar finds Madison and has him bring one into the country. Then we can arrange for him to be killed by the FBI. That'll solve our other problem with him."

Jenny sipped her drink. "I like it. We—"

The doorbell rang, silencing the conversation.

She looked to Archie and said, "Get the door."

Archie stood and started to the door, neither of the other two seeing the *drop-dead* expression on his face. Within a moment, he returned escorting Nassar. The four of them stood as Stew, being gracious, led them in several minutes of cordialities and small talk before beginning any serious conversation. The senator offered Nassar a beverage and pastries, and he accepted a coffee.

Stew motioned for Nassar to be seated in the chair beside Jenny and said, "I need your help."

The others followed suit as Nassar sat and replied, "Of course. How can I be of service?"

"You owe me a favor for allowing Kenworth to escape," Stew said as he locked eyes with the Muslim Brotherhood representative.

"Kenworth has proven to be a difficult problem," Nassar replied. "As I have told you, he will not leave Syria. What do you require of me?"

"I asked you before about Bart Madison."

"Yes, Trent Weldon's missing operative. Is he still missing?"

"Don't give me that shit!" Stew said, his face bright red. "The last time we talked, you said you were going to ask al-Ghazāli about him. You seem to have forgotten about him."

"No, no, I have not forgotten," Nassar replied. "Al-Ghazāli told me he is looking for him. These things take time."

"That's bullshit. My sources told me that he led the attack on Incirlik and al-Ghazāli hired him."

Nassar shifted in his seat. "No, your sources are wrong."

"Nassar," Stew replied firmly. "No more bullshit. I want you to tell al-Ghazāli I have a job for Madison."

"What is it?"

"I want Madison to bring one of the nukes into the US and set it off when and where I say."

In an incredulous tone, Nassar replied, "In the US? Your *own* country?"

"Yes." Stew's tone was cold. "I want to ensure Jenny's election."

Nassar shot a look to Jenny, then to Senator Chapman and back to Stew. Stunned, he forced the words, "I do not understand." He dropped his gaze to the coffee cup he held in his hands, then looked up to Stew. "You have fixed the election. You want to set a trap for Madison." He started to get up.

"No, please," Stew said. "I am serious, and it is no setup."

Nassar eased back down. "I do not understand."

"Madison tried to blow up the Hoover Dam three years ago," Stew continued. "He planned it and got away. I want him to do the same thing again but with a different target. I want it to happen about the middle of June. If he can do it and the bomb goes off, terrorists'll be blamed, of course. The president will denounce it first. Then Jenny'll give several speeches condemning the attack and blame it on the treatment of the Arabs in the Middle East. She'll speak to her strengths and her opponent's lack of experience. This'll solidify her election. We'll get it all worked out by the time we reach an agreement with Madison, but that's the concept."

ISIS and the Muslim Brotherhood would jump at such a chance, Nassar thought as he grasped his chin with the thumb of his right hand. *Al-Ghazāli is not going to believe it. Still seems like a trap.* "This will require several assurances. If al-Ghazāli can find Madison, he will require a substantial fee."

"Of course. He'll receive half up-front and half on delivery. We can work out all the details when you locate him and tell him what we want. Do not say anything to anyone else about this. Keep it *close hold*."

Nassar studied Stew for a moment, then said, his voice revealing his caution, "What about your border security, your CIA, and military?"

"They won't be a problem. All Madison will need to do is follow our instructions and be discreet."

Nassar nodded. "I will inform al-Ghazāli."

The doorbell rang again, and Archie—the dutiful servant—rose from the chair before Jenny could give the order. He made his way to the door, returning with Wes and Aaron in tow. As soon as Stew's pleasantries were completed, he said, "Please, be seated." He motioned to the two chairs next to Nassar's.

Archie offered them refreshments, but both declined.

Stew began laying out his idea to ensure Jenny's election. Archie finished his scotch, and Jenny, smiling and nodding, remained silent. Neither Wes nor Aaron spoke as Stew's words hit them. Stew sat back and finished the rest of his coffee. "What do ya think?"

Wes glanced to Archie and then to Aaron. "I think I'll have a scotch." He stood and stepped to the bar.

Aaron said, "I'll have one too." He stood also and followed Wes.

Archie stood, holding his glass, and before he could take a step, Jenny thrust her own glass in front of him and said, "I'll have another."

— ◆ ◆ ◆ —

Wednesday, June 1, 2016
Artisan Coffee on King Street
Hammersmith, London

Bart Madison stepped out of the Stamford Brook tube station, gave a slight tug on the brim of his hat, and donned his sunglasses, for the bright morning sun as well as to camouflage his appearance. A wedge he'd slipped in his shoe gave him a slight limp as he made his way to the coffee shop.

He ordered a coffee and took a seat facing the sprawling window with his back toward the wall. Withdrawing his smartphone from a pocket, he proceeded to log into the online account he used to communicate with Maurine when he was away. He accessed the message she had left for him, outlining her ordeal with the Israelis. The note didn't go into a lot of detail, just that she had been questioned about him for a couple of days and then released since she didn't know anything. She said she soaked in the tub for a long time, trying to wash away the experience. "I don't like those people," she wrote and then asked if they could schedule their trip to Italy as they had talked about. She closed by saying she needed him and couldn't wait to see him. The text was ended with her usual, "love and kisses, Maurine."

Sitting back in his chair, Bart glanced out of the window, then began to analyze what she had written. *It sounds like her,* he thought. *Nothing seems out of the ordinary.* He sipped the coffee and held it in both hands as he rested his elbows on the table. As his eyes scanned the street outside, his head filled with thoughts of Maurine—a smile that would light up the room, hair the color of wine cascading over her shoulders, she was a vibrant woman. The images were so vivid he could almost smell the perfume she wore. He longed for the one who had become his companion, needing her perfect body next to him. Suddenly, his eyes caught the back of a tall redheaded woman as she passed the window and turned the corner, jerking him back to the present. He felt his emotions spike. She was about the same size as Maurine, and her hair was the same color and style. *Impossible,* he thought. *Just a coincidence.* When her profile appeared in the side window, his excitement subsided. It was not Maurine.

The information in her note, although lacking in detail, was consistent with what his security guards had reported on her abduction. Senator Chapman's information wasn't as detailed but was consistent and identified the Israelis as the ones who had taken her. Nothing indicated that Maurine was being used as bait. Bart knew Mossad was good at their work, but he couldn't afford to take any chances. He sipped his coffee again, then set the cup on the small table and picked up his phone. *What could she have told them?* he thought. *Perhaps nothing, but then again…*

Bart began typing his response. "I miss you too. Meet me in Beirut Friday evening. A car will pick you up at the airport. Send me your flight details. Bart."

As soon as he sent the text, he stood and walked out of the coffee shop, then made his way back to the tube by way of an alternate route.

CHAPTER 20

Wednesday, June 1, 2016
International Waters off the Coast of Cyprus
Levantine Sea

THE ELECTRO-OPTICAL PERISCOPE of the Israeli Dolphin 2-class submarine *Rahav* broke the surface of the eastern waters of the Mediterranean Sea southwest of Cyprus. The captain scanned the area to verify his position and sent a coded message to the HMS *Bulwark* (L15) that was supposed to be on station northwest of Cypress. While waiting on the response, he searched the route the *Rahav* would take to a point closer to shore where Rav-Seren Beiser and his men would depart the submarine. Upon receiving confirmation from the *Bulwark*, the captain lowered the periscope and gave the order for the Shayetet team to prepare to deploy. The submarine went dark inside as the necessary white lighting switched to red to allow the team's eyes to adjust to the night before leaving. The submerged boat eased through the water to the release point.

The clandestine approach of the *Rahav* occurred under the noses of the Russian military. Khmeimim Air Base southeast of Latakia was operated by the Russian Air Force and home of their largest foreign signals intelligence surveillance facility operated by the Six Directorate of the Russian GRU. The Russian Air Force also used the Shayrat Airbase in Homs and had a repair and replenishment base on the north side of Tartus. The slightest error by the captain could alert the Russians, who in turn would notify the Syrians, foiling Beiser's mission before it even started.

Upon reaching the designated position southwest of Ruad Island (Arwad), the captain surveyed the area again through the periscope.

The island was three kilometers off the Syrian Coast south of Tartus. He turned away from the periscope to face Beiser and said, "You have a straight shot to the beach. I don't see any shipping traffic or small boats. However, the fishing trawlers will be out in a few hours."

"Understand," Beiser replied. "If there are any problems and we can't clear the beach before then, we'll postpone our pickup twenty-four hours. Is the weather overcast as forecasted?"

"It is, and seas are calm with a slight chop. You should have no trouble getting to shore undetected."

Beiser nodded.

The captain continued, "As soon as you are off the boat, we'll submerge. We have to get out of here and back into international waters. You will be on your own." He extended his hand and wished him success. "*B'hatzlacha.*"

Beiser looked him in the eye and, with a slight smile, confirmed he would see him later. "*L'hitraot.*"

Once the commandos reached the beach, a Mossad agent met them and introduced himself to Beiser as Jacob. Without hesitation, Jacob led them across the sand to the property he had appropriated. It was a walled compound—obviously a summer vacation home for someone. He stopped in front of a large, solid double gate in the stone wall and swung one side open to allow the team carrying the rigid-hull boats to enter. After the last man went through, he surveyed the beach to ensure no one was following them, then walked it closed. Inside the courtyard was a garage with four Toyota SUVs. He paused when they reached the front of the garage and said, "Put your equipment inside. The SUVs are for you."

Beiser gave a slight nod, then turned to the others and said in a low voice, "Get everything ready and post guards. I'll go with Jacob to get an update on the situation and latest intel." He turned and accompanied the man into the main house as his men began making their preparations.

Inside the house were two more Mossad agents, one on guard and the other observing a tablet screen. Jacob motioned to the man by the window and said, "That's Seth and Toby over there with the tablet."

Seth gave a slight nod, and Toby raised his hand.

Jacob stepped to a small table with a map spread out on it and began orienting Beiser to the area, showing him where a team of Hezbollah fighters was guarding the warhead. "Our sources have indicated the fighters plan to put the warhead onboard a fishing trawler first thing in the morning," he said. Placing his finger on a circled area, he continued, "They are in this vacant warehouse building, in the east end." He handed the Shayetet leader an aerial image of the building. "Toby is keeping an eye on them with a miniature drone. The building is on the main highway heading to Homs, but I don't anticipate any traffic on that roadway until about 0600. Commercial buildings are located across the highway to the east. Trees and light vegetation are on the south, west, and north side of the warehouse. There shouldn't be any traffic on this road coming from the west either. As you can see, it passes through a rural area. Where it approaches the intersection to the main highway, it is about forty-five meters from the side of the building."

Holding the image, Beiser said, "It looks like we can surround the building easy enough. Have you seen it during the day and night?"

"Yes. The vegetation offers good cover, and you should be able to get within fifteen meters undetected. The brush in the tree line along this gravel road hasn't been cut and is thick." The Mossad agent traced the road with his finger. "It is the last turn before the warehouse, right in the middle of the *S* turn on the east–west road. They have been keeping two men on guard in the front and two in the rear of the building. Here and here." He pointed to the southwest corner and the main entrance on the east side. "There are two doors on the west end, a large drive-through door and a personnel door on the side. The main entrance is a double door." The agent handed him sketches of the inside of the warehouse.

Beiser studied the drawings momentarily, then said, "I want to see the drone coverage." He laid the image and drawings on the table.

Jacob escorted the commando to Toby, and without hesitation, Toby turned the screen to show him the view. There appeared to be six men asleep, curled up on the floor with blankets. A large, wooden crate sat in the center of the room. When Beiser motioned, Toby rotated the drone's optical head to give him a view of the rest of the room. "I will launch another drone to keep an eye on the outside as soon as you depart."

"I'll brief the men, and we'll depart in a few minutes."

Wednesday, June 1, 2016
HMS *Bulwark* (L15)
International Waters, Northwest of Cyprus

On board the HMS *Bulwark* of the United Kingdom's Response Force Task Group, a team from the 22 SAS supported by a unit of the 42 Commando Royal Marines prepared their equipment to support the deploying Shayetet team if needed and for a boarding-at-sea operation. Intelligence reports indicated one of the warheads was to be placed aboard the Pakistani registered freighter, *Almira Mariam*, which was currently docked at the main port city of Latakia.

A small team from the SAS had previously infiltrated Syria to locate the nuke before it was taken into the port. Unfortunately, that didn't happen as Russian and Syrian Army patrols in the city and surrounding area restricted their ability to confirm either of two suspected locations, let alone attempt a recovery. They considered that the Syrian Army and perhaps even the Russian military may be assisting Hezbollah in getting the weapon out of the country.

The SAS team established an observation position outside the facility where they could see the freighter and dock. It appeared that loading of regular cargo had been completed several hours before. Intel reports stated that a black Toyota truck and SUV would be delivering the warhead just prior to the ship sailing, but vehicles matching that description had not entered the port. All the team could do was wait for the vehicles to arrive.

Thursday, June 2, 2016
Vacation House
Tartus, Syria

Rav-Seren Beiser led his heavily armed Shayetet commandos out of the gate en route to the Hezbollah fighters' warehouse. Based on the route they had to take, he estimated it would take approximately eleven minutes to get there. The four SUVs were spaced out and traveled at a moderate speed so as not to attract attention. Toby, the Mossad agent operating the drone at the vacation house, maintained constant communication with Beiser via secure radio as the four SUVs made their way along the planned route. As Jacob had predicted, no vehicles were present at that hour.

The gravel road that intersected the east–west route was approximately one-quarter mile before the warehouse. The last two Toyotas turned north onto that road and switched off their lights. Following the tree line, they stopped near one of the outbuildings. The commandos exited the vehicles and made their way to positions close to the west end of the warehouse.

The lead SUV and the one behind it slowed, then continued to the main highway, giving the other commandos time to get into position. Reaching the intersection, Beiser heard over his headset, "In position. Identified two guards at the rear of the building."

With a low voice, he replied into the radio, "Roger."

The two vehicles turned left and continued on the remaining forty-five meters to the main entrance on the east end of the building. Just as the lead Toyota approached the front drive of the warehouse, Beiser commanded over his radio, "Fire."

Two M4A1 suppressed carbines popped.

Beiser watched the front guards collapse as he heard over his headset, "Two rear guards neutralized."

The Toyotas stopped in front of the warehouse and the occupants sprang out. The commandos in the rear of the building entered at the same time as those in the front. Within several seconds, two pops came from the rear of the building.

Beiser heard the words in his headset, "Two down in the west end."

He replied in a low voice, "Roger."

Without so much as a squeak, the deadly men crept into the main area where the crate was located. Beiser signaled there were six people sleeping. Three of them woke and grabbed for their AK-47 assault rifles as they started to stand. M4A1 carbines of the Israelis popped, and the men collapsed back onto their blankets. The commotion rousted the other three, but their bodies fell limp before they could reach their Kalashnikovs.

Beiser motioned for three of his men to search the rest of the structure. "Be sure there is no one else hiding in here. There were just supposed to be ten of them, but we've got twelve."

Without speaking, the three began their task.

Another soldier approached Beiser and said, "There are two dead in the back of the building. There is a Toyota truck, a van, and Mercedes in the back."

Beiser said with a nod, "Make a thorough search of the bodies and vehicles. Photograph all of them and get DNA." As soon as the commando stepped away, he moved to the crate and opened it. He verified it was the warhead, then called Jacob on the radio. "We have it and will depart in about ten minutes. The men are collecting intel. There were twelve people, not ten, and the two extra ones are costing us little more time."

"Roger," came Jacob's reply through the headset.

Their mission completed at the warehouse, the Shayetet team loaded the crate into one of the SUVs, then got in their vehicles and returned to the vacation house. Jacob opened the gate as they approached the compound. Beiser stopped at the gate, and the other SUVs drove to the garage. The men went right to work gathering the rest of their equipment and headed to the beach with their rigid-hull boats. Beiser and Jacob drove the SUV, with the crated warhead inside, to the water's edge.

When the crate was in one of the boats, Jacob and Beiser shook hands, then the commandos departed to rendezvous with the *Rahav*. The team had executed their mission with speed and precision. The two unanticipated fighters at the warehouse were the one thing that bothered Beiser. Those two could have caused serious problems for the Israelis, but the commando's skill had overwhelmed their foe. He couldn't help but wonder who the extra fighters were.

———— ✦ ————

Thursday, June 2, 2016
HMS *Bulwark* (L15)
International Waters, Northwest of Cyprus

The SAS observation team watching the *Almira Mariam* notified the *Bulwark* that the freighter was departing the port. The British ship remained northwest of Cyprus, which blocked observation of the warship from the port area. To keep track of the freighter, a drone was launched from the *Bulwark* as the freighter entered the shipping lane. Since the Mediterranean Sea's depth averaged fifteen hundred meters, large ships could go about anywhere without fear of shallow water. Those ships destined for ports beyond the Strait of Gibraltar sailed to the south of Cyprus and along a route that was about in the middle of the sea. The British captain anticipated the freighter would appear normal and take this route.

As soon as the *Almira Mariam* rounded the southwest end of Cyprus, The HMS *Bulwark* approached the freighter from its starboard side. The sky had cleared, turning to a bright, sunny morning with a warm gentle breeze—a perfect day to be out on the Mediterranean with excellent visibility. However, this was not a pleasure trip, and it was all business for the commandos. Two Offshore Raiding Craft with sixteen 42 Commando Royal Marines exited the *Bulwark*, heading for the freighter at thirty knots. Two Lynx helicopters departed with the 22 SAS Commandos.

The HMS *Bulwark* hailed the *Almira Mariam*, ordering it to stop. Without a response, the order was repeated for the freighter to stop. Again, no response from the freighter. Ordering a third time without any effect on the *Almira Mariam,* the captain of *Bulwark* directed the gun crew to fire a short burst from the forward-mounted 20mm GAM-BO1 cannon.

High-explosive rounds impacted the water close enough to throw water across the bow of the freighter, which brought an immediate response.

As the freighter slowed, the frantic Pakistani captain's voice came over the speaker. "Stop, no shoot! We stop. No shoot! We comply. This international waters. Why you stop us? This international waters. This violation of maritime law."

The freighter captain's protests had no effect on the captain of the *Bulwark.*

Hovering above the freighter, forward of the bridge and approximately the center of the ship, the SAS commandos began fast-roping onto the ship. Engine exhaust fumes from the ship's stack greeted the men as they landed on the rhythmic rocking deck. In fewer than twenty seconds, they were on board and moving to the bridge. The marine team boarded the ship from both sides. Half of them immediately began assembling the crew and the rest started searching the vessel.

Major Basil Ainsworth, SAS Commando, stepped to the freighter captain and said, "I want to see your manifest."

The Pakistani shook his head and looked to the others, acting as though he didn't understand English.

Shoving his carbine into the man's chest, Major Ainsworth commanded, "The manifest!"

From behind the captain, an arm shoved the document into his hands, and he handed it to the major.

Ainsworth scanned the list of crew and one passenger, pausing at the name, *Khalid Safar.* He circled it and then looked at the Pakistani captain and, in a stern voice, asked, "Where is Safar?"

The captain shrugged. "I do not know. I have knowledge of one passenger. He possibly be in his cabin, or anywhere."

Ainsworth looked to Captain Poindexter, the marine commando next to him, and said, "Find Safar." He returned his attention to the manifest as Poindexter departed, taking three marines with him. The manifest listed general cargo consisting of vegetable oil, cotton, various fruits, pottery, tobacco, and two automobiles. The major looked back to the Pakistani captain. "I am looking for a crate that was loaded onboard just before you sailed. It is not listed. Where is it?"

"Everything is on manifest. I do not know what you talk about."

"Captain, I want that crate," Ainsworth said in a harsh tone, then he poked the man with his weapon. "My men will tear this ship apart looking for it. If you don't tell me now, when we do find it, I will sink your ship. Do you understand?"

The captain continued to deny any such crate was loaded, trying Ainsworth's patience.

The major started to step away when he received a call on his radio from Captain Poindexter. He listened, then replied into the radio, "I will be right there." Turning to one of the commandos, he said loud enough for everyone to hear, "Watch them. If they give you any trouble, throw them overboard."

Major Ainsworth stepped to the door of the cabin on the upper deck in the officers' section and was met by Poindexter, then looking past the captain, he saw the bloody body on the deck.

"Just as we stepped in, he went for his rifle," the Marine captain said as he pointed to the corpse. "He's dead."

"Any of our people hurt?"

"No, sir," Poindexter said, handing him the man's passport. "That's Khalid Safar, an Iraqi. The other cabins are clear."

Taking the document, Ainsworth flipped through it. "He was escorting the crate. Now let's find it. Is that his cell phone?" He pointed to the phone on the small desk.

"Yes, sir. I haven't checked it out yet."

"When you finish up in here," the major said, "see if there are any voice messages he saved." He turned and stepped out of the cabin.

Ainsworth's headset came to life again as he stepped onto the main deck, capturing his attention. "Sir, I think we have found it," the voice said. "I am in the number two, lower hold. I'll send a man topside to meet you."

"Roger, heading that way."

An SAS sergeant stood in front of a twenty-foot shipping container with the door open when Major Ainsworth arrived. Three bales of tobacco wrapped in jute fabric sat outside of the container. "Here it is, sir," the sergeant said, pointing to a crate camouflaged with tobacco leaves and wrapped to look like the other bales.

Without hesitation, Ainsworth examined the outside of the crate, then raised the lid to inspect the contents. Inside sat the warhead with several wires and a timer outside of the metal housing. It had obviously been modified to command detonate. Ainsworth reported to the HMS *Bulwark* that he had the nuclear device. He then directed Captain Poindexter, who was now on the main deck, to instruct the freighter captain to hoist the container topside.

By the time the crate was on the main deck, a Lynx helicopter set down, ready to transport it to the *Bulwark*. Major Ainsworth and his men departed the freighter on two other helicopters. Captain Poindexter and eight marine commandos remained on board as the rest of the marines departed in their Offshore Raiding Craft. The *Almira Mariam* was directed and escorted by the *Bulwark* to the port on the southern end of Cyprus.

CHAPTER 21

Friday, June 3, 2016
Beirut–Rafic Hariri International Airport
Beirut, Lebanon

RESTORED TO HER customary elegance, Maurine Rowen emerged from the crowd, pulling her carry-on bag. She had just arrived at the Beirut–Rafic Hariri International Airport aboard a KLM flight. Located nine kilometers south of the city, the aviation complex was Lebanon's only commercial airport. The modern facility handled over seven and a half million passengers annually and, like any other, bustled with people going in all directions.

Maurine paused and turned on her cell phone. She reviewed her last text from Bart. "We have reservations at the InterContinental Phoenicia Beirut Hotel. The limousine driver will meet you on the lower level by the baggage claim. Watch for him. I am looking forward to the weekend with you. I have some business to do, so I will be just a little late. You should be out of the shower by the time I get there. Love, Bart."

She gently touched the screen as though she was connecting with him. *I want to see him one more time. Hold him. Love him,* she thought as tears welled in her eyes. The Israelis are here somewhere, watching. *Can I warn him in time? Can we escape together?* Her jaw tightened. *I will find a way.*

She walked on, looking for the person who was to meet her. On the lower level, past the baggage carousels, her eyes locked onto her name on a white piece of paper supported by two driving-gloved hands. Her eyes followed the arms up to reveal an older man, stooped-shouldered, in the center of several other chauffeurs, each of them displaying signs. He was dressed the same as the others—white shirt that appeared too big, beneath an inexpensive black coat and tie. As Maurine got closer, she could see several scars covered by his heavy beard.

She stopped in front of the man and said, "I am Maurine."

The man tugged at the visor of the cap sitting on his coarse dark hair and reached for her bag, motioning for her to go with him. As they exited the doors, jet engine fumes, car exhaust, and a myriad of traffic sounds greeted them. The noise of aircraft landing and taking off was nonstop. A short distance out of the building, the two approached a dark E-Class Mercedes. The chauffeur opened the rear passenger door for Maurine and handed her an envelope as she slid onto the leather seat. He tipped another man who'd been standing watch over the sedan. The trunk lid rose as the driver closed the door and stepped behind the car. Another car pulled to a stop next to the Mercedes, then drove on.

Reading a note from Bart, Maurine didn't pay any attention to the other car. Nothing seemed out of the ordinary or aroused her attention. She never saw the driver shove her bag into the stopped vehicle. The chauffeur slammed the lid with a thump, then got into the driver's seat. He drove out of the passenger pickup area following a line of other cars.

"Excuse me," Maurine said, her tone incredulous. "This is from Bart?"

The man nodded.

"Do you know what this note says?"

The man nodded again and held a second envelope over his shoulder.

She took the envelope and read the contents. "Maurine, do as I have instructed in the other note. Do not say anything. Turn off your cell phone. Change all of your clothes, everything. Take off all your jewelry. There is a fresh change of clothes for you in the bag on the floorboard. Put everything in that bag, then give it to the driver. He will not leave the airport area until you hand him the bag."

She sat back, unsure of what was happening. She looked around the airport property, then switched off her cell phone. *Bart is always cautious,* she thought. *Sometimes a bit eccentric.* She pulled the small valise near her feet onto the seat, unzipped it, and looked inside. Laying neat and folded were a pair of panties and bra on top, just as she would put them on. Although she had removed her clothes many times before in her past profession, she was nervous, if not apprehensive, about disrobing this time.

Maurine paused as she remembered when she met Bart in Panama three years ago. She and several other girls had been hired for a weekend party at a Venezuelan rancher's estate. She didn't know who the men were, nor did she care—it was business. The girls were treated and paid well. She had just taken a dip in the pool when she saw Bart with two other men as they rounded the corner of the house. Standing nude, she'd asked Bart to help her with sunscreen.

We have been a couple ever since. Bart has given me everything I want, she thought. *He took me from that life. I am his forever. Maybe I can warn him after all.*

She wiggled out of her panties and slipped the fresh pair on. *I would have preferred to shower before putting these on,* she thought. *I want to be at my best when I see him.* Next, she slipped her arms inside her dress, released the catch to free her bra, then slipped it off. With her arms restricted, she felt clumsy as she laid it on the seat and picked up the one from the case. Again, with her arms inside her clothes, one arm and then the other slid into the pink, lacy bra and she nestled her thirty-four double-Ds inside it before fastening the catch. Next, she slid the garment she had on over her head and held it close to her chest while her hand dove into the satchel to withdraw its replacement. She held the item up, nodded in approval, and pulled the mini dress over her head, wiggling it into place. Sandals were the last items to be exchanged. After she stuffed her clothing inside the satchel, she placed it on the seatback for the driver.

He looked in the mirror at her, then tugged on his ear, reminding her to remove her jewelry. Taking the case back, she removed her earrings and bracelets, then, with a pang of regret, placed them in it. The driver took the bag when she returned it to the seatback.

The car drove onto the Beirut–Saida Highway heading north toward the InterContinental Phoenicia Beirut Hotel. Maurine sat back and watched the lights pass by. As the Mercedes sped down the highway, she began to relax, exhausted from the long flight. She closed her eyes. *Bart, I hate being away from you.*

The car braked hard, jolting her back to the present. Startled, Maurine grasped at the armrest, trying not to slide out of the seat. She fell over as the vehicle swerved to the right turning a corner, then shot forward as the engine roared like an angry beast. The Mercedes then decelerated and shot to the left, throwing Maurine onto the floor. Trying to resume her seat as the engine's power propelled the car forward, she was again forced to her knees.

With a voice loud and full of fear, she yelled, "Driver! Slow down. What the hell are you doing?"

He didn't reply.

The car slowed again, then swung hard to the left. Terrified by the chauffeur's hazardous driving—swinging around corners, speeding and then braking—Maurine wanted out. However, with the car's erratic behavior, she couldn't stay in the seat, let alone jump out. The car all but screeched to a halt next to a second vehicle. Maurine struggled back into the seat as the driver handed her valise to a man in another car, then the angry Mercedes engine launched the vehicle forward again. She was jostled around the backseat a couple more times, then the Mercedes slowed and turned into a vacant building. Maurine was able to sit up, then bolted from the car when it came to a stop.

After about four steps, she froze, realizing she was in a closed building but didn't know where. There was no place to go. She turned back toward the chauffeur and screamed at the top of her voice, "Where the hell are we? You were supposed to take me to the hotel and this is not a fucking hotel." Her hands trembled in fear. There were countless possibilities of what might happen, and none of them appealed to her. *I am not going to be an easy mark for this bastard,* she thought. *I need something, a weapon to defend myself. There is not even a stick in here. Bart, I need you.*

From the vestige of a forgotten light in front of her came the reply, "Maurine, I am sorry. I thought you might be followed."

A chill washed over her. Unable to comprehend for an instant, she said, "What? You know me?" The voice was familiar, but her brain couldn't process the opposing events fast enough. "Who are you?" She stepped closer to the figure, her guard high.

The man stood erect, removed the cap and wig. Next, he reached up and peeled away the dark beard, then the latex to reveal his true face. "Maurine, it is me, Bart." His voice was calm and reassuring.

Realizing it was Bart, she stepped to him. "Oh, thank God. I was so scared. I didn't know what was happening." She slapped at him, and tears welled in her eyes. "I almost peed my pants. Why didn't you tell me?"

"I'm sorry, Maurine. I couldn't take a chance." He wrapped his arms around her and pulled her close. The heat of her body rose, filling his nostrils with her scent. He kissed her long, a lover's kiss, full of passion. He felt the tears streak down her face as she trembled. Holding her close, he became lost in her red hair. She began to relax and placed her arms around his neck as he kissed her again. His right hand slid down her side, feeling her curves.

"Let's go to the hotel. I can't stand it. I missed you." Her voice was like honey. She kissed him again.

Bart thrust the four-inch stiletto up, just under her last rib. The thin, razor-sharp blade slid to the hilt into her upper abdomen, slicing into the inner chamber of her heart.

Her eyes widened as her heart stopped. She was dead before she knew what had happened.

Bart placed a light kiss on her lips and laid her body down. "I wish you hadn't become a liability," he said. "I'll miss you."

Bart stepped to a Toyota pickup he had parked in the corner of the building and removed the chauffeur's uniform. He stuffed it into a plastic bag, then pulled on a pair of jeans and a polo shirt. As soon as he was behind the wheel, he donned his ball cap and dropped the bag of clothes on the floor. Looking like most of the other local men, he eased the vehicle out of the building and closed the door behind him. He discarded the plastic bag somewhere along his route outside of Beirut.

———— ❖ ————

Saturday, June 4, 2016
Special Forces Forward Operational Base
Northern Syria

In the S2 shelter, Andy, Max, and Danya sat recapping the events of the past three days. The recovery of two of the warheads was critical, but also had revealed information regarding Madison's plan. It was in motion and meant the deadline was getting close. If Madison got the nukes to the targets, it would take a stroke of luck to find them before they exploded. The team believed one of the warheads was still en route to Israel, the Muslim Brotherhood still had one, and there were two they couldn't account for.

Max leaned forward, his eyes narrowed as he said, "We've gotta keep the pressure on Madison. When the parts move, they are vulnerable to discovery. Now is when mistakes happen. Watch for anything. Even something small could reveal a lot."

"I got confirmation on the identity of the two unknown men the Shayetet team killed in the warehouse," Danya said as she handed the message to Max. "Dawud Al'alim, a senior Muslim Brotherhood member. The other was just one of their fighters, probably Al'alim's bodyguard."

"It appears we might have been off just a little on our estimation," Andy said as he sipped his coffee. "Madison must not be ready for his target in the US, if he still has plans to attack there. I learned this morning that Madison was in London this past Wednesday."

"Wednesday? He was about to execute his plan for the UK," Max said. "Looks like we got that one just in time."

"Khalid Safar was delivering the warhead he had on the freighter to the UK. It was too valuable of a weapon to turn over to just any run-of-the-mill raghead. ISIS will probably use another senior guy to deliver one to the US. The same is true for Israel. I'm watching for anything on movements of senior people."

"We got lucky in our guess about one of the nukes going to Israel," Danya said as she shifted in her chair. "I'm worried about the one we don't know about. The Muslim Brotherhood bought two to use against Israel. We've still got one more to go."

"We've got four to go, Danya," Max said as he shot her a stern look. "I'm guessing the second nuke is headed to Israel overland. It looks like the Brotherhood didn't want to chance sending both by trawler. Splitting them up makes sense." He looked to Andy. "Has there been any indication that Madison has been to the US or made contact with anyone there recently?"

"No, nothing. I'm expecting a call from George anytime. I'm hoping he may have something. ISIS likes to brag and can't keep their mouths shut."

Max turned to the large map on the wall and studied it for a moment. Turning back to Danya, he said, "Start focusing your efforts on surface roads or even trails going from Homs to south of Damascus. If they are going by ground, they'll probably cross into Lebanon north of Mount Hermon and go south before they get to Jordan. I don't think they would chance crossing into the Golan Heights."

"I agree," Danya said. "I'll alert our people watching the known smuggling routes into Lebanon in that area and south Lebanon."

The S2 sergeant stepped to the table and looked to Max, then Andy. "Excuse me, sir. Colonel Johnston, you have a call on the secure line."

"Thank you," Andy replied and stood. Looking to Max, he said, "That's probably George."

Twenty minutes later, Andy returned and sat at the table with Max and Danya. "There's a lot of traffic about seizing the freighter and the operation in Tartus," Andy said. "ISIS and the Brotherhood are pissed that we cost them a lot of money. I thought one thing George told me was significant, though. Lieutenant General Devrim Çakmak, 6th Corps commander, has disappeared. At first, he was thought to be part of the opposition against President Kağan and was either hiding or Kağan's people had rounded him up. But he has simply dropped out of sight." He sipped his coffee.

Max and Danya were both intrigued by Andy's comments about Çakmak at this particular time.

Andy continued, "According to his sources, Erol found out that Çakmak left the country the night of the coup. Çakmak is supposed to be in South America somewhere and is still on the payroll. Erol is trying to verify the information and get a better location on him."

"That's a good lead and raises several questions," Max said as he scribbled on his pad. "I'll let Chugs know, and he can start working it from his end. Any idea what he is doing in South America? If one of the top generals in the Turkish Army goes out of the country during an attempted coup and is still on the payroll, we need to find out why."

"I thought the same thing," Andy replied. "I am pressing my contacts. Information flow out of Turkey is tight because of martial law and arrests at all levels. The CIA is a blackout."

Their meeting lasted another ten minutes, coordinating on Max's instructions.

Max looked at his watch. "It's time for me to call the general. I'm adding Çakmak to my talking points." The three stood as Max walked out of the shelter.

Max called Chugs at SOCOM Headquarters and told him what Andy had found out about Lieutenant General Çakmak. Special operations forces were heavily involved in the counter-drug and counterterrorist operations in Latin America in over sixteen countries at any given time. Chugs could focus his resources in the area and provide a lot of information on what is happening in the region.

"That's a pretty big area," came Chugs's words through the secure phone. "But it's more than we had. We've been trying to get information out of Turkey, but it's been damn near impossible. I'll have our people in Latin America try to find out about Çakmak and where he might be. It would speed things up if I had a specific country. Let me know as soon as you find out anything else."

"Will do," Max replied into the phone. "The two nukes that were recovered are on their way back to the US. I believe one of the other warheads is going overland into Israel. Danya is working that route. Andy found out Madison was in London last Wednesday."

"That means Madison is putting his plan in play," General Matherson replied.

"That's the way we see it too. I'll talk to you soon."

— ✦✦✦ —

Sunday, June 5, 2016
Sheraton Damascus Hotel
Damascus, Syria

Seated with Abdal al-Ghazāli on the terrace outside his room was Nabi Ulmalhamah al-Aqrab and Bart Madison. Al-Ghazāli refilled the men's cups with tea, first al-Aqrab, then Madison. As he set the pot back on the table, he shot a look to Madison and then to al-Aqrab and said, "It is unfortunate that we lost two of the nuclear bombs. The other one for Israel must not be lost."

With an air of confidence, Madison said, "I told you Kenworth was smart. I also told you there must be absolute secrecy. The slightest slip will tip him off. You need to find out which one of your fighters is bragging and get rid of him."

Al-Aqrab slid his fingers across the scar on his cheek as he nodded.

Al-Ghazāli sipped his tea, then said, "I have been contacted by Nassar. Stew Gareth wants to make a deal."

"Gareth?" Madison's tone was full of caution. "What kinda deal? Gareth was pushing the CIA to kill me."

"I know," al-Ghazāli said, then a slight smile emerged on his face. "His proposal is most interesting. He wants you to take one of the nukes into the US and explode it when and where he says. He thinks that will ensure Jenny is elected."

Al-Aqrab sat forward, his mouth gaped open and his eyebrows dipped, then he said, "Gareth wants one of the bombs to explode in the US? That is incredible. Is that true?"

With a scowl, Madison said, "Yes, but the word isn't *incredible*, it is *bizarre*. I didn't think the Gareths would stoop to that level. It doesn't sound right to me. It's a setup."

"Perhaps," al-Ghazāli replied. "Nassar doesn't think it is. He said Gareth assured him it was legitimate. He wants it to happen in a month."

His face lit up and, grinning, al-Aqrab almost looked like a pleasant person. He stroked his chin and said, "Yes, we will do it."

"Hold on," Madison said, his eyes narrowed and his hand shooting up as he looked to al-Aqrab. He was already considering al-Ghazāli's statement, but it reeked of caution. *Execute in a month,* he thought. *It's almost impossible. Very little time to recon, plan, and gather resources. When and where he says. Very risky.* "Don't be too quick to agree." He shook his head. "You could be losing more than you bargain for. I don't like it." The corner of his mouth wrinkled up and his brow furrowed. "I have a source in the US I want to check with. He'll know if it's a con.

Why would Gareth think he needs a nuke to go off in the US to ensure Jenny is elected? He has the election rigged. I feel sure it is a trap."

"If Gareth can provide assistance, we should accommodate him," al-Aqrab said with insistence. "Could you do it?"

Bart tapped the rim of his cup as he considered al-Aqrab's suggestion, then said, "I'll consider it, but first I'll check with my source in DC. I'll need more details, and of course, money up-front. Cash, and a lot of it."

Trying to hide his excitement, al-Ghazāli asked, "What do you want me to tell Nassar? When can I have your answer?"

"Don't tell him anything yet," Madison replied. "I'll get back with you tomorrow evening, day after tomorrow by the latest. I need to talk with my contact before I do anything."

CHAPTER 22

Monday, June 6, 2016
Senator Archibald Chapman's Office
Washington, DC

SENATOR CHAPMAN SHIFTED his chair as he sat down at his desk to get a better view of his young brunette staffer, busy at her desk replying to correspondence. Her skirt was hiked up, exposing her bare leg to midthigh. Mesmerized by the attractive woman, Chapman shoved a chocolate éclair into his mouth and bit it in half. Oblivious to the bits of chocolate icing that littered his desk, he grasped his coffee cup, almost spilling it, and slurped the drink without looking at the cup.

His cell phone rang, distracting him. Looking at the number, he contemplated not answering it. On the third ring, he swallowed and grasped the phone. "Senator Chapman," he said out of habit, although he knew who was calling him when he saw the number appear.

"Senator, no games. I'm in no mood," came the harsh words.

"Yes, Bart," he replied as he stood and stepped to close his door.

"You're behind in sending me the intelligence reports." Bart's tone was punitive. "I told you to keep me informed—"

"Bart, I—"

"I said I was in no mood for your shit. You didn't tell me about the British ship HMS *Bulwark* or the Israeli operation in Tartus, Syria."

"I was going to, but I—"

"You were going to, my ass. I give you a lot of money for booze, playthings, and information. I want fucking information!"

"Okay, Bart. I'll send you the intel report today. I need to go to a meeting now."

"You'll go when I'm through with you. There's another thing, I need answers on what you've omitted. I had to hear it from the Arabs. Gareth wants me to do a job for him. Is it true, and is it a setup?"

"We shouldn't be talking about this on the phone," Chapman said, trying anything to get off the phone and avoid his questions.

"All right, meet me in Damascus on Wednesday," Bart replied.

"I-I can't. I have—"

"You are trying my patience. I expect answers. Get me the complete details on what Gareth wants, what the Israelis are planning, and information on Kenworth. Call me back by three o'clock this afternoon your time. If I don't hear from you by then, we'll be meeting face-to-face."

The phone line went dead.

Chapman's hand trembled as he looked at his cell phone, then laid it on his desk. Turning to his credenza, he retrieved a bottle of Glenlivet and a glass. He set the glass—almost toppling it—on his desk, then sloshed it full, spilling almost as much as he got into it. When burning a candle at both ends, you are bound to be burned. The senator realized he was about to be burned, but by whom—Gareth or Madison? He knew it would be dicey, but sticking with Stew Gareth might be his best move, as Gareth wanted Madison dead and planned to set him up. In addition, with Jenny in the White House, he would have a cabinet position as long as he wanted, or if he remained a senator, Gareth would funnel *campaign funding* to him for as long as Jenny was in office. He knew well that, if he crossed Stew, he would meet an untimely demise, and betraying Madison would not lead to longevity either. Senator Chapman was faced with a Hobson's choice. He withdrew a notepad from his desk and picked up his pen when a light knock came from the door.

The attractive staffer's head appeared around the door as it eased open and she said, "Senator, you—"

Chapman didn't look up to ogle the woman as he normally did. In a harsh voice, he said, "Not now. You handle it, whatever it is."

The brunette withdrew and closed the door.

Gulping the scotch, the senator then scribbled on the notepad, trying to determine what to tell Madison. He would rehearse what he planned to say to him in order to sound convincing. His hand shook, making his notes difficult to read. He was unaccustomed to planning and making decisions on his own. Realizing he was a prostitute, he was in unfamiliar territory. Always before, his pockets were stuffed with money and someone told him what to do. This time he was making the decisions and the payoff was his life. Chapman was terrified he was about to be dealt a hand of aces and eights.

Chapman hustled to check with a few key people and made a number of phone calls demanding updates. When three o'clock rolled around, he called Madison back as instructed. As was his custom, the senator provided him with a summation of the report. The written version would follow by FedEx.

Madison's words came hard. "Why didn't you tell me about the British ship or the Israeli's plan for Tartus? I told you I wanted information and anything else that I should know about."

At the onset of the conversation, Madison derailed Chapman's planned narrative and he was thrown off track. His answers were vague, and he struggled with answering the first question. "I, well…the British were not forthcoming with the information until the operation was complete. They coordinated with Kenworth. It was all kept quiet. I was—"

"Lazy?" Madison interrupted. "Get your fat ass in gear and push them. I need information. Are you going to whine about the Israelis as well?"

"The relationship between the US and Israel is strained right now. The president and prime minister aren't speaking much these days. They are slow-walking information exchange. I found out about the HMS *Bulwark* stopping the freighter and the Israeli's raid on Tartus after they completed their missions, probably after you did. I did find out that Kenworth was calling the shots and coordinating both operations. He's your key."

"Your information is a bit flawed," Madison said, his frustration growing. "Kenworth may have been coordinating, but approval would have gone through NATO channels. Kenworth would have sought approval through SOCOM. You should have known about that. Israel doesn't do anything without US approval."

"I know, but I—"

With unmistakable anger, Madison shouted, "Fucked up? What's the deal with Gareth? What's he wanting?"

With a trembling hand, Chapman wiped the sweat from his forehead. "He wants you to do a job for him. He thinks if there's a major incident in the US, it will guarantee Jenny's election. He wants you to bring one of the nukes into the US and set it off when and where he says."

Madison replied, his tone cold, "Is he trying to set me up? He was pushing the CIA to assassinate me. Now he wants me to team up with him? I'm not buying it."

Chapman's voice broke when he replied, "Oh, no Bart. No, he's serious. Before, he thought you were going to ruin Jenny's chances of getting elected. That's all been settled."

"You're a terrible liar, Senator. If I did accept Gareth's assignment, it would be on my terms. I choose the time. What's the target?"

"I don't know."

"Information, Senator. You get me what I've asked for and be damn quick about it. Don't leave anything out this time."

The phone connection went dead before Senator Chapman could say another word. He upended his glass, then splashed it full of scotch again.

———— ✦ ✦ ✦ ————

Tuesday, June 7, 2016
Northwest of Damascus
Syria-Lebanon Border

In the rugged, mountainous terrain northwest of Damascus on the Syrian border, Max, Danya, Andy, and four special forces soldiers rendezvoused with two American YPG fighters. The four commandos were all that the S3 of the special forces forward operational base could send along with Max.

YPG had sent word back to the S3 that Dave and Sandy had located what Max was looking for. The two were on a hill overlooking a Bedouin herder's camp on the Syria-Lebanon border. In the message, grid coordinates were provided and a brief outline of the situation.

Chugs had talked to the YPG commander after Max and Danya were back in the hands of Americans. During that conversation, the commander had told him about Max's mission to locate the stolen nukes. Not long after the failed mission on the suspected bomb lab in Aleppo, YPG captured two ISIS fighters. The YPG interrogators learned from the two captives that one of the nukes was destined for Israel, carried by fighters disguised as Bedouins herding sheep. The YPG commander sent the two American YPG fighters to locate the suspected herd.

After a couple of false leads, Dave and Sandy had started following a herd of sheep south of Homs. From what they could safely observe, the indications caused them to believe it was the correct flock. The drove skirted the Damascus-Aleppo highway, staying in the valleys as it headed south. At the small village of Al Nabk, the flock turned southwest along the valley to their current location. For over a week of riding donkeys, they followed the herd at a safe distance. The Bedouin herder kept pushing his animals south, stopping only for water and camp for the night. As they neared other herds or villages, the older Bedouin man sold or traded sheep for goats.

Meandering herds of goats or flocks of sheep were a common sight. No one paid any attention to the old man and the six young men with him. They bothered no one and kept to themselves. Two of the young men rode on donkeys ahead of the herd. Two others walked alone with the animals, keeping them together and moving. The old man rode one of the camels, and two other men led a camel loaded with their belongings. By the time they veered to the southwest, they were herding only goats—common in the mountainous terrain.

The Bedouins made their camp where three ridges came together to form a bowl-shaped area. It provided them cover and made it easier to corral their goats for the evening. The mountain blocked the wind, but the temperature at that altitude of over thirty-five hundred feet dropped to forty-five degrees overnight. Under the cool, partly cloudy sky, the camp kept a small fire burning to help ward off the nighttime chill. One man appeared to be awake in the camp, stoking the fire and keeping watch.

Dave had established his observation position on the north ridge overlooking the camp approximately a hundred meters below. Sandy provided security below the ridge and waited for Max and his team. When he arrived, Sandy led them to the military crest of the ridge to meet with Dave.

The team closed in on Dave, then he briefed them on the situation. "There are seven men altogether," he said in a low voice, then pointing with his hand, continued. "They have the one tent beyond the fire. They act relaxed and unconcerned. One man usually tends the fire and keeps watch. They rotate about every two hours."

Max looked over the camp through night-vision goggles. "Have you seen the warhead? What weapons do they have?"

"No, sir, I haven't seen it," Dave replied. "It looks like each of the men is carrying a Kalashnikov under their robes. They try to be discreet with them. They do have something that could be the warhead. They keep it wrapped in blankets and carry it on a camel. They unload it each night and put it in their tent. The next morning, they reload it on the camel. I understand the warhead weighs about two hundred ninety pounds."

Max looked at Dave, then nodded. "That's right."

"What I see them carrying in the blanket is about twelve inches in diameter and I'd guess about thirty to thirty-six inches long. Kinda hard to tell from a distance. It's heavy, and they struggle with it. I think that could be it."

"Sounds like you've identified what we're looking for," Max said as he snugged his shemagh around his neck. "Have you seen any other fighters or people nearby who could support these seven?"

"No, sir."

"Have you seen them using any radios?"

"No, sir."

Max looked at the others along the ridge. "I don't like it. It's too easy. Is it possible they spotted you and Sandy following them?"

Dave dropped his eyes to the ground and paused. After a moment, he replied, "I guess it is possible, but I don't think so. They haven't acted like they spotted us."

Max coordinated with everyone on the plan and issued last-minute instructions. He also reminded them to watch for anything unusual as it could be a trap. "If it is," he said, "remember, the rally point is back down the ridge, in the ravine where it begins to curve."

Each one of them nodded. A final check of communications was made, then they adjusted their night-vision goggles.

Max turned toward Andy and said, "I saw you limping. Your leg is bothering you. After it starts, you stay here with Danya and cover us."

He sent one of the special forces soldiers back down the hill with Sandy to provide security, then spread the others out along the ridge with a special forces soldier on each flank and one in the center.

Dave returned to his position on the ridgeline. As he lay beside a large boulder, he snugged the shemagh around his neck and pulled up the collar on his jacket, then rubbed his gloved hands together to warm them.

Max looked to his right and saw Danya shiver as she lay along the rocky ridgeline. She had found her position in a depression with large stones to her front. He studied the camp again for a few moments. The lone young man, oblivious to what was about to happen, poked the fire. The flames rose and shed more illumination around the camp. Max had to turn away as the increase in light washed out his vision through the goggles. There was no other activity in the camp. He shot a glance to those on his right and then left to ensure they were in position. All signaled back to him they were ready.

Although Dave was confident that he was following the fighters with the stolen warhead, Max wanted to make sure he wasn't about to assault an innocent herder if he could help it. Killing innocent people would cause him a lot more problems and could derail his attempt to recover the rest of the warheads. If they were innocent victims, Max's legal problems would be insurmountable. He would be convicted in the media before any trial could be convened. It would also be bad for SOCOM and cost the careers of Chugs and the commander. Max had instructed Dave—because of his command of Arabic—to address the camp and seek permission to enter. He was to seem friendly but warily respectful. Dave pointed out to Max that he didn't know the local dialect and the men in the camp would recognize he was an American.

Max was well aware that the Bedouins would naturally be on the defensive when Dave called out to them. If the occupants of the camp were legitimate herders, they would be suspicious of anyone approaching them, especially at night. That was understandable because, as everyone knew, the country was filled with bandits, terrorists, corrupt officials, and military. Even fleeing refugees could pose problems for a herder.

Dave and the commando on Max's left were to enter the camp to inspect it when given permission. The rest of them would stay in position overlooking the camp as a security precaution. Of course, if the herders were actually fighters, they would try to defend themselves and their cargo. They could start shooting at any moment.

Max looked to Dave and saw the tension on his face, then nodded for him to call out to the camp.

Dave brushed dirt from his lips, then yelled to the camp below, "In the camp, we are friendly and want to enter."

Hearing the voice in the darkness, the drowsy man sitting by the fire jolted awake. He remembered the instructions that were drilled into him before they set out on their journey. The bewildered man jumped up, looked around, then darted into the tent. Within a few moments, he returned and replied in Arabic, "What do you want from us?"

At that moment, Andy, looking through night-vision goggles, spotted the others sneaking out the rear of the tent. He spoke into his headset just loud enough for Max to hear, "They're slipping out the back of the tent."

Max looked to his right and spoke into his headset, directing the special forces soldier on his far right to follow them. As he turned his attention back to the camp, he saw the lone man reach down, bring up his Kalashnikov, and fire off a quick burst. His attempted heroic actions of killing infidels and giving the others the opportunity to escape were to no avail.

As soon as the man made a threatening move, the special forces sergeant next to Andy fired his M4 carbine. A hole appeared in the guy's head, and blood spurted out as he fell backward. Max directed his team to focus their fire on the fleeing men. The hail of fire claimed three of them. Three others managed to escape into the ravine formed by an intersecting ridge.

To this point, the men had played their part as Bedouins. It had appeared that they fled in the face of the Americans. The typical response would be to rush into the camp since all seven men had been accounted for. The invitation had been offered.

Max looked over the situation, studying the tent, their escape route, and the area they'd picked for their camp. He looked left, then right to check each of his people. They began to relax their weapons as they anticipated Max's signal to advance into the abandoned camp. Two muffled shots penetrated the crisp night air, alerting Max's team. The sound of the shots came from beyond the campsite and were answered by an automatic burst. The team once again got low to the ground and focused their attention, ready to fire, in the direction of the ravine. They had no way of knowing if it was reinforcements to the fighters that withdrew from the camp or the one special forces commando taking out the three men. The radio signal between the commando following the three who had escaped was blocked by the ridge and low area of the ravine he entered. Max didn't have to tell his team to prepare for a counterattack, but he did.

Within a few moments, the harrowing sound of subdued gunfire reached them once again. Then silence returned like the slamming of a door.

Max checked his people, then raised and motioned for Andy and the special forces sergeant next to him to accompany him into the camp. As Danya stood, Max turned to her and said, "Wait here and cover us." He started to step down the hill without waiting for her response.

Overtaking the camp is too easy, he thought. *Just what the fighters want us to do—go into the camp and make an easy recovery of the warhead. One of Madison's traps.* Max suspected that since two of the warheads were recovered, Madison and his Arab employers might have instructed their fighters to set the bomb to go off if anyone attempted to recover it. Max stopped and shouted into his radio, "No, get back! It's a trap. The rally point." Then in a loud voice and waiving his arm, motioning to go back down the ridge, he commanded, "It's a trap! Take cover at the base of the ridge. Move!"

Hearing Max's command, the others started down the backside of the rocky ridge. Max grabbed Danya's arm, tugging her along as he started down. Kicking up dirt and rocks, everyone scrambled as fast as they could, not knowing what to expect or when it might go off. They were aware of their mission to prevent and recover a nuclear warhead before it could enter Israel. They also knew that an ISIS bomb scientist had worked on the warheads, converting them into functioning bombs. There was no way they could know if this was one of the nukes set to go off. All indications were that it was the one destined for a target in Israel. If it was one of the nukes, it would take a miracle for them to survive the blast, and even then, they would have to contend with the radiation.

Since the herder set up his camp in the bowl-shaped area, it was possible that most of the blast would be directed upward more than out because of the terrain, like a shape charge. However, there would still be a tremendous blast, blowing out much of the ridge and throwing dirt and rocks into the air—a very lethal place.

Sandy and the special forces commando with her looked back up the slope as they heard Max's shouts. Seeing them, not knowing what the danger was, the two began running to safety. Sandy looked back, searching for her battle buddy. Finally, she saw him scrambling down behind one of the other commandos. As Andy shuffled down the slope, he lost his balance and fell head over heels. The sergeant right behind him slowed, reached down, grabbed Andy by the shirt, and tugged him along as Andy tried to stand. Max and Danya reached the base of the ridge and ran into a ravine where it began to curve. They flattened on the ground. The sergeant, still tugging on Andy, landed close to them. Dave found his spot next to Sandy, followed by the commando with him, then the other sergeant landed.

They lay prone with their heads tucked under their arms and waited. Not a one of them was an atheist at that moment—they each said a prayer and prepared for what might happen.

Then a bright flash lit up the night sky.

Eyes squeezed shut in anticipation of what would reach them next.

CHAPTER 23

Tuesday, June 7, 2016
Special Forces Forward Operational Base
Northern Syria

C ONSTANT CONTACT WAS maintained between the S3 and Max's team. Because of the sensitivity of the nuke and that Max reported directly to Matherson, the S3 was to report significant events to the general. As usual, the S3 shelter buzzed with activity as other missions were ongoing. Although the tempo was high, order was maintained and each soldier responded to the S3 as required.

A sergeant approached the S3 and handed him the satellite phone. "General Matherson, sir."

After the usual greeting, the major began his quick brief to the general. "The team linked up with the two YPG mercenaries. They are set up on a ridgeline overlooking the Bedouin herder's camp below. Max said that it appears the herder has a device. They haven't actually seen it. They have identified seven men with Kalashnikovs. Max's last message said they are preparing to enter the camp."

"Did he say if there were any other people in the area that could support them?" Matherson said.

"They haven't seen any others. The camp has turned in for the night and one man is on guard, tending a fire."

The two talked for several more minutes. The S3 detected a hint of anxiety in the general's voice.

"Call me just as soon as you hear from Max."

"Yes, sir." The major ended the call.

Tuesday, June 7, 2016
Northwest of Damascus
Syria-Lebanon Border

There was no sound. Waiting, fear palpable in the air, Max eased his eyes open to see Danya, her arms still covering her head. Raising his head, he saw the others on the ground. There had been no nuclear explosion. One by one each of the others raised their heads and looked around. Seeing each face, he knew they were thinking the same as him. Everyone appeared unscathed. A dust cloud hung above the ridgeline, illuminated by the dull reflection of flickering light indicating a fire burned in the former camp.

A low-order explosion? Max thought. *One of Madison's traps?*

If it had been a low-order explosion, meaning that the nuclear bomb didn't function properly, that could be in their favor. However, radioactive material would be scattered around the area, making a hazardous environment—one they weren't prepared to deal with. If it was a malfunctioning nuke, that would account for another one of the warheads and indicate that the bomb scientist hadn't perfected his conversion. If not, they still had four to find.

Max rose to his feet and called out, "Is everyone all right?" As soon as the last one of them confirmed they were unharmed, he said, "Let's go."

His next priority was to investigate the camp and determine what type of explosion had occurred. He looked to his right and motioned, then to his left, indicating for the two sergeants to cover their flanks as they ascended the hill. Max knew the fighters would return to see the damage their bomb caused. He didn't know if the one special forces soldier was able to kill the three men who'd escaped into the ravine or not. If the soldier did kill them, it would take quite a while for Madison to send someone to inspect the damage.

At the military crest of the ridge, Max halted their advance. They crawled into position at the top to observe the campsite below without being seen. Although it was nautical twilight and visibility was improving, Max observed the camp with his night-vision goggles to keep his team from wandering through a radioactive area.

The campfire had been blown out, scattering burning firewood across the site. The first gunshots had spooked the animals. One of the camels was dead, and several goat carcasses lay scattered about, all of them still smoldering from the blast. The other animals had made it to safety by the time of the explosion. Remnants of the tent—strewn about—burned. A large hole in the ground occupied the spot where it once stood. The stench from what was left of the campsite rose up the ridge to meet them. The air was thick with the pungent odor of the smoldering carcasses, burning cloth from the tent, and chemicals, with a hint of sulfur from the bomb materials. From the signature left in the dirt by the explosion and absence of any of the nuclear components, Max was able to determine that the blast was not caused by a low-order nuclear explosion but by conventional high explosives. Madison's trap. As he panned the goggles, he saw the one commando emerge along the route the fighters had taken as they exited out the back of the tent.

Max spoke into his headset to the soldier, "Are you okay? Did you get 'em?"

"I'm okay, sir," came the reply. "I took care of the three who ducked into the ravine. Good to hear your voice. I got concerned when I heard the blast."

"We're going to start down the ridge and join you. Be careful, they could've left a few booby traps."

"Roger. I'll start inspecting what's left of the camp."

Max directed the three special forces soldiers and Sandy to take up positions along the ridgeline and provide security in case the fighters returned. Max rose and looked to Andy and Danya, then glanced in the opposite direction to Dave. "Spread out along the ridge and let's have a look at what's left of the camp. Be careful and watch for booby traps." Max led them carefully down the slope where they joined the other special forces soldier methodically searching through the debris of the former camp.

As the four reached the base of the hill, they began their examination of what was left of the site. Cautiously, they looked under the remains of the tent or any other item that could possibly conceal a booby trap, bomb fragments, or any other intelligence.

The sun was well above the peaks by the time Max and his team finished inspecting the camp and collecting intelligence. The fragments revealed a high-explosive bomb meant as a trap for Max and his team.

"Madison's ruse almost worked. If we had taken his bait, we'd be like that poor old camel, ripped to shreds." Max pointed to the remains of the mutilated carcass.

Madison's scheme had diverted Max's attention. For over a week, Dave and Sandy had endured riding donkeys through the hot and dangerous Syrian landscape. Max had been lured to the Bedouin camp but hadn't taken the bait to enter it. Otherwise, he and his team would have been added to the seemingly unending list of casualties in this part of the world.

Not wanting to waste any more time there, Max and his team returned to the forward operating base. It was the next afternoon before he was able to get in touch with Chugs and give him his report.

"Madison's elaborate deception was smart, typical for him," Max said. "He used a twelve-inch by thirty-six-inch piece of steel pipe stuffed with high explosives, nuts, bolts, and scraps of metal to simulate the warhead. It was heavy and about the size of the warhead. They kept it covered to make it look like they had the real thing. It was quite convincing. Andy suspects that the herder was keeping in communication with someone as the flock moved south, while trading or selling the sheep for goats as he moved. Andy thinks each stop was prearranged and is already working on that theory."

"Good," Chugs replied. "The Israelis found the body of Madison's girlfriend, Maurine Rowen, in a vacant building in Beirut. They'd lost her between the airport and the hotel where Madison had reservations. She was stabbed."

"Damn!" Max replied, frustrated. "Do you think Madison killed her? Any sign of him in Beirut?"

"No sign," Chugs said. "The Israelis think he killed her, but so far, no proof. I believe it's likely he did. We're getting close to him. The pressure is on, and he'll make a mistake."

"He doesn't leave loose ends and probably knew the Israelis picked her up," Max said. "That made her a liability. I agree. I just hope he makes that mistake soon, and before he can move the other warheads. Any leads on Çakmak yet?"

"Nothing solid yet," Chugs replied. "Tell Andy to look hard in the Damascus area."

"Yes, sir. Have you come up with something?"

"I'm not sure at this point." Chugs sounded cautious. "It could be nothing. I got a call from the NSA Director. A call was made to the US from Damascus, and he is requesting permission to unmask the person."

Max said, "I'm sure calls are made to the US from Syria all the time. What has raised the flag on this particular one?"

"It was made to a US person." Chugs paused. "The US person's number is a Washington DC number, area code 202."

"Are you thinking it could be Madison?" Max asked.

"It crossed my mind," Chugs replied. "It's too early to tell. I just wanted to give you a heads-up. The NSA Director told me there is a lot of pushback from the CIA. Most of the government is in election mode and nothing's getting done."

— ♦ ♦ —

Friday, June 10, 2016
Senator Archibald Chapman Residence
New York, New York

Senator Chapman was hosting another black-tie, high-profile fundraising reception for Jenny. Among the notable politicians, high-dollar contributors, Hollywood celebrities, key campaign staff, and media were the usual inner circle of the Gareth campaign. The men were traditionally dressed in tuxedos. Several of them appeared to push the limits of their waistcoats' fabric. Archie was no exception. He looked like a walrus with his prominent belly. The women wore varying types of evening gowns. The slenderer and more well-preserved ones tended toward plunging necklines. All of them used the opportunity to display their prized jewelry. Jenny wore beige palazzo pants that looked like they were the latest fashion from Omar the Tentmaker.

Approximately one hundred people had already filled the residence and the number continued to rise, overflowing onto the patio behind the house. A string quartet was off to one corner of the main room, a pianist played in an adjoining room, and a guitarist strolled around the patio. The catering staff refilled glasses nonstop with champagne. For those who preferred liquor, two dedicated bartenders provided a wide selection of scotch and bourbon. Servers circulated with silver trays of hors d'oeuvres through the mass of people crammed into the senator's house. Chapman had spared no expense in entertaining the guests. Only the best was served at the party, ranging from stuffed mushrooms to canapés with red and black caviar to assorted seafood delicacies. He hadn't overlooked the assortment of pastries either.

Everyone had an agenda, and the Gareths were no exception. The guests jockeyed for positions and favors. Both went hand in hand.

The consummate host, Stew worked the room, gripping and grinning, ensuring the guests were welcomed and had the chance for a few words with such a great man. After all, he was the main attraction, and Jenny was the second act. He was seen by everyone, and those who had not yet had the opportunity to press the flesh with him would eventually. At a quick glance of the crowd, he noted that everyone was engaged and sucking down the drinks and food nonstop as Jenny moved from person to person with the skill of a commando.

Jenny is doing fine, he thought. *Time to meet with the boys.* His gaze landed on the grandfather clock, and he noted the time. *Can't get carried away and lose track of time. Gotta get back in the room before she gets soused.*

Stew caught Archie's attention and with a slight nod of his head, his eyes shot toward his office, the signal it was time for the meeting. Archie went about his appointed errand of notifying the others to meet in his office, stopping en route to his office to fill a plate of hors d'oeuvres and pastries.

The last to enter the office, Stew closed the door behind him and took his seat in the vacant chair of the group surrounding the coffee table. He picked up one of the cigars from the humidor on the table and lit it, then encouraged Wes Brock, Aaron Fitzgerald, Archie Chapman, and Nassar to have one. Next, he poured two fingers of Garrison Brothers bourbon into a glass and motioned to the bottles of liquor on the table. "Help yourself," he said.

Although he appeared relaxed and cordial, the others remained cautious.

After taking a few minutes to cover some details of the campaign and ensure his key people were prepared for their upcoming speeches, Stew made a few suggestions and approved a couple of small, insignificant changes. Next, he covered the latest poll numbers. Compliments were dished out on their performance of keeping the news coverage positive and promoting Jenny.

Stew sipped his bourbon, leaned back, and said, "Archie, how're we doing on a replacement for Trent? It's been about three weeks."

Having taken a mouth full of chocolate tart, Archie covered his mouth with a napkin, chewed a little faster, then struggled with Stew's question. He swallowed and said, "Working on it, Stew. I thought we had a couple of candidates, but they both had too much baggage. I didn't think we could clean it up. I have another meeting on Monday with two more."

"Is the acting CIA director…Jonathan Wellington on your list?" Stew asked, then sipped his bourbon.

"Yes, he's one of the two I'm meeting with on Monday."

Stew nodded, then looked to Nassar. "What's going on with Madison? Do you need to offer him more money? We're getting short on time." He puffed his cigar.

"He is skeptical." Nassar sipped his bourbon. "Al-Ghazāli tells me that Madison believes you want to set him up."

Stew's eyes narrowed. "Didn't he tell him what I want, and it's not a setup?"

Nassar nodded. "He did. Al-Ghazāli tried to convince him, but Madison thinks your plan is bizarre. He said that something like that must be on his terms. He picks the time and place. Otherwise, no deal."

Wes, Aaron, and Archie breathed a sigh of relief and took a sip of their drinks, relieved that Madison had declined Stew's offer.

With a serious expression, Wes raised his index finger and said, "Stew, Jenny has the election wrapped up. Do we really need to create a disaster to get her in? Something like this is bound to get out."

Stew's face flushed and, through gritted teeth because guests overhearing shouting would not be wise, said, "God damn it, Wes! Are you on the team or not? We're going to win this election one way or another. This won't get out. We control it, and it'll be buried forever. If someone isn't loyal, we get rid of 'em. We're doing this. You understand?"

Wes's jaw tightened as he nodded.

Stew took a gulp of bourbon, his face revealing the stoutness of the drink. "Damn it, Nassar." He struggled to control his temper. "Okay, we could use one of the cartels to bring it in and explode it. What'll it take?"

"I do not know," Nassar replied. "I must consult with al-Ghazāli. I know it will be most expensive. I was informed that two of the nuclear warheads have been recovered."

"That's what I was told too," Stew replied.

"I was told by al-Ghazāli two days ago that a trap was set to get Kenworth but it failed."

Stew started to put the cigar between his lips but stopped. His gaze darted to Wes. "Did you know about that? Has it been verified? You didn't tell me."

Wes cleared his throat before answering, "I just found out this morning. Kenworth—"

"Kenworth, shit!" Stew said, then he stuck the cigar into his mouth. "What the hell's going on? The Turks and Trent Weldon's people couldn't get him. Now I learn that al-Ghazāli's people couldn't get him either. Why's he still running around?"

Nassar sipped his bourbon. "When Kenworth made it to the special forces camp, President Kağan pulled his team back. He was afraid that if something went wrong, he didn't want Turkey implicated."

"If something went *wrong*? Hell, it's going wrong now! Wes, what's the story on the CIA's Ops team?" Stew bit into the cigar. "Weldon couldn't get him with a Predator, and his team couldn't get him either. He had a contractor that was supposed to do the job before he was killed. Get on 'em and get 'em after Kenworth. If he gets the warheads back, that could be a problem. We'll also miss our chance for a national emergency."

Wes glanced to Aaron and then back to Stew. "When Trent was killed, my understanding is that the initiative stalled."

Aaron's gaze roamed over the others. "Nassar, there're four left. Where are they?"

"I do not know where they are." Nassar sipped his drink.

"I mean, who has 'em?" Aaron replied.

"The Brotherhood has one, but I do not know who has the others."

With the cigar between his first two fingers and holding his bourbon, Stew pointed to Wes and said, "Start looking over SOCOM's shoulder. Keep a close eye on 'em. Get in the loop on each of their moves. You may want to tell them that the president is very nervous about the stolen nuclear weapons. High priority and all that shit. Say all the right words. But be careful and don't let them figure out what you're doing. We need one of those nukes."

Wes nodded. "Yes, sir."

Stew picked a piece of tobacco from his lips. "It just occurred to me…Archie, after you talk to Jonathan Wellington, tell him I want to meet with him. I want a backbrief from you as soon as you conclude your meeting with him."

Archie sipped his drink, then replied, "Okay. What's on your mind?"

Gesturing with his glass, Stew said, "We use him. Right now, he's a second stringer. I want to see how he cooperates. I want him to get the contractors energized and go after Kenworth. If Madison doesn't want to cooperate, he gets rid of Madison too. Aaron, you and the acting director identify one of the cartels and find out what it'll take for them to do the job for us. If he screws it up, he's out." Stew shifted his gaze between Wes and Aaron, then said, "You guys got it?"

They each replied with a nod.

Ten minutes later, Stew stood up to indicate the meeting was over. "Time to get back to the party. Let's go press some flesh and bring in some money."

———◆◆◆———

Saturday, June 11, 2016
Abandoned House
Kozan, Turkey

In the small town of Kozan, sixty-eight kilometers northeast of Adana, George met with Erol in an abandoned house overlooking the Kilgen River. The rock and stucco two-story house was a typical middle-income dwelling. It was unknown why the owners had left. It could have been to escape the summer temperatures that reached as high as 104 degrees Fahrenheit. Or it could have been that the inhabitants fled because of the coup d'etat and subsequent purge. It didn't matter to Erol. Out of the way of the political and military facilities but close enough he could still get information, it suited his needs. For now, it was his temporary refuge.

The small vineyard on the side of the house and garden in the rear had been neglected and were overgrown. The house next door was a burned-out shell that Erol used to hide his car. The entire neighborhood, like the rest of the town, was quiet. Everyone stayed inside and only a few brave souls ventured out after dark because of the curfew and martial law that had been imposed.

Erol and George sat across the coffee table from each other in the living room with two candles providing light. A plate of figs, a tin of pistachios, a cool bottle of water, a bottle of raki, and two glasses sat on the table between the candles. The windows were covered for their privacy. Erol poured George a short drink, added water, then did the same for himself.

George lifted his glass and offered a toast. "Thank you. To your health and long life." Their glasses clinked. "You look much better than the last time I saw you." He then took a sip of the anise-flavored liqueur.

"I feel better as well," Erol replied as he picked at the pistachios. "I've been able to bathe and wash my clothes when the utilities come on. They are sporadic, but I make do."

George withdrew an envelope from his shirt and laid it on the table. "I thought you could use some money." He picked up one of the figs as he withdrew his hand.

"I can. I was almost out of lira." Erol sipped his raki. "It is rumored that Lieutenant General Devrim Çakmak is in Brazil. He is supposed to have a place west of Cantá, a small municipality located in the state of Roraima. It is the least populated and northernmost state."

"Brazil?" George questioned.

Erol nodded. "I have heard the same story from two different reliable sources. Cantá is thirty kilometers south of Boa Vista. Çakmak is supposed to have a big estate that backs up to the Branco River."

George's eyes narrowed. "He picked a good place to hide in. No one would think to look for him there. Do you know anything about it or his guards?"

"No. That is all I know." Erol popped another nut into his mouth. "The Muslim Brotherhood is angry that the US has recovered two of the warheads. They want to take one into your country and explode it."

George picked up another fig as he replied, "I know."

Erol lifted his glass and sipped his drink. "When Çakmak left Turkey on the night of the coup, he took two warheads with him to South America. Kağan's people wanted the world to think Çakmak was part of the opposition against them. But in reality, he was doing what the president told him, to take one of the warheads to Brazil. However, Çakmak didn't trust Kağan all that much and thought he might very well be the fall guy if something went wrong with Kağan's plan. He took a second warhead as an insurance policy against that. I do not know if the two warheads are together or stored apart."

George picked up several pistachios and started shelling them. "Where is the Brotherhood keeping the other nukes?"

"I do not know. They keep moving them around. I did hear that the Brotherhood is talking to someone in the US."

George held his gaze on Erol. "I don't think you mean to give it back to the US, do you? Who are they talking with?"

"No, not to return it. It is for inside help getting it to a target in your country. I do not know who they are talking with. Whoever the person is, they tried to make a deal with Madison to do the job, but he turned them down. I was also told that the same person in your country contracted to have Trent Weldon killed last month. All I know is that the person is powerful and high level."

George finished off his drink. "Try and get the name of that person." He paused in thought for a moment, then continued, "I want you to locate the warheads the Brotherhood has and keep track of them. Also, try to locate Madison and keep track of him too."

Erol nodded.

George stood and said, "I'll see you soon. Good luck."

"Thank you," he replied as he stood and shook George's hand. He then escorted George to the door.

George knew Erol's situation was precarious. The expression on his face as George departed told him the task put Erol more at risk—one that could cost him his life. *I hope to God he doesn't get caught,* he thought.

CHAPTER 24

Sunday, June 12, 2016
Special Forces Forward Operational Base
Northern Syria

GEORGE CALLED TO brief Andy and Max via a secured VTC on his meeting with Erol. Seated at a small table in the S3 shelter, the two listened to George as he relayed the information to them. His information provided them a new direction for their search of the four remaining warheads.

"The Muslim Brotherhood is moving theirs around, making it harder to locate," he said. "The indications are that they are still in Syria. He said that General Çakmak is in Brazil with two of the warheads. He heard it from three reliable sources."

"Brazil?" Max replied, making a note on his pad. "No one would think to look for him there. Did he say where?"

"He is supposed to have an estate that backs up to the Branco River, west of Cantá."

Andy searched Google for the municipality on his laptop. Once he had the village displayed, he turned the screen toward Max.

Learning that General Çakmak was in Brazil would allow SOCOM to narrow their search for him and acquire surveillance on him and his estate in short order. They had to verify he did, in fact, have the nukes before any action could be taken. Max believed Çakmak would keep the two warheads secured on his property and not move them around. He was smart and no fool. Taking them would not be a cakewalk.

"Erol told me that the Brotherhood is talking to some senior person in the US for help to get the nuke to the target in the US," George continued. "That same person tried to make a deal with Madison to do the job, but he turned them down. The same person contracted to have Trent Weldon killed last month. I told Erol to try and get the name of the person and find out where the Brotherhood is keeping the warheads."

"A senior person tried to make a deal with Madison to deliver the nuke to a target in the US and contracted to kill the deputy CIA director?" Andy replied, his tone incredulous. "Why would a US person want to set off a nuke in the US?"

"Good question. If we have a senior person wanting to commit treason against the US," Max replied, "we have a big problem."

The VTC lasted another ten minutes. George's incredible information was chilling. Max concluded the call and immediately made plans to call General Matherson. Andy stood and returned to the S2 shelter to organize the notes from the call.

George's comments about someone at a high level pointed back to Bart Madison. A senior political person in the US working to bring a bomb into the country made the recovery much more difficult. Discovering and eliminating an inside threat required immediate action, which was the FBI's responsibility. Madison was good at gaining access to powerful and senior people. He understood them and exploited them. That information signaled to Max that Madison was following the same pattern he'd used three years ago. Madison had been successful then and it would made sense to try it again. However, Max knew he was smart enough to be unpredictable and gave him credit for learning from past experience. But so had Max.

Max believed that the anger of the Muslim Brotherhood over the warheads would cause them to be more aggressive and make mistakes. He was confident that the Brotherhood would continue to push Madison to plan an operation using the device against the Americans. A powerful person in the US could be just the incentive the Brotherhood needed.

———◆◆◆———

Monday, June 13, 2016
Headquarters, US Special Operations Command
MacDill Air Force Base, Florida

It was 0732 hours before Max could get in touch with General Matherson. He gave Chugs the details of the intelligence George had discovered and his recommendations of what was needed to recover the remaining warheads.

"That a high-level US person tried to hire Madison and had Weldon killed is significant—treason at the senior level," Matherson said.

"Do you think that's why we're being blocked and stonewalled by the CIA?" Max replied. "They're a needed resource, but at this point, I don't know who to trust in the Agency—or in the government, for that matter."

"I feel confident we can trust the Defense Intelligence Agency and NSA," the general said.

"Why the hell would a senior US person want to set off a nuke in the US?" Max asked. "I've been trying to figure that one out ever since George told us."

"Good question," Matherson replied. "I'm going to lose a lot of sleep over that too."

"My gut tells me this is Madison."

"I agree with you," Matherson replied. "This puts even more pressure on us getting the warheads back sooner rather than later."

Max and Chugs had been talking on a secure line for almost thirty minutes when Max asked, "Have you identified the US person who received the call from Damascus? Andy's contact in Damascus told him that an American matching Madison's description is there. He's staying at the Sheraton Hotel. It looks like it was Madison who made the call."

"I anticipate finding out today. We'll turn it over to the FBI."

"No, don't turn it over to them. Well, I mean Andy insists we get someone we can trust and not any random agent. He doesn't have a lot of confidence in the bureau right now."

"Okay," Chugs replied. "What're you thinking?"

"Remember the agent who worked with us three years ago?"

"Not really."

"Gail Summers. She was smart, tough, and didn't take shit from anyone. We can trust her. She had an analyst working with her who was good, David Elsworth. We can trust him too. I don't know where they are or even if they're still with the bureau."

"I'll see what I can do, but I won't be able to sit on the information once the person is identified. If we can't get Summers right away, we'll have to deal with what we get."

"I know," Max replied. "I suggest we plant someone close to Madison but not from the Agency. If we could take him alive, we might be able to get whomever the Brotherhood is talking with in the US and who killed Trent Weldon. Risky, I know."

"Those types of operations are risky at best. If the plant gets into trouble, help must be available immediately. That'll be a big hurdle."

"I know. I have outlined my concept in the briefing material I am sending you. You'll have it in a few minutes."

"I'll look at it and discuss it with the commander. Thanks, Max. I'll be in touch."

— ◆ ◆ ◆ —

Wednesday, June 15, 2016
Gareth Residence
New York, New York

Nassar sat in the wingback chair across from Stew's desk. After several minutes of pleasantries, the two got down to business.

Stew sipped his coffee, then said, "What's it gonna take to bring one of the nukes in and set it off?"

Nassar sipped his tea, then withdrew a folded sheet of paper from his jacket. "From al-Ghazāli's lips." He laid the paper on the desk and pushed it toward Stew.

As he slid the paper closer, Stew held his gaze on Nassar, then picked it up and read it. His face flushed. In a slow motion, he raised his eyes and lowered the paper back to the desk. "That's a lot of money just to turn the device over to Los Zetas."

"There are many expenses to consider."

Through gritted teeth, Stew said, "Damn it, Nassar! That's too late. I told you when it needed to be here."

"Al-Ghazāli knows when you wanted it. However, it cannot be delivered before that date. Transportation must be planned and coordinated. Al-Ghazāli says there is a faster route, but it has more risk and will cost more."

"How much more?"

Nassar slid a second piece of paper across the desk.

"The date is not that much better. God damn it, Nassar! You guys are robbing me." Stew sipped his coffee. "I'll call you tomorrow with my answer."

Nassar nodded, then set his cup on the desk and walked out.

Stew picked up the phone and dialed Chapman's office. "Archie," he said as soon as Chapman answered. "I just talked to Nassar. They can't deliver the package for almost two months, and they want a fortune. We've already missed one date, and I don't want to miss another one."

"So, what's the plan now?"

"I did have a good meeting with the acting director of the CIA. He's on board. I have also talked to Los Zetas, and they agreed to make the delivery. They want money up-front. As soon as I can work out a deal with al-Ghazāli, half of the delivery cost is due. I don't trust just anyone to take that much money to them. I might want you to take it. You can slip in there and out better than I can. Fly on a diplomatic passport, 'cause if I go, too many questions will be asked."

Chapman sat back in his chair as the blood drained from his face. He started to speak, "Are…are you saying you are accepting al-Ghazāli's terms? What about Madison?"

"I'm working on it."

"Stew, I think there is another option. It's safer, and we can milk the publicity for a long time."

"What is it?"

"Get Madison on board, and when he is on the way, nail him. Jenny can play up the recovery of the device and killing a traitor. Think of the publicity. That way you get rid of a liability."

"I don't know. We'd still lose a great deal of money. I was going over the latest poll numbers, and Jenny is running neck and neck. She should have at least a ten-point lead by now."

"Oh, hell, Stew, she's got it. You know as well as I do that poll numbers are just a snap in time and will change with the wind. We'll get a positive news story out and the numbers will change. We can squeeze the donors for more money, especially if we can focus them on another shiny object." Archie wiped the sweat from his brow. "I'll check around and see if we can come up with some more dirt on Jenny's opponent, or we'll just invent something new. We get the news spun up and they'll have all the little old ladies giving up their last social security checks to Jenny's campaign. We'll play it up that the campaign needs more money now that we are entering the homestretch." He sat back in his chair.

"I'll think about it. But I still believe the disaster angle will give Jenny the advantage. It could be planned to take out Jenny's rival as well. Problem solved."

Friday, June 17, 2016
Sheraton Damascus Hotel
Damascus, Syria

A woman strode into the bar, her heels tapping on the parquet floor. The bar was two-thirds filled with patrons seated at tables. A hush came over the room as the men's eyes caught sight of her. Her skirt slid up her thigh as she settled in on the barstool and crossed her legs. Her gold bangle bracelets tinkled as she placed her arms on the marble top. When the bartender approached her, she ordered a drink in a soft voice that only he heard. Within a few moments, the bartender returned and placed a cocktail napkin in front of her, then set the drink on it. With a delicate touch, she stirred the beverage with the small plastic sword, then laid the sword on the napkin.

Bart Madison stepped into the bar and took a seat at a table. He saw the bartender standing behind the bar with a look of anticipation and motioned to him. As the man approached his table, Bart's eyes landed on the woman sitting sideways at the bar. Her exquisite legs were hard to miss. He glanced around the room and saw that the other men's gazes were fixed on her also.

"What would you like, sir?" the bartender said as he stopped at the table, breaking Bart's trance.

Looking up at the man, Bart said, "Crown Royal Reserve, please." His attention went back to the woman.

With polished French nails, she picked up the sword and pierced the cherry in her drink. Lifting the sword with a tender touch, she placed the cherry between her red, parted lips, then withdrew it as her teeth freed the cherry.

Bart looked around the room again. It was obvious the men were about to break out in a cold sweat. A slight smile emerged on his face as his gaze returned to the woman. She was alone. Her demeanor was relaxed. The former din of the bar returned as the men began to relax or the women accompanying them broke their trance.

Within a few minutes, the bartender set his drink on the table in front of him.

Bart looked at the man and, in a low voice, said, "Thank you. Who's the redhead at the bar?"

The man shrugged. "This is the first time I have seen her. She is nice to look at. I hope she stays for a while."

Bart smiled and nodded. "She *is* easy to look at."

The bartender returned to the bar as Bart's gaze shifted back to the woman. He scrutinized her from toe to nose. There were no obvious bulges indicating a weapon, nor did she have a clutch purse with her. Displaying diamond studs, her ears peeked through auburn curls. No earbuds were visible. She lifted the glass to her lips and sipped the drink. She was in no hurry. Once again, he looked around the room and as far as he could see into the lobby. No one outside the bar area seemed to pay any attention to the woman. It was just those men near him who were about to trip over their tongues. He grasped his drink and napkin, then stepped to the bar, stopping next to the woman.

She shot a glance at him, then returned her attention to her drink.

"Mind if I sit here?" he said as he stood waiting for her response.

Her eyes rolled up to his and she said, "Sit wherever you like." She sipped her drink again.

Bart placed his glass and napkin on the bar, then took the stool next to her. His eyes traveled up from her knees and, when they landed on her lips, he said, "Are you alone?"

Her head turned as she looked around, then back to Bart. When her eyes met his, she said, "Apparently." Her eyes moved to the bartender, who was busy mixing drinks.

"You're an American?" he asked.

Without looking at him, she said, "Another obvious observation. You are too."

He started to speak but just nodded. He was intrigued by this sassy, self-confident woman. *She's gonna be a challenge,* he thought. *But who is she?*

Her eyes, along with the corner of her mouth, rose to his. "Now that we've covered the obvious, names are next. Mine's Cheryl."

"You read my mind. I'm Bart."

"No, that's just the usual next question. Do you have a last name, Bartholomew?"

"Madison, Bart Madison. And yours?"

She sipped her drink. "Cheryl will do for now."

Bart's frustration level began increasing. All he could get from the woman was one- or two-word answers. Most often, the women he approached were always open and talkative. *Maybe I'm losing my touch,* he thought. *It was just Maurine for three years. I'm not giving up yet.*

He watched her lips settle on the rim of the glass as she finished off the drink. He ended his, then asked, "Would you like another one?" He set the glass down.

"Wouldn't say no," she replied with a quick flash of her eyes.

Bart motioned to the bartender for another round. It had been a long time since he was faced with such a difficult time in picking up a woman. After a couple more rounds of single word dialogue, the bartender set fresh drinks in front of them. Bart took a sip, then said, "Would you like to join me for dinner?"

She checked her watch, then a slight smile appeared on her face. "I believe I am previously engaged, Bartholomew."

He'd anticipated the rejection. "It's just Bart," he replied as he stood.

Without a word, she uncrossed her legs. A silky rush was all that was heard in the bar as she stood and walked out.

— ◆ ◆ ◆ —

Cheryl locked both locks on the hotel door behind her. She kicked off her shoes, opened a bottle of water, and sat at the desk. She retrieved her phone from the safe and powered it up. As soon as it was ready, she began tapping the keys. "Contact made. Will make myself available again tomorrow afternoon." As soon as the message was sent,

Major Scarlett Marsden, military intelligence, placed the phone on the nightstand and picked up the TV remote. She searched for an English Channel.

Max and his team infiltrated the Beit Zafran Hotel four-tenths of a mile away from the Sheraton Hotel. They were to provide support to Major Marsden. If she got into trouble, they would take appropriate action to extract her. They were to only go after Madison if their success was assured and if he could be taken alive, without casualties. The intelligence reports revealed that Madison was always accompanied by an armed security detail.

Scarlett was to develop the intelligence on Madison and find out where the warhead was held. It was anticipated that Madison would be a part of any planning to take the nuke to the US, so Scarlett was to keep track of Madison and keep Max abreast of his movements.

In order for her to get close to Madison, Scarlett's cover story for why she was in Syria had to be plausible. Andy and the Defense Intelligence Agency developed the cover that Scarlett worked for UNESCO, World Heritage. Their mission was to encourage the identification, protection, and preservation of cultural and natural heritage around the world considered to be of outstanding value to humanity. Damascus had 125 such monuments from different periods of its history. She was supposed to be an analyst from World Heritage, collecting and updating information on monuments that could be in danger. Her findings would be submitted to the World Heritage Committee who, in turn, would submit them to the Convention Concerning the Protection of the World Culture and Natural Heritage. The threat the war in Syria posed to the monuments was why she was there. Scarlett lived and worked out of the satellite office in Geneva.

Andy, through his assets, was making arrangements for Scarlett to visit a number of the monuments as they anticipated that Madison would eventually use his contacts to check her out and have her followed to verify who she was. Her cover had already been established. If someone at the senior level in the US government was aiding the Muslim Brotherhood, they certainly had the ability to check *Cheryl* out. As soon as she divulged her information, those wheels would begin to spin. Any slip in her cover story would end her life. Max and his team would maintain surveillance on her and remain as close to her as possible without being detected. Even though she kept in constant communications with Max on a planned schedule, there would be periods of time when they would not be near her.

Scarlett had read the dossier on Madison and knew all about him. That gave her an edge. She was already working on one of his weaknesses—beautiful women. She knew he was deadly and would kill her if he detected the slightest slip. She was as vulnerable as you could get—a beautiful woman in a war-torn Muslim country, unarmed and trying to attract a ruthless killer.

CHAPTER 25

Friday, June 17, 2016
Headquarters, US Special Operations Command
MacDill Air Force Base, Florida

CHUGS LOCATED SPECIAL Agent Gail Summers. The senior agent was on assignment at the southern border working drug and human trafficking. She wasn't told about this temporary assignment prior to her arrival at SOCOM, only to report to the headquarters.

The general's secretary greeted Gail with a smile as soon as she entered the glass doors of the general's office. "You must be Agent Summers?" Helen asked.

A tall blond wearing the typical black slacks, white shirt, and jacket, Gail produced her identification for the secretary.

Before Gail could speak, Helen picked up a folder with an orange cover and said, "This way, please. The general will be with you as soon as our other guest arrives. He wants you to start looking over this material while you wait." She led Gail into the large conference room and placed the folder on the table to indicate where she was to sit. "Would you like some coffee?"

"I would. Thank you," she replied as she slid the chair back, then sat.

Helen smiled and closed the door as she left the room. Within a few moments, she returned and set a cup of coffee in front of Gail. "Let me know if you need anything else," she said, and stepped out of the room and closed the door.

Gail's eyes traveled around the room. She noted the numerous plaques, pictures, and framed memorabilia that decorated the walls. They all told the story of SOCOM's history. Her eyes returned to the top-secret folder before her, and she began reading the summary. The door opened a few minutes later, breaking her concentration. She looked up to see Helen, trying to suppress a grin and holding the door open, then in a flurry, David Elsworth entered the room and stopped. Helen's eyebrows raised. It was a combination of his dramatic entrance and flamboyant choice of shirts—neon, light magenta. Her expression revealed that David was not the typical visitor to headquarters. She closed the door behind her.

In a dripping-sweet voice, David said, "Gail, *dahling*. I didn't know you would be here." He stepped to the table and grasped both of her hands in his. "It is so good to see you. Do you know what this is about?"

Gail's eyes rolled up and she said, "Hello, Sweet Pea. Sit down. No, I don't know what this is about. The secretary gave me this folder to start reading."

David pulled out the chair next to Gail and sat, crossed his legs, and placed his manicured hands in his lap. "This is so exciting. I—"

Gail slid the first page of the summary in front of David. "Start reading."

Major General Matherson entered the room, placed a folder on the table, and took his place at the conference table. After the introductions and greetings, Chugs got down to business. After giving a summary of the background information, he looked at each of them as he said, "Now the reason that you are here. Absolutely everything you have read and will hear is classified at the highest level. NSA intercepted a phone conversation from Damascus to a US person at area code 202. They requested and received the unmasked data on the call. The US person has been identified as Senator Archibald Chapman." Chugs looked at them, allowing a moment for that to sink in. "The call was from a throwaway phone. We believe it was from Bart Madison."

"Wait, General," Gail said with a look of shock sprawled across her face. "He's dead!"

"That's the problem, he isn't. All of this background is in your folder. However, we want to capture Madison alive. Your mission is to get proof that Chapman is working with a US traitor and terrorist. If you can get the senator, he will lead us to Madison. We believe Chapman is just the go-between."

Gail lifted the cup to her lips and sipped. Her expression was unchanged. "Chapman is working on Jenny Gareth's election campaign. This is going to be dicey."

"Yes," Chugs replied. "We don't know who to trust in the government. The CIA has blocked information and even sent a Special Ops team after Max. Deputy SecDef Wes Brock is looking over our shoulder, watching our every move. He could be in on it as well. Lieutenant Colonel Johnston doesn't trust the bureau either. He may be a bit over-cautious. However, we don't know who is involved. Find out. I feel confident that NSA and DIA are not involved."

Chugs spent the next half hour getting them organized and answering their specific questions.

━━━ ◆ ◆ ◆ ━━━

Saturday, June 18, 2016
Sheraton Damascus Hotel
Damascus, Syria

Danya and one of the special forces soldiers, posing as a European couple, finished breakfast at the El Patio Restaurant at the Sheraton. The outdoor restaurant had white linen-draped tables and was decorated with numerous palm trees. Four tables across the open-air restaurant had guests lingering, sipping tea. The morning rush over, the wait staff started making preparations for lunch. Large umbrellas stood erect, shielding the tables from the sun. Danya and her escort had arrived a short time after they were alerted that Madison was having breakfast. The couple had taken a table at a cozy spot across the patio from where he sat and now appeared to ignore the men while taking their time eating. The two seemed to be enjoying conversation that meandered like most couples—nothing important, just idle chat about the city, country, food, and travel.

Danya and the sergeant had placed earbuds on the opposite side from where the three men sat. An eavesdropping microphone was located in Danya's purse, which she had placed in the chair facing the men. The device transmitted the signal to Max's location, where it was recorded. Not only could Danya and her companion hear what was being discussed at Madison's table, they could also communicate with Max.

Seated with Madison was al-Ghazāli and al-Aqrab. The men had noticed the couple when they entered, but nothing signaled alarm. It was a popular international hotel that hosted visitors from all over the world. The most prevalent nationalities at the hotel were Russian, European, and Middle Eastern. Their meal finished, the men drank tea and talked. Their conversation was light but became serious when al-Ghazāli said, "Nassar informed me that we have an agreement to our terms." He then looked to Madison and said, "You must start immediately."

Madison leaned forward in his chair, placing his arms on the table, and said in a stern tone, "I don't like it. I think it is a setup. I am not taking it into the US and detonating it when and where he says. It smells like camel dung to me."

Al-Ghazāli sipped his tea, then said, "It is possible. Nassar informed me that if you do not accept, the CIA will kill you. Perhaps make your arrangements to the border, then let the Zetas deliver it. This is a lot of money, Bart. We will protect you."

"Right," Madison replied, his tone full of sarcasm. "If I agree, at some point I'll need to recon the routes. When you talk to the Zetas, set up a meeting. I'll coordinate the transfer and work out the details myself. Security will need to be worked out as well. Make sure they understand that they do the recon into the US."

Al-Ghazāli nodded. "Anything else?"

Madison shook his head. "Not for now."

Danya said in a low voice, "They're getting ready to leave. I can take Madison out. I have a clear shot."

"No!" came Max's voice in her ear. "We need him alive to get to the warheads."

Danya folded her arms on the table and watched the three men walk out.

— ◆ ◆ ◆ —

Saturday, June 18, 2016
Sheraton Damascus Hotel
Damascus, Syria

As Madison started to leave his breakfast meeting, Cheryl took her place in one of the easy chairs in the lobby, like a single rose on prominent display in the center of a large expanse. She wore a white linen blouse with cuffed sleeves at the elbow, a floral printed skirt, and a colorful emerald scarf draped around her neck. Knowing Madison would be in the lobby soon after breakfast and hoping he couldn't resist the beautiful woman seated alone, her objective was simple—attract Madison.

Andy had coordinated to have one of his contacts on standby to escort Cheryl to the Umayyad Mosque, one of the largest and oldest mosques in the world. He would act as a guide and chaperone for her. Since the mosque was already designated a World Heritage site, she was conducting a site review—a plausible duty for her cover. Although this was only the second encounter between Cheryl and Bart, Max anticipated she might be followed.

Across the lobby from where Cheryl sat, she saw the elevator doors open and Bart with two other men stepped out. With a subtle motion, she slipped the top button of her blouse free. *A little added honey for the trap,* she thought. She pretended to read from her notebook as she watched Bart. As anticipated, he stopped before her.

"Good morning, Cheryl," he said with a smile, looking down at her alluring cleavage.

She looked up and replied, "Good morning, Bartholomew. A surprise to see you this morning."

"I hope it is a pleasant one. It is for me." Bart sat in the chair across from her. "Are you heading out to see some of the sites of Damascus?"

"I'm reviewing the Umayyad Mosque."

"Aah, the Great Mosque of Damascus. A beautiful place."

"And you're off to where?"

"I'm meeting with clients all day."

"Too bad. You could have accompanied me. It might've been a bit boring for you though."

"My invitation to dinner is still open."

"I'll think about it. I might be in the bar about 5:30."

Bart smiled. "See you in the bar, then."

At that moment, another man walked up to Cheryl and said, "I am sorry I am late."

"That's okay," she replied, then looked to Bart. "My chaperone. I've got to go." She stood and walked out with the man.

Bart stood as she did and watched them leave. Curious about the young man who'd met her, he walked to another seating area across the lobby, to a man sitting in one of the chairs reading a paper. In a low voice, he said, "See where she goes."

The man nodded, then stood and walked out of the hotel.

———— ✦ ✦ ✦ ————

Saturday, June 18, 2016
Sheraton Damascus Hotel
Damascus, Syria

With high expectations, Bart entered the bar and was not disappointed. Cheryl sat perched on the barstool the same as she had been the night before—seated sideways with her legs attracting plenty of attention. Three other tables were occupied with men attempting discussions, but their attention kept drifting back to the redheaded woman. Bart stepped to the bar and sat down beside Cheryl.

Without looking at him, Cheryl said, almost sounding annoyed, "Make yourself comfortable, Bartholomew."

His gaze stuck on her legs as he scooted the barstool closer to the bar and said, "Thank you, I will." He looked to the bartender and ordered a Crown Royal Reserve, then returned his eyes to her.

She pierced the cherry in her drink with the plastic sword. With a delicate touch, she raised the skewered cherry to her red, parted lips. Her eyes met his. For a brief moment, there was silence in the bar. Around them, the men stared at her, no doubt envious of Bart. With her teeth, she slid the cherry from the sword, then placed the pick on the napkin. All the men in the room broke out into a cold sweat, including Bart.

"How was your visit to the mosque?" Bart asked.

"I enjoyed it. How was your day?"

"Productive. My clients are moving forward," he said as the bartender set the whiskey on a napkin in front of him.

As she faced Bart, one arm on the bar and the other resting on the back of her chair, she was relaxed. For the next few minutes, she was more talkative, carrying the conversation beyond the simple short sentences of before. The conversation moved to her visit to the mosque. Although Bart had been informed that she did, indeed, go to the mosque, the informant had not followed her inside. His attention was on her, but he also listened for the details that would verify she did tour the mosque.

"Did you see the shrine to John the Baptist?" Bart asked, waiting to analyze her response. "His head is supposed to be buried there."

"I did. The head is believed to have magical powers. They say if you press your head against the metal grill of the shrine, you'll have visions of the future. Before you ask, no I didn't press my head against the grill. The head is also supposed to be in several other places."

"I didn't either," Bart said with a grin. "Where're you—"

"Yes." She looked at him.

"Yes, what?" Bart replied, bewildered.

She tapped his shoulder with her French painted nails. "You want me to accompany you to dinner."

Without speaking a word, Bart finished his drink and stood, then stepped aside so she could stand.

The men's heads at the three tables followed her as Bart led her out. She looped her arm through his as they walked. Reaching the restaurant, the two were seated right away.

The conversation during their relaxed dinner was light and limited mostly to Syrian culture and history. Cheryl turned on her charm and used subtle cues throughout the meal—smiles, eye contact, a slight touch, an occasional dreamy look—all the ammunition a woman uses to attract a man. She had Bart on the testosterone superhighway in no time.

Their main dish was roasted lamb accompanied by small side dishes of makdus, a Syrian salad, hummus, haloumi, baba ganouj, and pita bread. They drank wine with the meal. The entire time, Bart studied the woman, looking for the slightest clue that might indicate she was more than a casual encounter or a threat. He had stayed alive by being cautious and was not about to let his guard down with this beautiful woman now. If she turned out to be a threat, beautiful or not, she would meet the same fate Maurine had. He labored through most of the meal to get Cheryl to talk more about herself and about something other than Syria. He needed to listen to her—any slight error and he would know. Even without a slipup on her part, she still needed to be checked out before he got too close to her. As they started their second bottle of wine, she did become a little chattier. She never asked Bart about himself, leaving him the frontal assault route of asking about her, which he postponed.

The waiter brought out baklava and coffee for their dessert. As soon as he stepped away, Bart sipped his coffee, then deciding it was about time to start probing, he asked, "What brings you to Damascus? It's not one of the top tourists' spots in the world, and the war makes Syria a dangerous place."

Her eyes locked onto his, and she said as she slid her fork down the corner of the pastry, "I guess it's questions time now. You've been dying to ask me all evening, what's a nice girl like me doing in a place like this, right?" She slid the small piece of baklava between her lips, paused to swallow, then continued, "I'll ask you the same thing." She sipped her coffee. "You'll find my job a bit boring. I work for UNESCO, World Heritage. I'm updating the list of National Heritage sites in Syria that are threatened due to the war. The information I submit will go through a couple of committees and end up at the Convention Concerning the Protection of the World Culture and Natural Heritage. Our organization tries to encourage the protection and preservation of cultural and natural heritage considered to be of outstanding value to humanity. We're working to prevent tragedies like what happened to the archaeological site of Palmyra from happening again. The damage the fighters caused is unforgivable."

Bart took a deep breath. "Whew! That's the most you have said in two days. I'll admit that it isn't very glamorous. That's what you meant this morning when you said you were reviewing the Umayyad Mosque."

"That's right." She smiled. "Told you my job seems dull to many. Now, your turn."

"My job isn't glamorous either. Foreign affairs is my specialty. I work with governments on external issues that affect their country. In some cases, the country wishes to influence other countries on their issues. In essence, I provide assistance to countries on certain matters."

She raised her cup as a toast. "Salut!"

Bart followed her move. "Salut." He sipped the coffee, then said, "UNESCO, part of the UN. You must live in New York then."

"No, UNESCO Headquarters is in Paris. I live in Geneva."

Bart smiled. "Are you going to tell me your last name?"

She sipped her coffee again. As she held the cup, looking over the rim, she replied, "Simmons."

Bart nodded. Cheryl Simmons, an American working for UNESCO, living in Geneva was just the info he needed to check into her background.

"Thank you for a lovely dinner, Bartholomew," she said with a smile and a stroke of his arm. "I must call it a night. I've got work to do." She stood and placed her napkin on the table.

As Bart also stood, he said, "The night is still young. Would you like to have a drink, or take a stroll outside and check out the night life?"

"That's very tempting, but I must call it a night."

"Will I see you again?"

"I hope so." She smiled. "I'll be here for a while. I've got a lot of work to do. Perhaps I'll see you tomorrow."

"I'll walk you to your room."

With a gentle touch of her hand to his cheek, she said, "That won't be necessary. Good evening."

She casually stepped out, her heels tapping on the floor. Once she was out of sight of Madison, she picked up her pace. Reaching the elevators, she cautiously checked to ensure she was not being followed. Satisfied she was alone, she pushed the number to her floor and stepped in. When the doors closed, she gave a sigh of relief. The doors opened, and she scanned the hall. Seeing only the vacant hall, she stepped out. Cheryl looked up and down the hall before she stopped at her door. Confident that she wasn't followed, she entered her room and locked the door behind her.

Scarlett retrieved her phone and sat at the desk. She typed the text, "The hook is set." She then typed a summary report and sent it to Max.

Within a few minutes, she received a reply. "Good. Be careful. You were followed to the mosque today. I want you to push it with him. We believe he has an agreement to move the nuke to the US and it could happen any time."

———— + ♦ + ————

Saturday, June 18, 2016
Sheraton Damascus Hotel
Damascus, Syria

In his room, Bart poured a glass of Crown Royal Reserve and then sat and propped his feet on the desk. He sipped the whiskey, set the glass on the desk, picked up his cell, and punched in the number to Senator Chapman's office. As soon as he heard the senator's voice, he said, "I want you to check out someone."

Chapman cleared his throat, took a sip of Glenlivet, and said, "What's the name?"

"A female by the name of Cheryl Simmons. Very attractive redhead. She is supposed to work for UNESCO, World Heritage and lives in Geneva."

"Bart, you know I can't check out a foreigner," Chapman said with a slight tremble in his voice.

"She's not a foreigner," Bart replied, his tone harsh. "She's a US citizen living in Geneva. Twist any arms you need to at the UN or wherever, but check her out."

Chapman took another swallow of his drink, trying to suppress his trembling voice. "Okay, Bart. I'll see what I can do."

"Be damn quick about it!" Bart's reply shot back. "You're late again with your intel update. I told you I wanted it every week."

"I was just about to send it to you."

"Yeah, I bet you were. Give me a quick rundown on what's happening."

The senator withdrew his notes from the desk and took several minutes to tell Bart the significant developments that had transpired since the last update. Items he emphasized were the election and that Jonathan Wellington, acting CIA director, was on board with Gareth. He was being considered for the CIA director position in Jenny's administration. Gareth told the acting director to get the contractors back on Kenworth. The last item he mentioned was the agreement Stew Gareth reached with the Muslim Brotherhood to deliver the nuke into the US. Chapman omitted that Stew Gareth instructed the acting director to get rid of him if he didn't deliver the nuke or that he planned to eliminate him after he delivered it. Wrapping up, Chapman looked over his notes, then said, "That's it, Bart."

Bart heard the senator attack his drink and said, "Are you sure?"

"That's everything, Bart."

"Find out about Cheryl Simmons right away."

CHAPTER 26

Monday, June 20, 2016
Tampa Marriott Water Street
Tampa, Florida

S PECIAL AGENT GAIL Summers punched in the number for David Elsworth.

On the fourth ring, David woke from his sleep and answered the phone. Recognizing it was Gail, he replied with a groggy voice, "Gail, *dahling*."

"Sweet Pea," Gail replied in a tone that would have jarred anyone awake. "Wake up! We've got to get to headquarters right away."

David peered at the clock. "*Dahling,* do you know what time it is? Call me back in an hour."

"Get your ass out of bed and meet me in the lobby in thirty minutes. We have an urgent message waiting for us."

"It's too early. I haven't even had breakfast yet."

"Thirty minutes, Sweet Pea, or I'm coming up to your room and dragging your ass downstairs. You can have coffee and a donut on the way."

Thirty-five minutes later, Gail and David pulled out of the parking garage and turned onto Bayshore Drive heading south to MacDill.

From the passenger seat, David looked at Gail. "What's the message?"

Gail shot a quick look at him and said, "NSA captured another phone call to Senator Chapman. They've sent us a copy of the transcript."

"That's wonderful. Can we stop at that donut shop up ahead?"

Gail wrinkled up the corner of her mouth as she glanced at him. "Yes, Sweet Pea."

As soon as they were back on Bayshore Drive, David bit a piece off his pastry and, with it in the side of his mouth, said, "Did the transcript provide any details?"

Gail sipped her coffee. "I don't know what it says, but they did say it was from Madison and was damning and we need to see it right away."

As soon as the two reached headquarters, they went straight into the SCIF to retrieve the NSA message. It was a summary and the transcript of the call between Senator Chapman and Bart Madison.

The SCIF was quiet except for the slight rush of the air conditioner as it cooled and dried the air. Only one other person was in the room, seated at a computer terminal against the far wall. David looked at Gail across the conference table and said, "Geez, this is bad stuff. I think there's enough here to lock the senator away for a long time."

"He'll raise a big stink too," Gail said as she laid her glasses on the table. "No doubt Gareth will make it tough as well. We've got to brief the general and see if he wants to go for a warrant."

Twenty minutes later, the two were briefing General Matherson on the transcript. "I want our attorney to take a look at this. Chapman is in deep on this, and Madison is relying on him. We've got to have an airtight case against him. I've told the attorney to expect you when we finish."

Gail looked at the general, her face expressionless. "You said you didn't know who you could trust. If I go for a warrant on the senator, the attorney general'll know about it."

"Correct," Matherson replied. "That's one of the things I'll ask our attorney. For now, get with NSA and make sure they keep Chapman's number as a high priority target. We need to keep monitoring him and collect all we can. He might very well give us enough to nab Madison and the nukes before they get to the US."

"Yes, sir," Gail said.

"Do you know anything about this Cheryl Simmons and why Madison wants Chapman to check her out?" David asked.

"Be very careful with that name," Matherson replied. "She's one of our assets that Lieutenant Colonel Johnston put there to get close to Madison. If you come across anything about her or if you suspect she is compromised, get with me right away."

"Yes, sir," David replied.

Matherson turned his attention to David. "Along with the Muslim Brotherhood, start watching the cartels. Madison used Los Zetas the last time. Don't forget about FARC either. They're active again. Remember, Madison worked for them for a time."

David nodded as he wrote on his notepad.

"I'll call Max and brief him on this," the general said.

——◆◆◆——

Tuesday, June 21, 2016
Sheraton Damascus Hotel
Damascus, Syria

Madison, al-Ghazāli, and al-Aqrab ate breakfast in the El Patio Restaurant as they had several times before. As Bart dropped a dollop of yogurt onto his plate, his gaze caught a couple entering the restaurant and sitting several tables away from him. He studied the attractive woman, then her well-fit companion. Although the couple paid no attention to Bart or the men with him, something about them held his attention. *What is it about them?* he thought. *Is it her or him? She's good looking, though.*

His cell phone rang, breaking his trance. It was Chapman's number.

He placed the phone to his ear and said, "Yes, Senator."

"Bart, I have the information on the woman, Cheryl Simmons. She checks out. She does work for the World Heritage."

"Good. Thank you, Senator," Bart replied. "You're up late tonight. Your wife must be out of town."

"No, I had a lot of work to do."

Bart noted the slight quiver in the man's voice. "Your Friday piece on Tuesday? Good for you."

"Oh, no! Work, honest."

Bart chuckled. "Right. Since you're working late, don't forget I am expecting your intel summary."

"I know. I'm working on it."

"Goodbye, Senator." Bart ended the call before Chapman could respond.

Al-Ghazāli made eye contact with Madison and asked, "The senator? Any problems?"

Madison sipped his tea and replied, "Everything is fine. I had him check out someone."

Al-Ghazāli smiled. "Ah, the woman with red hair. And is she acceptable to Bart?"

"Yes, she checks out."

"Who is the woman?" al-Aqrab asked.

"She works for World Heritage. She's over here updating a list of National Heritage sites." He smiled. "Yes. I like her."

"And the woman that just walked in with the man?" al-Aqrab said with a laugh. "I saw you looking at her."

Madison's expression turned serious. "No, there is something about her, and her companion." He looked back to the table where the couple was engaged in conversation. Then he said in a low voice, "I don't like it. Those two were in here before. We need to find out who they are. We should go."

Al-Ghazāli gave a slight nod of his head. "I will put a man on them."

The three men placed their napkins on the table, stood, and walked out.

— ◆ ◆ ◆ —

Tuesday, June 21, 2016
Sheraton Damascus Hotel
Damascus, Syria

Al-Ghazāli, al-Aqrab, and Madison rendezvoused in al-Ghazāli's room. He ushered the two men to the terrace as soon as they arrived. Holding out his hand for them to sit, he said, "Be seated." As soon as they sat, another man brought a tray of tea and set it on the table. "We will know soon about the couple."

Bart sipped his tea, then said, "I don't have a good feeling about those two. They could be tailing us."

Al-Aqrab's eyes shifted between the two men as he said, "We need to move the timetable up. Ship the bomb as soon as possible."

Bart leaned forward. "I don't have the plans finished yet, nor have I scouted the routes. I need to meet with the Zetas. There's just too much to do."

Al-Ghazāli looked across the terrace and on to the city below. "It will take some time for the bomb to reach Central America. Can you complete the planning during that time?"

Bart thought for a moment, then said, "Yes, but I don't like it. We need trusted people to handle transportation and security, but it feels like Kenworth is crowding us. He's forcing us to make changes to our timetable. We won't have time for rehearsals. That's when mistakes are made."

Al-Aqrab sipped his tea. "That is acceptable."

With a serious expression, al-Ghazāli replied, "That is true. We may not have another chance if the Americans are that close to us. I will employ our best fighters for this."

"Gareth is supposed to pay in advance," Madison said. "The agreement was *pay up-front*."

Al-Aqrab touched the scar on his cheek. "Gareth doesn't need to know where the bomb is. He will be told the money is due and he must pay us and the Zetas. Then he will be told when it will be delivered."

Bart nodded, looked to al-Ghazāli, and said, "Okay. I'll make arrangements to fly out as soon as I can. Contact the Zetas and have their representative meet me in Panama. Oh, Gareth will probably send a courier with the money. He won't want to use an electronic transfer."

Al-Ghazāli nodded and lit a cigarette.

＝＝＋＋＋＝＝

Tuesday, June 21, 2016
Sheraton Damascus Hotel
Damascus, Syria

Cheryl was seated at the bar—the same as she had been for the past several days. With a gentle twist of her wrist, she swirled her drink. Out of the corner of her eye, she watched Bart step up to the bar. As soon as he slid the stool back, she said without looking at him, "Hello, Bartholomew. What kept you?"

Bart grinned as he sat. "I was just working on a project, and it took longer than I thought. How—"

With a slight turn of her head, Cheryl said, "My day was productive. It was a good day. Yes, we can go to dinner."

"Do you always know what I'm going to say?" Bart replied. "You read my mind."

She wrinkled up the corner of her mouth as she looked at him. "No. But that's what you were going to ask me, right?" In a natural move, she lifted the cherry from her drink and placed it between her parted teeth, then tugged it free from the stem, her eyes never leaving him.

With a nod, Bart replied, "Right." He scooted his chair back and stood.

She slid off the stool, took Bart's arm, and kissed his cheek. The two walked out of the bar.

They were escorted to a linen-draped table as soon as they entered the Al-Mihbaje Restaurant. As they sat, the waiter asked, "Something to drink?"

Bart looked at Cheryl and nodded.

"I'd like a glass of wine, Sauvignon blanc."

Bart looked to the waiter and said, "Bring the bottle."

Cheryl was relaxed and charming. By the time their main course, *sayadieh*—fish with spiced rice and caramelized onions—arrived, Bart was already under her spell. Their casual chitchat meandered across topics bouncing between the two. They talked about their likes, dislikes, and travel. Nothing was specific.

"I imagine your job takes you to a lot of different countries." She lifted her glass to her lips.

"Yeah, I do travel a lot," he replied.

"What country do you like the best?" she asked as she held his gaze.

"Well, they all have pluses and minuses," he replied, his expression serious. "Probably Central America. I've spent more time there. Of course, Europe is fascinating. A lot of history and dynamics there. What about your favorite place?"

"Europe," she replied with a smile. "I love Switzerland. Tell me about Central America. I've never been. A friend of mine told me it's beautiful and the Panama Canal is fascinating."

"It is. I'd love to show it to you. I—"

The waiter appeared, delivering another bottle of wine.

"Thank you," Bart said as he glanced up at the man.

She smiled and said, as Bart filled her glass, "Thank you."

He filled his glass, and the conversation took another turn. She was a bit more overt this time in letting him know what she wanted—him. She was relentless with her flirts, smiles, and touching. Sometime during their second bottle of wine, their hands linked. More eye contact and less talk enveloped them. After they emptied their glasses, they ordered dessert. Both had *basbousa*—a sweet cake made of cooked semolina soaked in simple syrup—and tea.

Cheryl looked over her cup of tea, her eyes locking onto his. "Take me to your room."

A slight smile emerged on Bart's face as he nodded. He signed the check, then stood.

Cheryl laid her napkin on the table as she stood and stepped close to him. She grasped his arm as they left the table and said, "Thank you for dinner." She placed a gentle kiss on his lips. She looked into his eyes, holding his gaze hostage for several moments, and then the two walked on. Clutching his arm, she was as close to him as she could get as he guided her to his suite.

The elevator was vacant when they stepped in. The door closed and Cheryl turned, pressing her body firmly into him. Her kiss ensured he was on that super highway.

The man guarding Bart's room stood as the couple approached. He unlocked the door and held it open for Cheryl. Bart met his eye and commanded, "We're not to be disturbed."

The guard nodded. "Yes, sir."

Bart entered the room and allowed the door to close. A slight grin emerged from the guard as he heard the door latch.

After Bart locked the door, he turned back to Cheryl. Standing in front of him, she wrapped her arms around his neck and began kissing him before he could take a step or utter a sound. The kiss was full of passion—one he had not received in a long time. She left him with no doubts that her desires were the same as his. Her fingers roamed through his hair, then slid around to his back, her fingers exploring every inch of his back and then his arms. She withdrew, and her fingers found his chest as her gaze locked with his.

Without a word spoken, he guided her to the bed and laid her on it with her head resting on the pillow. Her red hair settled around her face as she pulled him close and kissed him again. She had him on fire.

Bart withdrew and in a soft voice said, "I'll be right back."

She smiled. "I'll fix the bed back."

Bart rose from the bed and stepped into the bathroom and closed the door.

As soon as she heard the door latch, she stood. *Whew!* she thought as she exhaled and turned the bed back. *Now's my chance. Make it look good.* She retrieved two eavesdropping devices from her bra and placed one beneath the drawer in the nightstand by the bed and another under the desktop near the phone. Still hearing Bart, she retrieved a micro-GPS tracking chip and placed it inside the sweatband of his cap. She then stepped back to the edge of the bed and sat. As soon as she heard the bathroom door open, she bent over with her head between her knees.

When Bart stepped in, he saw her doubled over and said, "What's the matter? Are you okay?"

Without looking up, she raised her hand and waved. Then she stood, bolted into the bathroom, and pulled the door to, leaving it ajar enough to ensure he could hear her. She took a deep breath, then placed two fingers down her throat. She gagged, and her abdomen tightened. Again, she placed her fingers down her throat. She gagged, her body convulsed, and she vomited. The contents of her stomach splashed into the toilet as the stench filled the small room. The acrid taste burned in her throat. She gagged and vomited again. When she finished, she pulled a washcloth from the shelf, placed it under running water, and wiped her face. Next, she rinsed her mouth. She flushed the toilet, then saw her reflection in the mirror. Through her tear-filled eyes, she saw that her makeup was streaked and smeared. Her hair was disheveled. She looked miserable. *Should do it,* she thought.

Stepping back into the room, Cheryl wiped her face and stopped in front of Bart.

With a concerned expression, he repeated, "Are you okay? What is it?"

She looked up at him to ensure he caught a whiff of her foul breath and said, "I'm so embarrassed. I feel horrible. It must have been something I ate or too much of the sweet things at dinner. I just hope I didn't pick up a bug." She stroked his forearm. She knew the odor from the bathroom and her breath would convince him that she was sick. Her performance was excellent, and she had succeeded in killing his mood.

"Can I get you anything?" he asked.

"No, I just need to lie down," she replied, her voice weak and just above a moan. "I'm so sorry. Perhaps tomorrow evening or the next?"

"We can link up tomorrow. I go out of town the day after."

"Okay, tomorrow afternoon then. How long will you be gone?"

"About a week, maybe two."

"Damn," she forced the words through a quick smile. "I'll miss you. Please, don't leave without me seeing you." She grimaced. "But right now, I need to go to my room."

"Okay," Bart replied, his voice full of regret. "Call my room if you need anything."

She nodded, slipped on her shoes, then left his room. As soon as she was out of sight of the guard by the door, she picked up her pace.

Cheryl locked the door as soon as she entered her room. She kicked off her shoes as she went straight to the bathroom. She brushed her teeth and rinsed her mouth out with mouthwash. Finished in the bathroom, she opened a bottle of water and retrieved her phone from the safe. She sat on the edge of the bed and punched at the keys. "Bugs placed and GPS chip in the sweatband." She then typed a summary of the evening and sent it to Max.

Within five minutes, Max sent a text back to her. "Great! Now get the hell out of there."

Scarlett read his text and shook her head, tapping at the keys. "No, I need to find out where he's going. I'll see him in the morning. I can find out."

Max's reply came in less than a minute. "No! Get out now. If he finds one of the devices, you'll not see the sunrise. Be downstairs in five minutes, or I'll drag your ass out."

In his room, Bart sat with his feet propped on a small table on the terrace of his suite, upended his glass of Crown Royal Reserve, then poured another. His mood had soured. As he started to lift the glass, his cell phone rang. "Yes," he said into the device.

"Your woman, the one with red hair," the man's voice said, "just left the hotel with another man."

Bart sat upright in the chair. "Who was the man? And where did they go?"

"I do not know the answer to those questions," the voice said.

Bart's face turned to a scowl. "Alert the others. Find her and kill everyone with her. Bring her to me. Search every building in the city if you have to, but find her." He ended the call and slammed the phone on the desk. It shattered and pieces shot across the room. He picked up the glass of whiskey and knocked it back.

CHAPTER 27

Tuesday, June 21, 2016
Beit Zafran Hotel
Damascus, Syria

W HEN MAX AND his team selected the hotel, one critical criterion had been to provide quick response to Major Marsden, if needed. The four-tenths of a mile between the two hotels was pushing the limit. Unfortunately, this was as close as Max and his team could get based on availability. It was the only one with a room large enough for them to work from.

The Beit Zafran was a former Ottoman mansion located in a historical neighborhood of churches, mosques, and winding streets. The luxury boutique hotel, with its high ceilings, had two levels of rooms and a rooftop restaurant. Each of the distinctive plush rooms had vibrant colors, elegant furnishings, and original hand-painted ceilings befitting Ottoman royalty. Built in 1836 around two inner courtyards with marble fountains, restoration to its former beauty was completed in 2010. During the restoration, the Syrian-Swiss owners had dedicated one of the courtyards to the private wing. This section was for the more affluent and had a private terrace and entrance. Both courtyards were covered with removable covers to allow for the enjoyment of beautiful evenings and mild days. The main courtyard was also used as the front entrance. Although the team was not there on holiday, the privacy and spacious rooms met their requirements.

Tucked away on a secluded side street of Old Damascus, the hotel was out of the main flow of traffic but offered easy access to the highway. Aside from the distance to the Sheraton, another drawback to this location was the parking situation. It didn't have dedicated, secured parking like one would find at major chains. The guests had to find parking where they could in the vicinity of the building. Max had opted to bend on this criterion since the street had little traffic, so their cars were parked in the open, within one block around the hotel.

When Max sent the text to Major Marsden, he also sent one of the special forces soldiers after her. In civilian clothes and only armed with a pistol, the sergeant bolted out of the hotel and headed to the Sheraton Hotel as fast as he could without attracting attention. He was to use whatever force needed to extract her from the hotel and get her back to Beit Zafran.

At a small desk near the window, Danya monitored the digital recorder. Dedicated to the eavesdropping devices Major Marsden placed in Madison's room, it would alert and start recording when an incoming call was detected.

In the adjoining room, Max talked with one of the soldiers and the other two took advantage of the down time, one asleep in a chair and the other stretched out on the bed, asleep.

The red light flashed, signaling the recorder detected a call.

Danya place earbuds in her ears to listen in. Upon hearing the call to Bart's phone, she said over her shoulder, "Max, we have a problem."

Stepping back into the room, Max stopped next to Danya. "What is it?"

"Madison just got a call." She pressed the button to replay the recording. "Someone saw Major Marsden leave the hotel with the sergeant."

Hearing that Madison had ordered the man to search for Major Marsden and kill everyone with her, Max said, "Alert the team. We've got to evacuate. They'll locate us in no time. Get everything packed."

A soft knock at the door jerked everyone's heads toward the entrance. Pistol in hand, Andy opened it to find Scarlett and the special forces sergeant. He admitted them and as soon as they entered the room, checked the hall to ensure they weren't followed. With only a few minutes to escape her hotel room, Scarlett had only grabbed her identification and cell phone, but there was nothing else that could be traced to her. While the other team members were busy packing and preparing to leave, Max briefed Scarlett and the sergeant on the situation.

"There is nothing else after the call," Danya said. "I did hear some rustling sounds, then nothing. He was probably searching his room and found the bugs. I don't know about the GPS tracker."

"I'm sure we spooked Madison," Max said as he pulled back the heavy drapes and peered out the window. "My guess is that they'll relocate somewhere else." He turned to the special forces sergeant on watch and said, "As soon as you're packed up, establish security and recon the road leading out."

The soldier nodded, then went to the other three commandos and briefed them.

Max glanced at Major Marsden, then to Danya. "Can you fix her up with a change of clothes? We can't have her in that dress. Be sure and cover her red hair with something. They'll recognize her in an instant." He turned to Marsden and said, "Sorry, Major, we've got to make you a little less attractive."

"I know," she replied with a smile.

Max looked to Andy. "Andy, get her a pistol. I don't want her unarmed."

Within a few moments, Max was leading the way as they slipped out of the hotel through the private wing. Once out of the light of the courtyard, they slipped on their tactical headsets and had their weapons ready. He halted them just before they exited the courtyard and contacted the team leader of the special forces soldiers who had left several minutes ahead of Max, Danya, Andy, and Scarlett to scout out the area and cars. When he received the message back that it was clear, Max and Danya left first, followed by Andy and Scarlett. They stepped out and strolled to their cars as though they were married. Although they were deliberate in their routes, they acted as if they were in no hurry. Should anyone see them, they looked like ordinary couples going out for the evening.

As Max and Danya made their way along the street, keeping in the shadows as much as possible, they were about a half block from their car when Max heard the sergeant's voice in his ear. "Two cars speeding toward the hotel. Could be trouble."

Max replied in a soft voice, "Roger. Everyone stay alert. Andy, keep moving and stay calm."

"Roger," came Andy's voice.

Max and Danya reached their car and got in, and he reported to the others that he was in his car. Within a minute, Max heard Andy's voice saying that they were in theirs. The soldier's voice sounded in Max's ear again, "Two cars just passed my location. Full of men. Weapons present."

Max saw the headlights approaching and replied, "Ease out and don't speed. Meet up after we get out of the neighborhood."

The two cars—a tan Toyota and a dark blue KIA—passed Max, and he watched as the occupants scrutinized him and Danya. Feigning calm, Max eased his white, Honda Civic out of the parking space and proceeded toward the exit. He checked his rearview mirror and saw the headlights of a car turning onto the street behind him. He identified it as Andy's silver Nissan as it passed beneath the light on the corner. The two cars headed toward the edge of the neighborhood and paused at the corner before merging onto Ibn Assaker together. As soon as Max saw the gray Hyundai carrying the soldiers ease up behind Andy, he led them out. Their planned route would take them north and onto the M5 highway toward Homs.

As Max crossed the Barada River after getting on the Ibn Assaker, his earpiece came alive.

"Headlights approaching fast from the rear."

Max checked his rearview mirror. "Keep an eye on 'em," he said as he shot a glance to Danya.

Already looking over the rear seat, Danya kept Max informed on the action taking place behind them.

A tan Toyota pulled in behind the soldier's gray Hyundai and switched on its high beams to get a good look at the occupants. The car then dimmed its headlights and attempted to pass to get behind the next car, Andy's.

Max's earpiece activated again with the commando's voice. "He's checking us out. He's not interested in us and going to pass."

"Roger," Max replied. "Andy, watch out. He probably remembers our vehicles from when they passed us as we were leaving."

"Roger, I see them."

From their actions, it became obvious that the occupants of the Toyota were searching for a man and redheaded woman but were not sure what kind of car they were in. When the two fake couples were leaving the hotel, they had not aroused any suspicion, but now, the Toyota was checking out a possible lead. The sergeant accelerated the Hyundai, preventing the Toyota from passing. His actions angered the aggressive driver, and the now belligerent occupants of the Toyota began shouting and waving their arms in anger, their interest in the couple spiked.

"Watch it, they're trying to come around," the sergeant said into his radio.

Again, the Toyota tried to pass and swerved toward the Hyundai.

The sergeant cut his wheel to avoid the encroaching car. "Damn!" he said as he slowed, which gave the hostile car the opportunity to slip in behind Andy.

The Toyota switched to high beams and sped up, trying to close the gap behind Andy so they could see the couple inside. The second advancing car—a dark blue KIA—had to slow down so as not to crash into the Hyundai as it swerved.

As the Toyota approached, Andy anticipated it would attempt to ram him from behind and he stomped on the accelerator, but his car couldn't react fast enough and the Toyota made contact.

The commando's Hyundai swung out wide and started to pass.

Max spoke into his headset, "Take 'em out."

"Roger," the sergeant replied.

The Hyundai gained on the vehicle behind Andy. One of the men in the left rear seat of the Toyota stuck a rifle barrel out of the window and it flashed several times. The soldiers on the right side of their car fired their M4 carbines as soon as they were beside the Toyota, emptying their magazines into the hostile vehicle. It slowed and veered to the right as the driver slumped over the wheel. The Toyota struck the guard rail, flipped over twice, and fire enveloped the upturned vehicle, killing the four occupants.

The two men reloaded their carbines as they watched for the KIA's rapid approach behind them. As his magazine was engaged, the sergeant glanced in his rearview mirror and saw the KIA closing in fast. "They're coming around!" the sergeant said in a loud voice, then he darted to the right lane to prevent the vehicle from getting behind Andy.

When the KIA was almost alongside the Hyundai, two men on the right side leaned out of the KIA, firing AKs.

The sergeant radioed to alert Max. "The guys in the second vehicle are shooting."

Max, followed by Andy, replied in crisp tones, "Roger."

"Roger."

Soldiers in the right and left rear seat turned, leaned out, and returned fire. Three bullets from the KIA shattered the Hyundai's rear window. The commandos slapped in fresh magazines and unleashed another volley of fire. The KIA swerved, then rammed the guard rail, flipped over, and slid to a stop.

The Americans didn't stop on their way out of Damascus.

⸺ ✦ ✦ ⸺

Tuesday, June 21, 2016
Sheraton Damascus Hotel
Damascus, Syria

Bart had spent several minutes searching his room for what the woman he knew as Cheryl may have hidden. He started with the obvious places, as she'd had only a few minutes to act. It didn't take him long to find the two bugs she'd planted. He placed them on the floor in the bathroom and stomped on them with the heel of his shoe, smashing the cases. As an added precaution, he filled the sink with water and dropped the devices into it to finally destroy the electronics if his footwork hadn't. He took a few more minutes to inspect his room, giving the water plenty of time to work. He returned to the bathroom sink, scooped up the remains of the bugs, and bolted from the room. As he ran toward the elevator, Bart startled the guard and almost bumped into him. Once inside, he hit the button for the floor two levels up. No matter how much he willed it or punched at the button, the elevator moved at its own unhurried speed.

Breathing hard, Bart rapped on al-Ghazāli's door. The Arab jerked open the door, shouting in a fit of rage, "How dare you pound on my door at this—" He was startled to see Bart standing in front of him.

"I was right!" Bart said as he pushed into the room. He held out his wet hand and opened his fist, revealing the destroyed bugs. "That bitch planted these in my room. We must leave now. I've sent men to find her. Kenworth is nearby."

Al-Ghazāli's brow dipped as he said, "I will meet you downstairs in a few minutes. Alert the others."

Bart nodded and left the room.

———◆◆◆———

Thursday, June 23, 2016
Gareth Residence
New York, New York

Archie had just nestled his large frame into an easy chair across from Stew's desk when Jenny entered looking like forty miles of bad road. The sack dress she wore was wrinkled and past due for the washer. Knowing what was coming, he set his plate of pastries on the coffee table as he said, "Good morning, Jenny."

Jenny flopped into the chair next to Archie and replied, "Ugh. Fix me a drink, Archie. In a tall glass."

Without speaking, Archie stepped to the cabinet and withdrew a tumbler and the bottle of Glenlivet. He poured the glass two-thirds full, dropped in a cube of ice, then strode back to where Jenny sat and handed her the drink as he returned to his chair.

With a stern look, Stew said, "Go easy there, Jenny. Nassar'll be here in a few minutes, and you're speaking at a luncheon today."

"I need this!" Jenny tipped up her glass. "I've given that speech a dozen times."

"Nassar is coming to deliver a message from al-Ghazāli," Stew said, grasping the remote and turning on the TV that hung on the wall.

Archie looked to the TV, then back to Stew. "Did he say what the message was?"

"No, just that it was important."

"Jenny is the presumptive nominee now that we've got the delegates," Stew continued. "The national convention is a month out. We can't let up for a minute. Archie, keep making the rounds promoting Jenny. Aside from her scheduled appearances and speeches, she's going to be giving more interviews from now until the national convention. It'll seem like she's everywhere. We'll keep hammering on her experience and the need to have her proven leadership in these times of uncertainty. That line has been resonating well. The donations have been good, but with this push, we'll need a lot more. I have the staff working overtime setting up interviews and squeezing people. The goal is to generate maximum enthusiasm for her going into the convention. I've got the media on board."

The doorbell sounded, interrupting Stew. He glanced toward the door, then to Archie. "That'll be Nassar. Archie, let him in." Stew turned his attention to CNN.

Archie pushed his frame out of the chair—stepping on crumbs and bits of frosting as they rained to the floor—then lumbered to the door and soon returned with Nassar. He went back to his chair, and Nassar took the seat on the other side of Jenny.

Stew picked up the remote and muted the broadcast, then got right down to business. "On the phone you said you had an important message from al-Ghazāli. What is it?" He locked eyes with Nassar and leaned back in his chair.

"Al-Ghazāli sends his regards," Nassar said as he withdrew a folded paper from his inside coat pocket and laid it on Stew's desk. "Your payment is due for the item and its transportation into the US. It is my understanding you wish to have the money delivered by courier. Is this correct?"

Stew leaned forward in his chair and rested his arms on the desk. "Where is the item now, and when will it be delivered?"

Nassar replied with a serious expression, "I do not know where it is. That is not important just now. You are to give me three acceptable locations. You will be told which one and when it will be delivered."

Stew's eyes narrowed as he said, "No, I wanna know when and where it'll be delivered *before* I send the money."

His expression serious, Nassar pointed his finger at Stew and said, "You will have your courier deliver the money within three days. He is to go to the Marriott Hotel in Panama City and call the number on that paper when he arrives. Tell me the name of the courier and reservations will be made in his name."

"If I send the money to Panama, what assurance do I have that delivery'll be made?"

"Al-Ghazāli's word. Just as he must trust you."

Stew held his gaze on Nassar, then looked down at a card on his desk with the latest polling numbers on Jenny—there was a significant drop. His jaw tightened. *Jenny's gonna be the next president,* he thought. He looked to Archie, then to Nassar and said, "Make the reservations in Senator Chapman's name."

Nassar looked to the senator, whose complexion had turned pale, and said, "You will be given instructions at the hotel." He looked back to Stew. "You will be notified of the destination and delivery date. Los Zetas must first recon the route and border. You are to ensure the border stays open."

Stew nodded as his gaze went to Jenny and then to Archie.

Trying to find a way out of making the delivery, Archie responded, "Stew, I'm not sure I can make it happen within three days. I have to make arrangements for the money to be shipped in a diplomatic pouch. I have several important appointments and an important committee meeting scheduled. I don't think I can make it that fast. You should have the acting CIA director deliver it. He can get it there faster than I can. Besides, you want to see how he works out."

Nassar looked to Chapman, then back to Stew and said, "*No CIA,* and no one else. Just the senator."

Raising his arms and turning his palms outward toward the senator, his eyebrows raised, Stew said, "You're the man, Archie. Make it happen."

"I will tell al-Ghazāli that Senator Chapman will bring the money," Nassar said as he shot a glance to Chapman, then back to Stew. "The senator can provide your three locations when he meets with our representative in Panama."

Archie looked to Nassar. "Who's your representative, and how will I know him?"

"Not to worry yourself," Nassar replied. "He will know you. You will receive your instructions when you call the number on that paper." He was pointing to the sheet on Stew's desk. He stood and said, "I must go now."

Stew nodded to Chapman, directing him to escort Nassar to the door.

As soon as Chapman stepped back into the office, Jenny said, "Well, that was kinda final."

Archie, looking like someone had run over his dog, sat back in his chair.

With a serious look, Jenny said, "Stew, that's a lot of money to turn over to those ragheads. It makes me uncomfortable. Al-Ghazāli'd better hold up his end of the bargain."

Stew raised his coffee cup to his lips, took a sip, and wrinkled his face. "Cold, damn it. Yeah, it's a lot of money, but I can't take a chance on the election. If they screw us over, we eliminate 'em. Label them terrorists, and you're a hero. I've already given Wellington his marching orders to locate all these guys, including Nassar. He isn't to do anything until I tell him. Hell, we'll even take care of our other problem—Madison. Jenny, you're *gonna* be the next president."

Jenny shifted her large frame in the chair and said, "That's good, Stew. I like it, but handing over the money on their word is a tough one to swallow."

Stew scribbled a note on the pad on his desk, leaned back in his chair, and looked to Archie. "When you go to Panama, try and pin them down to a time and place. If possible, have them show you the bomb. Keep me posted, and if you have any questions or problems, call me right away. Oh, and if you suspect it's a double-cross, don't give them the money."

Archie nodded.

———— ✦ ✦ ✦ ————

Sunday, June 26, 2016
Panama Marriott Hotel
Panama City, Panama

It was a beautiful summer day in paradise, with a bright sun and clear sky. Archie noticed several young women at the pool on the way to his room, some playing in the water and others sunbathing in lawn chairs. Once in his room, he dropped his bag and poured a glass of the Glenlivet that had been left for him. He sipped the drink as he explored the room, then he sat down at the desk in his hotel room, slid the phone closer, and punched in the number he'd been told to call upon his arrival.

On the second ring, a voice with a Spanish accent answered, "¿Senador Chapman?"

Archie paused, then with caution answered, "Yes, this is Chapman. I was instructed to call this number."

"Go to the Corvina y Caña Restaurante in the hotel at 6:00 p.m." The phone went dead.

Archie looked at his watch, took another drink of his scotch, then called Stew to give him a status report. Next, he called his office. His brunette staffer answered the call. He so cherished the sound of her soft voice that he made the phone call last as long as possible as he asked her for his messages and the activities of the office. With no other business to discuss, he ended the call, though the thought of her lingered with him for a few moments longer. With nothing else to do, he turned on the TV and lay on the bed.

His anxiety grew with each minute as he surfed the channels, but nothing was of interest. He tried to watch the news, but it too was dreary. He even tried to take a nap, but for over an hour and a half, all he could do was toss and turn. His mind raced from Jenny's election to his meeting in Panama. Finally, he got out of bed and changed clothes, then sat at the small desk for the next several minutes, contemplating his meeting.

At 6:00 p.m. Senator Chapman entered the restaurant as directed. The maître d' greeted him and confirmed he was Senator Archie Chapman, then escorted him to a table by a large window with a pleasant view and a man with a dark complexion seated there already. Archie glanced at the maître d' with a blank expression, then back to the stranger.

The man held out his hand, saying, "*Senador* Chapman, please, be seated." His unexpected host was well groomed and dressed in tropical-weight slacks and a white linen shirt. His eyes revealed a darker nature behind his smile. He filled a glass with Sauvignon blanc from a bottle chilling in the ice bucket next to the table, set the glass in front of Archie, and said, "I hope your accommodations are satisfactory?"

Chapman replied with caution, "They are. Do you have a name?"

"Everyone has a name." The Panamanian smiled and sipped his wine. "Mine, not important. I am just delivering a message, and I know who you are."

Chapman grew more uncomfortable, wishing he were somewhere else.

"Do you have what you were told to deliver?"

Archie replied, "I do. What message do you have for me?"

"Right to the point," his unknown companion said. "I like that." He sipped his wine. "You will be picked up tomorrow morning at nine o'clock. No cell phones, no guns, alone, and with what you were instructed to bring. You are not to call or communicate with anyone until after the meeting tomorrow. Do you understand? Oh, and you will be searched."

"I understand," Chapman replied, his hands beginning to tremble.

"Good," the man said, then stood. "Enjoy your meal. Your dessert is waiting in your room. I was told you like them young." He walked out of the restaurant.

Chapman drained his glass and filled it again. Not liking how his trip was evolving, he wallowed in nervousness and dread. However, the mention of the dessert in his room took his mind off the current situation.

CHAPTER 28

Monday, June 27, 2016
Headquarters, US Special Operations Command
MacDill Air Force Base, Florida

FOR THE PAST week, Special Agent Gail Summers and David Elsworth had been keeping tabs on Senator Chapman and sifting through his phone conversations, gathering information. Gail had also been communicating with her contacts within the US, especially along the southern border. Since she had been working drug and human trafficking, she knew who she could rely on for up-to-date intelligence on the drug cartels and who she could trust not to divulge what she was doing.

David, as a senior analyst, had focused his efforts in collecting intelligence through his contacts in Syria, Turkey, Beirut, and Central America. His primary interest was in the Muslim Brotherhood and Los Zetas. What he had developed over the past week produced a considerable amount of background information but not what he needed. Chugs had put him in contact with the special forces units operating in South America, and of particular importance was the twenty-four-hour surveillance SOCOM had established on Lieutenant General Çakmak's estate in Brazil ten days earlier. David had been in regular contact with them, but so far, no actionable intelligence had been discovered.

Thaddeus Nussbaum, chief of Mossad Station, Panama, had added David to his distribution list at the request of Major General Matherson when Gail and David arrived at the headquarters. David had read and filed the situation reports from Danya on a regular basis and talked with Thaddeus twice since he had been assigned to the headquarters.

Gail looked up from her computer and said, "David, are you over there?"

He looked over his cubicle. "Yes, *dahling*. What may I do for you?"

"Get your ass over here."

David stepped to her side and sat in the chair next to hers. "Yes, love?"

"Check with your contact at the State Department, but it looks like Senator Chapman went to Panama. Verify he's down there. A call was made from his cell phone to Gareth yesterday." She handed him the transcript.

David took just a moment to read it, then looked at her and said, "Oh, my. The senator is meeting someone and he's staying at the Marriott, geez! Remember the other transcript that said Gareth reached an agreement with the Muslim Brotherhood to deliver the nuke into the US? That's what this is about. They're about to execute. We need to alert the general. Are we going to Panama?"

Gail grasped his forearm. "Hold on there, Sweet Pea. First, verify he did, in fact, go to Panama. Then contact NSA and have them cover the Marriott in Panama, all calls in and out. Also, have them track his cell phone."

"Yes, ma'am."

——— ✦ ✦ ✦ ———

Monday, June 27, 2016
Panama Marriott Hotel
Panama City, Panama

A white Ford van with darkened windows pulled to a stop at the entrance of the Marriott Hotel at nine o'clock. The driver got out of the van, walked into the lobby, and stopped in front of Senator Chapman. He could not miss him—he was the only large man seated near the entrance with boxes stacked on a bellman's cart.

As soon as the driver identified the senator, he held out his hand and commanded, "Your cell phone."

Chapman stood and wrinkled up the corner of his mouth as he shoved his hand into his pocket and withdrew his phone.

Taking the senator's cell, the driver switched it off, removed the SIM card, placed both items in his pocket, and said, "This way." He led Chapman outside to the van, where he waved a metal detector over his body. Satisfied that he'd complied with the other instructions, the driver loaded the boxes into the van. "Get in," he said. "We will go now."

For almost an hour, the van sped eastward on the Pan-American Highway. The city was miles behind them, and the countryside was lush, dense jungle with only an occasional house or shack peeking out of the vegetation. The humidity hovered near one hundred percent, and perspiration saturated the back of Chapman's tailor-made linen shirt.

The senator leaned forward when he saw the sign for the village of Espave and said, "How much farther?"

When the driver didn't answer him, he asked again.

Still no reply.

Chapman's irritation increased. He wiped his face with his handkerchief, then sat back.

Another ten minutes passed, and the driver turned onto an unmarked trail. The van bounced and rocked as it plodded along with vegetation slapping at the sides of the vehicle like the brushes in a carwash. After a few moments, a small clearing emerged in front of them. Chapman wiped the sweat from his brow again with his handkerchief, more from nervousness of the intimidating setting than the heat.

The driver stopped in the center of the clearing and got out. Stepping around the vehicle, he slid open the passenger door and said, "Get out and wait here." Without waiting for a response from Chapman, he turned and stepped into the tree line in front of them.

Hot, humid air greeted the senator as the dense jungle prevented any breeze from getting to the large American. It was a sauna provided by Mother Nature. Chapman watched as the man disappeared into the jungle, then he worked his large frame out of the vehicle. He looked around but didn't see anyone else. Not knowing what would happen next, he wiped his sweaty face with his wet handkerchief. His saturated shirt clung to his back and chest. He stood beside the van and let his eyes scan the perimeter of the clearing, his fear and anxiety rising.

A small drone appeared overhead, capturing Chapman's attention. It followed the van's path from the entrance and circled around the clearing, then around the vehicle and Chapman. After two passes around the senator, the drone gained altitude and flew above the treetops, disappearing in the direction from which it came.

A few moments later, a figure emerged from the tree line where the driver had entered. The man wore jungle fatigues and hat, with a pistol strapped to his thigh and survival knife on his waist. Chapman recognized him as Bart Madison.

Bart stepped to Chapman and said, "Hello, Senator. Surprised to see me?"

"Uh, uh, Ba…Bart," Chapman said. "Hello."

"Did you bring the money?" Bart asked. "You were also instructed to give me three possible locations for the bomb. Do you have them?"

The senator nodded and handed Bart a slip of paper with the three locations listed. "The money is in the van."

Bart motioned to the rear door and said, "Open the door. I want to inspect it."

Chapman stepped to the rear doors and opened both, then moved to the side.

Bart stood beside the large man and said as he pointed to one of the boxes, "Open that one."

Chapman picked up the box on top of the one Bart pointed to and set it on the ground, then picked up the one Bart wanted to inspect and set it on top of the one on the ground. He fumbled with the packing tape, trying to find an opening on one of the edges.

"Let's not make a career out of opening the box," Bart said. "Move out of the way." The mercenary withdrew the survival knife from the sheath on his side and, as soon as Chapman stepped aside, slit the tape holding the flaps of the box closed. He picked up several bundles and inspected the money.

"It's all there, just as instructed," the senator said. "Now that you've seen the money, I want to see what we are buying."

"It'd better be. If not…well, it won't be pleasant." Bart pitched the bundles of cash back into the box, then looked at Chapman. "You can want all day, but it's not here yet. You're more than welcome to wait until it gets here, but you'll be waiting by yourself. I have things to do."

"When'll it be here?" Chapman replied.

Bart shrugged his shoulders. "It could be a few days to a week or so."

Chapman wiped his brow again. "Well, uh…so, what now?"

Madison retrieved Chapman's cell phone and SIM card from his cargo pocket, inserted the card into the phone, and turned it on. He held the phone in front of him and said, "Call Gareth and tell him the three locations and money have been delivered. That's all."

Chapman took the phone with a trembling hand, punched in the number for Gareth, and placed the phone to his ear. Madison stood in front of him, watching his every move.

"Stew, this is Archie," Chapman said into the phone. "The delivery is made." … "No, no problems." … "No, I didn't see it. It's not here yet. Do you want me to stay here until it arrives?" … "He said a few days to a week or so." … "Okay, I'll catch a flight out as soon as I can." He ended the call.

Madison held out his hand, indicating for him to return the phone. He removed the SIM card as soon as Chapman handed him the phone, then stuffed the card and phone into his pocket. "You haven't sent me the intel report you promised. Why do I have to keep asking for it?" His patience having run out with Chapman, he now considered the senator a liability.

Madison had paid a lot of money to Chapman for reliable and up-to-date intelligence. Madison was the consummate mercenary—if there was such a thing—and had achieved an excellent reputation as the man to call on for the most difficult assignments. His planning and execution had always been perfect. Accurate and complete information had been a key component for his success. He chose his information providers with extreme care, then kept detailed notes, recordings, and photo-graphs, using them to his advantage to get results. Politicians were his first choice as they were the easiest, since they had the information and influence he needed. He studied the possible politicians, then made his move to get them into his fold with a slow and methodical approach. He first found out all he could about his target—their likes, dislikes, weak-nesses, and sexual preferences. To Madison, politicians just like Senator Archie Chapman were nothing more than paid prostitutes. They would do anything if the price was right, including fringe benefits. Madison never fully trusted his information providers and knew there was always a time that someone else would appeal to them more and he or she would become a liability.

"I-I was," Chapman said. "I was almost finished when Stew sent me down here. I just ran out of time."

"Shit," Madison said with a smirk. "You're a horrible liar."

Chapman shifted his stance, and his complexion turned pale. His voice trembled as he struggled to say, "I-I…as soon as I get back, I'll send the report to you. I-I won't do a damn thing until I get it sent to you." He knew he was in deep shit and not convincing Bart.

Madison's steely eyes seemed to bore into Chapman. With a calm, cold voice, he said, "You have let me down, Senator. That's unfortunate. Your intel reports have been lacking and incomplete. You neglected to tell me about the British ship and the Israeli's plan for Tartus. I warned you about that." He withdrew his survival knife.

His gaze locked onto Bart's hand with a firm grip on the knife, Archie felt his body tremble and stepped back. He knew he was talking with the Angel of Death.

Pointing the knife at Chapman, Madison said, "You neglected to tell me that Gareth is setting me up. I know all about his plan to make me the fall guy. I take the nuke into the US, and the FBI kills me, then Jenny Gareth takes the credit for killing the terrorists."

Tears welled up in Chapman's eyes, his head fell, and he began to sob. He wet his pants and, through his blubbering, said, "Oh please, Bart!" He dropped to his knees. "Don't kill me. Please, please give me another chance."

Madison tapped him on the head with the blade of the knife. "Why should I? You'll just try to get me killed or set me up again."

"No, no, Bart! I promise. I'll do anything you say. Oh, God, please."

"You're pathetic. Just a worthless hunk of protoplasm."

"Yes," Chapman replied, tears streaming down his fat face. "I am. Just give me a chance, and I'll show you. I will do as you say. Anything."

"Stand up."

Hearing Bart's words to stand, relief that he might not die coursed through him. He raised his head and, through tear-filled eyes, looked at Bart's face. Then fear overtook him again with thoughts about Bart's knife slicing into his skin. He knew it would be excruciating. *Is he going to do it in my stomach?* he thought. *Or my neck. I never counted on this. I don't want to die this way.*

As soon as the senator was on his feet, Bart lunged forward, grasped Chapman's shirt with his left hand, and jerked it up, his forearm knocking Chapman's chin up. With a quick flick of his wrist, his razor-sharp blade cut a gash in his belly. He released the shirt and stepped back.

Astonished, Chapman looked down expecting to see his guts dangling but saw the blood saturating his shirt and locked his eyes onto Bart's. He had felt the sharp sting of the blade and was waiting for his body to collapse. He couldn't comprehend what was happening to him. He'd known Bart was going to stab him and felt the knife and seen the blood on his shirt, but he was still standing and not dead.

Or am I? Is this what it is like? he thought.

The look on Chapman's face signaled to Bart that he had Chapman's attention and had created the fear in him. For the time being, he needed him and figured with this warning, Chapman would do as he was instructed, at least until his wound healed.

"No, Senator, you are not dead and I didn't stab you. I just wanted to get your attention and give you something to remind you of our meeting. It would be just as simple to kill you. You'll do as I tell you, and your reports will be accurate and detailed. If you ever try to set me up again or not tell me of a trap, you will die. No warning, no escape, wherever you are, day or night, you'll cease to exist. Your allegiance is to me. Do you understand?"

"Yes, yes. Thank you. Anything you say."

Bart fished a plastic pouch from his cargo pocket and slit it open with the knife. He pulled out a gauze pad, wiped the blade on the pad, then handed it to Archie. "Hold this on the cut."

Chapman took the gauze and pressed it against the bleeding wound.

Madison shoved his hand into the cargo pocket again and removed a small electronic device that looked like a USB flash drive and handed it to Chapman. "This is a Micro Stick, voice-activated recorder," he said. "Every conversation you have with Gareth, I want you to record it. Just press the button to turn it on and drop it in your pocket. It will activate when it detects a conversation. Send me the voice files every evening after you have a conversation with Gareth. The battery will last about eight hours. It'll charge up when you connect it to your computer. It's very simple, and you won't have any trouble. Do you understand what I want?"

"I understand," Chapman replied, wiping his eyes. "You want me to record Gareth's conversations."

"Correct. I have written the address of my online account on the back. Turn on the device in the morning, stick it in your pocket, and you're set for the day."

Archie tried to sound sincere. "How long do you want me to record them?"

"Until I tell you to stop. And don't use your office computer to send the files."

Madison had already started building a file on the Gareths. The senator's recording would be added to the file. In the event that something happened to Madison, the files would be released, exposing the plot to detonate the bomb inside the US. Madison wasn't doing this because he'd suddenly developed a case of patriotism, though. He was doing it because Gareth wanted him dead and had tried to set him up. Madison was not a naive dummy. He would have evidence against Gareth when he was ready to strike. If you are swimming in shark-infested waters, you must be just as big and vicious as the other sharks.

"I understand."

"The driver will put a couple of stitches in that," Bart poked his finger on Archie's wound. "It won't look too good if you walk back into the hotel dripping blood and wet pants. I can't do anything about your pants. If anyone should ask, tell them you spilled your drink."

Archie flinched and groaned.

"Just a reminder of our meeting." Madison turned toward the tree line from where he originally emerged and signaled with his hand. Within a few moments, a green Land Rover appeared and pulled to a stop next to the Ford van.

— ✦ ✦ ✦ —

Monday, June 27, 2016
Headquarters, US Special Operations Command
MacDill Air Force Base, Florida

David received a call from NSA about a new telephone conversation they had intercepted from Senator Chapman. "What time was the phone call?" he asked.

"About an hour ago," came the reply. "We had him located at the Panama Marriott until about 0905, then we lost the signal. We locked onto him a little over an hour later, east of the village of Espave. He made a call to Stew Gareth, then we lost the signal again. We believe he removed the SIM card on his phone to keep us from tracking him. The call was short. He told Gareth the delivery was made, but he had not seen it. Chapman said it wouldn't be there for a few days to a week or so. Gareth then told him to return home. I'm sending you a copy of the transcript."

David thought for a moment, then asked, "If he was afraid of being tracked, why did he put the SIM back into his phone and make a call?"

"That's the puzzling part. We're not sure. He may have thought he wouldn't be tracked, or perhaps he may have wanted to be tracked, or he was just not very smart. We don't know. I'll let you know if we get anything else."

David stepped around his cubicle to brief Gail on the call from NSA.

"As soon as you get the transcript, send a copy to Thaddeus Nussbaum," she said. "Ask him to send someone out to that location to have a look around. They may find something. I'll let the general know."

With a serious look, David said, "This sounds like Madison. The senator goes to Panama to make a delivery. Madison removes the SIM card from Chapman's cell. I don't think Chapman is smart enough to think of that. Madison would though. But why would he put the SIM card back in the phone to make that call, of any call he could have made?"

Gail removed her glasses and laid them on the desk. "That's a good question. Perhaps it was a mistake, but I doubt it. Madison doesn't make mistakes like that. Perhaps he hoped the call was captured and wanted Chapman or Gareth on record."

"Gail, *dahling*, this is so exciting. We're about to get them, and we know the nuke is out of Syria and on the way to Panama."

"Calm down, Sweet Pea. You've got work to do. Now get back over there and get to it. I'm going to brief Matherson."

"Yes, ma'am."

CHAPTER 29

Wednesday, June 29, 2016
Lieutenant General Devrim Çakmak's Estate
Cantá, State of Roraima, Brazil

MAX AND HIS team linked up with the special forces unit conducting surveillance on Çakmak's estate. He was greeted by the team sergeant as he entered the perimeter of the camp nestled in the Amazon approximately one kilometer from the estate. After greeting the sergeant, Max introduced Andy, Danya, and the four special forces soldiers.

The sergeant said, "This way, sir. I'll take you to the commander."

Max nodded and stepped out with the husky man. Danya, Andy, and the others followed.

"I go by Bear," the sergeant said as he looked over his shoulder at them. Bear was a fitting moniker for the big sergeant. At just over six feet tall, he was lean, muscular, and looked like a bear. The tropical morning rain shower dripped from the brim of his jungle hat, and he wiped the water from his face. "The rain should pass soon, and it'll be steamy. It's going to be about ninety-five today."

They stepped into the center of the site where a wiry man of about five-foot-ten paced about, talking on a satellite phone.

"This is Captain Landry, the detachment commander," Bear said. "I'll get your people settled while you talk to the commander."

The captain paused from the phone, extended his hand, and said, "Good to see you." He then shook hands with Max, and he, in turn, introduced Andy and Danya. Landry handed Max and Andy folders containing satellite images of the estate with a sheet of paper clipped to each one. "Start with these. I'll be finished in just a moment." He resumed his call.

Max, Andy, and Danya stepped a few meters away, bent forward to shield the documents from the rain, and began inspecting the image.

After Max and his people had escaped from Damascus, he'd briefed Chugs on what had happened there. They both held the belief that Max had spooked Madison, causing him to move up his original timetable to deliver one of the nukes to a target in the US. David's intelligence research indicated one or two bombs were en route to Central America, and the uncertainty of the exact location of one of the nukes was troubling.

David had picked up information indicating that the Muslim Brotherhood was planning something, but he didn't know what it was. He feared that while the US was focused on Madison, the Brotherhood might be making a move to use one of the nukes Çakmak had or, perhaps, use the one that was unaccounted for. Since ISIS and the Brotherhood were working together, it made sense that the two organizations were sharing information. They knew Max was keeping pressure on Madison, but David couldn't find any indication that the Brotherhood knew about SOCOM's twenty-four-hour surveillance on General Çakmak's estate. Intelligence had led them to believe that Madison was successful in smuggling at least one of the nukes out of the Middle East, but there was no clue as to the method. Although the plan was to recover the nukes while still in the theater, that didn't happen. It would take time to locate the warheads again. Since David's analysis indicated the two nukes in Brazil could be moved, Chugs had directed Max to go for those two before the Brotherhood could act on them.

Captain Landry ended his call and stepped to where Max, Andy, and Danya were studying the image, sitting on a log beneath a large tree that provided some relief from the shower. The captain, as he approached, said, "That was my commander. He received a call from General Matherson, and I'm to tell you that Deputy SecDef Wes Brock is pressuring SOCOM. Matherson said we're to complete our mission in forty-eight hours; otherwise, we abort. They're stalling Brock and are to brief him on Friday about why we are in Brazil. Matherson doesn't like any of this and is uneasy with the entire situation. The reports seem to have dried up on the nuke you were hunting in Syria."

"Forty-eight hours doesn't give us much time," Max said. "I was hoping to have a C-130 gunship for support, but it looks like it'll be just us. Let's get to it."

The captain proceeded to brief them on the estate, covering every detail, although neither he nor his men had been inside the house. "The masonry wall around the estate is about eight feet high." He pointed to the image. "In the front is a double gate for the drive on the left and a single personnel gate in the center, a four-foot gate on the left side of the wall, about here." He pointed to each gate. "I have surveillance on the front and rear of the house around the clock. There appears to be six guards on duty twenty-four hours a day." He shot a glance to Max, Andy, then Danya, and went on to describe the swimming pool, garage, and a storage building at the rear of the estate and covered the guard's routine, time of shift changes, and meals.

Next, Landry passed out images of the airstrip and hanger, saying, "There's a private airstrip with an executive jet in a hanger about two kilometers from here. I believe that's the one Çakmak used to fly down here."

"Has the jet been moved since you have been here?" Max asked.

"No, sir. No one from the estate has gone near the hanger."

"Is General Çakmak inside the estate?" Max asked.

"Yes, sir." Landry replied. "We identified him the first day we were here. He usually comes out of the house about midmorning and talks to one of the guards, strolls around the grounds, then goes back inside. He has been coming out to eat with the guards when the noon meal is delivered. About 1400, he goes for a swim and goes back in about 1530."

Max looked at his watch and wiped the water from his face, then asked, "Have you seen any way we can get a confirmation that the warheads are actually inside the storage building? I don't want to risk getting someone hurt if they aren't there. I know we have good intel, but I need it verified."

The wiry commander looked to Bear as he shook his head. "There's no opportunity or way to verify what is in the building. Someone is always on the grounds and would see any one of us if we tried to get to the building. The only window is the one that faces the pool. You would have to be invisible to get in there."

Max looked at Andy and Danya, then said, "Any other questions?"

Each of them asked the captain several. Then Danya, with a serious look on her face, said, "Max, I know how it can be done. Since their meals are delivered, we intercept the van that delivers the food before it gets here. One of the soldiers and I will take the place of the caterers and deliver the meals. I'll provide a little distraction." The conviction in her voice was unmistakable.

Max glanced to Andy, then to the captain before answering, "No, it's too risky. Too many things could go wrong, and you could get killed. That would blow the entire operation."

Danya argued, emphatically disagreed, demurred with determination, and said, "Max, it's simple. We take the van, exchange clothes, then deliver the meals as usual. Captain Landry said the truck pulls into the front gate, one of the guards in the front looks in the van, then admits it. The two in the van remove the food from the vehicle and carry it to the back. They set it up on the end of the pool with the outdoor kitchen. That's the end closest to the storage building. It's simple. Once inside, we can identify all the guards and I can get a look inside the building."

Max lifted his jungle hat and ran his hand over his head and down his face. He then repeated, "It's too risky." He looked to the captain and hesitated, then back to Danya. "The outgoing and incoming guards'll be there. That's twelve of them we have to deal with, and you'd be right in the middle of 'em."

Reading his expression, Landry said, "It's daring, sir. It could work."

"We could also lose two good people." Max glanced to Danya.

He couldn't miss her expression of determination and confidence. He knew Danya, her abilities, and above all, her determination. His biggest concern was for her safety. They were supposed to meet in the Caribbean and then get married before all this happened. *If something goes wrong and she's killed...how do I live with that?* he thought. *There's no question she's good enough and can do it, but it's Danya.* Max looked back to Danya, noting her countenance, and, fighting against his feelings, said, "Okay. Don't take any unnecessary chances. Deliver the food, set up, look around, and get out of there. It's about twenty meters to the building. That's too far to try for a close look. If you can't see in the window, don't try it. If you do see it, just nod, then get down. Remember, stay on the route to the outdoor kitchen that Bear gives you."

"I can do it. I know what to do. Don't worry about me. You be careful and hit them hard," she replied.

Her confidence bothered Max. He looked to Bear and said, "They'll need to intercept the van and show up at the gate at the normal time. Pick one of your men to go with her. Rehearse them on the caterer's movements after they arrive. Choregraph it well and make sure everyone knows it. Select a place to stop the van."

Bear nodded. "Yes, sir. Staff Sergeant Sanchez. He's good and is fluent in Spanish and Portuguese. He's also about the same size as the caterers who have been delivering the food. There's a place a couple of kilometers back up the road, around the bend. It dips to a low place. We'll stop 'em there."

Max pushed his jungle hat up and wiped his forehead and face. He shot a look to Danya, then said, "Get 'em ready. We'll do it at this evening's delivery. Half of them'll be occupied with the meal. Any questions?"

Everyone said "no" with a shake of their heads.

Max stood and said, "Let's go take a look at the estate."

⸺ ♦ ♦ ♦ ⸺

Wednesday, June 29, 2016
Abandoned House
Kozan, Turkey

George met Erol again at the abandoned house overlooking the Kilgen River, parking his car two blocks away—far enough not to reveal his destination but close enough if he needed to make a fast getaway.

The two sat at the coffee table in the living room with the curtains drawn, two candles flickering between them with just enough light for them to see each other. Although the conditions were sparse, Erol was still a gracious host. A plate of figs, cheese, a tin of pistachios, a cool bottle of water, and raki were spread across the small table between them. Erol picked up a glass, poured it half-full of the raki and added water, and handed it to George, then did the same for himself. The two touched their glasses with a clink.

Even in the dim light, George noticed that Erol looked rested and a little more relaxed as he picked up a piece of cheese and sat back. "What information do you have for me?"

Erol took a sip and said, "I've been here too long. I am clearing out."

George leaned forward. "You didn't ask me to come here just to tell me you're moving. What do you have?"

Erol placed a pistachio in his mouth, then said, "The Muslim Brotherhood has not shipped the warhead to Central America. I have this from several reliable sources. The Brotherhood has been very quiet on the nukes. The information they leaked—that the nuke was shipped—was a ruse. They hoped the US would turn their attention elsewhere, but in fact, the nukes are still in Syria. My sources are unsure if they are going to ship both out of the country or not. I got the feeling they wanted to see what the response would be before committing. The Brotherhood might ship one and keep the other one hidden for a while. That is just a gut feeling on my part. They believe they have a better chance of getting at least one out of the country while the US is chasing the 'rabbit' elsewhere."

George's eyes had widened as Erol spoke. He replied, "Are you sure? Do you know where they are?"

"I verified this with two others," Erol said. He retrieved a piece of paper from his shirt pocket and handed it to George. "They are in Syria… Aleppo. This is the location. I will take you there tomorrow night. But first, I must go to the new location I have found. It is in a small town of Karsi, which is about two hours south of here, on the coast. We can leave from there tomorrow night just after dark."

George nodded and sipped his raki.

Erol stood and stepped across the room to another table. He picked up a map, then returned to his chair and unfolded it as he sat. He proceeded to show George the route they would take to his new quarters and then on to the location of the nukes. They planned their reconnaissance in detail. Erol knew very little about how the warheads were guarded or who was guarding them. They would have to determine that when they got there and submit it to SOCOM so an assault could be made to recover the bombs before they left Syria. Unfortunately, preparing a complete briefing package would take more time than they had.

George stood, walked over to a window, and peered out as he withdrew his cell phone from his pocket. He punched in the number for SOCOM and, when Major General Matherson was on the line, relayed to him what Erol had told him. "Yes, General, Erol said it was a ruse and we're going to check it out tomorrow night. It might take me a while to get back with you. The initial report seems credible."

"Get back to me as soon as you can," Matherson said. "I want to recover them in Syria, if possible. If they manage to ship them out of there, we may not be able to find them again in time."

"I understand, General. I'll get you an update as soon as possible." George ended the call and returned to his chair.

— ◆ ◆ ◆ —

Wednesday, June 29, 2016
Lieutenant General Devrim Çakmak's Estate
Cantá, State of Roraima, Brazil

The special forces team, augmented by Max's team, each eased up to their assigned locations around the perimeter of the estate, selecting a position with good visibility of their assigned sector. The thick foliage shielded them from any breeze, holding in the humidity. The morning rain had ended several hours ago and, as the sun replaced the clouds, the jungle had turned into a sauna. Sweat soaked their uniforms. It didn't take long for the normal order of the jungle to return after the humans were settled in, insects, reptiles, and animals going back to their routine.

Max and the captain lay prone next to each other and observed the estate, scrutinizing each detail. Their position provided good visibility of the rear of the house and a portion of the double gate in the front.

Bear, via his radio, checked with each position. Receiving confirmation, he looked to the captain and nodded. "No change. Everyone is ready." He placed the mouthpiece of the drinking tube between his lips and sucked water from the hydration pack.

With binoculars, Max studied the estate and compared it with the satellite image Landry had provided. Two guards were visible on the rear grounds, one slouched in a chair by the pool and the other meandering around. Although Max couldn't see the front, he received periodic updates from the soldiers on what the guards were doing.

"They're getting lax," Max said in a low voice as he lowered the binoculars and turned his head toward the captain. "There's the third guard coming around the far corner of the house."

"I see him," the captain replied. He turned and motioned to a soldier behind and to the right of him.

Seeing the captain's signal, the soldier gave a slight nod in reply that he saw the guard come around the corner of the house too.

The captain turned back to Max. "My men in the front have identified the three guards in that sector. We have all six in sight. The relief will be straggling out in a few minutes. They'll set up the area for the food and a couple of tables to eat on. When they finish eating, they'll relieve the other guards. The outgoing shift eats, then cleans up," Landry said, then looked at his watch. "Danya and Sergeant Sanchez are in position, waiting on the van."

Max checked his watch, then took a deep breath. "Is everything still the same as before?"

The captain replied, his voice just above a whisper, "Yes, sir. They've always set up on the end nearest the storage building and eaten around the pool. When they finish eating, the next shift takes over."

"Good," Max replied. "I want eyes on all six of the on-duty guards and as many of the oncoming ones as possible. We'll go just as they start to eat. There'll be enough chaos to minimize our risk."

"Roger," the captain replied.

Sweat streaked the faces of the Americans, more from the tension than the heat, as they remained motionless around the perimeter of the estate, waiting to execute. Their eyes were the only things that moved as they scrutinized the estate, except for the occasional slow turn of their heads. The jungle can be a noisy place when it is undisturbed. When it goes silent, trouble is lurking. The absence of sound would be a signal to the guards of the estate that something or someone is in the area. They would be alerted to a possible threat. Stealth was an integral part of how the special forces operated, and they would not violate it that day.

Calculating that Danya and Staff Sergeant Sanchez should have commandeered the van by now, Max checked his watch and then looked to Bear.

"They've got the van and will be leaving in about three minutes," Bear said in a low voice.

"Roger," Max replied with a nod. He surveyed the estate again. From all appearances they were still undetected. He took a deep breath and controlled its release.

"The van is en route now," Bear said as he wiped sweat from his brow.

"Roger," Max replied, looking to the captain.

Landry, anticipating Max's command, made eye contact with Bear and in a low voice said, "Notify the men they are on the way and to get ready."

Each of the Americans focused on their assigned zone and targets. The double gate at the entrance would be the first test for Sergeant Sanchez and Danya. If there was any trouble at the entrance, Sanchez would give a prearranged signal to his teammates to engage the guards so the van could escape.

Sanchez had watched the caterer's routine numerous times—arrival, set up, serving the meals, and clean up afterward. Although he'd briefed Danya in detail, he would coach her as if she were newer in the job, establishing himself as the lead so the guards would focus on him. He would speak Portuguese to everyone at the estate except when instructing Danya, when he would speak Spanish. He looked as you would expect a food service person to look, wearing a black chef's cap, white jacket trimmed in black with a company logo over his breast pocket, and black utility pants. The bulky jacket hid the abundant waistline of the pants. He'd done the best he could, and although not a tailored outfit, it didn't look all that bad. Danya was dressed in black, with a chef's beanie over her hair that was pulled back in a ponytail. Her chef's jacket, with a company logo on the pocket, provided ample room and did not flatter her trim figure. It did conceal the waist of the pants she had to gather up. As long as Sanchez and Danya stuck to the same procedure, they anticipated the guards would be none the wiser since the occasionally different caterers showing up was nothing out of the ordinary.

Bear said in a low voice as he looked to Max and the captain, "Here they come."

Max and the captain nodded, keeping their attention on the front gate. A gray van with *Lulite Festas e Eventos* painted on the sides rolled to a stop at the gate. One of the guards walked out and approached the driver.

Max tensed as he watched the guard, unable to see Danya in the passenger seat opposite his view. The guard and Sanchez appeared to have a brief exchange, then Sanchez opened the door and walked to the rear of the van. He stood to the side as he opened the rear doors, allowing the man to look inside. Resting his left hand on the door, Sanchez gave a slight signal with his hand to the soldier behind him, in the dense foliage that provided cover for him, that so far, all was going as planned.

The guard, after seeing the hot boxes containing food, stacks of beverages, dishes, and supplies—the same as he had seen time and again—closed the doors, then motioned for Sanchez to enter the gate. Following the instructions, the sergeant got back in the van and eased it inside, stopping about fifty meters in, where he'd been told to park.

The Green Beret who'd observed Sanchez's signal radioed to Bear, "So far so good. They're inside. Sanchez kinda looks like he's wearing his brother's clothes."

"Roger," Bear replied. "I don't think these guys are fashion experts."

Sanchez and Danya exited the front and stepped to the rear of the van. Without hesitation and doing exactly as they'd rehearsed, they began unloading. Danya, her knife roll slung over her shoulder, wheeled the first dolly of hot boxes around the house to the pool. As she made her way, she scrutinized the area, looking for possible cover, where the guards were, and mentally planning an escape route in case she needed it. She knew she was covered by the American soldiers every step she took, but she also knew all too well that anything could go wrong and she could wind up shot or dead.

At the end of the pool, several guards were setting up tables and chairs for the meal. As Danya guided the dolly up next to the table, she made eye contact with one of the guards nearby. She smiled and went about her duties, placing her knife roll on one of the boxes she then placed under the table. Sanchez moved in position right behind her, pushing a loaded dolly. As soon as he reached the table, he unloaded it and then returned to the van to get the next load of food. Danya started placing the stands for the chafing pans on the table and cans of Sterno beneath each one. She shot a glance to the guard again and smiled.

The guard stepped closer to her and said in Portuguese, "Would you like some help?" He handed her another can of Sterno.

In Spanish, Danya replied, "I am sorry, I don't speak Portuguese." She took the can from him, touching his hand as she displayed a smile.

He repeated his question in Spanish.

Danya replied, "Thank you. You have nice hands. I like strong men with nice hands." She winked.

A grin appeared on the guard's face as he caught her flirt. He handed her another can. For the next few minutes as Danya turned on her charm while arranging the serving line with utensils for the food, she gave instructions to the man. Her trifles and occasional touches increased. She stepped around the table and stooped over at the first hot box to remove a tray, taking her time removing the tray to give the man a long look at her from the rear. She anticipated the testosterone was taking control of him. As she rose, she caught a glimpse of the guard looking her over.

She set the tray of food in the stand, then said, "Light the cans." She made sure she touched his hand again and brushed against him.

Several more minutes passed until she saw the expression on his face and knew he was envisioning how she looked beneath the chef's jacket. Danya looked into his eyes and said in a soft voice, "130 reais."

"100 reais," he countered.

Danya shook her head. "130 reais. I promise to be the highlight of your day."

He nodded with a slight smirk.

"I must finish setting up first. Help him, I can take care of the rest of this," she said as she pointed to Sergeant Sanchez. Just as he turned and stepped away, Danya bent over and reached under the table where she had placed the knife roll. She opened it, grasped her pistol, and slipped it into her cargo pocket.

No one saw what she did.

Once the guards were lined up and shuffling down the buffet line, Sergeant Sanchez scanned the six men, taking a mental note. Each man was armed with an M4 carbine slung over his shoulder and a Taurus PT92 pistol on his hip. He felt vulnerable as he stood unarmed in front of the guards he and the other Americans were about to engage, serving them a meal. He had been assured by the caterers whose van he was using that no one ever checked their knife rolls. Feigning his role as the dutiful employee, he made his way to where he and Danya had hidden their weapons in the knife rolls placed under the table.

Three on-duty guards were dispersed across the back property, two on either side of the pool and one between the pool and main house. All were in open positions and visible to the Americans. Sanchez glanced toward Danya and gave her a slight nod.

Danya eyed the guard she'd made the deal with, who was standing at the end of the line, and stepped to him. In a low voice, she said, "130 reais, and we can go now."

A slight grin emerged on the man's face. He retrieved his billfold from his pocket, opened it, and fingered the contents. He withdrew three bank notes—R$100, R$20, and R$10—folded them, and handed them to Danya. She took the bills and shoved them into her pocket as casually as if she had just received the change for purchasing a loaf of bread.

Danya turned on her charm, dragging a finger down his chest. "Can we go in that little building?" She pointed to the storage building.

He looked to the shed, then around to the other guards, then back to her. "We are not supposed to go in there."

"Well, I'm not going to do it right here. We could go in the house, but I doubt your boss would approve. If you want it in public, it will cost you much, much more. Otherwise, no deal."

He looked her over from head to toe, seemingly measuring the risk to reward.

Knowing his testosterone was in control of him and wanting to prevent him from thinking about it too long, she withdrew the notes and held them in front of her and said, "What's it going to be?"

He looked around, then said, "Come on."

Danya stroked his arm and pulled him closer as the two stepped toward the shed. Reaching the door, he opened it, allowing her to precede him in. He looked back to the table where the others were eating and saw one of his teammates grin as he held his thumb up in front of him.

As soon as she entered the door, she scanned the contents of the small building. Two wooden crates were against the back wall, and a broom that had not been used in some time stood by the door. Two cylindrical objects covered by tarps sat against the two adjoining walls. They appeared to be supported on stands. She stepped closer to the objects and grasped the edge of the tarp.

The guard turned back toward Danya and closed the door. Catching her with her hands on the tarp, he said, "Looking for something?"

"Yes, something to block the window. This is private, remember?" Without waiting on a response from him, she removed the tarp and exposed the silver warhead. The quick glance was all she needed to verify it was what she was looking for. "Here, place this over the window." Without showing concern for what she had just seen, Danya tossed the tarp to the guard, turned around, and before he could object, yanked the corner of the second tarp, exposing the other warhead. The sound of the tarp hitting the floor was the only sound left in the shed.

"What are you doing?"

"The floor is filthy. I'm not rolling around in it, and I don't want to get all that in my hair." She began slipping free the buttons to her chef's jacket. "Don't take all day."

The guard's expression signaled his confusion. He was struggling with his emotions—one for his duty and the other for his craving. Danya had pegged him as one who liked the ladies and wasn't an intellect. Although he was duty bound to prevent access and discovery of the two warheads, he couldn't resist the attractive woman who had offered her body to him. Seeing her free the buttons of her jacket and expose her breast where it nestled in its lace bra kept him focused on sex.

She stood still and said, "The window." She pointed to it. "I do not have all day."

He turned and fastened the tarp to the window. Satisfied it was secured in place, he turned back to her.

Crouching, Danya had her pistol aimed at him. In a cold, stern voice she said, "Not a word and don't make any sudden moves. Take off your clothes."

The man's desire turned to rage. His knuckles whitened as he squeezed the sling of his carbine and stood motionless evaluating his position.

Danya's eyes locked onto his. "Don't underestimate me. Do as I say, and you will live. Remove the magazine and put your rifle on the floor."

He eased the carbine from his shoulder and released the magazine, allowing it to fall. Maintaining eye contact, he bent over and placed his carbine on the floor.

"Now the pistol," she said. "Unfasten the belt and let it fall."

He complied, and the pistol hit the floor with a thud.

"Now your boots."

The man hesitated, then bent down and reached for the lace of his right boot. In a quick move, he grasped the pistol belt and flung it toward Danya. Anticipating it would distract her, he lunged in an attempt to deflect the pistol and overpower her.

Danya fired twice. The first bullet struck the man in the chest and the second one hit him in the forehead. His lifeless body crumpled to the floor. Shooting the man was not what she had planned. She knew the shot was heard by the guards outside and all hell was about to break loose. She had a front row seat. She stepped over the body to the door and stood to the side as she opened it and peeked through. With a quick look, she saw one of the guards sprinting toward her with his carbine ready. She squeezed off two more rapid shots. Seeing him fall, she signaled with her hand, then slammed the door and grabbed the M4 carbine and magazine as she stepped over the body. Max gave the order for the Americans to fire as Danya took refuge behind one of the wooden crates, slapped the magazine into the carbine, and leveled it at the door.

Terror descended on the grounds of the estate. From around the perimeter, the special forces soldiers delivered death with precision fire. Although Danya's shot had alerted the guards at the table, events happened so fast that they were cut down before they knew what was taking place. The on-duty guards tried to identify the positions of the aggressors but were caught in the open. Though it seemed like an eternity with gunfire from all directions, it lasted less than a minute. Once the guards in the front were neutralized, the Americans began rushing through the gate.

Three lay dead on the front grounds near the gate while nine more littered the grounds at the rear of the estate. The first three commandos who entered the open gate burst into the house and began searching it for threats. By the time Max and Captain Landry arrived at the rear of the estate, two soldiers were escorting Lieutenant General Devrim Çakmak out of the house with his hands bound behind him. Like a trapped animal, his eyes were full of fear. He knew his life of luxury had ended. Spending the rest of his life behind bars was the best he could hope for.

Max headed straight for the shed, and as he neared it, Danya stepped out. "Are you all right?" he asked, stopping in front of her and pulling her into his arms, hugging her tightly.

"I'm fine. It got a little tense for a bit. There are two warheads inside," she replied as she squeezed him back.

"I told you not to take any unnecessary chances and you took a big one with that guard."

"That was the only way I could find out what was in there." She kissed his cheek, then released him.

Max stepped into the little building and looked down at the body. Blood was pooled on the floor around the corpse. A slight chill enveloped him. *That could have been Danya on the floor.* He pushed the thought from his mind and verified the two warheads, then called the general to report the successful capture.

CHAPTER 30

Friday, July 1, 2016
Bombed-Out Building
Aleppo, Syria

GEORGE AND EROL had found the location of the building where the Brotherhood was supposed to be keeping the nukes, and now they had to confirm the warheads were there. The night sky offered a clear view of the millions of stars in the Milky Way and a moon bright enough to read by. Unfortunately, the bright moon had an adverse effect on their stealth, making it easier for them to be seen by any of the Brotherhood guards. They had to use extreme caution and travel a meandering course to get to their destination, several times having to alter their route when they spotted fighters along the way. The two men snuck into a bombed-out building about two blocks away from the target. Climbing over the rubble and debris to the third floor, they were able to see into the courtyard of the suspected building.

Using night-vision binoculars, George said, "I think they've got about thirty to forty guys in there. Give me a minute, and I'll try and get a good count."

Terrorists in various fighting positions covered the property from street level to second and third story windows of the surrounding structures. The presence of that many armed individuals meant it was an important place—so far, Erol's reports had proven correct. Even with the high security, George still wanted to get into the building and verify that the nukes were there, so they continued to study the building and surroundings, seeking a way they could get in.

Men with Kalashnikovs meandered around the courtyard. Many of the window positions were also equipped with machine guns or RPG-7s.

About an hour after their arrival, three Toyota SUVs and a van arrived at the entrance to the courtyard.

Erol looked to George and in a low voice said, "This is not a good sign."

"Did you hear anything about them moving the nukes?" George asked as he lowered the night-vision binoculars from his eyes.

"No, nothing," Erol replied.

Inside the courtyard, two men with rifles slung over their shoulders walked the iron gates open and admitted the vehicles into the compound. The gates were closed as soon as the last vehicle entered. The Toyotas circled around and parked pointed toward the gate. The van backed in close to the doorway of the building. Three men got out of each vehicle and walked inside while the drivers stood beside the driver's doors. One of them stepped to the front of his vehicle and urinated. Another lit a cigarette. It wasn't long until George and Erol watched four men struggling to carry a wooden crate pass through the door and wrestle it into the van. One man backed out of the way as the remaining three men strained and pushed it farther into the van, then closed the doors.

George turned his head toward Erol and whispered, "Look. Just one. I'm afraid your feeling was right. They've split 'em up. I just wish we had the opportunity to verify that's one of them. Let's try not to lose this one. We'll never get back to the car fast enough to follow them, so I'll alert SOCOM. They might be able to locate the van and track it. When we get back to Turkey, I want you to find out where they're taking it just in case SOCOM doesn't find the van and where they have the other nuke. Lean hard on your contacts."

"We may be too late," Erol replied. "It looks like they are making their big push. We should go now."

Without speaking, George eased back from his position and raised to a crouch. Erol followed his lead, and the two worked their way down through the rubble, then made their way back to their car.

⸻ ✦ ⸻

Friday, July 1, 2016
Headquarters, US Special Operations Command
MacDill Air Force Base, Florida

FBI agent Gail Summers entered her work area at headquarters and said, her tone forceful, "Sweet Pea, are you in here?"

Senior Analyst David Elsworth replied, "Yes, Gail, *dahling.*"

"Get your ass over here," she said, then sat in her chair.

David stepped around his cubicle and sat in the chair next to hers. He crossed his legs, placed his hands in his lap, and said, "Yes, love. What can I do for you?"

Looking over the top of her glasses, Gail said, "The general told me Max has recovered the two warheads that were at General Çakmak's estate in Brazil."

In a sweet voice, David replied as he clapped his hands, "Oh, *dahling*, that's wonderful news. Is Max all right?"

Gail, trying not to roll her eyes, said, "Yes, he's fine. He's on his way back here. George called Matherson and told him the Brotherhood just moved one of the nukes that was in Aleppo. He believes they are shipping it to the US but doesn't know anything else or where they have the other one. Have any of your contacts mentioned anything that might indicate when or where it will enter the US?"

"No, it has been very quiet," he replied.

Gail removed her glasses and said, "Get back with your contacts at every port of entry and lean on them. Make sure they tell you everything, no matter how trivial it seems. Tell them you have creditable reports that a very dangerous cargo shipment is expected to cross the border. But don't mention a word about the warhead. Be careful who you talk to and what you say." She held a stern gaze on him before continuing. "If they hear or see something suspicious, have them call you immediately."

"Yes, ma'am."

"I'm going to check up on Senator Chapman and Gareth. We haven't heard anything out of them except trivial shit since Monday. That bothers me. I'm also going to call a friend I have on the border. I think I can trust him. He's always been truthful with me, and he knows a lot of people."

A smile emerged on David's face as he replied, "A friend? Are we going to take a trip to the border?"

Gail's brow furrowed, and her eyes narrowed as she replied in a harsh tone, "David, get to work!"

David stood, swiveled on the balls of his feet, then stepped back to his cubicle.

———•◆•———

Friday, July 1, 2016
JW Marriott Panama
Panama City, Panama

Nassar, al-Aqrab, and Bart met with al-Ghazāli in his suite to discuss the current situation.

"The bomb is on the way to Panama," al-Ghazāli said. "President Kağan called me. The Americans attacked General Çakmak's estate in Brazil and have taken the two warheads there. General Çakmak was able to call Kağan when the attack started, but the line went dead, and he is sure the Americans got him."

Sipping a glass of Crown Royal, Bart said with a serious expression, "What's Kağan going to do about Çakmak? He needs to be eliminated right away."

Al-Ghazāli sipped his tea and said, "Kağan is to call me. I will know soon. You have the locations from Gareth for the bomb?"

Bart set his glass on the coffee table, his eyes shot to al-Aqrab, then to Nassar and back to al-Ghazāli. He leaned forward and said, "I do, but I don't like any of them. That's what I wanted to talk to you about."

Al-Aqrab motioned with his hand. "Proceed."

"Gareth wants to set me up. If I go to any of those locations, Gareth will have the FBI there waiting on me. They plan to take me along with the nuke. Our objective will be lost. I recommend we keep everything the same except go to a different place. I have a plan, and the result will be the same."

"You know this to be true?" Al-Aqrab asked.

"Yes," Bart replied. "Senator Chapman keeps me informed."

"What is your plan?" Al-Aqrab asked, again sipping his tea.

"We use the Zetas to deliver the bomb. Nassar will contact Gareth and tell him the bomb is en route, but it will cost him the rest of the money. He should say there are more expenses. Gareth may throw a fit and say he'll threaten to walk. Don't believe him. It'll be a bluff. Count on him sending Chapman with the money. Gareth'll think it is one of the three sites. If Gareth presses Nassar, he'll tell him one of the locations Gareth gave us and the time when we have the rest of the money."

Al-Ghazāli's eyes narrowed as he said, "He will still set you up. The FBI will have time to get to the location. I do not understand."

Bart glanced at the others. "That's right. They'll have time to get to the location and set their trap. However, that's not where the bomb will go off. I plan to set it off in New York. Chapman is keeping me updated on Gareth's itinerary. I'll choose a location close to Gareth."

"New York?" Al-Aqrab asked. "Three years ago, you were against New York. What has changed?"

Bart answered in a matter-of-fact tone, "This time it's personal. He's tried to have me killed. That didn't work. Now he wants to set me up. Two can play at the double-cross game."

Nassar held up his hand. "You will end one of our resources in the government. We get a lot of money and favors from Gareth. When Jenny is elected, we will get a lot more."

"No," Bart said. "We tell her to cooperate or end up like her husband. We'll help make her a martyr and keep her in power. She'll cooperate."

Al-Aqrab stroked the scar on his cheek as he lowered his dark eyes in thought, then he looked to Bart and said, "New York. Tell me what the nuke will do to New York."

"Aside from the massive destruction," Bart replied, "a detonation on the East Coast will knock out the electrical grid and be followed by a large electromagnetic pulse, doing more damage. The massive fallout, along with the pulse, will hit DC as well, depending on the winds. Transportation on the East Coast will be cut off, the financial markets will collapse, and the government will shut down. Of course, the blast and radiation will have a devastating psychological effect on Americans throughout the country. I can go on and on, but you get the picture. We'll have our money *and* achieve our objective."

Al-Ghazāli sat motionless. After a moment, he sipped his tea, looked to al-Aqrab, then back to Bart.

"What would the American response be?" al-Aqrab asked.

"Nothing. If the president starts making threats, we remind him that we have another one. The president is favorable to the Muslim Brotherhood, some say even a member. We'll have the Brotherhood control him. Since we are using the Zetas to deliver the bomb, I can make sure there is enough evidence leading back to them, even a couple of bodies with evidence. Jenny won't be in office until January but will be an influencer until then. We'll own her. The administration will make a big show with the help of the news media, but I think we can control them. The Zetas are in Mexico, and the US will need approval from Mexico to take action against them."

"What about Kenworth?" al-Ghazāli asked. "He has been right behind us for a while."

Bart downed the rest of his Crown Royal. "Yes, Kenworth. I'm going to set a trap for him as well. I'll leave him a trail of breadcrumbs he won't be able to resist—right to the nuke. He'll be vaporized in the blast."

Al-Aqrab made eye contact with al-Ghazāli. It was as if they were locked in mental telepathy, both motionless for a moment. Then al-Ghazāli looked to Bart and said, "New York is acceptable."

Al-Aqrab nodded in agreement.

—◆◆◆—

Saturday, July 2, 2016
Gareth Residence
New York, New York

Stew had been on the phone with Senator Chapman for several minutes when he said, "I got a call from Nassar. He told me the item has been shipped. I want you to come up here in the morning. We have a few things to discuss."

"Stew, I can't make it. I am giving a speech on the fourth, and I'm trying to get ready for it. My staff hasn't even finished my speech yet."

Stew replied through clenched teeth, "Archie, get your ass up here in the morning. I don't have time for your shit. The convention is in three weeks, and Jenny has dropped in the polls again. I wanted this to have been taken care of by now, but it couldn't be delivered any sooner. Everything is in motion, and I can't change it."

"Stew, really, I—"

"Tomorrow morning." Stew slammed the phone down.

———— ✦ ✦ ✦ ————

Saturday, July 2, 2016
Headquarters, US Special Operations Command
MacDill Air Force Base, Florida

Gail received another call from NSA alerting her that they'd captured another conversation on Senator Chapman's cell phone. "That's right," the watch officer said. "We got it about two hours ago. I'm sending you the transcript."

"Good!" Gail replied. "What're the details? Skip the *I love yous*, just give me the details without all the shit."

"Yes, ma'am," he replied. "Gareth told Chapman he received a call from Nassar saying the item has been shipped. Then he instructed Chapman to go to New York in the morning as they have things to discuss. Chapman protested. Gareth mentioned the convention in three weeks and said it couldn't be delivered any sooner. Everything is in motion, and he can't change it."

"Shit!" Gail replied. "It's the nuke. I want Chapman's and Gareth's conversation captured tomorrow when they meet. This is it. I want every word, and get me the transcript ASAP."

"Will do," he replied.

CHAPTER 31

Sunday, July 3, 2016
Gareth Residence
New York, New York

I CING ALREADY LITTERED Archie's shirt. He picked up his coffee and sipped it, dripping a new stain onto his shirt.

Anxious to get to the point of the meeting, Stew said as he picked up the remote and turned on the stereo in an attempt to block any eavesdropping, "Madison didn't give you any indication when the nuke would be in the US?" The senator had become problematic and required stronger coercion and finesse to get him to cooperate. Stew needed him for the time being and knew how to work him. Stew—ensuring plenty of pastries and scotch were on hand—took a slow approach with him. He avoided any topic related to the campaign until Archie started eyeing the Glenlivet on the counter. He knew the bulky senator would opt for a drink in no time.

Archie lowered his coffee and said, "No, not a word. He was just vague about everything."

Stew sipped his coffee, then leaned back and crossed his legs. "You gave him the locations. Did he indicate which one would be the target?"

Napkin in hand, Archie dabbed at the coffee on his shirt as he replied, "Like I said, Madison didn't say anything. I've told you everything."

Stew uncrossed his legs and slid his chair closer to the desk, resting his arms on it. "Three weeks until our convention in Philly. The locations we gave to Madison were Cleveland, Toledo, and Denver. Madison will need to go to each location and plan his operation. That gives him very little time to set it up. I don't think he will make it to Cleveland the week of the eighteenth. But the following week in Toledo or Denver are possible. We'll be in Philly at the convention the week of the twenty-fifth."

"Unless he has already visited his target," Archie said as he stood, ambled to the counter, and poured himself a scotch.

"Good point," Stew replied. "We've got to figure out which target he is going to hit. We go on a two-state tour right after the convention in the Rust Belt—Pennsylvania and Ohio. Jenny is also scheduled to be in Denver on the third. If Denver is the target, we'll need to reschedule the event. We don't want to be in the same state when he sets that thing off. Jenny isn't doing well with blue-collar and older voters."

"Have you asked Nassar?" Archie asked as he returned to his chair. "Perhaps he can find out."

"I have," Stew replied. "He doesn't know either. Speaking of Nassar, he wants the rest of the money." He held his coffee cup with both hands and looked over the top of it. "I need you to deliver the rest of it to Panama on Friday."

Archie's face flushed. He took a drink of his scotch and set the glass on the end table. His hand dropped to his lap and bumped the cut Bart had given him a week ago. It was still tender, and Archie flinched. The memory of that day in the jungle flashed in his mind. Bart terrified him, and he didn't want to have another meeting with him. "I can't deliver it on Friday," he said. "The week is packed with the holiday being tomorrow. I have meetings every day. It is—"

Setting his cup on the desk, Stew said in a harsh tone, "Archie, knock off the shit! Cancel whatever meetings you have and make that delivery. We've too much riding on this. The election is in the home stretch. You're the only one I can trust to do it. Fly down there Thursday and come back Friday night or Saturday."

"Stew, really, I can't. Not this week."

Stew slammed his fist down and the coffee cup almost turned over, then through clenched teeth said, "I'm in no mood to put up with your shit, Archie. You're going. I'll give Nassar a call and tell him to have a nice treat waiting for you in the hotel. I'll lean on him to get the details of the delivery. I want you to tell the acting CIA director to focus on Madison. I want to know his movements and who he's meeting with.

The CIA should be able to find out where he's going in the US and when. I don't want him taken out yet."

Archie nodded, then said, "What about Kenworth? He could upset everything."

Stew's eyebrows raised as picked up a cigar from the humidor on his desk. "I've been so busy, he'd slipped my mind. Wes Brock called and briefed me on his meeting with SOCOM. Bottom line is that they recovered two of the nukes and have General Çakmak in custody. If Kenworth finds Madison before he can get the nuke to the target, he could cost us the election. I told him to slow Kenworth down. When you talk to the acting director, remind him to take care of Kenworth."

— ✦ —

Monday, July 4, 2016
Headquarters, US Special Operations Command
MacDill Air Force Base, Florida

Max, Danya, and Andy were back at headquarters after returning from Brazil, their first duty was to brief Chugs on that operation and get his guidance on recovering the last two warheads.

"Max," Matherson cautioned, "once the nukes enter the US, our problems get a lot bigger. Remember, the Posse Comitatus Act prevents the use of military forces from operations inside the US. We'll need both presidential and legislative approval for SOCOM, which includes you, to operate on US soil. We sure as hell can't ask them for their approval."

"But the FBI can," Max replied. "If the nukes do cross the border into the US, we put Gail out front as the lead. If she discovers them, she calls it counterterrorism and askes for our help with surveillance, intelligence gathering, observation. She'll make the arrests."

"That might be thin ice, Max," Matherson replied. "But it's easier to ask forgiveness after the fact than permission beforehand. Let's hope we don't need to find out. Okay, brief her."

As soon as their meeting ended with the general, they met in the SCIF conference room with Gail and David. After the greetings, they got down to business. Max provided an update on their current situation and shared the general's guidance. Each of them, in turn, gave an update on their area of responsibility.

Max sipped his coffee, then said, "We know one warhead has left Syria but don't know the status of the other one. Finding the one we know about and recovering it before it gets into the US is a must. If Madison gets it across the border, our job becomes more complicated. Gail, if that happens, you become the lead and we are just advisers. We've gotta be careful with Posse Comitatus."

"I understand. I'll take care of the admin stuff on my end," she replied.

"Remember, we don't know who we can trust, " Max said. "We know Senator Chapman, the Gareths, CIA, attorney general, the assistant SecDef, and there is no telling who else are not to be trusted on this. Be careful who you talk to or what you submit electronically. We must keep this close hold. If word gets out, the attorney general will shut us down and you know what that means."

Gail scribbled on her notepad and said, "I'll keep everything quiet and not submit anything until I have to. There are a couple senior FBI Agents I can trust."

Max looked to Danya. "Get with Thaddeus Nussbaum and tell him we need to use him for our intelligence. You can tell him why. Have him ramp up his coverage of the Zetas, MS-13, and the drug routes through Panama."

Danya nodded. "David has maintained contact with Thaddeus and kept him updated. I'm sure he'll provide the support."

"When talking to someone, make sure you phrase your information as counterterrorism," Max cautioned.

Their meeting went on for another half hour with Max providing instructions and guidance on the situation and what to do if the warhead were to make it into the US. Based on the intelligence David had developed, it would arrive in Panama. He anticipated it would be transported along one of the drug routes into the US. Max was aware of the sophistication of the cartels' transportation capabilities and made brief comments about them.

Gail opened a folder. "Here's the transcript of the meeting Gareth and Chapman had yesterday. Gareth provided three locations for the bomb—Cleveland, Toledo, and Denver. He doesn't know which location Madison will pick. He's sending Chapman to Panama on Friday with the rest of the money. He seems to believe Madison will visit the locations to scout out the targets. Gareth is timing this to occur with one of the political rallies."

"That sounds like Madison," Max said. "He'll scout out the target and keep it quiet up to the end. Those're good starting points. Look for anything that might reveal the actual target. Anything, no matter how trivial, could be the clue we need."

Gail pushed the folder to the center of the table so the others could read the transcript. "In the conversation, Gareth told Chapman to get with the acting CIA director to locate Madison and find out which location it is and keep tabs on him. Wes Brock is to slow us down. Chapman is supposed to remind Wellington that he is to take care of you, Max."

Max nodded, then looked to Andy and said, "Get with your contacts at JIATF-South and alert them. Then see what you can come up with on the CIA in relation to Panama and on me. They'll probably use contractors." He was referring to the Joint Interagency Task Force South, Key West, Florida.

"Got it," Andy replied.

Max looked to Gail. "There'll be a lot of security and intelligence gathering in those three cities in preparation for the political rallies. David might be able to pick up some intel if he spends a couple of days at each city. He'll fit right in." Max looked to David with raised eyebrows and said, "Counterterrorism."

Gail turned to David. "Well, Sweet Pea, what do you think?"

With a smile spread across his face, David replied, "Oh my, yes. That will be so much fun. Do I get a gun?"

Gail rolled her eyes. "No, David. You are just going there to collect information."

Max shifted his attention to Danya and said, "Tell Thaddeus that Chapman is going to Panama on Thursday for a meeting Friday. See if they can tail him as soon as he gets off the plane. We need to know where he goes and who he meets. If he meets with Madison, apprehend both and the money. Provide Thaddeus with all the details on Madison."

Gail removed her glasses. "I could follow Chapman to Panama and assist Thaddeus."

Max sipped his coffee again, then said, "No, I need you here."

For the next three days, Max and his team spent long hours trying to develop intel on the location of the warhead, the planned route into the US, and the target. The only lead they had to Madison was Chapman. NSA placed a high priority on capturing Chapman's phone and Madison's number they had captured earlier. DIA informed Andy they hadn't intercepted any cell-phone transmissions from al-Aqrab or al-Ghazāli since 21 June. They believed the two ditched their phones when Madison discovered the bugs left in his room in Damascus. Also, DIA had not picked up the signal from the GPS tracking chip since Major Marsden planted it. They didn't know if it was discovered and destroyed, or the signal was being blocked. They did confirm it was working. If it was blocked, the device would go to sleep and wake up when a signal from a cell tower was available.

With each passing hour of each day, and the lack of intelligence on Madison, Max and his team's frustration increased. They knew that he was getting closer to achieving his goal. So far, all the information they had led them to the three cities mentioned in the Gareth transcript. Max had placed a large cork board with a US map pinned to it next to the wall and put red map pins on each location. He compared the dates with the political rallies and scheduled conventions. Cleveland being just over two weeks away, he sent David there first. Gail was going over the police reports and newspapers from each of the cities but found nothing out of the ordinary. Max and Andy had also been scanning the papers over the past several days, so they expanded their search to other major US cities that Madison might target as well. Max clipped articles from newspapers he thought might provide clues to Madison's target. One article reported that a Los Zetas gang member was apprehended at the southern US border. Another reported on an MS-13 gang member who was apprehended south of Baltimore on I-95, and another that a Los Zetas gang member was arrested on drug charges on I-95 south of New York. He pinned each article next to the map and placed map pins on the location mentioned in each article.

———◆◆◆———

Thursday, July 7, 2016
Panama Marriott Hotel
Panama City, Panama

An attractive, petite Panamanian woman greeted Senator Chapman as he approached the registration desk. "Your room is ready, *Senador*." She eyed the small overnight bag and boxes stacked on the bellman's cart, then motioned to the bell captain and said, "Help the *Senador* to his room."

Chapman shoved the keycard into his pocket as he looked to the bellman. "That won't be necessary. I can manage, thank you."

"*Senador*," the young woman said, "you have a message." She handed him a small white envelope.

Knowing the message was taking him closer to Madison—the evil man he didn't want to meet with—he had to muster up all his strength to maintain his composure. He looked at the envelope as his hand began to tremble, then shoved it unopened into his shirt pocket and walked to the elevator, tugging at the cart. It was a beautiful day, but Archie Chapman knew he was caught in the middle of a horrible thunderstorm.

Once inside his room, he shoved the cart against the wall and dropped his overnight bag on the king bed. As he turned, he saw the bottle of Glenlivet XXV on the desk with a glass next to it. He stepped to one of the large windows and opened the curtains, allowing the bright sunlight to burst in. Then he stepped to the next window and opened that curtain. He took a moment to gaze out on the picturesque view of Panama City and tried to lose himself in the tropical paradise, but it was useless. Memories of his previous trip flooded his mind.

He stepped back to the desk, flopped into the chair, and opened the bottle, then poured the glass full. He sucked half of it down before he took the envelope from his pocket and opened it. Extracting a folded piece of paper, he unfolded it and read the message. *Call this number when you arrive.* He glanced at the number, then dropped the paper and envelope onto the desk and lifted the glass to his mouth, filling it with sufficient false courage to make the call.

On the third ring, a familiar voice with a Spanish accent answered, "*¿Senador* Chapman?"

It was the voice of the man he had met in the restaurant the last time he was in Panama. Chapman replied, "Yes."

The voice replied, "Be in the Corvina y Caña Restaurante at 6:00 p.m."

Then the phone went dead.

Chapman dropped the phone into the cradle, grasped the bottle of scotch, and filled his glass again. He felt as though a shroud of darkness had just enveloped him. The chair squeaked under his formidable weight as he leaned back. He took another mouth full of Glenlivet and sat motionless for a moment, then fished his cell phone from his pocket and set the glass on the desk. He rubbed his face, then punched in the number for Stew to report that he was in his hotel and had made contact.

"I am meeting with him this evening," Chapman said. "I will call you tomorrow after the transfer."

"Don't forget to press him on the delivery details," Gareth replied.

Chapman lifted the glass to his lips and sipped. "I will."

He ended the call, dropped his cell phone on the desk, then stood with glass in hand and stepped to the window to gaze out. He tried to think of his brunette staffer, but all he could think about was meeting Bart again. Stepping back to the chair, he picked up the remote and switched on the flat-screen TV atop the dresser.

Chapman was restless, flipping through the channels, not really paying attention to what was showing. Realizing that he had been through the channels three times, he stepped to the bed, set the glass and remote on the nightstand, and lay down. With each sound of someone in the hall, he looked over, expecting Bart to be at his door. He finally got up from the bed and got ready for his meeting.

At 6:00 p.m. Senator Chapman stood in the doorway of the restaurant and looked around. He saw the same dark-complected man he'd met before seated alone by the large windows. Ignoring the maître d', he ambled toward the man.

As he approached, his contact held up a glass of wine and said, "*Senador*, welcome to *Panamá*. Have a seat."

Chapman slid into the chair, and the well-groomed man filled a glass of Sauvignon blanc from a bottle chilling in the ice bucket next to the table just as he had the last time. His demeanor was casual and nonchalant, not what one would expect for a clandestine meeting. It was more like a meeting of old friends. He handed the glass to the senator and held his gaze on Chapman for a moment. His dark eyes unnerved the senator.

"Thank you," Archie said with caution. He sipped the wine and waited for his host to speak.

The man leaned forward and in a low voice said, "You were followed from the airport."

A chill came over Chapman. He turned his head and scanned the dining room, seeking anyone who seemed interested in him, then he looked out of the large window. No one seemed to care about his presence.

"Relax, *Senador*," his contact said. "We are watching them. I have ordered you dinner. Enjoy your meal. Your treat will be in your room when you finish." He emptied the remainder of his glass, looked at Chapman, and said, "Don't leave the hotel. You will be contacted and told what to do." He smiled, stood, and walked out of the restaurant.

Chapman watched the man leave, then gulped his wine. His hands began to tremble. The waiter brought out his meal and sat the plate in front of him, then filled his glass from the wine in the bucket.

The senator looked up at the man and said, "Bring me a whiskey."

The waiter nodded and left.

Chapman picked at his food and drank more than he ate, his nerves having the best of him about what would happen tomorrow. Soon he wandered up to his hotel room and sank into denial so he could enjoy his company.

At seven-thirty the next morning, a knock at the door rousted Archie from his slumber. He looked around the room and saw the boxes still on the cart. His toy had vanished. Again, a knock came from the door. He grabbed the robe from the closet and slipped it on. Groggy and disheveled, he shuffled to the door. Opening it, his eyes focused on a trim, dark-haired man of about forty wearing a blazer with the hotel logo on the breast pocket.

The man stepped past Archie as soon as the door opened, then closed it behind him. "At 9:00 a.m. a car will pick you up. You are to take a tour of the Miraflores Locks. You brought what you were instructed?"

"Who are you?" Archie asked, then waited for the man to speak. When he didn't, Archie got the message. This man scared him almost as much as Madison. In a nervous voice, Chapman said, "Yes. Yes, it's right here. All of it." He motioned to the boxes on the cart. "Do you want to count it?"

"No," the intruder replied. "If it is not correct, you'll hear from us. Everything is in motion now."

"When and where will it arrive in the US?" Archie asked.

The man shrugged.

"You have the money. Tell me!" Archie said in protest. "Am I still being followed?"

"I'll take care of everything here. Enjoy the tour and don't worry about being followed," the stranger snapped as he stepped to the door.

As soon as the door closed, Archie flopped into the desk chair. He rubbed his stubbled face with trembling hands, then picked up his cell and punched in Stew's number. When Stew answered, Archie said, "I am being followed. A guy just came to the door and told me to take a tour of the Miraflores Locks. He asked about the money but didn't want to see it. What do I do?"

"Calm down, Archie," Stew replied. "Who's following you?"

"I was told by the man I met with last night that I was followed from the airport. The guy just now told me not to worry about it. He didn't tell me anything else."

"Did he tell you the details of the delivery?" Stew asked.

"No, he wouldn't tell me. He just said everything was in motion."

"Damn it!" Stew said in frustration. "I'll check with the CIA and see if they know anything. I'll let you know what I find out. Just do as he told you and stay calm. You don't have anything to worry about."

CHAPTER 32

Friday, July 8, 2016
Erol's New Location
Karsi, Turkey

"Erol," George said, his voice just above a whisper as he closed the door behind him.

Hearing a moan in the darkness, he stepped to the center of the room. As his eyes adjusted, he saw a form laying on the couch. He picked up one of the candles from the coffee table and lit it, raising the candle to shine light on the motionless form.

Even in the dim light, George could tell that Erol was in bad shape. His clothes were dirty and crumpled. Dark stains marked his pants and shirt. George's eyes were drawn to the bandage, the center darkened, on Erol's side. Erol's head rolled to the side, revealing sunken eyes in a dirt-streaked face.

"I came as soon as I could," George said in a soft voice as he knelt beside him. "How bad is it?"

In a weak whisper, Erol replied, "Not good."

"I brought an aid bag, but I think you need a hospital."

Erol rolled his head from side to side and mumbled as he struggled to lift his limp hand.

George couldn't understand him. He began his examination, and it was apparent Erol had a fever and the bandage needed to be changed. He was too weak to answer any of George's questions. With care, George peeled the dressing, caked with dried blood, from the wound. He cleaned the damaged tissue and applied a fresh bandage. Next, he took an eight hundred milligram Motrin in his hand and with his other hand under Erol's head, lifted it, and placed the capsule in his mouth. He then grasped the water bottle in the bag, opened it, and put it to Erol's lips so he could drink.

"How long has it been since you've had anything to eat?" George asked.

Erol lifted his hand to motion and shook his head.

George stepped into the kitchen and searched for something to fix for Erol. Within a half hour, he was feeding him soup with a few crackers.

As sunbeams penetrated the curtains of the dark room, George—asleep in the chair next to Erol—woke. He changed the dressing on Erol's wound and wiped his face.

Erol stirred, but his eyes were slow to open. In a labored whisper, he said, "Water."

George slid his hand under Erol's head and lifted it, placing the water bottle to his lips. After a couple of sips, he eased his head down and said, "I've got to get you to a doctor."

Erol rolled his head and lifted a limp wrist. Struggling with the words, he said, "You must call SOCOM. Tell them—"

"Tell SOCOM what?" George replied. "What am I supposed to tell SOCOM?"

After several moments passed and no reply came, George wiped Erol's face again. His fever was high, and George knew it was caused by the wound and infection. There wasn't much else he could do for him other than first aid, water, and something to eat. He allowed Erol to sleep for a while and hoped the next time he woke he could tell him what he needed to tell SOCOM.

Just don't die on me, he thought.

When Erol woke again, George gave him water and another pain killer. Again, he heated soup and encouraged Erol to take some as he held the patient's head. Once finished, he eased Erol's head back down to the pillow.

In a low voice, George asked, "You said I needed to call SOCOM. What do I need to tell SOCOM? Tell me what happened."

Erol struggled until he managed to get the words out in a weak voice. "The bomb is going to New York. They just talked about one."

George winced. "New York? Are you sure?"

Erol nodded. "I heard them talking. I was on the floor above them in a damaged building. I heard them laughing and celebrating." He licked his dry lips and muttered, "Water."

Again, George lifted his head and placed the bottle of water to his lips.

As soon as George eased Erol's head down, the wounded man continued, "Madison knows Gareth is going to set him up. He tried to do it before and has tried to have him killed. Madison is going to double-cross Gareth and take him out. It is a personal vendetta." He moaned, "I need to rest."

"When is Madison going to set it off?"

Erol struggled to respond, "Next Friday or Saturday."

"Where in New York?" George asked.

Erol rolled his head from side to side and breathed, "Somewhere near Gareth's house. That is all I know. The floor collapsed after I heard that. I had to fight my way out. That's when I got shot. I believe I hit al-Aqrab with one of my shots."

George squeezed Erol's shoulder gently and said, "I'll call SOCOM and then I'm getting you to a doctor."

— ♦ ♦ ♦ —

Friday, July 8, 2016
Headquarters, US Special Operations Command
MacDill Air Force Base, Florida

Max pinned a copy of a police report about a Los Zetas gang member charged with assault on the map just above the one he'd pinned there the day before. The incident had occurred in Wilmington, Delaware just off I-95. The report from the previous day was on a Los Zetas gang member charged with attempted rape north of Philadelphia, off I-95. He stepped back from the map and looked at the other reports and articles posted on the board, noting that MS-13 and Los Zetas gang members had been arrested along I-20 in Texas, Georgia, and South Carolina as well as those on I-95. He looked at the three locations Gareth mentioned in the transcript—Cleveland, Toledo, and Denver—but no reports or news articles mentioned MS-13 or Los Zetas gang members in the past two weeks in either of those cities. The only articles posted were in reference to the political events.

Max turned and said, "Andy, Gail, Danya, step over here for a moment."

As soon as they were standing next to him, Max began to point out the locations where the gang members had been arrested. Then he reminded them that only political news had been reported on the three cities. "Gail, has David reported anything unusual?"

"He's checking in regularly and sending notes but hasn't come up with anything," she said. "He's only been in Cleveland two days."

"Those gang members you're concerned about," Andy said as he pointed to the map, "they're following a drug route into New York. Do you think they're doing more than just moving drugs?"

"Exactly!" Max said. "But there're no reports along the routes to the three cities. Something doesn't seem right. Could this be one of Madison's deceptions? Are the reports on the gang members to throw us off?"

"Maybe not," Danya said. "Perhaps Madison doesn't have that tight of a control on them and they go wild along the way."

Gail posed, "Something this big and Madison doesn't have control of his people? That doesn't sound like him. I think those arrests are a ruse or a coincidence."

"There's no such thing as coincidences," Max said.

"Are you suggesting Madison is telling us where he's going to detonate the nuke?" Gail replied.

"I am," Max said. "He's set up red herrings for us all along. He could be trying to draw us in. As you know, he and I don't exchange Christmas cards." He made eye contact with each of them. "Andy, you and David include New York in your searches. Look for anything." He looked at Gail. "See if you can get Gareth's itinerary for the next ten days."

"What about Chapman?" Gail asked. "Do you want me to pick him up?"

"Not yet," Max replied. "I think he's just the stooge in this. He may lead us to Madison yet."

Max looked to Danya. "Contact Thaddeus and tell him what I think. See if he has heard about either of the gangs making a big shipment into New York or making a big delivery into the city."

———— ♦ ♦ ♦ ————

Saturday, July 9, 2016
Headquarters, US Special Operations Command
MacDill Air Force Base, Florida

Major General Matherson entered the SCIF where Max and his team were working. It was a den of activity with muffled phone conversations, computers and printers humming, and the occasional conversation. Although the air conditioning cooled and dried the air, providing a pleasant environment, the tension was high and perspiration evident.

Seeing Chugs enter, Max stood and stepped to him. "Yes, sir," he said, noting Chugs's unusual visit to the SCIF. "What's on your mind?"

"I got a call from George," the general said. "The nuke is headed for New York, and Madison is supposed to set it off Friday or Saturday."

"Shit! That doesn't give us much time. Do you think the information is reliable?"

Chugs nodded. "I do. His contact, Erol, overheard al-Aqrab and al-Ghazāli talking. Gareth is going to set up Madison at one of the three locations. Madison knows Gareth is trying to set him up and plans to double-cross Gareth and set it off near his residence in New York, taking him out with New York. Madison is making this personal, so be careful."

"Any indication where in New York?" Max ran his hand across his head.

"Just somewhere near Gareth's residence," Matherson said. "George said that Erol was eavesdropping from the floor above where the two were talking. The floor collapsed under him, and he had to fight his way out. He was shot and thinks he hit al-Aqrab. George said Erol is in bad shape and is taking him to a doctor."

"This's damn dirty business we're in," Max said. "Thanks for the update. We'll be going to New York as soon as possible."

Matherson nodded. "Remember what I said about Madison making this personal." He turned and left the SCIF.

Max relayed the general's update to his team. As soon as he said *New York*, glances were shared between them.

"Son of a bitch," Gail said. "Of all the places…New York. You were right, Max."

He looked to Gail. "Send David to New York, and we'll meet him there."

"New York is a big area with countless places to hide it," Andy said. "There's no way in hell we can cover the entire city. Where the hell do we start?"

"Within one mile of Stew Gareth's residence. Madison'll use a vacant house or building. Someplace he can get into and out of with little notice. Develop a list of every vacant or recently rented building or residence that might have been leased in the past three weeks. We've gotta work fast on this. We only have five days. If we can't find it by then, we evacuate."

"Would he use a rental truck or car?" Danya asked.

"I don't think he'd use a car. He wouldn't have much room if it was in the trunk of a car. A box truck or boat are possibilities. I think he would go more for the privacy of a building. However, check for anything."

"He could also use the business of a Muslim Brotherhood or ISIS sympathizer," Andy said.

Max replied, "Good point. Stay alert."

Gail asked, "When do we warn the people?"

Max shook his head. "We don't. There won't be enough time to evacuate the city. We'd need the government's support and that would hamper our efforts. They'd just turn this into a political show. We have to find the nuke and fast, without their knowledge. If word gets out, the hysteria in the mass exodus would kill half of the population, and gridlock would be more than you can imagine."

Max was aware of the impact of his order. More than twenty million people in New York City alone would die in the initial blast. Untold numbers would die from radiation. It was a decision he and Chugs had agreed on earlier that no matter where the nuke was going to be taken, no one could be alerted. He was unsure if he could live with himself if he couldn't find the device in time. He wrestled with his conscience—if he should fail, would it be better to die in the blast or not? However, he also knew he likely would not get to make that decision. They were searching in one hell of a haystack.

———— • • • ————

Wednesday, July 13, 2016
Manhattan
New York, New York

Max and his team relocated to New York Sunday evening. With preparations made before they arrived, they were able to hit the ground and go straight to work. Needing someone who knew their way around Manhattan, Gail tapped her trusted FBI friend working on the Mexican border for a contact. Max arranged for Gail to meet Sally Davidson for coffee Monday morning. All he told Gail about Sally was that she was a private investigator, could be trusted, and knew her way around New York.

Gail, skeptical of private investigators—and one named Sally—met the woman. Sally was not what she'd expected, and Gail was impressed when they met. Sally was ex-FBI and an army veteran, physically fit with a great figure, and stood about five-foot-six with light brown hair. She didn't elaborate on why she was no longer with the FBI, but after talking with her, Gail thought she'd either beat up one of the young, stud agents or hadn't been politically correct enough. When Sally leaned closer to the table, Gail smiled to herself when she saw a SIG Sauer semi-automatic beneath the woman's jacket. Gail liked her and brought her onto the team.

The mile radius around Gareth's residence was divided up, and each one of them had a section they were responsible for. Gail continued to get police reports, none of which seemed to be relevant to their mission. For three days, they did not turn up any clues to the location of the nuke. Sally had identified several Muslim-owned store fronts ranging from pastry and coffee shops to grocery outlets, dry cleaners, tailor shops, and various eating places that she thought needed closer scrutinizing. Gail spent the first day checking with the property rental companies, and most of the second day, she was consumed with the discovery and investigation of a body reported to be a member of Los Zetas. However, that afternoon, she returned to her sector and continued visiting store fronts.

Max, Danya, and Andy contacted rental companies and questioned Middle Eastern shops in their sector that Sally had identified. David was kept busy parsing the police reports Gail provided and working his contacts while keeping in routine contact with DIA.

Wednesday evening, they all met before dinner, which was their routine, to discuss the results of the day and plan the next. All of them reported about the same information—no one remembered seeing anyone resembling the photograph of Bart Madison. And as expected, no one at the Muslim-owned shops would talk to them. The properties reported as rented in the past three weeks seemed to check out as legitimate business rentals, and none of them appeared to have ties to the Middle East. Showing on their faces and their mood, the tension they felt in knowing they had only hours left—and that was an approximation—was obvious. All they knew was that George had been told by his contact who was in Turkey and seriously injured that the bomb was to be detonated Friday or Saturday.

Turkey was eight hours ahead of New York. Although no one brought up the subject, they all were thinking the same thing. How much time did they have? Was the timeframe based on Turkish time or New York time?

Max began to doubt his decision to limit their search to just one mile around Gareth's residence. Even at two miles, the potential blast could still take out Gareth and destroy the city. *Have I missed something? Did I miscalculate and condemn millions of people to die?*

"Gail," Max said as he shot her a look. "Anything more on the gang member's body?"

"Nothing," she replied. "NYPD believes it was a drug deal gone bad."

Max nodded. "We have twenty-four hours left. If we don't find Madison and the nuke by then, Chugs has ordered us to evacuate the area. We'll rendezvous in Pittsburgh. Stay on the interstate, and you should be there in about six hours." He looked at David. "Get us rooms, then send a text to everyone with the information."

"Yes, sir," David said as he scribbled on his notepad.

"Pittsburgh is far enough away, and the mountains will give us protection," Max continued. "Check in with me as soon as you get there. Any questions?"

In a somber mood, each of then shook their heads.

"Madison is here, somewhere," Max said. "We've got one day to find him."

———— • ◆ • ————

Thursday, July 14, 2016
Manhattan
New York, New York

Everyone had been working their assigned sector since eight-thirty that morning. It was a beautiful day, but they couldn't help wishing to be somewhere else. They didn't have the luxury to enjoy the day or even the time to think about it. The city people were going in all different directions, cars, trucks, and buses competing for space on the streets. Work was ongoing in the offices and shops as usual. It was like any other day in New York—busy.

At 4:05 p.m. Max's cell phone rang, and he looked at the screen and saw that David was calling. He pushed the button to answer and said, "Max."

"Max!" came David's voice. "I can't get ahold of Gail or Andy. Danya told me to call you. He's here."

"David," Max replied, his voice was calm. "Slow down. What did you say? Who's here?"

"I just got a call from DIA," David replied, trying to contain his excitement. "They're getting a signal from the GPS tracking chip Major Marsden put in Madison's cap. We got a location on *him*. Gail's and Andy's phones went to voicemail."

"It could just be a false positive," Max remarked, his voice calm. "What's the location?"

"It's about four blocks from you. I think it's in a bakery shop." He gave the address and directions to Max.

"I'll check it out and let you know what I find."

"Oh, good," David replied. "Max, please be careful. What should I do? Do you want me to tell the others to meet you there?"

"Hold off until I check it out," Max replied. "It could be nothing, or one of us might be getting close to Madison and he's trying to draw us away from him."

It took Max about ten minutes to get to the location David had provided. He took his time as he got close to the shop, looking over the area, trying to find anything or anyone out of place. He didn't want to charge in with his pistol drawn until he knew what the situation was. He peered through the window and saw one woman behind the counter. She soon disappeared into the back. Max eased through the door and stepped close to the counter. Just as he sensed someone behind him, he felt the unmistakable muzzle of a pistol in his back.

"Don't turn around," a man's voice said. "In the back room. Now!" he said, nudging Max with the pistol.

As Max entered the back room, Madison appeared from the shadowed depths and said, "Kenworth. Welcome to the party. I've been expecting you." He looked to a woman standing in the doorway of an adjacent storeroom and nodded.

She and a man behind her scurried out through the front door.

Max's eyes darted around the room, landing on Danya seated with a gag tied around her mouth. He resisted the urge to rush to her but saw her give a slight nod to her right. He shifted his glance and saw what she'd wanted him to see. A shiny, nuclear warhead rested on the floor. A ball cap and the GPS tracker next to it sat on top of the counter behind the warhead. It was a signal from Madison to Max that meant, *You can't fool me.*

"That's right, Kenworth," Madison said. "That's the GPS tracker your redheaded bitch put in my hat. Is she with you? She's good. I want her to join us as well."

Max held his gaze on Madison. "Nope! This is all of us."

"Too bad," Madison said. "I was hoping to have a party. Well, you'll have to excuse me. I must be going now. Have a blast!" His gaze shot to the man holding the pistol on Max. "Cuff him to the pipe over there." He nodded to the wall across from Danya, then watched as the man cuffed and gagged Max.

CHAPTER 33

Thursday, July 14, 2016
Gareth Residence
New York, New York

S TEW AND JENNY returned from the campaign trail for the weekend. The effects of the long, hard grind showed more on Jenny than
on Stew. Aside from her clothes needing to go to the laundry, the bags
beneath her eyes were more pronounced, her hair was limp, and she
struggled to carry her large frame. The constant consumption of alcohol
hadn't been kind to her either.

Jenny followed Stew into his office and flopped into the wingback
chair in front of the desk. "My feet are killing me," she said as she kicked
off her shoes. "Fix me a large scotch and bring me my pills."

Stew filled two glasses with scotch and handed one to Jenny along
with a bottle of pills. He stepped behind his desk and took a sip before
setting the glass on the coaster. He sat down and reached for a cigar.

Jenny dumped four capsules into her hand, then locked onto Stew's
eyes and said, "Don't light it. I've had enough of body odor and smoke
from the little people for one day. I don't want to smell it anymore."

Irritated, Stew ignored her remark and placed the Padron 1926 Series
No. 9 in his mouth. "Before Archie left, did he give you the updated
itinerary for Sunday afternoon? There's a meet 'n greet at some museum
he wants you to attend."

"Right now, I don't want to think about it," she said, then she
washed the pain pills down with scotch. "Any big donors going to be
there? If not, I'd just as soon not go. I'm beat. I might just stay in bed all
weekend."

"I don't know. I need to call him anyway," Stew replied. Calling Archie next, he discussed Sunday's itinerary with him. "What about the donors? Big or small money?"

"I'll send you the list," Archie replied. "There'll be a couple of large donors there."

Stew promised to get Jenny's confirmation to him in the morning, then asked, "What did the acting director have to say?"

"They're looking for Madison, but so far, they haven't been able to locate him." Archie closed his eyes and anticipated the response.

"Damn it, Archie, what's their problem? What the hell does he mean they can't find Madison? The CIA is that inept? Get on his ass and tell him I need to know where and what Madison is doing. What's Wes Brock's story?"

"Wes said that Kenworth is back at SOCOM and he's pushing them for a briefing from Kenworth. He's expecting a call back. The acting director didn't know Kenworth was back in the US until I told him. The contractors are balking at taking care of Kenworth on US soil."

"The CIA is getting skittish? What's the problem? Does he need to offer them more money? Tell those two guys to get the lead out of their pants and do as they were told." Stew slammed the phone down before Archie could reply.

— ❖ —

Thursday, July 14, 2016
Manhattan
New York, New York

"I thought about killing you right off," Madison said as he looked down at Max. He picked up his ball cap and placed it on his head. "Then I thought that was too good for you. You've been a pain in my ass for a long time. I want you to think about what you've cost me while you're waiting to die. I don't have a country or a lover. You've cost me everything. You'll have plenty of time to think about it. I hope you feel about Danya the same way I felt about Maurine. It was because of you I had to kill her. She was a beautiful woman and a fantastic lover. She meant a lot to me. So, you see, you'll be killing Danya too. You can look into her eyes just like I looked into Maurine's. Well, almost. The circumstances require you two to be separated. For the time you have left, you'll just have to remember her scent and how she feels in your arms. I want you to be in agony for the little time you have left. When the counter on the nuke reaches zero"—Madison pointed to the nuke—"you'll cease to exist. No pain, no agony. Just gone. It's the period of time before you vaporize that I want you to suffer. Knowing the exact instant you are going to die puts a different perspective on life."

Max jerked on the handcuffs, attempting to reach Madison. The cold steel dug into his wrists, and no matter how hard he tugged, he couldn't free himself. Although he heard Madison's words, he refused to contemplate them. He would fight to the very end.

"Yoo-hoo!" a woman's voice came from the front of the shop. "Is anyone here? I've come to pick up my order. Hello!"

Madison looked to his cohort standing beside him and nodded toward the front.

Stepping to a place where he could peer into the front of the shop without being seen, the accomplice glanced at the entrance of the shop. After a quick look, he turned back to Madison and held up two fingers as he whispered, "Two, a man and woman. They don't appear to be a threat. The woman is a knockout, and the guy…well, he looks fruity."

"Tell them to come back tomorrow. The shop is closed," Madison said in a low voice, then readjusted his cap.

"You'll have to come back tomorrow," his henchman said as he stepped into the doorway. "There's a water leak, and the shop's closed." He looked at the woman to his left and the man to his right. Eyeing the man's bright magenta shirt, he perceived him as no threat. He shifted his scrutiny back to the attractive, well-built woman in tight pants and displaying lots of cleavage, looking her over from head to toe.

"Well, damn!" Sally said. "I needed my order for a party tonight." She reciprocated his gaze with one of her own.

"Put your hands up!" David ordered.

The man shot a glare to David, finding a .45 automatic aimed toward him, and didn't move.

Sally pulled her SIG Sauer from beneath her loose-fitting blouse and motioned for him to step out from behind the counter. "On the floor."

Gunfire erupted from deep inside the back of the shop as the man knelt. One shot followed by two, then two, then two more.

"Against the wall, David!" She motioned toward the backroom entrance. She removed the man's pistol and knife, then thumped him on the back of the head. "Don't move. Do you understand?"

He nodded.

Sally looked at David. "Keep an eye on him. If he tries anything, shoot him. Stay alert. Madison might have other friends in the area." With caution, she entered the back room and saw Max and Danya gagged and their arms tied behind them, sitting on either side of the room.

Gail and Andy entered from the rear door, their pistols held at the ready. Gail's gaze landed on Sally first, with her pistol in hand. "Are you okay?"

"Yes," Sally replied. She saw the blood on Gail's side. "How about you?"

"I'm okay," Gail said as she looked to Max, then Danya. "Take care of Danya and I'll get Max." She removed the gag around Max's mouth, then went to work on the handcuffs.

Max looked up to her. "I appreciate the rescue, but why aren't you and the others on your way out of here?"

"When we didn't hear from you, we thought you might be in trouble," Gail replied. "It seems that you are."

"Just a little. Did you get Madison?" Max looked at the blood stain on her shirt and asked, "How bad is it?

"It hurts like hell, but I'm good. Andy fixed me up. Madison got away. He had a backup in the alley, but he may also have two bullets in him. He started out the door and shot when I challenged him. We exchanged a couple of shots. That's when his backup opened up on us. Andy and I both think we hit him."

A slight smile started to emerge on Max's face.

"We're in for more trouble," Gail continued. "The police will be here any minute. They'll have lots of questions and take up precious time."

"You've gotta run interference and take care of 'em, Gail," Max said. "I gotta get to work on the warhead. I don't know if I can do any good. I might just kill us all." He looked toward Danya and said, "You, David, and Andy get the hell outta here as fast as you can. Gail, you and Sally go as soon as you can."

"Save your breath, Max," Andy replied. "We all decided to stay."

"Danya," Max said. "Please go."

"Max!" Danya replied. "We're here to help. Get to work on the nuke. What do you need?"

"See if you can find any tools—pliers, screwdriver, wire cutters… whatever you can find," Max replied.

Max looked to Andy. "Andy, see if you can find a flashlight."

Max began studying the device, his first concern the possibility of booby traps.

The wail of sirens punctuated the ambient city noise, emanating from two directions and converging in front of the shop.

Over his shoulder, David said, "Gail, *dahling*, the police are here."

Gail marched through the shop to greet them. She saw the officers in defensive positions with shotguns across the hoods of their cars, pointing at the front of the shop. Holding up her credentials, she said loud enough for them to hear, "Special Agent Gail Summers. We're secure."

Identifying the FBI agent, one of the other officers—a corporal with revolver in hand—approached the door with caution.

Gail began by saying, "This is an FBI case. Search the alley. I think we hit one of them, and he could be down in the alley. There's one alive on the floor you can process."

The officer looked into her eyes, then saw the blood on her shirt. Over his shoulder, he said, "Call for EMS." He faced Gail again. "Excuse me, ma'am, we need to check the situation and verify it is secure."

"I told you, it is secure. Call for your captain," she said, her tone unyielding. "I'll need to talk with him first. While we wait for him, we can start out here."

"Ma'am, please step aside so we can enter," the officer said with insistence.

"I told you, it's secure. We'll wait on your captain." Gail didn't budge and, with a stern expression, stared into his eyes.

Getting the message, the corporal turned and said, "The agent requests the captain. It's secure here, and one suspect is on the floor. Come get him and put him in the car. Another suspect is possibly wounded and went into the alley. Start to work there." He faced Gail and withdrew his notepad. "Please give me the details and who else is inside?"

Gail proceeded to provide everyone's names and the details, not mentioning the nuclear bomb. She stepped aside as two officers approached to get the man on the floor, then turned her head toward David and said, "David, give your weapon back to Sally." Her head swiveled back to the inquisitive corporal now attempting to enter behind the two officers, and she stepped back in front of him.

"I need to assess the situation, ma'am."

"We'll wait for your captain."

"I need to see the others and take their statements," he said.

"As soon as your captain gets here," Gail replied, almost daring him to try.

One of the other officers approached and said, "Excuse me, ma'am. There isn't anyone in the alley."

"No body?" Gail replied. "Did you search the alley?"

"Yes, ma'am. There's some blood, but that's all."

"Well…son of a bitch!" she said, drawing out the curse. "We put two bullets in him. Find that piece of crap *now*. He couldn't have gotten far!"

Soon, Captain M. Taner Mackenzie arrived in a black unmarked sedan, followed soon after by EMS arriving. Taner was six feet, two hundred pounds with broad shoulders and reddish-blond hair cut short. He stepped toward the corporal standing at the doorway and started to speak when Gail said, "Hello, Marion."

Mackenzie's face flushed as his eyes landed on Agent Summers. A smile broke across his face. "Hello, Summers. I don't know if it's good to see you or not."

David grinned, his curiosity piqued to find out about the apparent history between the two.

"Why does it not surprise me that you're here?" Mackenzie said. "And it's Taner or Captain Mackenzie, if you don't mind. Whatta ya got?"

"Whatever you say, Marion," Gail replied. "Step in here, and I'll tell you." She turned and led him into the front of the shop, then looked to the corporal and said, "Wait outside for a few minutes."

Taner looked to the officer and nodded for him to comply.

David, knowing Gail wanted a private meeting with the captain and suspected what was about to happen, retreated to the back room.

She continued as soon as they were alone in the front of the shop. "I need to get something straight with you."

"I knew it. Shoot," he replied.

"This is classified, and I need you to trust me."

Mackenzie nodded. "We're not starting out very well. With you, that is asking a lot. Tell me what's going on and why you didn't notify us of your operation?"

Gail proceeded to tell him the background and how it was connected to the Gareth presidential campaign and that Bart Madison had planned an attack on the US. At times during Gail's info dump, Taner raised his voice and scolded her. She went on to tell him that they had chased Madison around the world and caught up to him in New York, but they weren't sure where he planned to strike until a few days ago.

With that statement, he erupted again, "And you were so busy you couldn't find the damn time to even make a phone call?!"

"Marion, I know," she said, attempting to calm him down. "Everything must be kept close hold until the operation is complete. There's a lot of senior people we can't trust."

"Including me?" he replied.

"You know better than that, Marion." She continued until the mention of Madison bringing a nuke into New York sent him reeling again.

Taner's face reddened. "Wait, you said *nuke*? A terrorist brings a nuclear bomb into my city, and you didn't bother to inform us! What the hell're you doing? We need to start an evacuation. This is unbelievable. Tell me you found it."

"Hold on," Gail said. "You need to talk to Max first."

Sally stepped back into the front where Taner was giving Gail the third degree. Before she could speak, he looked toward her and said, "Davidson, what did you do to get mixed up in this?"

"Living right, I guess," she replied.

"Come on," Gail said. "I'll introduce you to the others." She led him into the back and made the introductions.

Max told him about the nuke and what he anticipated if it detonated. "We don't have time to evacuate the city. The panic would kill a lot of people, and it would also hamper our efforts here. What I'd like you to do is have your men block off either end of the street and clear everyone out. Tell 'em there's a gas leak and above all, don't mention nuke. Finish up here with whatever you need to do as fast as you can."

"We can't just let that many people die," Taner said.

Max looked him in the eye and in a cold voice said, "You don't have any choice. If you have a suggestion, I'm open. I'm in constant contact with our nuclear bomb disposal technicians and just sent them pictures. We're doing everything we can."

"What do you need? Do you want me to call for our bomb experts?" Taner asked.

"No, I've got all the help I need," Max replied. "The fewer who know about this the better. If your people get involved, the media will be next. Then we've got mass panic."

"If you can't get it disarmed in time?" Tanner asked.

"Then it won't matter," Max replied. "I'd appreciate it if you would let me get back to work and you do as I asked."

"What am I supposed to tell the chief?"

Gail said, "You'll think of something. Whatever you come up with, make sure it is kept quiet. I'll work with you on the after-action report."

"My retirement too?" he said with sarcasm. "I'm probably going to lose it." He and Gail started to walk back to the front.

"Taner," Max said. "Thanks. Can you get me some better tools? All that were in here are worn out, chipped, and rusty. A better light too."

"You got it," Taner said as he walked out.

"Andy, as soon as the police clear out, take the others to where they block off the street."

Max received a photo annotated with notes back from the bomb technicians, then his phone rang. The officer explained the photo and advised him on how to proceed. "Slow and steady," he said. "We've studied as best we can on what they have done to rig the warhead to explode. There is one wire that leads down and out of sight, and we're not sure what it is. It could be that the bomb is rigged with a booby trap. We've got to be very careful with this."

"That is an understatement. If it's booby trapped, any way to disarm it or bypass it?" Max asked with concern in his voice.

"Not yet," the officer replied.

Max took several more photos with his cell and sent them to the bomb techs.

"It's possible they have a redundant system on the timer," the tech said.

"I've got the tools you asked for," Taner said as he stepped into the backroom of the shop.

Max had no idea how long he had been gone but knew it was longer than it seemed. "Thanks."

"I'll be at the intersection if you need anything else." He didn't wait on a reply before walking out of the shop.

It was all or nothing. If it was nothing, he would never know nor would anyone else in New York or the surrounding area. If it was all, just a select few would know.

The tension was thick and the sweat on Max's face caused him to have to stop and wipe it away. He grabbed a small towel and tied it around his head to absorb the perspiration and keep it out of his eyes. He picked up another, wiped his hands, then laid it beside the warhead. He listened with intent to the technician's calm voice.

"It appears from the photo," the tech said, "the timer cannot be disconnected as it will close the circuit as soon as it is disconnected."

"And that's not a good thing," Max replied. His years of training had sharpened his ability to focus and given him unwavering concentration on the task at hand. He was able to push the impending doom out of his mind. He continued with a steady hand and determination. As long as the counter hadn't reached zero, he had a chance. The tech instructed Max to follow the wires to the end of the casing and try to determine whether it had been opened.

With the gentlest of touches, Max followed the tech's instructions and opened the access panel, then described what he saw and took more photos. He was instructed to probe deeper through the wires and take several more photos. Max was acting as an extension of the officer's hands. He had never met the soft-spoken man whose voice was sounding in his ear, but he trusted him and did exactly as instructed. At the direction of the voice, he snipped one wire and then another.

Max eased back, wiped the sweat from his hands, and looked at the counter. He said, "We've got a problem!"

"What is it?" The tech asked.

"The counter has gone crazy. It's ticking down so fast I can't make out the numbers."

"Get out of there now!" the officer said. "A booby trap has been activated. Get out of there now."

Max bolted out of the shop toward the intersection where Andy had taken Danya.

Pumping his arms and pushing as hard as he could, Max ran. "Take cover! Get down!" he shouted. His gaze found Danya standing next to Andy, and he watched as they sought protection behind one of the police cars.

Not knowing how much time until the explosion or how destructive it would be, he wanted to be with Danya when it happened. With each of his pounding steps, he knew it could be his last. His lungs struggled to take in enough air, his heart thumped hard in his chest, and time seemed to slow.

Thoughts of Danya flashed in his mind. Their plans to marry and spend time in the Caribbean had been put on hold when this started. Neither of them were strangers to danger, and both had had several brushes with death along the way. Sooner or later, everyone's number comes up and no one ever knows when it is their time. He couldn't help but wonder if this was it for them. He and Danya had talked several times and agreed that they would always be together, to the very end.

He prayed, *Please, give me time to be with her.*

Max strained and pushed himself harder. It seemed that an eternity had passed since he darted out of the bakery. He anticipated the blast coming at any moment. His lungs felt like they were turning inside out as he demanded more from his body. Breathing so hard, he couldn't speak when he reached the police car. He dropped next to Danya behind the vehicle and pulled her close, trying to shield her from the blast.

A flash of light silenced everyone, followed by a thunderous explosion.

Max opened his eyes and met Danya's, reading the question in her mind. *Are we still alive?* He smiled as he caressed her cheek. Still pant-ing hard, he looked over and saw Andy raise his head, then Gail, Sally, and David. He made a quick visual survey of the area. Smoke, dust, and debris littered the street. Windows were blown out and flames licked the large opening of the former bakery.

"Andy," Max said. "Check to see if everyone is okay."

Andy signaled with a wave of his hand and went to work.

Max stepped to Captain Mackenzie as he stood and brushed at his pants. "Notify your fire department and the hazmat team that the area is contaminated by radioactive material—plutonium and uranium. They'll need to establish a safe zone as soon as possible."

Mackenzie started to step to the patrol car to use the radio.

"One more thing," Max said. "What's left of the components or physics package is classified and will need to be guarded until the military arrives to take control of it."

"I'll tell 'em," he said.

Max called General Matherson to give him a report on what had happened.

Chugs asked with concern, "Are you and the others all right? Injuries?"

"We're all okay. I don't know of any casualties. NYPD is checking."

"What happened?" Matherson said. "Did a booby trap set it off?"

"It's too early to tell exactly. We do suspect it was booby trapped, but I can't tell you now if I tripped it or it was something else. We'll have to wait for the scientists to examine it before we know for sure."

"I understand. Tell me what you think happened. I need to get the information to the commander before the SecDef or POTUS calls him."

"I believe I was able to affect the functioning of the primary stage," Max said. "I most likely interrupted the equal compression of the explosive material, preventing the fission in the first stage. It appears the high-explosive material blew out the side of the outer case. In this instance, there was no fission of the first stage."

"If that had occurred, we wouldn't be having this conversation, right?" Chugs replied.

"Yes, sir," Max said with a smile. "Without the equal compression of the nuclear material to cause fission of the first stage, the explosives ignited and blew out the side of the canister and scattered the nuclear material of both stages. In essence, it became a dirty bomb."

"I've alerted the Nuclear Accident and Incident Response Team," Matherson said. "New York will be busy cleaning up the mess for a while."

"Yes, sir, it is indeed a mess."

"What about Madison? Is he dead?" Chugs asked, anxious to know if the terrorist had been eliminated.

"Gail thinks he was hit twice," Max replied. "He had a backup in the alley who covered his escape. Gail has NYPD looking for him."

The general was quiet for a moment. It was painful for Max to report that Madison had eluded them once again. It was also painful for the general to hear the terrorist had escaped again.

"I'm sure we haven't seen the last of that traitor," replied Chugs. "We can talk about him when you get home."

"The hazmat team will be here any minute," Max said. "I'll brief them on the situation and provide any help I can until the Nuclear Accident and Incident Response Team arrives. That's about all we can do here, unless NYPD finds Madison or Gail gets a solid lead."

CHAPTER 34

Thursday, July 14, 2016
Gareth Residence
New York, New York

"S TEW, TURN ON the TV," Jenny said as she rushed into his office. The fabric of her caftan trailed behind her like a luffed sail. "The news just came on with a breaking report about an explosion and fire in a bakery a few blocks from here." She turned a chair to face the screen, then plopped into it.

Stew pointed the remote toward the TV on the wall and pushed the button.

The screen came to life with an excited reporter describing the incident. "There's conflicting stories about what happened. Initial reports indicated there was a gas leak at a bakery, then it exploded. I was later told by one of the police officers that there were several gunshots before the explosion. Just a moment ago, I was told that NYPD is looking for a terrorist who was shot in the exchange of gunfire and another one is already in custody. The hazmat team is on the scene, and the entire area is blocked off. I can't get close enough to see what's going on, but I was able to see that the team members are suited up and using radiation detection monitors."

Stew muted the broadcast to make a phone call.

"Find out what's going on," Jenny said as she pushed herself out of the chair and hobbled to the bar to refill her drink.

Stew sipped his scotch as he punched in the number to Wes Brock. As soon as Wes answered, he asked him what was going on in Manhattan.

Wes hesitated, then answered, "It appears that a terrorist was trying to or did set off a dirty bomb. The Nuclear Accident and Incident Response Team has been called in."

"Would that be the same item we've discussed?" Stew asked in a cold voice.

"It looks like it," he replied. "I've just had an initial brief, and more is expected as the details are sorted out. We need to get on top of this before the investigation gets very far. I suggest we meet."

"I agree," Stew said. "I don't want our asses exposed on this. You and Jonathan Wellington get up here first thing in the morning."

"It's going to be next to impossible to break away with all this going on."

"I don't give a damn! You two be here first thing in the morning!" Stew slammed the phone down.

The phone rang before Stew removed his hand. He answered to hear the agitated voice of Senator Archie Chapman.

"Things are going wrong. What're we going to do?"

"I'm working on it, Archie. Just sit tight until I get back to you. It'll be taken care of." He talked with Archie for several more minutes to calm him down before he ended the call.

Jenny stayed glued to the TV for the next hour, trying to sift through the changing updates. She emptied her glass twice during that time. Listening to the TV and Stew's phone calls, she mumbled in slurred speech. Very little seemed to differ from the initial reports other than that they were reporting it now as a dirty bomb attack and the police were looking for the terrorist.

The next morning, Wes Brock and Jonathan Wellington—looking like two schoolboys who had been called to the principal's office—were seated in front of Stew as instructed. Both knew the meeting would be uncomfortable. They provided Stew with an update on the official report of the Manhattan bombing.

After about twenty minutes of questions, Stew said, "Keep your damn mouths shut, and we stay in front of this. There're a few loose ends that need to be tied up." He fixed his gaze on Jonathan. "Archie Chapman is a weak link—arrange an accident. I don't give a damn how you do it. I want Madison dead too."

Jonathan hesitated, fearing he was sinking even deeper into the abyss than he already was, and glanced to Wes before he replied, "Senator Archie Chapman? I don't know, Stew. Trying to get the contractors to take out Kenworth on US soil is hard enough, but Chapman is going to be damn near impossible. What if something goes wrong?"

"Damn it, man!" Stew's face reddened. "It already has gone *wrong*! Your guys couldn't find Madison, and he tried to blow up the city *with me in it*! Get your head out of your ass and light a fire under your people. Chapman'll spill his guts and get us all hung if Madison doesn't kill us all first."

Wellington seemed to slump in his chair as he gave a slight nod.

"Wes," Stew said, "take out Nassar, but not in the US. He'll be the fall guy. The story is that he and Bart Madison tried to blow up New York. Stick to that story. I'll watch to see how the situation develops. If need be, we'll release a report that Jenny's opponent is fabricating a story that she had something to do with the bombing. I'll have all the networks work this angle and saturate every broadcast. That'll keep the focus off us for a while. If your guys can get Nassar and Madison, it'll be easy to keep the focus on them until after the election."

＝＝＋＋＋＝＝

Monday, July 18, 2016
Headquarters, US Special Operations Command
MacDill Air Force Base, Florida

Gail, David, and Andy returned to headquarters to create a plan for finding Madison and the others responsible for the Manhattan bombing. Gail received approval to seek an arrest warrant for Senator Chapman. The SOCOM lawyers wanted Chapman arrested before they tried to get a warrant for Stew Gareth. Chapman's statement and cooperation was necessary to solidify their case before they went after Gareth, and even then, they knew it would be a tough slog to get him indicted. The evidence had to be overwhelming and corroborated. Otherwise, their careers and probably their lives could be over.

Gail obtained the warrant for Senator Chapman's arrest and coordinated with Captain Mackenzie, NYPD, and the FBI Field Office, New York City, for assistance. Her plan was set, and she was to fly to

New York the next morning. Mackenzie provided her with his report on Madison. None of the hospitals or clinics in New York had admitted or treated a patient matching Madison's description.

David and Andy were busy trying to find Madison and the remaining nuke, and sifting through intelligence reports, looking for anything that may help them. Andy had received a message that George got Erol to a hospital outside of Turkey and treated in time, so he was expected to make a complete recovery.

Late that afternoon, Max called and said that he and Danya were returning the next morning. He had done everything possible and briefed the chief of the Nuclear Accident and Incident Response Team. He relayed that Captain Mackenzie was mystified by how Madison could disappear with two bullets in him. Max had given Mackenzie a copy of a photo and description of Madison, which he included with his report. Taner had also contacted the coroner's office without success. They, like the other facilities, had no knowledge of processing a corpse matching Madison's description.

Max was frustrated that Madison, once again, had escaped. Finding him was a priority, and Max wanted to be there when he was found. The special forces teams operating throughout Central America had been alerted to take Madison if they found him. Danya sent her report to Thaddeus Nussbaum, Chief of Mossad Station, Panama, and he, in turn, provided Madison's photo and description to his agents throughout Panama. Unfortunately, Madison knew the jungle very well and had contacts throughout Central and South America. If that was his destination and he made it back to that part of the world, he likely would never be found.

The next morning, Gail took David to headquarters on her way to the Tampa Airport, after spending a few minutes in the SCIF collecting the material she needed in New York. She shoved the material into a briefcase, then stepped toward the door.

"Gail, *dahling*," David said with a wide grin as he looked over the cubicle wall. "You have a phone call."

Without looking back, she replied, "Take a message. I'm on my way to the airport."

"It's Marion."

She hesitated, then stepped back to her desk. Placing the receiver to her ear, she said, "Hello, Marion. I was just on my way to the airport. What's up?"

"I'll save you a trip," he replied. "Senator Chapman is dead."

"What did you say?"

"Chapman is dead. It appears he fell down the stairs in his house and broke his neck."

"Shit! How convenient. I was wanting to see that fat bastard swing. Are you sure it was an accident?"

"Yep, pretty sure. Nothing to indicate otherwise."

"I'm willing to bet Gareth had something to do with it."

"Could be, but you'll never be able to prove it."

The intelligence had dried up about the one nuke still missing, but the team remained in constant contact with their sources around the world, trying to find out anything they could that might lead them to the missing one. Turkey remained under martial law, and the terrorists continued with their rhetoric against the West. Madison was crazed with rage when Max came face-to-face with him in Manhattan and wanted revenge on Gareth for trying to set him up. Max suspected Madison had added him to his revenge list and was keeping in contact with the terrorists as he recovered from his wounds. He feared Madison was not far away and making his revenge plans.

Major General Matherson directed Max to take time off and get married. Although Max protested, Chugs had held firm. The rest of the team would continue seeking information that would lead them to the missing nuke in Max and Danya's absence.

EPILOGUE

Friday, August 18, 2016
Sandals Grande St. Lucian
Saint Lucia Island, Caribbean

A GENTLE BREEZE DANCED about as it carried the fresh tropical scent of the island. A few puffy clouds dotted the blue sky. Max and Danya relaxed in chairs beneath a large umbrella and watched the rhythmic waves lap the beach. Two sailboats cruised by in the distance, beyond a catamaran sitting at anchor a short distance offshore. Several people were in the warm, turquoise water, some sunbathing on the sand, and a few others strolled along the beach. But for Max and Danya, they were alone in the tranquility of tropical beauty. They both pushed the events of the past several months from their minds.

Danya dug her toes into the sand as she clasped Max's hand. He gave her a lingering gaze. They didn't speak—they didn't need to. It was the perfect place to unwind. No matter what else was going on in the world, love still prevailed.

Their wedding was scheduled for Sunday, and the guests were trickling in. Although there was much work still to be done, no one, including Max and Danya, could put the remaining nuke or Madison completely out of their minds. However, everyone looked forward to getting away from their dangerous world for a bit to enjoy this destination and wedding. Thaddeus Nussbaum and his wife along with several friends from the Panama office arrived the day before. Most of them were either on tours or were scattered along the beach, soaking up the sun, or in the water. Major General Matherson, his wife, and a few from the headquarters were due to arrive that afternoon.

Carrying a large tropical drink, a newspaper tucked under her arm, and sliding a chair across the sand, Gail strolled to where Max and Danya lounged. She sat, her sun dress sliding up to her thigh as she stretched her shapely legs out in front of her. She remained silent for a moment, sipping her drink and looking over her sunglasses. "I brought a copy of the newspaper, if you want to see it."

Max turned his head toward her. "No, we've put the world on hold for the next couple of weeks. Anything of importance in there?"

She adjusted her wide brimmed hat. "Not really. Same old nauseating shit."

Max just nodded. "There's a trash can over there by the bar."

The Gareth's were the darlings of the media and were constantly featured. It was reported that Jenny had dropped in the polls, again. However, she was confident she would be elected in November. She kept attacking her opponent on his leadership and how there would be more Manhattan-type incidents if she was not elected. Stories were circulating that she had something to do with the bombing, which she continued to deny and blame her opponent for fabricating.

New York's mayor grabbed his portion of the media and was constantly campaigning with Gareth, often mentioning the Manhattan situation. He stated that it had been estimated to take about two to three years to complete the slow process of cleaning up the contamination. All of the construction workers had to wear protective suits and their time was limited in the work zone. Several buildings had to be demolished and about six to eight inches of the surface had to be removed due to contamination. Monitoring and decontamination of the buildings surrounding the area was on going.

"I haven't seen Andy or David this morning," Max said as he turned his head toward Gail.

"They took some tour."

"Something is bothering you. What is it?"

"The attorney general took my evidence on Gareth. She's considering a special prosecutor."

"That could be a good thing, right?"

"I'm reading the tea leaves, but I don't think anything is going to happen. I'm sure that was just a pat on the head and 'get the hell out of my office.' What a scumbag! Gareth is getting away with everything."

"You've done everything you could." Max squeezed her arm.

"I know, but it's damn infuriating." She sipped her drink. "I'm gonna have a bunch of these," she said, upending her glass.

"I've seen several good-looking guys around here," Danya said.

"You sound like David. Maybe later, but now I need another round, or two, of these." She stood and made her way to the beach bar.

TO BE CONTINUED...

DID YOU ENJOY READING
ACTS OF TREASON?

Please take a quick moment to let everyone know by posting a review at your favorite online bookstore. Your feedback will mean the world to me, and I will be forever grateful.

Best Regards,
Patrick Parker

ABOUT THE AUTHOR

Patrick Parker received his bachelor's degree in management and his master's degree in international relations. He joined the US Army and spent five years in Italy, then spent an additional fifteen years in the defense industry. Now retired and living in Texas, Parker enjoys writing, astronomy, traveling, and going to the gun range.

ACKNOWLEDGMENTS

A big thank you to my wife and best friend, Carole, for your confidence and support. You have been my best critic and provided invaluable input.

New Braunfels Writers Guild—Deborah Ellison, Don Burquest, Donna Heath, Dr. Lefter Baklas, James Whelpley, and Lewis Sarkozi. You are a great group and helped me bring my story to life. Through the many writings, critiques, edits and rewrites, thank you. I appreciate your candor, support, and confidence.

Bob Sabasteanski, a big thank you for your critique, suggestions, and attention to detail. My go-to guy for a reality check and a weapons expert. Thank you.

Scott Kotowski—F16 pilot with over 1600 hours in Iraq and other locations overseas and currently a pilot for FedEx Express. Thank you for your input and attention to detail of the F16 Viper and Air Force. Harrumph!! Thank you.

Thank you, all.

BOOKS BY PATRICK PARKER

Six Minutes Early: A Max Kenworth Suspense Thriller (Book 1)

Acts of Treason: A Max Kenworth Suspense Thriller (Book 2)

War Merchant: A Dydre Rowyn Suspense Thriller

Treasures of the Fourth Reich